DANCING INTO DANGER

DANCING INTO DANGER

— BISMA ALDANE —

Copyright © 2020 Bisma Aldane
The moral right of the author has been asserted.

Apart from any fair dealing for the purposes of research or private study, or criticism or review, as permitted under the Copyright, Designs and Patents Act 1988, this publication may only be reproduced, stored or transmitted, in any form or by any means, with the prior permission in writing of the publishers, or in the case of reprographic reproduction in accordance with the terms of licences issued by the Copyright Licensing Agency. Enquiries concerning reproduction outside those terms should be sent to the publishers.

Scripture quotations taken from
The Holy Bible, New International Version (anglicised edition)
Copyright ©1979, 1984, 2011 by Biblica (formerly International Bible Society)
Used by permission of Hodder & Stoughton publishers, an Hachette UK company
All rights reserved
'NIV' is a registered trademark of Biblica
UK trademark number 1448790

This is a work of fiction. Names, characters, businesses, places, events and incidents are either the products of the author's imagination or used in a fictitious manner. Any resemblance to actual persons, living or dead, or actual events is purely coincidental.

Matador
9 Priory Business Park,
Wistow Road, Kibworth Beauchamp,
Leicestershire. LE8 0RX
Tel: 0116 279 2299
Email: books@troubador.co.uk
Web: www.troubador.co.uk/matador
Twitter: @matadorbooks

ISBN 978-1-83859-366-7

British Library Cataloguing in Publication Data.
A catalogue record for this book is available from the British Library.

Printed and bound in Great Britain by 4edge Limited
Typeset in 11pt Minion Pro by Troubador Publishing Ltd, Leicester, UK

Matador is an imprint of Troubador Publishing Ltd

*This book was inspired by, and is dedicated to,
Luke and Carol without whom it
would not have been written.*

*Special thanks go to Frank for the music
in the supplementary book.*

CONTENTS

Foreword		ix
Chapter 1	Trysts and trysts again	1
Chapter 2	A voice from the dead	37
Chapter 3	A reluctant spy	71
Chapter 4	Mind games	99
Chapter 5	Caught in the web, worldwide or otherwise	137
Chapter 6	The jailor becomes jailed	159
Chapter 7	Battles without – at Blackfriars Bridge	177
Chapter 8	Battles within – the search for Sarah	201
Chapter 9	Out of the frying pan	247
Chapter 10	The ebb and flow of life	298
Epilogue		352
Appendix		355
Acknowledgements		360

FOREWORD

A book with a difference that can be read three ways:

1. A straight read.

2. A slower reading journey, dwelling on the moods from the included verse and lyrics. Snippets of some of the music (albeit of poor quality but enough to give a gist) will be available on YouTube to help the imagination. All the associated music is printed in the supplementary book, *The Music of Dancing Into Danger*. If you wish, you can create your own musical by selecting a personal choice from the lyrics and published music.

3. Create your own choreography to your chosen music either to express the mood or tell the story.

TRYSTS AND TRYSTS AGAIN

The sensuous touch of his hand on her face as he gently stroked her cheek and slowly drew her to him made her want even more to surrender to her deep, stirring inner desires. He caressed her cascading hair. Together they sank to their knees. He then placed his forefinger on her lips to signal the continuance of this silent special moment. They gazed into each other's eyes longingly. This was their moment. Then with unbridled passion they…

THE TRAIN LURCHED AND THE READJUSTED BODIES made it impossible for Sarah to see over the shoulder of the seated lady whose book she had surreptitiously been attempting to read. This was despite craning her neck to the fullest, letting her long hair flow fully down in the process. She tried standing on tiptoe for a moment in the squashed central aisle that ran along the middle of the coach but to no avail. It was an old type of rolling stock which had been substituted for a vandalised modern one. Long, continuous seats stretched across its whole width at either end of the coach. The springs on these seats, like the carriage in general, had seen long service and better days and over every large bump the six passengers at either end bounced together in an exaggerated fashion by virtue of their combined weight. This sight struck Sarah as funny and she felt the beginnings of a titter. The more they bounced the sillier it looked and the harder the giggle became to stifle.

Though quite shy, some might say timid or at least reserved in nature, Sarah had always had a tendency to laugh when nervous, and she was nervous, very nervous about the job interview she was going to. She looked around the carriage, anywhere to avoid the scene of the synchronised bobbing passengers. She could only see bits of misted-up window over a man's shoulder, so she decided to close her eyes and listen to a conversation going on in the next group of seats along. Several girls were talking about a previous night out, their Estuary English becoming more pronounced with their repetitive speech patterns and vocabulary. Sarah unconsciously started to count the number of times one particular girl said the word 'like' but shook herself out of it once she realised what she was doing.

'Anyway, I goes to him, I goes, no thanks I've just been up dancing. Anyway, I got my friend waiting for me.' The speaker then gesticulated. 'He was like, and I was like. He didn't like it, you know.'

'Was he the one with the black, straight hair?'

'Yeah, that's right. He was like, and I was like.'

Sarah thought, if only she'd brought something to read. Then the vision of the bouncing passengers popped into her mind again. She could even visualise them moving to music and a grin forced its way onto her face. *Oh no, no, stop it*, she thought. Someone at the distant end of the carriage, hidden from view, was talking loudly on their mobile and seemed to have a case of verbal diarrhoea, much to everyone else's annoyance. Thankfully Sarah could not discern what they were saying. *Quick, think of something else, anything else*, she thought. At last! Fenchurch

Street station. She wished that she had stayed in her flat in Tooting at the weekend to save on this awful journey but she had so wanted to attend the weekend course on dance, which she had greatly enjoyed.

Having allowed plenty of time for possible train delays and cancellations she was way too early for her appointment. So, before catching the tube at Tower Hill she thought to wander around the war memorial in Trinity Square to calm herself before the imagined impending grilling. It was the Monday after Remembrance Sunday and there were many flowers, little crosses and notes of love for the lost. She felt a tinge of sadness for those remaining, living but still grieving, losing but still loving. Some of the notes were so heartfelt. Perhaps one day there would be nobody left to mourn, no one left to sense the pain of loss, she mused. Sarah then stopped at the memorial for those killed at the scaffold on Tower Hill and wondered how many less influential men were killed there but with no memorial.

A bright shaft of sunlight briefly broke through the cloud cover from a wintry red sun, giving gold and red hues in the reflections of the tall glass-dressed office blocks, making some of them look as if they were actually on fire. These sobering thoughts now made her feel quite calm, which was just as well as she still wanted to arrive with a little time to spare, and so she walked past the old Roman wall and fountain. Eventually she found the tube station and caught a relatively empty westward train. Unfortunately, she had just witnessed the scene of two commuters turning the same corner travelling in opposite directions colliding, as both were texting on their mobile phones whilst walking. A nervous smile inched a little onto her face.

Sarah sat reading the advertisements displayed throughout the carriage. When the doors opened at Mansion House station, a pigeon hopped on and waited by the doors until the tube stopped at Blackfriars, at which point it hopped off as the doors opened. Sarah could not believe this. She started to giggle, but with a little self-control she managed to quiet herself again.

The train was stationary for quite a while and just as the doors were closing a man dashed into the carriage. He sat down heavily, on what was had he noticed, a vandalised seat. This slid off its mounting and he landed with an almighty crash in an embarrassed heap sprawled on the floor with part of the seat still under him. This was just too much for Sarah. She burst out laughing. He went very red and got up quickly, placed the seat back on its mounting, sat down on a different seat and hid behind a newspaper, trying to blend in as if nothing had happened. Apart from Sarah's response, there were a few brief isolated smiles before people resorted to the normal commuter malaise of nondescript blank expressions, texting, listening to music in their earphones or reading, but above all, carefully avoiding of any sort of eye contact.

When it came for the man to alight, having been clearly preoccupied in an article, he quickly placed the newspaper in his briefcase, shut it and got up to leave. Unfortunately for him, he had not closed his briefcase properly and as he got up its contents spilled out onto the floor. Sarah just shrieked with unconstrained laughter at this. He hurriedly scooped up the papers, inserted them into his case and dashed off the carriage. However, Sarah noticed an envelope still on the floor, which he had missed. She quickly picked it up and ran after the man, calling to him to get his attention. She caught up with him at the foot of the stairs.

'You dropped this.' He turned around and for the first time fully looked at her and noticed straight away her attractive eyes. He glanced down and saw her clasping the brown envelope with a solicitors' marking stamped at the top. As he reached to take the envelope their hands briefly touched.

'Thank you, thank you very much,' he said as his furrowed brow loosened and he once again looked into her eyes. There was a moment's silence as they stood looking at each other, commuters dashing up and downstairs around them.

Sarah felt a little uncomfortable at this so she ventured, 'I am sorry for laughing at you.'

'Well, come to think of it, it was rather funny,' he said as his face broke into a smile. Sarah was struck by how handsome he looked when he smiled.

'Look, I'm running a little late at the moment but I'd like to thank you for saving something very important to me. Here is my business card, please call me and I'll buy you lunch.'

'I'm not sure,' Sarah began.

'Please, I'm very grateful and, well, you did laugh at me. You probably think me a bit of a picnic short of a sandwich but surely you could make amends by coming to lunch. Where you like, you choose somewhere you'll feel safe meeting a stranger like me.'

'Maybe,' she said hesitantly, her curiosity aroused.

'OK. I'll pretend that was a yes then,' he said, his smile broadening. 'Thanks again, I must dash,' and with that he ran up the stairs. Sarah's train had gone but there would be another in three minutes so she stood, inspected his card and pondered. It read, '*Luke Aylmer, Research and Development Department*,' and then gave a business address and telephone number.

Hmm, what a morning already, she thought. Thankfully she still had plenty of time before her personality and ability tests were due and the interview booked for afterwards. She was intrigued, however, in questioning herself and determining if she had detected a slight West Country twang in his voice. Maybe. No matter, she dismissed the thought while catching the next train and concentrating on what was to come and the likely questions she would get in her interview.

– FOOD FOR THOUGHT –

Three people latched onto the end of the queue of the restaurant-come-cafeteria on the sixth floor of the Admiralty building. Edmund Athelstan Weston was studying the large placard displaying the menu while standing at the head of this threesome. He was a man in his late fifties, part balding, part grey and a little bit neglected around the edges. He was a true gentleman though, still clinging to his old values. In the section he ran of the department, people were still addressed by their surnames.

'Anything catch your eye, Bowers?' he asked the attractive woman behind him in the queue while still studying the menu in front of him. Marwenna Lesley Bowers was in her mid- to late twenties, had spent time in the services and had now moved on to work in intelligence. She was very keen to become operationally involved but had so far only been assigned back office tasks during her eighteen months in the department.

Knowing Setford was behind her in the queue she deliberately looked around the restaurant, making it obvious she was looking for a handsome man that caught her eye and replied, 'No, sir, not particularly,' her slight Cornish accent less discernible since working in London. Marwenna, having been brought up with three brothers, loved to gently tease Setford as she knew he was sweet on her but struggled to talk to her as he was quite shy. She was confident, bright, serious about her work, knew what she wanted and what terms she would accept it under, and had a really mischievous sense of humour. Her gutsy, steely resolve contrasted well with her vivacious nature. Setford, for his part, could be really great fun to be with when he opened up, which was rare at the office.

Perhaps without realising it deep down she had a real soft spot for Setford. She just could not resist making him squirm and blush a little and felt she could read him like a book. A suppressed smile started to creep onto her face as she reflected on the time she was in the back of a crowded lift and Setford, without seeing her, entered it with a large press of people, turning around to face the doors as they closed. She managed to pinch his cute behind without detection. He did his best to turn around but did not know who of the two people directly behind him it could have been. To this day, he never knew it was her, hidden from view. Her smile grew.

They collected their meals; Weston had insisted on paying for all of them. At his direction, they sat down in a corner area away from other diners.

'Sorry to bring you here but we needed to meet away from the office somewhere secure but where no one from our department visits. What I am about to tell you is totally unofficial and you have total freedom to walk away after this meeting with no comeback. It is not part of your normal duties or job description, I know, but it is important.' He momentarily subconsciously touched a small square of embroidery kept in his left jacket pocket before picking up his fork and his conversation.

Marwenna was already interested; Setford wasn't but became interested when he realised that Marwenna was. After all, it might mean some time spent with her even if it was on operations. Marwenna's mind raced with excitement at the potential implications of working undercover. Perhaps an office somewhere in a high-powered position, monitoring decisions and sussing out personalities with the possibility of planting bugs and surveillance work after hours.

'We don't have the resources or political will for this but I think it is worth investigation,' continued Weston. He withheld the fact that he had been politely warned off this case by a senior officer in the division, or that he suspected that someone in the upper echelons was stonewalling any further official investigation. He had more than a gut feeling that some misinformation had been cascaded down within his own department.

'If this assignment does come to something and the investigation is successful then it will be more than a feather in your cap. I will of course cover for you at work. It is an information-gathering only role. Any sign of danger or discovery and you are to get out immediately. You, Setford, are to be technical backup. Bowers, I have managed to get you employment with some access to all floors but not all areas of the building. You are ostensibly an agency worker. Not very glamorous, I'm afraid. Just keep your ears and eyes open particularly around the Research and Development section. Find out as much as you can about the personnel who work there or have worked there. I do know there has been a death recently but there has been a spurious link to some terrorist chatter from the Corporation in general.'

– A DARK OFFICE ON A DARK EARLY MORNING –

Very early on the same day a meeting had taken place between two Savile Row-suited executives sitting in a subdued lighted office somewhere high in one of the many soaring, characterless office blocks cramping the city skyline – edifices perhaps to monetary success, housing mega global corporations with designer identities that shout their achievements to the world, but whose smoked-glass windows allowed only filtered daylight in and very little light out. Was this for purely aesthetic taste or had it a convenient double use to mask some less acceptable public dealings with suspect motives, or maybe just to cover occasional mistakes? The two men spoke in low voices and could barely be seen in the semi-darkness. Nichols chose not to confide to his subordinate security officer, Fazul Arif, that he had already arranged weeks ago for a bug to be planted inside Luke Aylmer's phone. Had Arif known, it would have made him suspicious enough to check his own phone for bugs. This, Nichols had previously engineered, the implanted bug being secreted at the very start of Arif's employment. It was easy enough to arrange as each member of staff working for the Corporation had to lock away their personal phones into personalised security phone lockers for the working day as part of corporate security policy. In addition to this he also withheld from Arif the fact that together with the original base salary data he was now monitoring all financial transactions on Luke Aylmer's building society and financial accounts as well as recording all the physical geographical locations of Luke Aylmer's mobile phone. He had also, again unbeknown to Arif, had his top operative place a secret device still in development in Aylmer's office to affect his brain behaviour. Arif started his report.

'My technical staff's search has proved fruitless so far. We've tried all our standard checks of logs, hidden files, directories, access history, and now we are trying the more technically exotic approaches. We checked for cloud access just in case he went against corporate policy. You should see some the equipment they have got in there. He must have been a real enthusiast. Some of the gear is decades old. All sorts of obscure operating systems and languages as well. We even took the really old VDU they had there and checked for imprints on the screen, as on old models, if they were left on overnight they could cause heat damage on the actual screen and hence the outline of a display.'

Dave Blagdon's death, though arranged, had come too late for Nichols' purpose, as Blagdon's project work had disappeared without trace. How Blagdon had anticipated his own death and had planned accordingly was a mystery. More frustrating for Nichols was that because of Blagdon's popularity, his funeral was packed with over a hundred people, none of whom he could link meaningfully with his work for the Corporation. Arif continued his report.

'Our nocturnal visit to Aylmer's flat while he was away on the course you had arranged for him has showed up nothing.'

'Spare me any more of the details,' replied the short, fat – some would politely say portly – bearded Nichols, adding with a little dismissive wave of his hand, 'I'm aware of that, nor did your search of Blagdon's place immediately after his death. Just arrange the monitoring of Aylmer from a distance. You've had two months and you have turned up nothing, either on the project work disappearance or on this Aylmer who shared an office with Blagdon. So, I have adopted a new strategy. I am passing the problem on to another department. Now, I suggest you read these notes and await Aylmer at his office.' He handed some notes to Arif. 'Your final part in this phase is to go to his office this morning under the guise of corporate security and brief Aylmer according to these instructions here,' he said as he handed a further covering note to Arif. 'I've arranged for our target to be out of the office for part of this morning. Ensure that you delay him a tad so he feels under pressure.'

Arif didn't like the fact that he was deemed to have failed. He made a mental note to himself that he would think of something else to achieve success. That would show Nichols a thing or two.

'One final thing before you go. I'm having to move your fifth secretary in two years. You really must control your attitude. Even in my position I cannot keep covering for your outbursts. Human Resources are becoming difficult to placate.'

This mild condemnation rankled Arif; already slightly perspiring, his pride dented, he managed to quell and control his anger. Nichols waited for Arif to leave and then picked up a phone and dialled a number.

'Ah, Ruby. Did you enjoy your last foreign jaunt?'

'It was successful as you well know. I gather you are recruiting a new assistant for my office,' she said, her voice as beguiling as it was appealing.

'Nothing but the best for you, of course. I trust your rest and recreation break went well. Are you pleased with your new jewellery purchases? Collection complete yet?'

'There are a few pieces I still have my eye on to complete my collection,' she said as she placed her hand in front of her to view the new rings she had bought.

As her collection had grown, her pleasure in it had started to wane a little. Each new acquirement had less of a thrill compared to the previous ones and even less so compared to the earliest. Nothing quite eclipsed her very first trophy. In monetary value it was comparatively low, being far exceeded by her later purchases. However, she did not buy the first one. It was a gift which always reminded her of her first major success and the power she could wield. Each item represented a job done or a conquest taken, and not all items were jewellery, which would have been a surprise to Nichols. Ruby knew what he was leading up to and sometimes wished he would cut the flannel. She was surprised, though, that he was not using their normal coded wording but knew that he always ensured that his corporate phone conversations, though recorded, were wiped and destroyed.

'I have another job for you and if it pans out right, then I'm sure we can remedy that. I'd like you to work undercover in the Research and Development office in the city. If you remember, it's the office you placed the bug and gamma device in before your last assignment. Obviously remove the device while you are working there. We can't have you becoming clumsy and less effective, can we? But leave the bug. The target will be out of the office when you arrive. I've already sent you the usual file on him so if you could build up a dossier of his further movements and contacts and size him up, creating a profile of weaknesses etc, it will prove useful. You can set the scene with him when he returns this afternoon. Ostensibly, you are auditing and trying to rebuild Blagdon's project work in minute detail, which gives you lots of leeway in asking questions of Aylmer. See what you can wheedle out of him. You might need to turn on your indefatigable charm if need be. In addition, I want you to start planning for another possible termination to take place.'

'Won't that arouse suspicion? It'll be a second death in that section. Besides, isn't it a little too soon after the others in the same field in the other research labs across the globe?'

'Admittedly the first was "encouraged" to take his own life, but he was in Brazil. The second in London we had to make it look like suicide. Having said that, the target I have in mind does not work in research but he is becoming a bit of a liability.'

After his previous conversation, Nichols had made a mental note that Arif was getting too risky; maybe he was getting to the end of being useful and one day his 'secret' terrorist agenda would actually come to fruition. Nichols had known for some time that Arif was plotting to snatch Corporation technology when the opportunity arose.

'When do you want the termination done?'

'Not till I give the word, let's keep our options open in terms of timing and method, possible accident or overt assassination. Either might serve our purpose.'

After the conversation Nichols replaced the telephone, smiled and sat back in his chair. His long journey from being a bully that had been allowed to get away with it had morphed into becoming someone hooked on control. As the years progressed, he had attained power and status but he had hungered after more. In the business world he had always been very competitive and aggressive but now his ambition was way beyond the purely commercial. Initially he had lapped up the status, the trimmings and trappings of his achievements, the fact that he could bask in his lordship over people and companies. They, though, no longer held any shine or satisfied him as they once did. They had become merely trinkets of the past and of little value or pleasure. Now his desires centred solely on control of larger entities.

— ALL BEFORE MORNING TEA —

When Luke Aylmer got to his office the light was already on and Arif was waiting for him. He rose and greeted him with a handshake.

'Hi, I'm Fazul Arif. I work in the Corporation's Security and Audit department. I need to chat to you about how things have been left since the demise of Mr Blagdon. Such a sad business. Did you know him well?'

'Yes, he was a very good friend.' Luke dumped his case and took his coat off. 'I was interviewed soon after his death by your section.'

'Yes, I am aware of that but we like to cross the T's and dot the I's. Did he ever talk to you about Project Crescent?'

'Well, no, I've not heard of that. We did share some projects but both of us are, I mean were, assigned to different projects most of the time. When we were on different projects, we were not allowed to talk about the work. Of course, you know the Corporation security drill concerning separate access, filing and the locking up of any research notebooks on a daily basis. If we were on different projects, we could not discuss it with each other or anyone else for that matter. The last thing I knew that he was working on was virtual reality headgear to help people with depression. They were running trials in conjunction with a university, I believe.'

'Well, keep this under your hat. This is strictly company top secret but we think that Blagdon was under pressure from industrial or foreign government spies, possibly the DGSE of

Rainbow Warrior fame. We think he may have been blackmailed and could not cope with the consequences. Hence the suicide. It is, of course, well known about the stress IT staff often work under so the additional pressure of outside coercion may well have tipped him over the edge.'

Luke cast his mind back to how Dave was. He briefly remembered the zany things they would do at an opportune time to relieve the pressure from their intense workload. He could still picture them pretending to Cossack dance while both seated on their office chairs awaiting computer jobs to finish. Another flashed into his mind of their backward-rowing races across the office while still seated on their five-wheeled chairs. He stifled a smile as another memory replaced the previous: their silly competition to see who could get the furthest across the office without touching the floor. This involved clambering over desks, chairs, filing cabinets, whatever was convenient. They had a real laugh with that one. His mind refocused.

'I still can't believe it. I'm sure he would be the last person to think of that. He was always so honest in all his dealings,' Luke stated.

'We feel he may have been forced to take something out of the company. Something very valuable but secret. Hence our not using the police. If you can think of anything or come up with something, however minor, then let us know immediately.' Arif passed him his business card and scribbled a private number on it as well.

'Of course, it goes without saying.'

'As you know we sent people over to clear up most of his research work quickly. We'll be sending a forensic security auditor to help evaluate and summarise his work in total. I believe they may be starting today. Did Blagdon leave anything with you at all?'

'He left me his bible he sometimes used in his lunchtimes.' Luke pulled it out from his desk drawer and handed the book over to Arif.

'Do you mind if I borrow this for a short while? About a week or so. I will return it undamaged.'

'Be my guest.'

'Can you tell us if he did or said anything out of the ordinary in the final months?'

'Not really, because in so many ways there was nothing ordinary about Dave Blagdon. I mean, to all intents and purposes he appeared very normal,' Luke confirmed and then added, 'totally average in fact, but when you got to know him his interests were varied and deep.' Arif, knowing the time, now felt he had delayed Luke Aylmer long enough.

'Oh, by the way, I believe you have to deputise for an interviewer this morning as they are off sick. The receptionist mentioned it to me when I left this morning.'

'Really? Where?' said Aylmer, hurriedly logging in and accessing his diary.

'Shellac building, South Bank, I think.'

'What time?'

'I'm not sure.'

'In less than half an hour. Blast, I'm behind as it is,' stressed Luke.

'Oh, so sorry to have kept you. It doesn't give you a lot of time, does it?'

Luke dashed out of the office with sour thoughts of having to miss a brew to start the office day, noticed the lift was busy, probably due to the tea round, and started to descend the stairs.

Edna, the tea lady, was showing the ropes of delivering tea and sundries to multiple floors in the same building and giving the lowdown on all their client base, floor by floor, to her newly arrived protégée – which ones to watch out for, who not to trust, those that would take a mile if given an inch and the like. They had just exited the lift on the Research and Development floor and Edna had started describing the clientele and their usual orders.

Luke Aylmer, already running late for his newly discovered appointment, retraced his steps up the staircase, having forgotten his briefcase. Unfortunately, while just trying to catch his breath he misjudged his stride on the final step and tripped, causing him to go sprawling. With unerring accuracy, while reaching out to save himself he collided with the tea and sandwich trolley that Edna and her new assistant had parked close to the stairs. His reaching out managed with expert ingenuity to push the tea trolley into one of the lifts that were diagonally opposite, much to Edna's chagrin. With perfect timing the lift doors then closed and the lift proceeded on an upward journey. This left Edna wondering which floor the doors would open at and hoping that it wasn't the fourth where some of her regular 'gannets' were liable to pilfer the unattended trolley of its riches. As Luke fell, his shoulder managed to knock the noticeboard off the wall, which, with inextricable bad timing and lack of luck, landed corner first on his foot. He apologised profusely to Edna while holding his painful foot and hopping on the other one.

'I'm so sorry, Edna. I'll get it back for you.'

Edna's new assistant stood motionless for a moment, mouth agape as the lift doors had closed. Then, seeing on which floor the lift stopped, volunteered to run up and get it, and as she started to climb half heard Edna exclaim, 'Don't worry, Mr A, I can see you're in a hurry. We'll get it back. I think I've got some porn plasters for your foot if you need them.' The assistant wondered if she had heard right as she lightly ascended. *Surely I misheard. She couldn't have said 'porn'.*

Edna quickly pressed the button to call the lift while checking from the lights above the lift which floor it had stopped at. She waited for Luke to collect his briefcase and disappear down the stairs again, and remarked to her new trainee who had emerged with the trolley from the elevator, 'That nice Mr Aylmer has not been quite the same since Mr Blagdon died. You know, I think we could do with one of those dead waitresses.'

'Dead waitresses?' questioned her new helper.

'Yes, you know, dead waitresses,' repeated Edna and gesticulated pulling open doors and pulling on ropes.

'Oh, I see. Dumb waiters are what we call them where I come from.'

'Yes, that's the ones. That's what I meant,' confirmed Edna.

– THE INTERVIEW –

Having just arrived with five minutes to spare to conduct the interview, Luke Aylmer checked with the receptionist as to where the interview room was and collected the corporate question list and interviewer notes. He then stopped off in the gents' to freshen up. He washed his hands and face and started to comb his blond hair when he was interrupted by the alarm on his watch so he dashed to the interview room, forgetting to take the comb out of his hair, and zoomed straight past the receptionist into the interview room. Looking out of the window with his back to the door he heard it open and started to speak as he turned around.

'I take it you have already been to Human Resources.' He hesitated as Sarah came into full view. 'Erm, before we start the formal interview do you have any questions at all?'

She put her hand to her mouth and muttered 'erm' and then pointed to the comb in his hair.

'What?' He started to turn around to see what was out of the window she was pointing to. Again, she pointed to his hair.

'Erm.' By this time, she was so nervous she started to giggle. Trying to get some restraint back she said, 'There's a comb in your hair, I am so sorry for laughing. It's just that I'm nervous.' Then added, 'Is this an observation test?'

'Oh drat, sorry about that. I was running a shade late and, well, you saw the outcome.' He took the comb out of his hair and nervously smiled as he sat down. There was an uncomfortable silence as he gestured for her to sit down. Sarah's heart sank. She had really wanted this job. Finding silences uncomfortable, his mouth went dry and he started to sweat as the sensation of hot blood rising to his face took effect. After a thoughtful, if uncomfortable, pause he resumed.

'It's OK, so am I. Let me assuage your worries. I'm afraid I'm filling in for Ms Fenwick.' His smile became far more natural. 'Maybe I'd better say the result of your interview won't be based on our encounter this morning or whether you have lunch with me or not. Please don't worry, you won't be working with me or near me as I have been seconded to conduct your interview on someone else's behalf. I work in a different building at a different location anyway. So, let's just start afresh and treat our interview professionally as if we have seen each other for the very first time. If you do decide to ring me for lunch, wait till after the result of the vacancy filling has been passed on to you. You may not want to come. Have you any questions before we start?'

'Why did I have to hand in my mobile phone when entering the building?'

'Corporation security policy, I'm afraid. Mobiles have cameras, the Corporation has commercial secrets and due to the special communication insulation in the buildings they don't work too well anyway. It's company policy to use the landlines. We are at liberty to make free personal phone calls, within limits, using their phones though. Your phone would have been locked away in its own small cubicle and will be returned when you leave.'

With that he went through the questions set for all the candidates, making occasional notes on her answers. They shook hands in a business-like manner at the end of the interview and Sarah travelled homeward not sure how she felt. One moment she was hopeful, another downcast, another curious to see him again. She thought him a very proper, polite man, if a little out of sync with things around him, and caught herself starting to daydream about him on the train home.

Luke, for his part, took pains to deal with Sarah's interview fairly, as he did with the two other interviewees after her. The other two candidates were good, but did not quite match Sarah's experience. Thankfully, he could generally compartmentalise his thoughts and feelings and made the recommendation on merit, experience and best fit for the job, but he did make a mental note that actually, he really did want to see her again. Luke found himself thinking about her laughing eyes and the smell of her scent. He then left his sealed recommendations and paperwork with Human Resources and travelled back to his office.

– THE VICAR AND THE IMAM –

'You are in my way,' said vicar Peter Hones to Martha, his wife, this being an ongoing mock complaint between the two of them that had run for years when domestic chores were to be done and shared.

'Who was here first?' she replied.

'Well, first there were the dinosaurs and...' he started to reply flippantly.

'You were here first then, you old relic!' Martha got her riposte in very quickly. They both smiled as they completed their housework chores. Like any successful marriage they were part lovers, part friends and worked well as a team, each aware of the other's limitations. Any creaks or strains in their relationship were well oiled by love and respect, and their bond had grown and been shaped by all that life had thrown at them, producing a unique joining so that one half would not fit with anything or anyone else. The vicar had enjoyed the distraction but then returned to his desk to attempt his umpteenth version of the welcoming speech to the symposium he had been trying to organise.

'Friends, Romans, countrymen. Lend me your money!' he joked to himself. The doorbell rang.

'I'll get it, Peter.'

Though a vicar, a lot of his congregation nicknamed him 'Pastor' because his gifts and ministry were really concerned with pastorship. He was never too good on administration, which was one of many maddening shortcomings Martha had coped with over the years. Fortunately, she in contrast was very organised. Martha opened the door.

'Hello, Mo, how's Mrs Noor?'

'Oh, she's fine. I know you two have not met yet, have you? You will have to come over and meet her. Her name is Ayesha, by the way.'

'He's in his study. I'll just get him. Is it work or chess today?'

Overhearing, Peter shouted, 'It's a little of both. We can multitask, you know! Could we have some tea, please?'

'Why is it you men have so much tea?' she shouted back.

'We have bigger engines to keep going, Martha. Besides, it takes a lot of tea to make me this handsome and maintain my beauty regime and Adonis physique,' came his reply.

'You are obviously not drinking enough then, are you, because it's not working,' she bellowed back.

'Exactly, O she of the tantalising teapot.'

'Would you like some tea, Mo?' Martha asked in her usual quiet, calming voice, ushering him in.

'If there's enough, after all that Peter needs,' replied Mohammed with a grin. She showed Mohammed Noor into

Peter's study, which was rather similar to Mohammed's study at the local mosque. Having delivered some tea she exited saying, 'Right, well, I'll leave you two to it but don't let Magnifi in through the window or you'll teach her bad habits.'

'Magnifi?' queried Mohammed.

'It's our new cat. Family joke in naming him,' replied Peter.

'Oh, I see. How are the speeches going?'

'I have just been working on my opening welcome address: *"Friends, Romans, countrymen, lend me your lugholes. Once more unto the breach, dear friends, once more, or close the English Channel up with our waste and rubbish. Nothing so becomes a man as plastic bottles"* etc.'

'That bad, eh?!'

'Actually, a bit better than that and crucially I still have time. You're a bit quieter than usual and look a bit, well, preoccupied,' observed Peter Hones. 'What is it? Mrs Noor OK?' he asked, concerned.

'Ayesha is fine.'

'Everything at the mosque OK?'

Mohammed hesitated. Such was his relationship with Peter that he knew he could trust him but still was a little reticent to admit what was deeply troubling him. Finally, he spoke bluntly.

'Did you ever have trouble with extremists in church?'

'Not personally but there have been cases in the past, though more to do with politics than religious misinterpretation. Our minister licensing system is meant to deal with the threat and ensure a certain degree of responsibility and consistency. Why, what's happened?'

'I found some literature that has been distributed to some of my mosque members. I'm not sure it is just literature either as I think there have been some fringe meetings, DVDs and internet contacts as well. Our mosque administrators are considering the options available to deal with it but it is worrying. We've contacted the police, of course, but it's weighing heavy on my heart.'

'I'm sure. The last thing you want is negative press and an undoing of all the hard work you have put into educating on the Koran.' Mohammed was pleased he could share a little of what worried him, and knowing that he had done all he could for the present time decided to change the subject.

'What's the progress on the symposium? Is everyone coming?'

'Yes, the environmental groups were no problem and some are going to produce the latest research and scientific facts for us. The Jewish representatives, Buddhists and Sikhs are on board. The biggest trouble I had, believe it or not, was with the Humanists. I think they were worried about their street cred being associated with religious types like us. I had to invite their representative round to convince them to commit. We talked about what we were attempting to do and then meandered off into the usual criticisms about organised religion. You know the sort of thing, about religion causing wars to which I countered about godless regimes, like Stalin's and Pol Pot's, responsible for even more deaths and suffering. Then about people claiming God on their side to which I countered that the question should be "Are we on God's side?" not "Is God on our side?" We sort of partially agreed that mankind can be a pretty selfish and untrustworthy animal and I hope we parted with a bit more respect for each other's position. It does bug me a bit that people never seem to raise the subject of all the good that has been done because of religious views. I'd like to think that my arguments swung him round concerning our project, but I more than suspect that it was Martha's angel cake that was more convincing. Another unsung victory for women's persuasion! One of her special smiles was always my undoing but I've never told her which one for fear of total capitulation.' They both grinned. 'The venue is booked. It's at the Queen Elizabeth II Centre,' added Peter.

Peter and Mohammed had been childhood friends and had chosen similar paths albeit one was a Muslim path and the other Christian. Both men had been classmates at the same school and both had been through the faith mill in terms of form criticism and the various theories espoused by esteemed and not so esteemed theologians and philosophers. They both had had to battle through in their separate ways the philosophical problems raised when violence in history had been done in the name of religion.

'You know this idea of yours reminds me a little of the House of Wisdom in Baghdad, not so much of collecting and translating for knowledge but getting people of different outlooks to care about one thing plus the added bonus of taking out several layers of politics,' Mohammed ventured.

'Well, politicians have failed, though for some not for the want of trying. As for removing politics, not all politics, I'm afraid. Limiting it to environmental issues has helped greatly though. Mind you, you would have thought it should be blindingly obvious to everyone that the planet is too precious to be left solely in the hands of politicians and big business corporations. We all have a vested interest in the planet's survival and therefore its stewardship. There still are the personal political levels of getting everyone to work together and of course where necessary supporting legal, peaceful action. For instance, I'm proposing if we discover companies behaving in an irresponsible way, we could either use consumer buying power or buy token shares and raise issues at their annual shareholders' meetings. Grant you, it has been done before, if memory serves, with sugar cane companies and how they were treating their workers in the Dominican Republic. In those cases, it did work. The companies did change their behaviour. Consumer buying power is usually the stronger influence though. If we can pull this off and it proves successful it could be a blueprint for other nations.' He paused and then questioned, 'House of Wisdom?'

'Yes, during the time of the Ummayads and Abbasids, great minds from diverse backgrounds, many of them Christian as well as Muslim, were devoted to translating great philosophical, medicinal, scientific and theological works and developing knowledge. This contributed greatly to Islamic civilisation throughout the fourth to seventh centuries.'

'I'm sorry, I don't follow the correlation.'

'They were aspiring to one thing irrespective of their diverse outlooks on life. Don't you see? We may well be starting something similar. When you have the chance, look up Hunayn ibn Ishaq, the Gondishapur Academy etc.'

'You name dropper you!' Both men laughed.

'Where did you learn about the House of Wisdom?'

'In my all too short a time at Al Azhar in Cairo, I used it as part of a module for my PhD. A bit like yourself in studying Protestant, Roman Catholic, Orthodox, Eastern and all those in between and beyond your faith. It was part of my studies into Sunni, Shia and all the other offshoots of my faith.'

'Ah, he who has not endured the stress of study will not taste the joy of knowledge,' quoted Peter.

'Where did you pick that up from?' asked Mohammed.

'Comparative religion module at university, though personally I still hold to *"much knowledge increases sadness"*. I suspect we have both come to a similar conclusion in our search for illumination.'

'Which is?'

'Why, we have found faith in the most surprising places which challenges our own personal small faith in very practical ways. I fancy a break, especially while we have some tea. White or black?'

'Tea?'

'No, chess pieces,' clarified Peter. Mohammed chose black as he loved to counter-attack.

'How is this making yourself available on a lunchtime going?' asked Mohammed.

'Nothing so far but I'm obviously praying about it and feel it is right to make the time available.'

'Well, if it works, let me know and I might try it.'

'Sure thing, now to a hopefully different opening gambit which might knock your socks off.'

– TROLLEY TALK –

It was the end of the afternoon tea trolley round and Edna continued to show the new starter her duties. If ever there was a mother figure it was Edna Aetheldreda Bass, the Aetheldreda being a throwback from a Victorian aunt. Edna was at an age and stage in life where keeping up with and after her children sometimes left her a little flustered. She would on occasion search in vain for the correct words or would get her statements muddled. She had always been maternal, even from an early age. Though she maybe lacked imagination, and sometimes spoke before she thought things through, she had a steely resolve when it came to things that mattered to her, namely her family. If put to the test she would leave many people in her wake when the chips were down. Edna took to her new trainee with an open heart, thinking more of her as a slightly older daughter than her own offspring. She was impressed with how conscientious her new protégée was and was pleased that her new help was so eager to learn.

'What with the to-do here this morning with the trolley, I think we'd better park it well away from the stairs,' guided Edna before launching into a further introductory spiel. 'Well, dearie, we occasionally do conference teas of an evening as well as the usual day work. That's why we advertised for a trainee, as when my Bert is home I like to be there with him and the family. I really don't want to be at work in the evening, even though my youngsters can look after themselves now. Done much of this before?'

'No, not really,' stated Marwenna.

'Marwenna, that's a pretty name. I've not heard of that before. Is it Irish?'

'No, it's Cornish. What's that suite of offices there?'

'That's the Research and Development lot, you remember from this morning. Live on tea they do, well did. Very nice and polite they are but it's not been the same since Mr Blagdon died. So tragic. He was such a cheery chap. Really pleasant. I can't believe he would have committed suicide though, what with him being religious an' all. They said they found him with, oh, what are they called now?' She mimed injecting someone frantically while searching for the correct term which she knew was on the tip of her tongue. 'Hyperdeemic nurdles,' she stated with an air of pride. 'Right by his body.'

'Syringes, my word,' Marwenna said with a straight face not quite believing what she had just heard.

'Yes, I think it had those drugs, what do you call them now? Don't tell me, I'll get it in a second.' She hesitated searching for the right terms. 'Anna-bollock stair-rods!' she said triumphantly.

'Oh, right, steroids eh?' replied Marwenna just about successfully stifling a titter.

'All that is left in their office now is Mr Aylmer. Another nice chap, single, I think. Though he has not been the same since his colleague died. He's got very accident prone lately. Are you courting, dearie?'

'No, not at all, I mean, no, no one at present.'

'What, no one caught your eye? I'm sure some nice young fella will snap you up. I think that nice Mr Aylmer is single. Oh sorry, I already said that, didn't I, dearie.' By this time, they had transferred all of the leftovers and dirty cups from one trolley onto the urn trolley ready to be put into the lift.

At this moment, Luke exited a database technical support office while reading a manual but unfortunately marginally misjudged the door surround, his foot catching on it. He sprawled head first onto the empty trolley, the manual flying out of his grasp. The trolley then proceeded to progress down a flight of stairs with him on top of it voicing a bump-controlled, low, syncopated operatic 'argh', coming to a stop at the stairwell wall and him in a crumpled heap.

'See what I mean, dearie, not quite the same,' Edna observed and shouted after him, 'Not again, Mr A! Not your day, is it? Are you alright?'

'No worries, Edna, it's only a few bruises and what's left of my dignity that's hurt.'

Luke got up quickly, returned the trolley and then collected his partly damaged manual. He could not believe how clumsy he had become. Maybe his balance had become poor due to his body belatedly dealing with the psychological impact of his experience in Afghanistan, he surmised. He made a mental note to see his doctor about it. Returning to his desk he was surprised to find a young attractive woman seated at Dave Blagdon's old desk.

'Hello, I'm Sapphire, Sapphire O'Connor. I'm from Computer Audit. You must be Luke Aylmer.' She smiled and offered her hand. As she did so Luke noticed she seemed to wear a lot of rings and jewellery.

'How do you do.' They shook hands.

'I am here to try and tidy up the loose ends of Dave Blagdon's work. Sorry for taking over your office.'

'No worries,' he replied.

'You have an awful lot of outdated equipment here,' she observed.

'Yes, that's mainly down to Dave. He rescued bits and pieces thrown out. That old box over there holds what Dave called the Rolls-Royce of mainframe operating systems, ICL's SCL, and that one is a very primitive PC with an old version of CP/net.'

'What's that over there?'

'Ah, that's an old arcade machine which Dave rescued and adapted. We occasionally played on it of a lunchtime.'

– DAY'S END –

The world appeared to turn slowly as the winter lights already on in many homes and offices blotted out the panoply of Milky Way stars above. People were starting to ready themselves for night-time shifts or early bed. The night cold began to cut into the homeless whose makeshift shelters were far from effective. City traffic, always busy, had by now subsided a little, perhaps lulled by the cold grip of the season before it would grow again in the morning. The ancient Thames fulfilling another cycle of ebb and flow was particularly cold this night, its slow immense power acting as an eerily silent backdrop to the noisy transient traffic on its banks.

Sarah finished her two-hour evening dance practice at her local church hall, feeling a lot better for it, and went home to her Tooting flat. She wondered how long before she would hear the result of her interview, while putting her business clothes in the washing machine. Luke Aylmer's business card fell out of one of the pockets. She picked it up, examined it again and carefully put it in a bedside drawer. After showering she slipped into bed and turned her lamp off. About half an hour later, not being able to sleep, she switched on the light, turned on the radio[1], opened the drawer and reread his card and thought of his smile. She

---

[1] The radio plays, 'We slumber, the world turns, while God watches over us', a simple lullaby on piano.

then put the card back, turned the lamp off and, with a bit of a struggle, finally succumbed to slumber.

*

What a day this had been for Marwenna. First the exciting possibilities of operations and then the loss of sundries from the trolley, and her hands were now sore due to having to wash items which could not go into the Corporation's dishwasher. Ho hum. The downside of operations, but you have to start somewhere. Maybe after this successful assignment she will be considered for more important operations. After a shower she turned the radio on just before turning in, and relaxed to some quiet piano music[2].

*

After a bit of a shambolic day Luke Aylmer finally sat down to relax having tidied the dishes away from his evening meal. He felt too bushed to practise on his drum kit so decided to watch the 'Salt and Peanuts' brush duet of Steve Smith and Jeff Hamilton, hoping to glean more insight into brush technique on the snare drum. Though enjoyable, he was even too tired to concentrate on that. He still could not believe how uncoordinated and clumsy he had become. Again, his best assumption was that maybe it was the after-effects of him serving in Afghanistan. A sort of delayed battle trauma maybe. For the second time that day he made a mental note to book a doctor's appointment. He showered. Tired, he just closed his eyes and let his mind wander. It was then that he thought of Sarah's eyes. That was far more enjoyable.

*

---

2   The radio plays, 'We slumber, the world turns, while God watches over us', a simple lullaby on piano.

Edna snuggled into Bert in bed.

'All the tin lids in bed?' he asked.

'They went ages ago,' Edna said dismissively. ''Ere, guess what, Bert?'

'The chap who invented the steam engine,' he replied flippantly.

'No, silly, I've got a new helper at work. She's very keen and bright as a button so it won't be long before I won't have to do any evening work.'

'That's great, Duch', more time with the family and maybe a bit more time for how's your father.' He always called her his duchess.

'Give over, you daft thing, and give me a cuddle, you old codger.'

Within a minute Edna turned the light on again. 'Bert?'

'Yes,' said Bert keeping his eyes closed but guessing what was liable to come next.

'I'm worried about Joan. She's growing up far too quickly. She's already taking an interest in boys.'

'You worry too much. She'll be OK.'

'She's at a dangerous age, Bert. All those – what do you call them? – "ferro-moans" rushing through her veins.'

'I thought they were hormones.'

'No, I think that's what men have.' Science was not Edna's strong point.

'Oh, I see. No wonder I'm slowing up. My hormones have gone AWOL. That's why I need my sleep.' He turned the lights off.

A few minutes later Edna turned the lights on again.

'I've had the conversation with her but I don't think it's done much good.'

'Conversation?' asked Bert knowing he was going to regret asking.

'Yes, you know, when women grow into, well, women?'

'Well, surely that has prepared her.'

'I wish it had, Bert, but I think you need to have a conversation with her.'

'What conversation?'

'You know, *the* conversation.'

'I'm having enough trouble with this one. I repeat, what conversation?'

'A father's conversation with his daughter warning about boys. She always listens to you. She's a proper father's daughter, that one.'

'Honestly, Duch', if you could keep them at home till they were OAPs, you would. She's very sensible. She'll have a few hurts and break a few hearts in her turn on the romance front but she won't do anything foolish. If you think it will help, I'll have a word. Happy now? Now, can we go to sleep?' Bert turned the light off again.

''Course, darlin'', she added while cuddling up once more and then after a minute in the dark added, 'Tomorrow.' Bert quickly but briefly opened his eyes with an element of shock and fear. He had faced angry mobs in Northern Ireland when in the Royal Green Jackets but talking to his daughters about life with all their awkward questions and supposed superior logic was something else.

*

Weston worked late as he didn't fancy going home and facing an empty house. He spent time completing much of Marwenna's work in her absence, she being away information gathering for him. He had already completed the official formalities of her absence of leave. Finally, when he was tired enough, he returned to his abode to sleep as best he could. It had taken him a very long time to adjust to sleeping in the middle of the bed again.

*

After working on some of his music compositions, Setford had run out of inspiration. He looked at the forgotten dirty dishes in the sink and dismissed doing them till the morning. He settled down in bed with one of his favourite science fiction books, *Operation Blacklight*, from a series he was steadily working his way through. However, he had found himself revisiting this particular one often. Eventually tiredness won the day and he nodded off with the light still on.

*

Nichols looked out at the night sky from his penthouse while savouring a nightcap, the myriad lights representing so many lives in the city, lives he was already partially controlling. He thought of the minor setback to his plans that had occurred in Brazil, which as a consequence had spread to London. He could wait to see the outcome. At worst he would lose a piece of technology for the time being. A useful tool in his grand scheme. His mind wandered to the other irons he had in the Corporation fire. They were ticking away nicely. He took a final swallow and turned in for the night.

*

Fazul Arif waited patiently for his distant cousin Abdullah Alam to introduce him to a Daesh operative. Alam was a recent convert to the ISIS philosophy and his recruiter was interested in what Arif could supply in terms of technology from the Corporation that could help in the war they were waging against much of the planet. Once Alam had introduced them he left. Arif, for his part, was keen to see what money they would be offering and what provisions they could make if he needed to make a quick exit from the country.

'What device is it and what is its capability?' asked the imposing Daesh character. Fazul outlined what he knew. 'Can you accelerate its retrieval?'

The Daesh operative was keen not to show the desperation his organisation was increasingly experiencing by giving the impression of confidence drawn from a position of strength. The two men discussed the monetary reward, the escape plan and what could be done to bring the device into Daesh's hands quickly. Towards the end of their conversation the Daesh operative even tried some subtle coercion for Arif to join their cause. Arif implied he was sympathetic but not committed, well not just yet. He did emphasise that he would be more useful as a sleeper in the Corporation to see what else could be obtained for their cause. After the Daesh operative left, Arif reviewed their conversation. He felt he had done enough to convince this contact of his worth and possible later recruitment. In reality he did not believe in their cause but could see a way of making money, causing some grief to Nichols and the Corporation and eventually, at his own convenient choosing, disappearing.

*

Mohammed and Ayesha were cuddling in bed. They had only been married seven months but it felt as if they should always have lived like this. They had previously discussed the problem at the mosque and Ayesha did her best to reassure Mohammed that all would turn out well and gave him an extra tight squeeze. It didn't take long before they drifted off to their shared Land of Nod.

*

Martha and Peter had been privy to a late meeting concerning pastoral affairs. Both were tired and as they retired for the night Peter pinched Martha's behind as they climbed the stairs.

'Oi, pervert, have you put the cat out?'

'Of course,' Peter countered.

Too tired to read they snuggled close together in bed. Martha dropped off first, emitting her usual gentle snore and Peter followed soon after.

– SETTLING IN –

The next day Edna arrived at work to find Marwenna already getting things ready. There, too, was a bunch of flowers on her worktop.

'Flowers?' exclaimed Edna.

'They're for you, Edna.'

'For me! Oh, thank you.'

'No, they're not from me. You have an unknown admirer perhaps,' said Marwenna mischievously and then added, 'It's actually from Mr A with an apology for the trolley incident yesterday.'

'Ah, bless him. He's a real sweetie. They both were in that office,' stated Edna.

'Yes, he is quite cute. You sure nothing is going on between you two?' Marwenna couldn't resist pulling Edna's leg.

'No, I love my Bert. Mind you, if I weren't married and at least twenty years younger he would have turned my head. Has he turned yours?' Edna added, trying to turn the tables.

'Shall we have a cuppa before we start?' Marwenna changed the subject.

'Yes, and I'll turn the radio on.'

As they got the tea things and trolley ready, they hummed along to 'Always Something There To Remind Me' on the radio, singing the one or two lines they knew.

'This is one of my favourite music writers. He writes such good songs,' explained Edna in a louder voice.

'Who is the composer then?' Marwenna asked raising her voice too.

'Oh, for a minute I forget, but don't tell me, I'll get it in a second,' said Edna hesitating. Marwenna nearly spit out her tea when Edna triumphantly exclaimed, 'Burt Back-ache!' and carried on humming.

– ONE WEEK LATER –

One week later Sarah looked out of her bedroom to see the postman disappearing from her front door. *Funny*, she thought, *I normally hear him. I wonder if he has left the usual flyers and bills*. Donning her furry slippers, she ambled downstairs to the front door. Among the usual advertisements was a letter with a Corporation franking mark. She opened it quickly and there to her relief was a job offer, a contract and terms and conditions. Excitedly she read it through at least three times, signed the contract and made sure it caught the midday post.

She had a brief lunch and sat down just to calm herself when the thought of Luke Aylmer's business card entered her head. Umming and ahhing she wondered what to do. It would be useful to glean something more about the Corporation, she thought, and he could be a useful contact. And, it would be nice to say thank you for recommending her for the job. She did a very good job of convincing herself with logical reasons while ignoring the fact that she just really wanted to see him again. A little nervously she picked up the phone and dialled the number on his card.

'Luke Aylmer, Research and Development. Can I help you?'

'You already did,' she blurted out not meaning to say that as a first remark.

'Pardon?'

'Sorry, it's Sarah Manning here. I just called to say thank you for the job offer.'

'Oh, right. Glad to hear from you, though you needn't thank me. You were the best candidate by far for the job. By the way I have not forgotten my meal offer. It could be a celebratory meal. That is, if you are accepting the job. Are you?'

'Oh yes.'

'Where and when would you like to eat?'

'Is it difficult for you to get to Tooting in the evenings?' asked Sarah.

'Not at all.'

A VOICE FROM THE DEAD

Luke Aylmer woke up in a sweat after another night experiencing a recurring nightmare. Not a good start to the day when he was looking to a new beginning in the evening. Initially a variety of bad dreams had started after his second tour of Afghanistan. It was there he had served as a captain, having originally been a second lieutenant in the Royal Green Jackets and then after the amalgamation of regiments and promotions, The Rifles. Over time the horrors of what he'd seen and lived through were replayed and merged into one particular dream. As the months had passed into years, the dreams had become a lot less frequent but occasionally more intense. They would always start in the same way.

He would be viewing himself from above as he and his patrol passed through a ramshackle village. The village was the furthest they would patrol from Marshall's Post in Sangin district, a temporary strongpoint built with meagre resources at the sacrifice of riflemen's lives. A boy of the village turned around and greeted them smiling and waving. Towards the end of their previous tour they had bought and given some cricket gear to the local children. There he was, this little boy, as pleased as punch with the gift, holding the cricket bat and trying different shot poses. His sister had come out to look and laugh, she a little older than him, picking him up and hugging him as he was much smaller than her. Then setting him down, they held hands, smiled and waved as The Rifles walked through the village main street, such innocence shining through in their bright little faces in such heat and squalor. In his dream, Luke would try to shout to them from above to run with every fibre of his being but no sound would come forth. He would shout to his men and to himself but again no sound would be produced. Then he would try to run from above to any of them but his legs were like lead and would hardly move.

An incoming rocket-propelled grenade exploded in the village main street, carnage ensued, instant shock and devastation. He watched as a powerless witness from above, yet still experiencing the event as himself below, the training kicking in, fear being put in abeyance, compartmentalised like the memories that later would come back to haunt him. All round defence was adopted till the enemy could be located. Small arms fire commenced immediately as the Taliban followed up trying to make best use of their surprise attack.

He saw himself, partly deafened by the grenade, shouting orders or rather in his dream mouthing them as no sound seemed to register. The radio operator was already contacting base; several riflemen had spotted the source and immediately worked as a team in fire and movement to obtain the best defensive positions until they could glean something of the enemy strength. Within fifteen minutes air support was pounding the enemy position. Once the fire fight was over and the enemy in full retreat carrying their wounded and dead with them, Luke surveyed the scene as his section checked the situation to ensure it was secure. Discipline had been key. They'd been incredibly lucky having no casualties from this attack.

Caked with dust, tired by the adrenaline, the fear, the concentration, the heat, the heavy body armour, he turned to where the children had been. He felt sick yet in control; the limited dressings they had were applied to those still alive in the little village street. Then the background scene would darken and the boy's face and outstretched imploring arms would fly slowly, silently towards him from a retreating blackening backdrop, his mouth moving but no sound could be heard from his anguished shouts.

Luke had loved the army life. The regimental family, the loyalty, the professionalism, the teamwork, the friendships and the laughs and banter. There would be the leg-pulling, the wind-ups and so many things shared, sometimes hard, tough, funny, and sometimes sad. It would always stay with him as with most servicemen and women.

He had been incredibly proud of his men but when serving his final tour, the tension had started to wear him down; early signs of mood swings had been starting to appear as well as flashbacks. He knew then that for the sake of his men and for himself it was time to finish. Gone was the dashing officer in his No 1 dress about to start on his first tour; now a seasoned soldier knowing this current tour had to be his last. His compartmentalised emotions were always something he thought to be faced later on when he was still in service but now that he was on civvy street, Luke had chosen to deal with them sooner rather than later. He was very grateful for the support from his regiment, the army benevolent society, the British Legion and the army in general on his departure. They too were having to adapt in aftercare of servicemen with battle trauma.

He knew he was so much luckier than previous generations of servicemen. Other ex-soldiers he knew, or heard of in the past, were not always so fortunate to adapt back into civilian life, many not wanting to leave the army in the first place. It was not so surprising that many of the 'gentlemen of the road' have been ex-servicemen. Some had even committed suicide becoming estranged from their families who increasingly were unable to cope with their errant behaviour and mood swings as they grappled with the fallout of conflict experience. Because Luke was single and had no immediate family, he had not had that hurdle to overcome. He was helped to retrain in information technology and was found to have a real aptitude for it. After a tough time at first, and still occasionally a little hesitant, he was adjusting to civilian life very well considering.

– THINKING THINGS THROUGH –

During his years of service and for some time afterwards Luke Aylmer had tried to come to terms with the ethics of his role in the war and struggled with some of the paradoxes, not just of his part in it but with the mentality and attitudes of some of the Afghan people, particularly the Taliban. The mix of bribery, intimidation, drug trafficking, family debts and family honour infused by tribal loyalties made his head spin. He could and never would get his head around the mother who found it acceptable for her daughter to be a suicide bomber but was concerned about her female body bits being exposed in public after the explosion. It struck him as peculiar how they would accept and adopt new technology to wage war but ban other new technology for storing music etc. This was acceptable in their interpretation of Islam. How convenient. Of course, the better pay from the Taliban compared to the Afghan army renumeration he understood to be a major inducement for impoverished young men.

The Afghan tribe with which he had had most contact wanted no part in the conflict. They just desired to be left alone, to raise crops, not be in debt to drug runners or warlords, or have to barter off their daughters to pay debts. They neither wanted the soldiers nor the Taliban. After all, both disrupted their way of life and so they tried to be noncommittal as either side in turn held sway in the area. All he knew was that the more he saw, the more it appeared that those who had no real agenda suffered the most – the poor farmers, shopkeepers, especially the children and women whose voices were rarely heard and had little power themselves. They were the real victims who bore the brunt of the power struggles of ideology, sheer greed and corruption. They just wanted to live in peace and be left alone. Yes, he had been a soldier and was hardened to the realities of war, but why was it so often the innocent that catch it, that suffer?

Having attempted to rationalise and think it through he had also tried to empathise and sympathise as best he could with respect to their way of life. In the end, though, no matter what conclusion, if any, he had come to, these things were out of his control and the best thing was to focus on the job in hand. His men were his first priority and any issues aside from them he would have to deal with later. This he did with so many of his emotions too, as part of his training was to control his reaction to fear, panic and anger. Progressively over time he became worn down by the nature of the conflict and the frustration with the limited and unsatisfactory structures in place, whether they be political, tribal, social or even military.

In the end, he had to leave it all largely unresolved but did feel justified in the actions he had taken and was responsible for, in his small part in the conflict. Now he had started a new chapter in his life trying to leave behind the pain and the paradoxes. His IT research job, his friendship with Dave Blagdon were a massive boost. Sure, it was tough at first but it was getting easier. Then there was Dave's sudden death. That really knocked him back a bit. In the army, you would half expect it but in civilian life, it can be a shock. That was something else.

Dave had been a great help to him, particularly with his zany sense of humour. It had really helped him cope early on. Luke really missed him and still found it difficult to come to terms with the circumstances of his death. Even now with Dave gone he was getting better, but it was taking time. He sometimes found himself reminiscing about the times when there was a natural pause for both of them in their work and they would do something really silly to let off steam. There was the time they stood on their chairs and pretended to surf while singing the melody of 'Point Panic'. With that pleasing memory he began to look forward to his first date with a woman since leaving the army, but first things first, to work, and what a productive day it had turned out to be.

His research progressed well and he found Sapphire very friendly, though grew a little tired of her questions. Edna properly introduced him to her new helper and made sure he got an extra-large mug of tea. The day passed by very quickly.

– THE FIRST DATE –

Luke glanced at the clock as he arrived home from work and entered his flat's sitting room. Drat, he was a shade late and he would be seeing Sarah tonight. *Better get my skates on*, he thought. Before starting to shower he switched on the radio to hear the disc jockey say, '*This is John Watermain on Radio Upney and I'm just bursting to play this new song already high in the charts, so let's take it away with "The First Date*[3]*".*'

How apt, Luke thought, particularly as he too was running late. He very briefly pondered while showering, *I wonder whether this is what they call piped music. I suppose it could have been Handel's Water Music*, but dismissed it in an instant. Abluted and dressed, the upbeat tune and associated video clip that he

---

3 'The First Date' – an upbeat shuffle on guitar, drums and bass

had previously seen of it stayed in his mind as he journeyed across the city on his way to meet Sarah, his memory repeatedly replaying the track and video while travelling on the tube. It partly soothed him as he felt a little nervous apprehension mixed with exultation at the thought of meeting her. He wondered why the video had stayed in his head so readily. Probably, he thought, because of the relevant subject or maybe because the video was funny too and did not contain the usual sort of fashion-conscious sexualised dance moves or the supposed cool gangster poses cynically targeted at a teenage audience. He dismissed his musings as being unimportant and irrelevant as he alighted from the tube.

Sarah, who had chosen the restaurant close to where she lived, had the luxury of plenty of time to choose what to wear from the limited outfits she had. Eventually, she settled on an old favourite because it was one of the few with a matching ensemble.

THE FIRST DATE

Dashing home, he slips into the shower.
First date tonight. A little lady on his mind.
Soap smarts his eyes, he stumbles from the bathroom.
Rips his best shirt, in his rush to keep time.

Jumps in the car, bibs to gardening neighbour.
He's grooving now, easing back to relax.
Cruising along, glances down at the fuel gauge.
It registers low, where to get a full tank.
                    She's so nice… She's oh so very nice.

              Driving to the nearest gar-age.
              For his wallet has to for-age.
              Rush-es home for missing money.
            Gardening neighbour thinks it's funny.
    Signs on station forecourt saying sorry we are closed.

Speeding along, at last an opened garage.
'Filling up' with thoughts of her.
Motors right on, he makes her door to the second.
Misery, her mother says she's not there.

Called away on domestic crises.
'Won't be long, come inside, have a chair.'
Time goes by. Mum talks to entertain him.
At last she arrives. What a night for going out.
        She's so nice… She's oh so very nice.

        Sweating in anticipation.
        Fears of dried-up conversations.
        Trying hard to be so cool.
        Will she take him for a fool?
Small talk's not his forte nor chatting up his line.

Time for a drink, swift chat and some laughter.
A packet of crisps, too late for a meal.
Goodnights said, nervous tension makes him tired.
Laughs at events, against him conspired.

        Some date!

They both arrived spot on time to their surprise and relief, and met outside the restaurant. Though their conversation started a little awkwardly it soon picked up as they relaxed. The restaurateur kept a careful fatherly eye on all his regular single lady customers and took the opportunity to cast an eye over her date and from a distance managed a discreet wink and thumbs-up to Sarah. After initial niceties and polite inconsequential small talk, they finally relaxed enough to begin meaningful conversation.

'So, at your interview you mentioned you like dance,' Luke ventured inquisitively. Sarah took a deep breath.

'Oh yes, all sorts.'

This was true, but she refrained from saying her main interest was, in fact, dance in worship. Sarah already instinctively liked him but wondered whether if she spoke about it there and then he would think her a bit weird and be put off. As it turned out, the conversation moved on and she didn't have to say.

'Well, you know a fair bit about me from my interview,' began Sarah. 'So, what about you?'

'Me? Well, there's not much to tell really. Like you, my parents died quite a while ago and, like you, I have no siblings. I used to be in the army and after that trained in information technology, eventually working for the Corporation in one of their research laboratories. It's been about four years now. Dave Blagdon, who I used to work with, became a really good friend and helped me a lot when I was first out of the services. Sadly, he died earlier this year.'

He gazed into the distance with real sadness in his eyes as soon as he mentioned Dave Blagdon but then snapped out of it and began to look at her and smiled. He decided not to mention the anguish of recovery after his service life not only due to the operations he was on but the fact he had been forced to relive some of the actions he and his men had been involved with due to dubious court cases brought by money-making lawyers. Some of these lawyers had been encouraging supposed victims to complain in order to use the compensation justice system for their financial gain. The real cost in psychological trauma to his men and himself in recovery was never taken into account.

'Don't laugh, but I've taken up an interest in drumming after a distant uncle left me his precious drum set and a pile of drumming music books, DVDs and CDs in his will. I really enjoy it. A bit like you with dancing, I dare say.'

'Isn't it noisy?'

'Well, for the most part I use synthetic silencers on the kit, and practice pads so I don't annoy the neighbours. In fact, I'm definitely quieter than someone learning the saxophone or cornet. Besides, if you are taught well, you play off the top of the drums and not through them. I always try to remember a practice adage: first wrists, second finger control, finally arms with the least amount of movement possible for the arms and upper body and stay relaxed.'

'Oh, what colour is the set?' asked Sarah.

'It's green, terraverdi green, to be precise. It's from one of the original manufacturing runs by Premier of its Genista Birch range. I had to do a fair bit of research to find out about it actually. The snare drum is seven and a half inches in height. I know it's silly, but I've come to love it. I've tried other makes that are a lot lighter and made of maple and other woods but for me there is no comparison.' When he spoke, there was wide-eyed excitement in his face like a fixated passionate teenager.

'Why do men do that?'

'Do what?'

'Go into so much technical detail about things.'

'Don't women do the same about dresses, shoes and handbags?'

'I suppose we do.'

They soon discovered they had the same broad sense of humour, which ranged from whimsy to surreal, and both particularly liked humorous wordplay.

The evening went far too quickly for them both as they chatted and learnt more about each other to the point where the restaurant wanted to close. Luke walked her home and as he turned to go, he looked deeply into her eyes and said, 'I'd really like to see you again but if you're not keen then, well, thanks for a lovely evening.'

Sarah took two steps towards him, gave him a quick peck on the cheek and replied, 'I'd like to meet again too,' and quickly slipped back to her open door and disappeared inside. Luke returned home with a broad smile on his face.

– ROMANCE BLOSSOMS –

Six weeks had passed by so quickly for Sarah and Luke, during which the pair saw each other as often as they could. Aside from their initial physical attraction they really enjoyed each other's company, taking in concerts, art galleries, museums, films, books and walks in the parks and countryside.

Both thought it a nice idea to learn something together so decided to do a very short course on Lindy hop and explore a crash course on the visual arts, as both were interested but knew very little about the vast subject. They talked about anything and everything, though Luke didn't say much about Afghanistan and Sarah, sensing his reticence, never broached the subject. Sarah often talked about her love of dance in general but was more than a little hesitant to talk about dance in worship. After all the time they had spent together she really did not know why. She did, however, chat about her church life and contacts, even though she felt that recently in England it had become unfashionable to be a churchgoer, especially the way the media seemed to always portray them in such a negative light.

Luke, however, had soon put her at ease concerning his feelings about church and religion. In the army he had known all sorts of men, from devout Christians, Muslims, Buddhists, those who never thought too much about it to Humanists with attitude and even the odd Pagan. As far as he was concerned it did not matter. Much depended on their own understanding of what they stated they believed in, but they all had to get on with each other as a team. He always thought that's how life should be – people working together because of, and in spite of, their different beliefs.

Without letting on to the other, they both started researching each other's main interests. Sarah wanted to know all about him. Intrigued, she researched The Rifles, on more than one occasion catching herself daydreaming about how Luke must have looked in his regimentals.

As for his part, his balance and co-ordination had improved a smidgeon but it was still a major hindrance to them enjoying dance together, particularly when attempting Lindy hop. He did his best to compensate by trying to understand ballet and other types of dance that Sarah was interested in. Luke admired the dedication of the dancers to their art but he was never able to experience the joy of it which he knew was to his own personal loss. He was struck by how noisy the feet, particularly when landing, were above the music. Sarah did try to teach him about ballet on various occasions but he found it difficult to understand the language of shape, movement and gesture. Eventually the penny dropped a little when he realised about the body shapes telling stories and expressing emotions, but it was a struggle for him to even grasp that. Mentally he acknowledged it, but he could not feel the emotion of it. He just could not identify and express his emotions in that way.

Sarah could not understand how he would enthuse about the subtleties of different finger positions in the left hand when playing different types of rolls, and associated sticking and brush techniques. *But folk with passion are like that, aren't they,* she thought, *whether it's cars, engineering, sport, football teams, they have to pursue it to the nth degree.* At the same time, she found very attractive his passion for the drum set, his eyes lighting up when discussing the different nuances of technique. Having thought that, she realised she was just as bad with her interest in dance, or some of her acquaintances that collected handbags and shoes. She questioned herself as to whether she would become bored like the women who watch their husbands or boyfriends playing football or cricket and often fall asleep. Sarah did, however, make a point of seeking out the 1938 Benny Goodman version of 'Sing, Sing, Sing', Louis Bellson's 'Skin Deep' and Steve Smith's 'Salt Peanuts' which Luke kept raving about. He would get quite animated about them.

– LUKE AND THE VICAR –

Luke's colleague and best friend Dave Blagdon had been a Christian and on discovering that Sarah was too and that her faith was important to her Luke decided to read up on it. He did not know quite where to start but happened to spot a small board outside a city church stating a vicar was available one lunchtime a week for anyone interested in the Christian faith.

When Dave was alive Luke had listened to him out of trust and respect for the man and their friendship. Originally, Luke, though respectful, had taken an intellectually condescending attitude to the Christian faith, but army experience had taught him much about intellectual perceptions contrasting with reality and that belief was a strong weapon. He was, however, astonished at how many people had attended David's funeral from all walks of life and beliefs, and how celebratory as well as how sad it was. The funeral oration was extraordinary, not least because Dave had requested that if available, a newly created lay reader conduct it and he or she merely had to read what Dave had written about music, faith and life. Typical of Dave, even in death he had thought of others' progressions.

Luke ventured into the church on the appropriate day and was greeted warmly by the vicar. Having introduced themselves the Reverend Peter Hones asked, 'So how can I help?'

'Well, being honest, I'm not sure why I'm here really.'

'Is that for this instant or a deep philosophical question or both?' He gave a friendly quizzical look and then a reassuring smile.

'I'd better own up straight away and be frank with you. I've met this girl, well, woman actually, and she's a Christian and takes her faith very seriously.'

Peter Hones raised his other eyebrow with a knowing look.

'And what do you want from me? Marriage counselling?' he said with an even broader smile and lowering both eyebrows.

'Oh no, nothing like that.' Reverend Hones then raised both eyebrows, part teasing. Luke continued, 'Well, I suppose to help me understand some of the things that are important to her. My very limited experience is really of a few church services in the army and, well, her faith doesn't seem like what I experienced in the army. Don't get me wrong, I mean, well, I'm not sure what I mean. I did have a friend who was a Christian though, and he taught me a bit, however he has since died.'

'Well, let's start by chatting a little bit about ourselves.' After they chatted for a while Peter asked, 'Where shall we start then?'

'Well, maybe Genesis and evolution.'

'OK, we'll start with the old chestnut in Genesis if you believe that science and the Bible conflict. There are various interpretations, of course, depending on whether you class yourself creationist, fundamentalist, evolutionist, rationalist, etcetera, etcetera. In general, science tends to want to ask the question how, whereas scripture tends to be more concerned with why. Think of a car. There is a maintenance manual and an owner's handbook. Both are about the car but one is about maintenance and how it works and the other is how to use it. For me, I find the most useful approach is to put yourself in God's position. If you were God, how would you explain the beginnings of the universe in a way that every human could understand and relate to, whether technologically or scientifically ignorant or advanced?'

Luke thought for a while. 'I'm not sure,' he replied.

'Light is a form of energy everyone understands. The birth of a baby involves the breaking of the waters. Hence the description of the dividing of waters. It's a messy business being born but everyone knows something of the process. God is basically saying, "I did this," and there were passages of time between the phases of creation just as time, or the concept of time, marches on through all of nature. Not all cultures have had the same concept of time as we do but every culture would have been familiar with the time span of a day.'

'I've never thought of it like that before,' stated Luke.

'My personal favourite bits that are in chapter one are, let "*us*" make man in our image and "*God saw that it was good*". Have you ever made something that you've been really pleased about? You stand back and look at it, pleased that it is good. Another way to look at it is that it is breathed in pictures, in words, according to the intellect and understanding of the time.' The vicar started laughing at himself.

'Why are you laughing?'

'I've got carried away and I am rambling.'

'No, not at all. It's very interesting.'

'Well, even Jesus chose simple stories we call parables to teach. Stories that everyone can relate to on at least one level, though there is often the underlying specific message to whoever he was talking directly to or knew that was listening.'

Over the course of the weeks they skimmed the surface of many topics, covering such subjects as religious hypocrisy and coming to the conclusion that 'within any group of people there may be some, but if they know they are hypocrites and want to change, then surely for them the place to be is in the church and if they don't know they are hypocritical then there are always plenty of accusing fingers outside the church that will challenge them'.

They then progressed to judging the judges by today's standards, the self-justification of the psalmist and the nature of sin by way of how to approach the different types of literature in the Bible, including wisdom literature. They skirted the relationship between God and time, and man's understanding of the concept of time. As their chats developed, they became good friends and enjoyed the illumination of ideas in their discourse, even when there was no definite complete answer to be found and thus underlining the need for faith. Finally, they were just starting to sink their teeth into the life of Jesus and his teachings when events intervened.

– COLLUDING COUSINS –

Arif was concluding a conversation with Abdullah who had just updated him on the amount of money they were making from the women they had coerced into prostitution. Finally, Arif spoke of their illicit work for the Corporation.

'I think it's time to scare, I mean shall we say encourage, Aylmer to disclose what he knows, or what he has of the Corporation's and thereby escalate our taking it for the cause, my brother.'

Arif smiled as he spoke to Abdullah about the idea he had in mind. He calculated that he could impress Daesh with the plan and explain to Nichols that he was being proactive and it would soon produce some results. In addition, Abdullah, in turn, would feel that he would be making a contribution to the cause in carrying out Arif's wishes.

'I want you to follow Aylmer from work and when an opportunity presents itself put the frighteners on him with a car. Either just miss him or give him a glancing blow. Put false plates on the car and check for CCTV cameras in the area.'

– THE UMPTEENTH DATE –

It was the start of another workday and Luke Aylmer, usually cheery at the prospect, felt a pang of impatience as he was especially looking forward to seeing Sarah in the evening. They were planning to meet at the Bouncing Banker pub before going on to a meal at Church House restaurant above the bookshop in Westminster. He left work punctually for once and made it home in plenty of time. Apart from getting ready, he had managed to wash and clear up the breakfast things without delaying himself. While doing so he switched on the radio. The radio disc jockey announced, '*It's John Watermain signing off from my new broadcasting slot with "Persona in Excessia Part 2", a number from mainstream pop. Have a great evening and I look forward to talking to you again tomorrow at the same time.*'

Luke found himself drying the cups, glasses, dishes and teapot in time to the beat of the bright, quick, breezy love song played on the twelve-string acoustic guitar emanating from the radio. The melody kept playing in his head as he travelled from his flat to the Bouncing Banker. Sarah arrived shortly after. On their journey to the restaurant they chatted about their daily work and this and that, and Luke suggested that they try clog dancing as something else they could learn together. This was even though he knew he would struggle to learn it, particularly as he had been so clumsy lately. They sat down and were ready to order when he launched enthusiastically into talking about Albert 'Tootie' Heath's drum solo midway through Sonny Rollins' version of 'St Thomas' when Sarah stopped him.

PERSONA IN EXCESSIA PART 2[4]
(Extremes of Love CD track 2)

From brokenness can come new life.
Welcome to the human race.

I think you, I dream you, I live, sleep and breathe you.
Woman I'd die for you.
I love you, I want you, I won't live without you.
Take what you want of me.
Our relationship's growing, trusting and knowing,
sharing the knocks and the trials.
I'm so proud of you.

Each facial expression, your eyes glint suggestions
That fire deep feelings within.
Your voice and your laughter, your conversing gestures.
I'm entranced when you walk in the room.
Voluptuous lady, quintessence of woman.
You permeate all of my life
Like a sweet-smelling perfume.

---

4   'Persona in Excessia Part 2' – a bright celebration of love on guitar and voice

[Music intro repeated]

I'm besotted, euphoric and almost psychotic
With the love that I have for you.
I'm ecstatic, quixotic and feeling erotic
With the passion of love's full bloom.
Each day I discover, new depths of you lover.
New facets of the true you.
You continually surprise me.

The curves of your body, milk skin of such texture.
Apt vehicle for your beauteous soul.
Your faults, imperfections endorse my affections,
assured to know you're human too.
All your creations, our deep conversations
Expressions of the real you.
All the love you put in life.

'Before we start our meal, there is something I simply must say. I've been putting it off for quite a while but I feel impelled to say it.' He looked at her somewhat surprised.

'OK,' he offered slowly, feeling more than a little concerned.

'I've a confession to make. Let me first say, I have really enjoyed all the different nights out you've taken me to concerning dance.'

Luke looked quizzical as he ventured a surprised, 'Oh,' beginning to think and fear she was going to end their relationship.

'You know when I said I like dance. Well, I'm really only into a special form of it. It's fairly obscure.'

'You mean all the times I've taken you to barn dances, line dances, the ballet and folk dances you weren't that keen? Why didn't you say, especially before we enrolled into the introductory classes for Lindy hop?'

'Well, of course I'm interested in them, and enjoyed them immensely, especially as I was with you and I love learning something together with you. But what I'm really into is something else.'

'I don't get it. Why didn't you say?'

'Please don't be angry with me.'

'I don't understand. Why couldn't you just tell me?'

She looked sheepish and then confessed what was on her mind.

'I really don't know. I have no logical explanation really except… I thought you might think me very weird and go off me and being honest I didn't want to lose you.' He looked at her for a while a little stunned and then started to laugh.

'Why are you laughing?'

'Just thinking about all my feeble attempts to impress you at trying to dance and all the time it wasn't that important to you.' He reached over and took her hand and gently squeezed it.

She smiled, relieved at his reaction.

'Wait a sec, let me see if I can guess,' he added. 'Tango?'

'No, it takes two to tango!'

'What about Morris?'

'Pull the other one, it's got bells on.' She put her other hand on his lips and said very quietly, 'It's dance in worship.'

'What's that exactly? I mean apart from the obvious.' Sarah then began to explain what it was for her, but found it difficult.

'Well, I express my praise for God with body movement. Sometimes it's emotional, other times cerebral. Sometimes communal or in small groups or sometimes as a lone dancer. I tend to fall into the latter category. Apart from the communal ones there aren't set ones to learn as such. I create my own. I get inspiration from the words of a Bible verse, sometimes a melody or rhythm, sometimes a mood or all four.'

After the meal they walked and joked. They started to play a silly game the way people in love sometimes do, trying to outdo each other with apt names for dentists, their verbal sparring gradually increasing their laughter and dottiness.

'Phil McCavity,' offered Luke.

'Paula Molar,' proffered Sarah.

'Mr I. Teeth,' he countered.

'Miss D. Kay,' she ventured.

'Miss Flossie Mouth,' he retorted.

'Mr E. Namel,' Sarah exclaimed.

'Mr Algy Gum,' he playfully competed.

'Mr I. N. Ciser.' This continued as they walked to the tube station.

As they crossed the road a car came speeding around the corner. It headed straight at them. Luke pushed Sarah out of the way and went to dive in the opposite direction but fortunately for him his foot got caught and his arms moved as if to dive to the left but he ended up sprawled on the right. The car drove through the place he would have landed and it carried on. They embraced each other out of shock and checked to make sure they were unharmed. It all happened so fast neither of them got any details of the vehicle or driver. Having recovered, their mood gradually improved. Cheerful again, they set off to the tube on the way to Sarah's place in Tooting.

At the station, they stood underneath a destination sign. Unfortunately for them, a pigeon perched on top of the sign. With expert precision as well as consummate timing, which only a London pigeon could have, it defecated on Luke's shoulder whilst taking off.

'Yuck!' said Sarah. 'Let me get a tissue.' She started to rummage in her bag.

'What good is that, the pigeon will be miles away by now!' replied Luke grinning broadly and added, 'It must have been a female pigeon,' while Sarah wiped his shoulder with the tissue.

'What makes you say that?' she asked.

'It was multitasking, leaving a message and taking off at the same time.'

She playfully slapped him on the shoulder and then placed both arms around his arm as they moved to a safer place on the platform, both laughing. The rest of the journey was uneventful and after some late-night tea, a goodnight kiss and embrace, Luke made his way home.

– A LATE-NIGHT VISIT –

Just outside Luke's flat he was approached from the shadows by an elderly-looking man. Luke for an instant thought he was about to be mugged, having only glimpsed the slightly portly figure out of the corner of his eye.

'Excuse me, Mr Aylmer,' the figure said while raising his hat, which revealed a fairly balding pate. 'My name is Weston; may I have a word with you, please?'

'It's a bit late, isn't it? What about? Can't it wait?'

'No, I'm afraid it can't. It's about your friend Mr Blagdon who died recently.'

They entered the flat, Luke switching on the light to reveal a fairly neglected room with piles of books everywhere and a drum kit in the corner. There was a picture of Sarah on the mantelpiece and there were odd bits of computer hardware and wire scattered around. Weston stood by the doorway a little outside of the room and carefully looked around the room suspecting that there might be bugs. Knowing what to look for he spotted a small camera, pointed to its location and put his finger to his mouth, then beckoned Luke outside again.

'You have at least one camera in your flat and there is likely to be an associated microphone hidden there too. I suspect your landline phone is bugged and probably your mobile as well. Leave them where they are, carry on as normal, but obviously don't divulge anything of our meeting.' He continued as Luke stood astonished. 'There was an attempt on your life tonight, wasn't there?' Weston began. Luke threw him a questioning glance. 'It was not accidental. You were targeted,' continued Weston.

'You mean that car was deliberate, but why?' Luke exclaimed disbelievingly.

'Mr Aylmer, I believe you are in great danger and that your friend did not die accidentally. We think your friend had discovered something that, shall we say, is very unethical going on in the upper echelons at your employers. I'd like to have an official chat with you about the death of your colleague and the work you are involved with. Such a sad business was Mr Blagdon's demise.'

'I see, and who is we?'

'Her Majesty's Government.' Weston produced an identity card.

'How do you know so much?'

'We have been watching you for some time as has someone from your employers and until now we thought you were in no immediate danger but after the attempt tonight, we think you could be now and by association so is your friend Ms Manning.'

'If this is true it would go some way to explain Dave's death but not why they would wish to kill me or Sarah, especially as neither of us knows anything.'

'As for Ms Manning, she knows you and that is enough.'

After the initial conversation Luke paused for thought.

'How do I know that you are who you say you are? Why should I trust you?'

'I can arrange for you to visit my office at Thames House but we must do it so that your employer does not suspect. Can you make tomorrow lunchtime? It would be ideal if you could both make it. If you can, make sure you are not followed. Here is my card with contact details. Call me either way, from a public call box of course. Just don't trust anyone at work and don't take your mobile phone with you to our meeting. That goes for Ms Manning too.' With that Weston left.

I'd better call Sarah, thought Luke but then something made him stop. He reflected on all the new people in his life. The security guy, the auditor, Weston, Sarah, the new tea trolley trainee for that matter. Sarah had held the letter in an envelope for a very brief period, hadn't she? His heart missed a beat. The Corporation had arranged the interview with Sarah, hadn't it? He thought about the Sarah he knew and loved, at least he thought he knew. What about the attempted hit and run? Could she knowingly live a lie? He tried to think rationally, fighting the emotions that were welling up inside him. A feeling of stabbing cold gripped his stomach. Heart in mouth he could not face eating but managed a couple of mugs of tea before going out for a walk. Luke focused on what had gone on in the last few months and reflected on how happy he had become. Before, he had been under some stress, with the long hours and mourning Dave Blagdon. Who could he go to? Who could he trust? What was it that the Corporation was after? Were there really rogue elements within the Corporation?

His thoughts raced but then he calmed himself. What would he have done in the army? To know your enemy, you need to information gather. So, a bit of reconnaissance was in order. He then decided to call Sarah after all but from a call box.

'Hi, Sarah, can you meet me at Millbank tomorrow lunchtime?'

She knew she could organise her work in order to take an extended lunch hour if need be.

'Yes, I think I can do that. Are you OK? You sound very serious.'

'Great! Make sure you are not followed and don't tell anyone where you are going.'

'Are you in trouble?'

'We both might be. Sarah, you'll have to trust me.'

Sarah could hardly sleep wondering what the mystery was, but glad that she would only be kept in suspense until tomorrow.

– SARAH AT WORK –

Because Ms Fenwick, Sarah's boss, was away nearly all of the time Sarah had been seconded to a small administration section which supported Human Resources. It was located a few floors below the main HR suite and dealt mainly with travel arrangements and hotel stays for Corporation staff as well as being close to the store room of historical personnel data. This consisted of paper copies required by law, archives and data not originally stored on computer. In all the weeks she had worked for the Corporation she had still not met her boss.

Ms Fenwick did request the occasional job or errand, mainly by email but only once by phone. The latter seemed to have a dream job, often travelling to different parts of the world on secondment or on short projects for the Corporation. It seemed as if on a phone call or whim from the boardroom she would globe-trot to troubleshoot at project and business level wherever requested. At least, that was what everybody thought, though no one really knew what she did in these places. It seemed a very glamorous lifestyle. Ms Fenwick's one hobby appeared to be collecting jewellery, particularly unusual rings and necklaces. This Sarah discovered as she was occasionally directed to collect items from jewellers and send them on to various places. Apparently, Ms Fenwick was very attractive but rarely put in an appearance and if she did, it was usually very late at night.

Two executive suites adjoined the sides of Sarah's office. One, Ms Fenwick's, was always vacant and the other was where another manager would intermittently attend. Yvonne, who shared the office with Sarah, worked for the other manager. On one of their occasional chats Yvonne had intimated that there had been a whisper that Ms Fenwick had been romantically involved with a high-flying ex-employee. He was sacked for alleged embezzlement. The chap could never work in the same circles again and took to the bottle and no one had heard of him since. This may have been one reason for Fenwick's meteoric rise in the Corporation. At least that was the rumour.

Yvonne's temporary boss was not at all nice and had a history of a bad attitude to women who had to work for him. His previous secretary had complained because he insisted on holding her passport and once slapped her face. Again, rumour had it that Human Resources had to move him several times previously but they never did sack him, nor was he subject to verbal or written warnings. He appeared to be vital to the Corporation, or someone it seemed was protecting him. Sarah observed to Yvonne on experiencing his manner for the first time, 'You know, he strikes me as being a very lonely man.'

'Lonely! Why, he is a misogynistic chauvinist who thinks women have been put on this earth just to serve him. He is an arrogant sexist toe rag who only cares for himself and has a nasty controlling cruel streak.'

'You see, no wonder he is lonely,' remarked Sarah. They both had a good laugh at her last remark.

— REPORTING BACK —

'Sorry for the position at the Corporation but that was the only opening for recruitment there was for access to the building at such short notice,' Weston stated quietly to Marwenna and continued, 'So how has it been since the first week? Any leads? What did you find out?'

'None definite, sir, but I know the building layout and the research lab's position. A new person has started in the R&D section as an auditor. She is worth checking out; she seems to arrive late and work a lot of late hours. I'll follow this up as best I can, sir. Oh, also, I discovered a new woman has started in the human resources admin section in Shellac House when I was shown around it, sir. She might be worth investigating too.'

She passed their names and what details she had accrued about them to Weston as they walked into Setford's part of the office. He then gave these to Setford with the request, 'See what you can find out about these folk, Setford.' Then turning to Marwenna again he asked, 'Any problems with your line manager?'

'Only that I'm being mothered by Mrs Ackroyd,' reported Marwenna. Setford grinned. 'She definitely is not a suspect, sir. You already know the background to Mr Aylmer, sir. He's quite dishy if a little clumsy,' Marwenna added to wipe the smile off Setford's face.

Weston half ignored her last comment having already immersed himself in the data they had on the auditor.

'Hmmm, we have some information on the auditor but it's very sketchy. She is some form of free-roaming troubleshooter for the Corporation but she does not actually work in Audit as far as we can make out. See if you can find out more, Bowers.'

'Yes, sir.'

'Bowers, this assignment is starting to get a little bit riskier. There was an attempt to endanger Aylmer last night. There's still time to withdraw if you want to. No one would think any the less of you if you wanted to return to normal duties.'

'I know, sir, but I want to see it through.'

'Let me know if you think you need to plant surveillance equipment or need to be wired.'

'Will Setford personally attach and demonstrate it, sir?' said Marwenna with a hint of a twinkle in her eyes.

Setford went red. Weston replied, 'That's enough, Bowers.' Several years ago, Weston would, ordinarily, have picked up on the badinage of this quirky relationship between Bowers and Setford, but his bereavement had dulled his senses to a great extent. Now his sole preoccupation was with the job in hand. In the past he had been avuncular and protective of Setford throughout Setford's short career, Setford being technically brilliant but not too hot on social interaction. Government, along with many other commercial management structures, tends to reward financial responsibility rather than technical brilliance.

'So, what are you doing?' Setford asked Marwenna.

'Information gathering, of course,' Marwenna said with a hint of disdain.

'No, I mean what is your role in the Corporation?'

'I'm a personal assistant to an executive departmental manager,' she replied, deliberately not disclosing her real job title and then added defensively, 'It's a very big Corporation.'

'Anything you need, Bowers?' asked Weston.

She drew Weston aside out of Setford's earshot. 'Could I put a chit in for some hand cream, sir?'

Weston initially looked nonplussed but then showed a questioning countenance. Could this be a new tool in accessing key conventional locked areas? he wondered.

'My hands, sir.'

'Your hands?'

'Yes, sir, they are very sore, from all the extra washing-up that can't be done in the dishwasher, sir. A woman has different priorities in her personal life to men, sir.' She'd be blowed if by working on assignment her beauty regime would be compromised when it was routine information gathering with no imminent danger. HM Government could blasted well pay for it! Weston left the room after acquiescing to her request with a sigh.

'I've managed to wangle working late, sir,' she shouted after him.

Setford did overhear part of the conversation and, shy though he was, found it amusing enough to give a wry smile and a hesitant laugh.

'And you can stop sniggering or I'll knock your block off,' scolded Marwenna. She often treated him just like her youngest brother.

She liked him, not just because she knew he liked her. He was funny, though mainly unintentionally, and there was just something about him, though she had never consciously thought about it. He certainly did not appear overtly like an alpha male which many women look for, and what she thought she needed, if she thought she needed anyone. Maybe it was because he reminded her of one of her brothers, or indeed her father, or maybe she just sensed that there was something of real worth in him. It was the constancy at his core being that brought her so much reassurance. For he was like a rock that she took for granted; he was just there, overlooked and not noteworthy aside from his technical brilliance.

– A VOICE FROM THE PAST –

It was 6.30 in the evening and Luke was starting one of his inspired sessions. That's what he and Dave used to call them when the logic, testing plans and solutions seem to appear serendipitously whilst grappling with some problem and pursuing a very productive solution. Most staff had left and there were none of the bothersome phone calls that could interrupt problem-solving in full flow. Sapphire had moved to the general office to get some photocopying done; the rest of the offices on the floor were virtually empty. She could still see Luke's profile through the frosted half-glassed section of the dividing wall. Sapphire had always lingered a little longer in the evening than Luke, which he put down to keenness to learn the job. He had just devised a solution to a problem similar to a database deadly embrace scenario and so decided to chill out for five minutes while waiting for several jobs to run. He sat down at one of the more unusual pieces of equipment hosting access to a game at a remote site when something bizarre happened. Dave Blagdon had known that Luke preferred it to any other game they had played together.

Luke was not a proficient typist. He'd always got by using two fingers only, rarely looking at the screen because his gaze was nearly always on the keyboard, but in this case, it being a game he knew well, he stared at the screen. When Luke glanced back to the screen, having checked how his first job was going, what he saw took him aback.

'Hello are you alone?'

Luke glanced round before typing Y. Was Sapphire playing games with him? He thought for a second so checked to see her still photocopying.

'*It's Ratfink here. What's your corresponding password?*'

Luke could not believe his eyes but with hesitation he typed in 'Crabfface', with two f's. These were names he and Dave Blagdon used to light-heartedly insult each other. He could still hear Dave's voice all those months before as they had set the game up between them.

'*Check to see if the camera in the corner of the office is still in the place opposite you. Thought something might happen to me hence this delayed program triggered by time and your remote access to the game. It must be over seventy days after my death. At least you have survived! Trust no one especially from the Corporation. No time to explain now. Have hidden device and research notes and log. You know, or rather knew, me and how I thought. Call my solicitors, Argue and Phibbs, and they will send you something in addition to what went out before concerning bequests. I have already sent associated info to other sources. Be careful. Repeat. Trust no one.*'

The screen continued slowly scrolling upwards.

'*I never told you because I did not want to endanger you. You need time to learn what I know, or rather knew, and time to think. As an extra precaution, it is written down as a puzzle should it fall into the wrong hands. Different unofficial access codes and passwords will be given to you along the way. This message will destruct together with the program after you have viewed. Have a good life! As you know, I'm now permanently logged off this one. Dave.*'

The message disappeared. Luke, still stunned, sat staring at the screen as questions arose in his mind. Was Dave still alive? No, he couldn't be. Luke had been to his funeral. Luke reminisced on Dave and the times they had descended into schoolboy humour. If one of them was giving a demonstration the other would send spurious messages to the screen. He smiled on remembering some of their office banter and wacky moments; some of the tricks they would play on each other – changing the mouse from left- to right-hand control or changing the screen display by 90 degrees; the time Dave convinced Luke that it was a fancy-dress party they were going to, having hidden a secret stash of normal casual clothes to change back into so that Luke was the only one in fancy dress.

The new auditor returned to the room.

'You look a little white. Are you OK?' she asked.

'Er, yes… Well, no… come to think of it I do feel a bit odd.'

'Anything the matter?' she asked inquisitively, placing her hand on his shoulder and bending closer to him to give him a chance to gaze down at her cleavage. She had already started the charm offensive that had been the downfall of many of her male victims.

'I think I'm a bit tired. It's been a hard day. I think I just need to go home and get a full night's sleep.'

'See you tomorrow then,' she replied, withdrawing her hand with a show of sympathy.

On his way out he asked, 'Any news on tracing the outside subversive organisation whose coercion may have been involved in pushing Dave over the edge?'

'At this moment in time our latest report still suggests it could be DGSE or the Russian GRU but who knows, it could even be the Chinese or Iranians.'

'Corporation propaganda,' he muttered to himself.

'Sorry, I didn't quite catch that. What was it you said?' she asked.

'I said I'd like to have a proper gander at the report when I get the time,' he responded quickly. After Luke had received the screen message from Dave, he decided to contact Dave's solicitors, Argue and Phibbs, from a public phone box and ask them to send his envelope to an old army friend's address. This he would collect about a week later, having prearranged it with his friend.

3

A RELUCTANT SPY

THE MAHOGANY-PANELLED WALLS WERE IN TASTEFUL contrast to the brash chrome office accessories in Nichols' office. Fazal sat a little nervously opposite him, he being a bully, like all bullies, cowed when challenged.

'Maybe Blagdon had left him something you could have missed,' stated Nichols.

'No way. We checked every inch of that office after we searched his flat when we put the listening and camera bugs in there. We checked every directory and file he had access to. We even ran one of those search engine algorithms on a variety of Bible concordances for different Bible versions to see if he had left a code in one of his programs that correlated,' replied Fazal trying to appear reassuring.

'I take it you have arranged the shadowing of Aylmer's new girlfriend,' Nichols probed.

'Not yet, but I put the frighteners on Aylmer and his girlfriend in the hope that he will come directly to our security for support.'

'What did you do?'

'I arranged a near miss.' Nichols thought for a moment, reflecting that Fazal had probably used one of his naïve idealist extremists, convincing them it was part of a greater plan. He refrained from letting Fazal know that he knew about his secret extremist agenda, at least part of it, though he did not know of the latest developments on that front.

'What, using a car driven by one of your heavies? That was a little careless and foolhardy!' stated Nichols. 'Was there any result?'

'No, so I think he knows nothing.'

'But according to my other sources he has behaved suspiciously. One of our agents thinks Aylmer has found something.'

'Other source?' Fazal was surprised by this. He started sweating; how he was beginning to hate working for the Corporation. He thought it demeaned him but it was a means to an end.

'Of course, you don't think you are my only operative, my only eyes and ears. The report I have is that he behaved suspiciously last night, not to mention that he has been seeing a cleric of an occasional lunchtime. There could be a link there bearing in mind Blagdon's circle of acquaintances. I'm sure he has discovered something.'

Nichols loved power, no matter whether it was interpersonal, political or latterly over regimes. Originally spurred by the craving for status and the accumulation of wealth he had now grown out of such mere trappings and become totally consumed by the love of control and manipulation. He had well and truly left his previous weaknesses to those he could use for his own purposes. Now the principle pleasure was control of others, the more the better.

Fazul's network of contacts had grown from his early years of grooming vulnerable girls, raping and then pimping them out. He had progressed to drug pushing around the areas of Rotherham, Huddersfield and further afield. Now he had heavy muscle when needed. His initial network was first with his cousins and friends and then via the drug routes to some Romanian gangs from overseas. From the latter came contacts with extremists. With Daesh he could make all the right noises when required to, in order to get what he required. It was easy for him to feign his hatred for infidels, as he hated Nichols, but was frightened of him. Fazul despised Nichols because in working for him he was forced to confront his own failures.

He also took much kudos from making the 'sacrifice' of being a sleeper in the despised Western capitalist unbelieving world, a fifth columnist in the enemy's camp of which the Corporation was an icon. Deep down Fazul's real agenda was for himself, as it had always been. He genuinely thought he could outsmart his Daesh handler, just as he was outsmarting Nichols, and when the time was right, he would just disappear. The bottom line was that he had no intention of being someone else's cannon fodder and he already had someone in mind to make the sacrifice on his behalf. When the time was right Fazul would cover his own tracks and disappear. He was starting to make provision for a new life under a new identity. All he needed was the money to set him up for life.

Fazul saw how easy it was to manipulate people just as he had groomed all the young vulnerable girls he had sought out in local authority care over the past decade. From this knowledge he spotted how easy it was for Daesh to pull the right psychological strings to recruit men feeling isolated or alienated in a different culture. They always highlighted the things wrong with Western society and held up an idealistic golden caliphate of the past and future. It was easy to sell a perfect dream fed by the discontent and disenchantment in people's lives.

Abdullah Alam was Fazal's chief henchman and had a similar background but was not greatly skilled at disingenuity and manipulation, besides, he was very much devoted to his new cause. Abdullah looked up to Fazul as he had the prestige of being a bigger player in both the legitimate and criminal worlds. The Corporation stood for all he was told to sneer at and despise. He often told himself that he would make them all pay when the time was right and all of Western civilisation was destroyed. After all, his limited understanding of Allah and Islam, coloured as it was by ignorance and dubious interpretation, could justify anything and suited his criminal lifestyle. No matter what he did, however cruel, in his mind he would be justified. He consoled himself with the thought that he would still be in paradise at the end of his personal jihad. At least, that was what he thought, having been allocated the role of supporting the sleeper in the Corporation by his Daesh handler.

Fazul, in the meantime, tried to look cool while receiving this minor condemnation from Nichols. He was cunning but not that clever in reality and was easily outmanoeuvred by Nichols in what some would say was a parent-child transaction relationship. Indeed, he could grasp technology but to a large extent only its uses.

'What if Blagdon illegally accessed something in a remote machine?' Nichols postulated rhetorically while looking out of the window.'

'I'll recheck the remote machines he had access to and double check the logs,' offered Fazul.

'No, I think it's too late for that, don't waste your time, he would have ensured no saves were taken and rewritten the logs by now,' Nichols continued and then changed the subject. 'Sorry you've had to move to a new office again and your new assistant is having to share the outer office. I will try and get you something more permanent but you keep letting the side down in dealing with your assistants. It's getting harder to find someone willing to work for you.'

Fazal wasn't overly concerned at this as he thought, in his arrogance, that he was too valuable to Nichols. After all, Nichols could hire and fire who he wanted, and what do mere assistants mean in the scheme of things? They are two a penny.

Nichols, however, had already been revising his opinion and plans for Fazal. His usefulness was coming to an end and he thought it might be time to retire him permanently, sooner rather than later. This sleeper jihadist was becoming too expensive. Let him have his 'martyrdom'. With any luck Nichols could engineer the situation to kill multiple birds with one stone.

'I want you to check out this vicar. He could be a handler! Or he may be taking Aylmer's confession, though I don't think Aylmer is the religious type. In which case, we may have to visit and interrogate him.' Nichols handed Fazul the location details.

– THE BEGINNINGS OF A PLAN –

Sarah and Luke carried out separate elaborate journeys to ensure that they weren't followed before meeting outside Thames House. Weston was waiting for them at the security desk in the foyer. He then led them along a gloomy government corridor to a meeting room with a long table along its centre. The room's décor, which must have been depressing even when new, was now giving off vibes of neglect and stagnation. Waiting for them was a youngish-looking, thin, blond man who rose to greet them.

'This is Setford,' Weston announced as they all sat down after shaking hands. 'First things first. We know you have signed the Official Secrets Act, Mr Aylmer, from looking at your service record days. Ms Manning, my dear, would you mind doing the same?'

'Of course, and it's Sarah, call me Sarah.' Weston filed her dutifully signed document away into a manila folder and then proceeded.

'I suggest for any future meetings we change venue to somewhere like the Royal Festival Hall restaurant,' stated Weston, mindful of the fact that he'd registered them into the building under false identities as his investigation was still not officially sanctioned. 'As mentioned to Mr Aylmer before, we believe that he may now be in imminent danger from someone or some part of the Corporation you work for. And now by association, Ms Manning, I mean Sarah, you are too.'

'Couldn't we both just resign and move away?' asked Sarah innocently.

'I'm afraid not, and even if you did, these people would consider it highly suspicious and probably shadow you and become even more threatening.'

'Can't you do something about this, protect us or something?' Sarah enquired.

'I'm afraid we don't have the resources. They have so many fingers in so many pies we cannot keep up with all that the Corporation is doing with the resources we have. Plus, of course, we are stretched at the current time coping with counter-terrorism and other issues. We've managed to trace much of what the Corporation does through its maze of shell and subsidiary companies that it operates through. These are not obviously trumpeted about as part of its global image but we don't have people on the inside with your sort of connections to investigate further. As I previously said, our department's resources at present are stretched due to work on monitoring political and religious extremists. The latter's spurious chatter indirectly links to someone within the Corporation but we don't know who, and as to whether this is the main driver to what is emerging or is a separate issue we just don't know. I suggest Setford updates Mr Aylmer concerning some of the technical aspects we know of, while I fill you in concerning the Corporation's movements, Sarah.'

With that Luke and Setford moved down to the other end of the table and spoke in quiet tones.

Luke asked Setford, 'Why do you want me to work for you if you know so much anyway? I'm sure you have abler computer professionals than myself.'

'As Weston said, we don't have anyone on the inside with your sort of access levels.'

While Setford was imparting the technical aspects of his discoveries to Luke, Weston addressed Sarah.

'HM Government fast became interested when a number of research and defence workers met with sudden deaths or "committed suicide" over a short period of time worldwide. Virtually all of them worked for, or had contact with, the Corporation you work for. Aside from the normal marketing business weapons of FUD, which is legal, we know they have definitely strayed into corporate spying but which we unfortunately cannot prove nor wish to follow up at this juncture.'

'What do you mean by FUD?' Sarah asked.

'It is short for fear, uncertainty and doubt. For instance, casting doubt on your competitors' ability and capacity to deliver and support products by raising fear, uncertainty and doubt in the customer you are trying to sell to. If that doesn't work on the people you are directly dealing with then you try the next level of management up with the same tactics,' answered Weston.

While Weston was informing Sarah, Setford described to Luke the largely unsuccessful attempts at gaining corporate technical information due to the Corporation's internal security procedures and the type of building insulation they had deliberately fitted.

'Technically I have only been able to use our more primitive tools. For instance, I've been unable to Tempest scan because of conflicting signals and even when I got within 250 metres of the relevant buildings there appears to be some form of aluminium and marble shielding blocking signals. When I do get some remote access, they are streets ahead in terms of encryption. I suspect they have implemented Shor's algorithm for encryption. Even their corporate rules concerning use of personal and corporate phones on their premises is very restricting to us. Key sniffers don't seem to work either and as you know they have their own anti-industrial spying software which is very sophisticated.'

Weston waited for a convenient break in conversation to speak to both of them again.

'We think the danger to you is directly as a result of the demise of Mr Blagdon, among others, and concerns the research work he was doing at the time. We are fairly sure his death was made to look like suicide because he had discovered something untoward. Most of his research was ostensibly for humane purposes, we know. However, there have been one or two instances of supposed suicides and accidents in other research teams that work for the Corporation around the globe in the last couple of years that were involved in similar work. What endangers Mr Aylmer is that Mr Blagdon has hidden his research papers and a device he was either working on or obtained from one of the other teams.'

'He did receive a parcel from Brazil some time back, initially giving the impression that some of his research work had been completed by someone else to his surprise,' Luke offered.

'Why didn't he destroy it and his own research papers?' asked Sarah.

'That would have given him away and while they were still in existence, they bought him time to plan. Maybe he didn't have enough time to put in place a strategic one but had enough for a makeshift one,' replied Setford.

Weston continued, 'As with your work, Mr Aylmer, the Corporation has different research teams in different locations, in different subsidiaries, all working on similar subjects but independently. And like yours they know nothing about each other's work. This is where you and Mr Blagdon fit in. You were unusual in that you worked as individuals on different projects in different fields but were in the same team for the convenience of management. The UK part of the Corporation, being typically British, underinvested in research and was more focused on management structure and on-costs.'

'Tell me about it,' said Luke, very well aware of the plight of much research due to financial constraints.

Weston postulated further, 'Putting ourselves in Mr Blagdon's position as best we can, maybe he wanted a chance to hand over his discoveries to the right people. We think that he learned about the existence of the parallel research team which was unethically working in his area and of their subsequent terminations when their project finished successfully. We don't know how yet. Surmising on his behalf, who initially could he trust? Nobody at the Corporation with the exception of Mr Aylmer here. It seemed that apart from his faith in God it also appears he had faith in you, Mr Aylmer.' Weston turned to look directly at Luke.

'It's Luke, please.'

'We can try and trace the package source. If you narrow down dates and can remember the courier that would be excellent,' added Setford.

'How much do you know of what he was working on?' Weston enquired.

'We didn't work in the same areas or projects. We weren't really in the same fields either. Neither of us was allowed to say too much about what projects we were involved with. As far as I am aware his research was into mental health solutions and it ranged from the way the brain works to the effect on the brain of various types of waves.'

Luke continued, 'Let's see, his research on psychiatric help for the depressed was always within ethical boundaries. I know one of his projects was working on virtual reality for treating depression and the use of subliminal images within that remit. Once he mentioned flicker fusion rates in connection with it.'

Weston nodded sagely and postulated further, 'Now we suspect this is where your colleague Mr Blagdon became suspicious that they were initially revisiting the subject of intermittent subliminal messaging, possibly not only to individuals but via satellite to populations watching TV. Of course, that's only conjecture at this stage.'

Luke Aylmer then continued, 'A second project was to develop firmware to help combat mental health issues exacerbated by, believe it or not, full moons. Presumably this may have been linked to neural lacing. I vaguely remember him researching magnetic and gravitational effects on the brain as well as brain mapping network fingerprinting. Then there was some work on technology that allowed modification of DNA non-dividing cells, to fix broken genes in the brain, heart and liver. He even joked concerning jelly behaving a little like the brain when it comes to physical trauma. If memory serves, so to speak, I do now remember him having some disquiet about the possible future research direction of the use of organoids.'

Setford asked, 'Did he ever mention the theory of connectivity?'

'He may have done,' answered Luke, 'but you'll have to refresh my memory.'

'We think that some of his work was based on the mathematical theory of connectivity and a simple algorithm.' Setford looked for reassurance from Luke that he was following his line of reasoning.

'Please, go on,' Luke offered with genuine interest.

'Basically, it's the idea that human intelligence and thought is rooted in a power-of-two-based permutation logic, N = 2i-1. This relates to how groups of similar neurons come together to handle tasks such as recognising food, shelter and threats. These cliques then cluster together to form functional connectivity motifs (FCMs), which handle additional ideas and conclusions. The theory suggests how we acquire and process knowledge and this can be explained by how different neurons interact and align in separate areas of the brain. If his research had gone beyond this development,' Setford postulated, 'then he may have artificially produced perceptions, memories, generalised knowledge and flexible actions. You can see the potential of this?'

'Absolutely!'

'A further speculation would be a device that could target and bombard small relevant parts of the brain by magnetic pulses or some other type of wave to temporarily or even permanently change them.'

'What sort of devices?' asked Luke.

'This sounds all very far-fetched,' stated Sarah, 'after all, this is just conjecture, right?'

'Not at all. During the Cold War the Russians used to bombard the West with radio waves in order to make people's brains less efficient. If you tuned in on the appropriate frequency you could actually hear the sounds, that is aside from the usual spying numbers stations broadcasting on the radio that are still in use today. Indeed, sonic waves can be used to actually shatter objects and there have been instances of ears being affected in foreign embassies by being bombarded by waves, even though the range may be beyond human hearing. These methods were very crude though,' assured Weston.

Luke suddenly looked very grave and pensive.

'What are you thinking?' said Setford picking up on Luke's expression.

'Could it affect the motor part of the brain? What would happen if this was targeted?'

'Theoretically, yes. I guess it could make one clumsy, uncoordinated, with a poorer brain performance and maybe the added side-effect of less effective memory,' confirmed Setford.

'Thinking back, I'm reasonably sure it was only after the package arrived that both Dave and I started getting clumsy and poorly co-ordinated. When he died, I was still affected. Presumably it was triggered accidentally. I've always put my clumsiness down to the after-effects of my service years in Afghanistan gradually surfacing. Maybe Dave eventually worked out what the device did and planned to dispose of it safely,' Luke stated, beginning to feel angry and then apprehensive wondering about long-term effects on an individual.

'So, this device tuned to other areas of the brain together with subliminal messaging could have devastating effects on an individual!' suggested Sarah.

'Carefully targeted either on an individual or community. It's possible,' stated Weston.

'Those who have come into contact with the research have met with accidents, disappeared or have supposedly committed suicide. Maybe they could tune the direction and pulse to cause depression and suicidal tendencies rather than countering them. Just think polarity changes of memory, blink timings coinciding with subliminal message attempts,' ventured Setford.

'Why don't they just build a new one?' interrupted Sarah.

'The designer died in a fire together with the designs, discs, hard copies and backups, and because no one has ever possessed one for any length of time with the possible exception of Luke's colleague Dave Blagdon,' answered Weston.

'My bet is the original designer of it deliberately tried to destroy the research just before the full research team were killed so that another device couldn't be built. I don't know what must have been in their minds to send the device to Blagdon but it might be due to a personal connection if we can find it,' said Setford.

'How did they make the connection to him?' asked Sarah.

'That's where we still need to fill in the gaps on Mr Blagdon's interests and contacts,' reflected Weston.

'I am due to collect a letter from Dave Blagdon's solicitors which might shed more light on what's happened. I've had it sent to an old army contact,' informed Luke.

'You can guess what I'm going to ask, can't you?' ventured Weston.

'Investigate at work, see what leads I can come up with as well as share anything useful from the letter,' replied Luke realising that he had little choice if he wanted Sarah and himself to eventually escape the danger.

'We would like you to see if you can find out what has happened to one of the other research teams in your particular area of research too. Setford has a couple of names,' added Weston.

'Oh, so there is another research team working along the same lines?'

Weston ignored the question and continued, 'As regards the Corporation, we are not sure at this stage as to whether this is a strategy at board level or an internal organisation within the Corporation. The board members check out OK as far as we can tell, which suggests that they are very good at deception or that it's someone in the upper echelons of the company that has access to all the research work via the shell companies and subsidiaries.'

'So, to sum up, we have a likely device for brain manipulation and a possible subliminal image emitter that someone in the Corporation had developed but tried to stop being developed and that Dave Blagdon may have received,' Sarah summarised adding, 'I have access to some personnel documents. I could try digging around in those, at least the ones on paper.'

'Excellent,' Weston exclaimed. He went on, 'One final thing, only use the phones I have given you for communication with us and when we meet do not bring your personal mobiles along as these are likely to be GPS-traced, but keep using them for the rest of the time to keep the pretence of normality.'

After they left the building, Sarah turned to Luke and uttered, 'I'm scared.'

'Are you?' he answered.

'Well, I've never danced the Watusi but my body is shaking like I am,' she replied trying to make light of it.

'So am I if it's any comfort, but even if we were to refuse that still does not mean we won't be a target. Besides, I don't like the fact of Dave's death as well as my clumsiness being due to the Corporation. Dave has entrusted this task to me and I don't want to let him down.'

Then Sarah saw that Luke was smiling.

'What are you smiling about?'

'Just thinking about Dave.'

'And?'

Would she think less of him, if he confessed?

'Sometimes our work would get very intense and we would do silly things to ease the tension.' He then recounted the time Dave put a CD on with a track by the Surfing Safaris and they both stood on their chairs and pretended to surf while singing along to the tune.

'You did what?'

He repeated it somewhat sheepishly, thinking at the same time, *Well, if she wants me, she'll have to accept the small child inside of me as well.*

'You are an absolute noggin!' She smiled, squeezed his arm and gave him a peck on the cheek before they went their separate ways back to work, she, smiling, visualising Luke and Dave pretending to surf on chairs and he, smiling, pleased that she had reassured him with her touch and kiss.

— SPYING IS VERY SYSTEMATIC —

If Setford was correct about the sophistication of the machines Luke was accessing, Luke reasoned that the whole network would be monitored. Therefore, in order to conceal the trail to himself, he hacked into different machines, at different sites, at different times, to temporarily hide his access while setting up a dummy regular session of his normal work to cover while he was investigating. Sometimes Weston would provide access codes, although Luke never knew how he managed to get them. He wondered what timescale was involved before security would suspect anything untoward, knowing that if he kept at it, then it would be just a matter of time before he would be detected. But how much time? On each occasion, he felt he aged somewhat, but in a curious way he enjoyed the controlled tension. It was a little like being on patrol in the army but without the physical element.

He checked the archived images of diaries and engineer's logs and hardware maintenance records before and after the Brazilian team's death at their site. Four names occurred out of the usual pattern. He then, by searching back, checked the other sites where Weston had told him about other deaths. The same engineers or visitors' names cropped up. On closer inspection of the signatures he noticed that two of the female names, Cynthia Garnet and Amber Smith, had the same handwriting. He was sure he had seen that handwriting before. But where? On re-examining the male signatures, these again were remarkably similar to each other. One of the names was the security chief who had briefed him after Dave's death. Luke passed the names on to Weston who was extremely grateful.

'If he's responsible then that was careless of him. This is the first definite lead we've had. We'll investigate,' came Weston's reply.

Sarah and Luke liaised over dinner most evenings that week, swapping information, the exception being a drink on the Monday night after Sarah's dance practice. They always ensured they were at a different venue each night as a precaution. Luke then always made sure Sarah was safely ensconced at home before retiring to his flat.

Sarah knew that all her computer access would be monitored so had to research historical personnel data held on paper. Fortunately, much of the historical personnel, legal and financial paperwork was located across the corridor in a large store opposite her office. She was very careful when she entered the store to always go for a legitimate reason, but she would always bring back additional files in between her normal work folders. Sometimes she would wait till Yvonne had gone home if an extensive search was required to trawl through the expenses and travel records as well as perusing archived diary appointments. Usually the more recent documents were close to hand. She memorised the observations she made as she didn't want to leave anything written that might be incriminating. At the end of each day at home she would write down all that she'd memorised.

Her discoveries proved very useful. She cross-checked the names Luke had discovered and confirmed that as far as the Corporation was concerned, they did not exist, with the exception of the security chief. She was puzzled too that her boss's salary wasn't sufficient to buy all that jewellery that she had collected. Admittedly her boss might have other sources of income or a sugar daddy or something else, but Sarah thought she would flag it up to Weston anyway, when they met up to report back. In a strange way, as each day passed Sarah's confidence grew.

– A WORKING DINNER –

It was early evening when they all met for dinner at the Royal Festival Hall. As requested by Weston, their table was away from the windows and other guests. Sarah and Luke again had taken independent diversionary routes and left their personal phones at home. Weston insisted on paying, saying it was the least he could do for volunteers on state business. After ordering, they got down to reporting their findings.

Weston confirmed that the package Dave Blagdon had received had indeed come from Brazil and in fact was from the now defunct research team, the sender of which was the last to meet with an untimely fate.

Sarah's research results were a little surprising. She found that the security officer that had interviewed Luke had several different job titles as well as aliases depending on where he worked and that his office location was moved quite often. He seemed to have an awful lot of assistants over a short period of time compared with anyone else. It was only that very day that she realised Yvonne was now his secretary and so decided to try to monitor his movements closely.

Weston confirmed Sarah's suspicions about her own prospective boss, whom she had still not seen, stating that apart from large cash payments going into her account infrequently there was no other legitimate income stream. He added that the information from the jewellers was that she always paid for jewellery either by cash or her own credit card. This left only the possibility of a generous suitor or payment for some unknown service. He furnished a series of payment dates for Sarah to check against her boss's foreign jaunts to see if the payments were linked to her trips for the Corporation. Sarah also raised the subject of a new agency worker in catering that could be a suspicious appointment and might be worth following up.

Weston and Setford briefly looked at each other and said nothing initially then Weston quickly volunteered, 'Leave that with me. I'll check it out.'

Setford reported that he had details of a secret research laboratory of the Corporation's in Japan that was working on the same issues as Luke. There was phenomenal investment for it in comparison to Luke's research budget. This was corroborated by Luke who added some disturbing discoveries.

'As you know, my research has been into quantum computers.' Luke continued after Setford's affirmative nod, 'My research covered trapped ions, superconducting qubits, light particles and vacancy centres in diamonds. After your tip-off regarding the other research team I have uncovered some secret research papers and test results via a trap door. Sarah has managed to find out that two of the team have met tragic accidents in the last eight months. The team in Japan were trying to solve the problem of synchronisation using a quantum effect known as entanglement.'

'Ah, spooky action at a distance,' Setford offered with a smile to show he was following closely what Luke was reporting.

'Quite!' Luke answered, momentarily pausing as if put off his stride before recognising the quote from Einstein. He then went on to update Setford further with the technical details. Finally, Luke informed them of his most disturbing discovery to date. Namely that a quantum computer had now not only been created but was being developed for mass production. But to what aim? They speculated about the usefulness of this.

'It is unlikely that it would be produced for PCs and laptops so what use could it be for on such a roll-out scale?' Weston posed out loud.

'It could be that if a molecular-level quantum computer was piggybacked onto all computer chips then the Corporation could be party to all information passing through those chips.

These minute devices could detect, collect and send data from every piece of hardware the Corporation makes and sells. Incorporated onto bog-standard chips it would be almost undetectable. No one would suspect, particularly as it is at the molecular level. Unless you had specialist equipment, and knew what you were looking for, you wouldn't know it was there,' theorised Luke.

'The computing power, storage and processing speed to handle and interpret this type of data must be immense. Who but the Corporation has that sort of resource?! The Corporation has profits greater than some countries' expenditure,' affirmed Weston.

'But surely the Corporation is not party to all the global information floating around?' Sarah questioned.

'Not yet,' Setford added.

'How small is this thing?' asked Sarah.

Setford jumped in enthusiastically with an explanation. 'Quite a few years ago, a logo was made of xenon gas atoms on a patch of nickel crystal 14 by 12.5 millionths of a millimetre thick. At that time, it was the smallest engineered creation. Following on from that it became possible to store data of 1 billion bits per square inch. Later recent work has been done where they have demonstrated a new method of storing computer memories which require only a single electron per bit of information. The method uses gallium arsenide semi-conductors working at extremely low temperatures, mind. It exploits a phenomenon known as quantum tunnelling, quantum annealing and the like.'

'Never mind the technobabble gobbledegook, Setford,' Weston stated, a little exasperated by now but then continued, 'Basically, it is miniscule. That is what you are telling us. More to the point, what are they going to use it for? Though half guessing, their ultimate aim, I think, is…'

'World domination?' Luke interrupted half joking.

'Of a sort,' replied Setford and went on, 'They could use it to collect, monitor and/or change information.'

'The potential of this is huge,' exclaimed Weston and then elaborated, 'Governments have initiated regime change in the past and meddled in other countries but this looks like a global agenda, not just a continental area of influence. Nothing so mundane as creating conventional dictatorships or puppet administrations but rather control by economic forces and the massaging of information influences to remotely steer governments and their economies using disinformation when needed. Control the world by redefining the information fed to people and governments and influencing the world economy. You would need phenomenal software models and computing power to handle it. But it could be done. Nowadays, you don't need to march an army into a country or even set up a puppet regime to guide its direction. Just think of it. Different bits of misinformation to different countries destabilising some. It's been done before by national governments seeking to influence their neighbours or a region but not on the scale the Corporation or some element of it is attempting. To quote Gleb Pavlovsky, *"All politics is information politics. There is no difference for us between facts and perceptions."*'

Sarah sat pensively. Weston observed this and patiently looked for a response from her. Eventually she looked at Weston.

'Sorry, I was just thinking. All that data. How do you sift the truth out? I was also thinking on a much simpler level too, of someone who once asked "what is truth?" when he was looking at it.'

'Who was that?' enquired Weston.

'Pontius Pilate.' Then after some further thought she added somewhat reluctantly, 'And I suppose I can't wash my hands of the situation I find myself in.'

Luke chipped in, 'Oh yes, there was the case of various co-ordinated texts sent on social media to the local population before attacks in Ukraine. It caused fear and confusion in the local population.'

Sarah added a further sixth pennyworth of deduction. 'Setting up counterfeit user accounts with posts of fake information or out-of-context data. People wouldn't know what or who to believe.'

'In fact, you could create crises from which wars could start. Foment rumours and manipulate cultural attitudes that result in criminal acts by mobs at local levels or orchestrate riots based on part facts and rumours on social media. If you could orchestrate all these strands of information to create a false reality upon which national governments try to act and govern, even a stable government will crack. It looks as though their ambitions are growing beyond global commercial dominance, though even at that level just think. Like it or not, the world is run on finance which in turn is based on confidence and calculated risk. If you influence business confidence by fake news, well, need I say more?' elaborated Weston.

Setford observed, 'It is incredibly complex dealing with the real world and applying different economic models and tying that in with the sophisticated advanced weather modelling but if you could, then you could manipulate the food markets. No matter how well-meaning a government, if it does not put food in the bellies of its people there will be unrest and it is likely to fall. Sophisticated weather prediction models could be used to profiteer on annual crop storage and famine relief.'

'It becomes easier as the Corporation is the only one with a true picture of what is going on. You can predict or, better still, guide by misinformation the decisions and paths governments and countries will take,' Weston added.

'Yes, there will always be the odd happening outside the predicted behaviour but the divergence would likely be temporary and with a little patience and manipulation at the opportune time, your plan would be back on track,' Sarah postulated further.

On that alarming conclusion they finished the main course with a greater resolve to find out more in order to ultimately negate the likely Corporation plan. It was at this point that a waiter hovered, seeking their dessert orders. They lightened the mood accordingly by conversing in polite chit-chat taking time to choose desserts while digesting their latest conclusions. Weston took the opportunity to put his brain into overdrive trying to conjure a plan for the Corporation's just desserts.

– MEMORIES OF DAVE BLAGDON –

Finally, Luke furnished copies of a puzzle in verse he had received from Dave Blagdon's solicitors. They each gazed at the verse till Weston commented, 'He probably felt he not only could not trust the Corporation but technology in general because of the likelihood of detection and so resorted to this "old"-style method of communication, hence the puzzles in verse.'

Luke added, 'He certainly could not leave it in technical or ancient languages because he knew I would struggle with that.' He continued, 'Dave, I mean Mr Blagdon, must have been totally convinced about the danger he was in. By nature, he always checked the facts before acting.'

'What was Mr Blagdon like? You must tell me everything you know concerning your friend. His thought processes and interests?' asked Weston.

'Well, the quality of his work was beyond reproach. He could be painstakingly ultra-careful in his work, sometimes to the frustration of others. He was born in and commuted from Essex and bemoaned the fact that everyone assumed that Estuary English was the Essex accent.'

Setford pricked his ears up and immediately enquired, 'Whereabouts in Essex?'

'Little Dunmow, I think.'

'Shame I didn't know him. I'm from Great Dunmow.'

'Go on, please,' said Weston impatiently glaring at Setford.

'Dave was a Christian, just like Sarah, who loved mind games, word plays and puzzles. He did not say too much about church but often talked about the Bible. I know he had a smattering of Old Testament Hebrew and New Testament Greek because he sometimes talked about root meanings and stuff. You know, like our word "love" actually describes four different Greek words, each with a different emphasis.'

'Oh, right, hence from some of his early published research I've read, there seemed to be a strong emphasis on data analysis and normalisation,' Setford added.

Luke, spotting that Sarah and Weston did not see the relevance, added quickly, 'To properly name a data item you needed to fully understand its meaning and relevance to every part of a business or system, which harks back to the old-world concept that knowing the true name of something gave you power over it!'

Luke pondered on what he could add to describe his many faceted ex-colleague.

'Let's see now, he talked about the Bible's picture language.'

'Picture language?' repeated Setford quizzically.

'Yes, you know like, oh, for instance the creation story in Genesis. If you were God, how would you explain the beginning of the universe to mankind? You would use something they could relate to no matter in what age or level of knowledge they had. Hence the dividing waters like the breaking of the waters when a baby is born. Apart from his faith, his passions were English culture and science, particularly astrophysics. You know the sort of thing. Music, literature, visual art and dance. You name it.'

'You picked up a lot from Dave!' exclaimed Sarah.

'Oh yes, he explained a lot,' replied Luke, not wanting to admit to Sarah that he had got a fair bit of information by asking questions on his visits to Reverend Hones. He was just not quite ready to confess that.

'Anything else?'

'There is a phenomenal amount. I've never known someone to have so many friends with different interests. At his funeral there were people from all walks of life and pastimes. I know he had contacts in a variety of churches throughout the country as well as overseas due to various voluntary projects he was involved with, from youth work to working with down-and-outs. I think there was a strong connection with some Midland churches. I know he did go to a lot of Christian festivals.'

'Like Greenbelt, the Dales, Spring Harvest, Ashburnham?' Sarah offered.

They were all a little nonplussed at her specialist knowledge and didn't know how useful this information was at that juncture.

'Some of them sound familiar,' Luke confirmed. He then spoke of all he knew about Dave Blagdon's work just as he had done previously but filling in the gaps he had missed on his initial explanation. 'All I can say is that in Dave's spiritual search for enlightenment he had travelled much and made many friends in churches of different denominations from Quakers to Roman Catholics, Plymouth Brethren to aesthetics, Eastern Orthodox to free and house churches up and down the country and had attended all sorts of conferences, YMCA and charities, some of them international. I'm sorry it's very general but that's the best I can do.'

Towards the end of their discussion it was agreed that Sarah and he would investigate the verse further. They decided that in order to follow the puzzle clues they would need to book time off from work, ideally for the following week.

Dave Blagdon had foreseen and prepared for his own death by leaving with his solicitor handwritten letters to be sent to a variety of people at set times after his death. Some letters were purely to say goodbye, while others not only said goodbye but had some enclosures of a photograph, of him and Luke at work, and instructions to pass on an attached smaller envelope only to the man in the photograph, if he showed up. His instructions to his solicitor were that letters with enclosures were to be sent at least three months after his death.

The four diners, having finished their dessert, sat for some time considering the verse that Blagdon had provided:

First rays of hope, now rays of death
Disorientate for more ugliness
Concrete encased polluted Rom
Trickle past in Rush to be Green
Triangle Red that welcomes not warns
Speak inside for clue to glean

'Rom could be read-only memory?' suggested Sarah.

'That's what I thought,' Setford enthused.

'Could he have encased the device in concrete, do you think?' surmised Weston.

'It's a possibility but the trickle in the next line maybe suggests not. You're an Essex man, is there a river Rom in Essex?' asked Luke of Setford thoughtfully.

'Well, yes, but I think you'll find there is more than one Romford in England,' offered Setford, aware of other possibilities.

'There are at least two Romfords according to the index on my phone from Weston,' observed Sarah.

'Where did he commute from again?' asked Setford.

'Somewhere near Hainault,' Luke replied.

'We can check that with his address,' stated Weston.

'Where did he attend church?' enquired Sarah.

'A place called Havering-atte-Bower, I think. I don't know the name of the church, I'm afraid,' answered Luke.

'Let's look on a larger-scale map within a radius of say eight miles of these two places to see if the Rom passes nearby,' offered Weston.

'Hey, there's the river Rom and looking further south the river appears to be passing through a Rush Green,' stated Setford.

'Well, that narrows our search,' affirmed Weston.

'What about the warning red triangle and the welcoming bit?' asked Sarah.

'I'll google Red Triangle Rush Green,' replied Setford. 'It's a YMCA place!'

'Any chance of taking a half day off on Friday afternoon?' asked Luke of Sarah.

'Well, my boss is away and I've no backlog of work so to speak, so it should be OK. I think we should plan for the following week as leave as a contingency, or at least see if there would be any difficulties in getting it. You never know where this verse might lead us,' she replied.

Friday afternoon leave proved no problem to either of them, which they managed to arrange the next day. The following open-ended week for leave was a bit doubtful for Sarah concerning office cover. Sarah did lay the seeds with Yvonne about an extension of leave with the pretext of it being for a romantic mini-break which might need to be furthered. This was enough to persuade Yvonne to cover for her. Luke and Sarah quickly tied up loose ends at work before going away.

– PETER POSTPONED –

When Luke called in on Peter Hones two days after the restaurant meeting, he greeted him with, 'I'm afraid I can't make our usual weekly chat next week as I am away.'

'That's a shame. I was looking forward to getting stuck into the Book of Job. Anywhere nice?'

'Not sure yet but I might be away for several weeks.'

'With your young lady? What does she think of our chats?'

'Well, yes, it is with Sarah but she does not know about our chats. I haven't told her yet.'

'Oh, I see, well it might be worth listening to what she has to say about what we have discussed. Let's see now, we've covered an awful lot. The end times, what the Bible says about suffering, difficult sayings of Jesus.' During mid-summation Reverend Peter Hones noticed an impatience in Luke. He stopped and allowed Luke to interrupt.

'Tell me, what do you know about dance in worship?'

Reverend Hones was a little flummoxed to reply at first, expecting some deep philosophical question. He quickly adjusted from his initial judgement.

'Well, it's a big subject. I've seen it with children before services and with adults or family groups, though sadly it's mainly only ladies during services. There is the spontaneous sort in individuals as is often the case in Pentecostal churches, or prepared group or solo ones as in some of the establishment churches. I'm sorry to say, we don't have it at our church. Much as I'd love it to take place. I can't dance for toffee but I love watching it and sometimes I manage to understand what they are saying with their bodies.' He reflected and then reminisced for a moment before continuing, 'Martha, my wife, used to be involved in dance worship. In fact, that's where I first clapped eyes on her. In dance, that is. Boy, that takes me back. I think I may have fallen in love with her there and then. I can still see her now, her face shining and her graceful moves. I still can't believe she took on an uncoordinated mover like me.'

'Does she not dance now?'

'Not since our children were born. Maybe I'll suggest to her that she reacquaints herself with it when I get back. Is your lady into dance then?'

'Very much so.'

'Why are you smiling?' asked Luke noticing the vicar's broad smile.

'Just thinking about how we first met. We were both in our early teens. Neither of us were Christians then but Martha was very much into dance and doing very well. I didn't dance and didn't have a lot of achievements to try and impress her with. Boy, did I want to impress her. So, I pretended that I had done some modelling for some artists. I don't know why I chose that. Stupid really. But at that age you say and do some really dumb things. I still don't know why I said it or where it came from but when she asked where the modelling work was, I said Cerne Abbas. When she found out what it was, I thought she was going to punch my lights out.'

Luke laughed heartily finally stating, 'But here you are happily married for how many years?'

'Quite a few, the children are grown up and have left the nest.' He then flippantly exclaimed, with a broad grin, 'So, I won't book your marriage classes just yet then!'

'No, I wouldn't if I were you, not just yet anyway. Besides, I thought you would be extolling to me that patience is a virtue,' he replied laughing.

They then got stuck into an overview of the Book of Job. At the end of the half hour Luke had to return to the office.

'Have a safe journey and keep in touch,' Peter called after him.

4
MIND GAMES

– FRIDAY AFTERNOON –

Sarah and Luke met up and travelled by tube and bus to Rush Green and easily found the YMCA red triangle building.

'Oh well, here goes!' Luke remarked to Sarah as they entered the building.

'Excuse me, I wonder if you could help me. My name is Luke Aylmer and I used to work with a chap named Dave Blagdon. You might know him or of him. I think he may have left a package or envelope for me. Would you check for me, please?'

'OK, I'll just go and check.'

The receptionist went into another office, pulled on a filing cabinet drawer and looked at a photograph, reread the attached instructions and compared Luke's features with those in the photograph before returning to the reception desk.

'Yes, there is,' as he handed him an envelope. 'Sorry for not acknowledging our mutual friend earlier but I had strict instructions about the envelope and who I was to give it to.

Obviously, it's not my business but is this some kind of treasure hunt with clues?'

'Sort of,' replied Sarah.

'Dave was a bit of a character, wasn't he? I bet he's having a last laugh on you now. You can't get your own back now he has gone, can you?' stated the receptionist.

'Oh, you could definitely say that. Thanks very much,' answered Luke turning to leave.

Once outside the building Luke and Sarah opened the envelope and were met with another simple rhyme. It did not make much sense to them so they phoned it through to Weston.

Laureate not averse to lie in a place he loved to reside
Not too far from seaside tide
A place of worship once buried in sand
Your start clue however could well be inland
But stay on course to get in the swing of it
Holed up in a county renowned as Stannic.

'Swing? Could it be music or dance?' questioned Luke out loud.

'Course and swing seem linked. A golf course maybe?' suggested Sarah.

'This county Stannic, I'm not aware of any county of that name,' stated Luke.

Weston racked his brain. Where had he heard that word before or something like it? He tried various variations: 'stannary', 'stenery', 'stannim', 'stannic'.

'Stannic is another name for tin, isn't it? What counties have tin mined in them?' asked Weston.

'Well, mainly Cornwall and Devon,' answered Luke.

'Wasn't there a Stannic parliament?' Weston mumbled rhetorically then answered himself aloud, 'Yes, there was. Where was it now? Cornwall! What do you know about Cornwall, Setford?'

'Pasties, mining, er, the Lizard and Land's End, of course. There's a seal sanctuary there too, I think, but it's all Gweek to me,' Setford partly muttered while preoccupied with a technical problem he was dealing with. Weston scowled with irritation at Setford's flippancy. Unaware of Weston's response Setford continued still mainly absorbed in his ongoing equipment conundrum.

'My esteemed colleague is from there of course. She sometimes blathers on about it and how she misses the sea.'

Hand covering the phone Weston uttered, 'It's a shame Marwenna isn't here, I'm sure I'd get more sensible answers from her.'

Setford thought for a moment on Weston's remark having given the subject more of his attention.

'Actually, sir, did you say something about a golf course and a place of worship?'

'Yes. Why?'

'I'm sure Marwenna mentioned that her childhood church was like that. We could ring her, though she might be in some high-powered management meeting,' suggested Setford.

'We can't contact her on her mobile, I could try her office landline, but I suspect she could be on her travels.'

Setford was puzzled by this last comment but assumed it was part of her new, exciting, hectic executive schedule.

'Before we check Marwenna's personnel record, look up poet laureates and see if any lived, died or were buried in Cornwall, would you, please, Setford,' requested Weston.

'There must be dozens of them!' Setford exclaimed.

'I think about a score. What do they teach in schools these days?!' grumbled Weston under his breath. After several minutes of various data retrievals and data matching Setford replied confidently, 'One is buried in Cornwall at Trebetherick, in the parish of St Minver. A Sir John Betjeman is interred at St Enodoc Church.'

'That's got to be it!' Weston relayed the news to Luke and Sarah on the phone and asked, 'When and how are you getting there?'

'If this is going to be a long puzzle then I think we will need to expand our mini-break from work. We'll discuss it and get back to you. Though we really don't know how much time we have if, worst case scenario, someone from the Corporation is closing in on us.'

After a bit of liaising with people still at the office, Sarah and Luke managed to wangle further time off, Yvonne only acquiescing with the request by insisting that Sarah was to '*fill her in on all the romance she got up to*'. Together, Sarah and Luke drove down to Cornwall on the Friday night. They booked into a hotel that had been an old school in Port Isaac for initially a couple of nights. Very early the next morning, they motored to Trebetherick and after some searching found St Enodoc and Sir John Betjeman's grave but the church itself was empty of people. Eventually they found a churchwarden contact number, only to discover on telephoning that the warden was out for the day but would be in on the Sunday.

'Well, we have a whole day to enjoy. What shall we do?' asked Sarah.

'I've heard the beach at Perranporth is quite something. I think there used to be an army camp at the back of it.'

It was a bright, clear, but very windy day and the constant roar of the distant waves as well as the wind reminded them of how powerful nature was. The beach was very long and expansive with the tide out. They stretched their legs by walking along the whole length of the beach and back. Just as they were leaving the beach, they witnessed a charming little episode of a small dog dropping his ball into the river from the top of the bridge and running down the slope to retrieve it again as it flowed out to sea, repeating the feat many times and having great fun doing it. The lazy owner just stood and watched it from the bridge. After their bracing walk, they had a pasty each for a very early lunch and decided to try to take in some other places of interest before it got dark. They just managed to make the Arthurian Centre at Slaughterbridge as well as Tintagel. Back at the hotel they ate a sumptuous meal, washed down with a bottle of sparkling wine from Camel Valley and then stood looking at the stars and the harbour before retiring for the night. The next day they called in on the churchwarden who took a long look at Luke.

'Did you know Dave Blagdon well?' asked Sarah of the churchwarden.

'Not too well. He would sometimes bring groups of mainly Christian painters and photographers to the area to stay for a week or so. Something about the light and the dramatic coastline that would inspire them, I guess. Some of them would come to services on Sunday or attend other local churches. Would you excuse me just for a moment?'

'Sure,' affirmed Luke as he and Sarah swapped quick glances while the woman disappeared inside to emerge after a minute or two with a photograph of Luke and Dave.

'I just needed to check,' she said as she handed over an envelope to Luke.

'Thanks very much, sorry to have troubled you.'

'Aren't you going to open it? I have to confess I've been curious about it ever since it arrived. If it is legalese, I might be able to help as I know a fair bit of Latin.'

'Thank you for your kind offer but it is not legalese. It is puzzling language, though not Latin, and I'm afraid it is for my eyes only.' As soon as they got back to the car Luke opened the letter and read it aloud.

> *Island in sea that you might wear*
> *To get there you need weather so fair*
> *Keep to the track though Spartan in scene*
> *Tis but a stone throw from Island Green*
> *Overcome hurdles to join the club*
> *Though visiting, you are due no sub.*

'What do you think?' asked Sarah.

'Cardigan? Cardigan Bay?' offered Luke.

'But Cardigan Bay is not an island. Let's look at the map to see if there is an island off it,' Sarah ventured as she scoured the large-scale atlas they had brought with them. Luke made a further suggestion.

'Well, Eire is known as the Green Isle and it is off Cardigan Bay.'

'Here on the map there is a very small island in the south but I'm not sure it is technically in Cardigan Bay.' Sarah continued, 'Mind you, there does not appear to be anything on it, anyway. What else might you wear?' Sarah frowned while asking.

'Italy looks like a boot.'

'Well, that ties in with a plot being afoot! Did Dave visit Italy?'

'Not that I know of.' They both racked their brains, making alternate suggestions.

'Let's see now, there are jumpers, socks, pants, tights, stockings,' listed Luke.

'Vests, blouses, skirts, dresses, ties, hats, berets, boas,' continued Sarah.

'Scarves, gloves, petticoats, shirts, shoes, jerseys, coats,' proffered Luke.

'Jerseys,' they both exclaimed at the same time.

'Jersey or New Jersey?' queried Sarah.

'Time to look at a detailed map of Jersey and New Jersey, I think.'

'Did Dave ever go to either of them?' asked Sarah.

'It's unlikely that he went to New Jersey, at least he never mentioned it. But who knows?'

'Hey, there's a Green Island off the south-east coast of Jersey.'

'There are also loads of single-lane roads and tracks.'

Between them they researched and booked the most convenient flight to Jersey and a stay at the hotel Somerville in St Aubin. Throughout the journey and flight, they learnt as much as they could about the island of Jersey and from the new information gleaned, reduced the area of search considerably. Once settled in at the hotel they arrived at a joint conclusion, namely to investigate the athletics track at FB fields not too far from Green Island. Catching two buses they then walked to the fields. Here, they managed to find a helpful groundsman who advised them to contact Jersey Spartan Athletics Club, the clubhouse of which was aside the running track. This they did and arranged to meet the chairwoman at the clubhouse in the early evening before the start of training sessions.

'So, we have lunchtime and an afternoon to kill. Let's go for a walk. I don't know about you but I could really do with stretching my legs.'

Walking along the beach to Green Island they then took the coast road and ended up at the Le Hoc pub. After a fine meal, washed down with some Somerset cider, they rested and enjoyed the wintry sunshine. Sure enough, the club chairwoman was there to meet them when they eventually sauntered back, arriving spot on time for the rendezvous. She looked very closely at Luke before going into the club office and taking out an envelope and double-checked the photograph.

'How did you come to know Dave Blagdon?' asked Sarah.

'He had financed several coaching courses for our club members. He seemed to take a real interest in each coach's development, though the recipients never knew him.'

As Sarah and Luke worked out each step of the puzzle to bring them to a different location they were always met with a comparison of Luke and the photograph before the next verses were handed over. If the holder of the envelope knew Dave Blagdon, they would often remark on what a character he was and what a loss to them. Some would reminisce about the fun times they had had in his company with notable affection. In this case the welcoming and helpful chairwoman had only met Dave Blagdon once. Luke opened the envelope as they walked towards a bus stop but they were so engrossed in the puzzle that they just kept walking.

It's on to St Helier, a Holy place of light
To a welcome of warmth not aware of your plight
Apart from the clues there's a gift for you
Though years will pass till its worth you'll enthuse

As they walked past Howard Davis Park, they could hear instruments being tuned up. As most of the churches in St Helier would not be open at this time, they decided to investigate the sounds. A free concert and marching display by the Band of the Island of Jersey was due to start so they found a seat and rested their tired feet waiting for the band to begin in the concert bowl. Luke did his best to watch what the drummer was doing but found it difficult as the drum set was placed at the back of the bowl. Midway through the concert a singer was invited on and sang 'The Island Games Toasting Song'. This was to promote a collection in aid of travelling expenses for the athletes from Jersey due to take part. Gradually some of the audience cottoned on to the chorus and started singing along with gusto. Sarah and Luke joined in as best they could. At the end of the concert the marching band display commenced.

THE ISLAND GAMES TOASTING SONG[5]

Through the pain, the wind and rain, excellence we seek to gain.
Shared aims, common goals, personal bests and team golds.
Coach's shouts, winging moans, encouragings in the freezing cold.

Open hands across the sea
Makes a friend of you and me.
Exchanging views helps us to see
The people God calls us to be.

Chorus

Tests in sport, trials in life
Can be a shared experience.
New targets set, new tests to face,
Taking part in this human 'race'.

— TOASTING CHORUS —

Bless your friends and
bless your family
May your life be rich in
good deeds
Bless your home, good
health and happiness
May your life be full and
complete
Treasure each moment of
this fleeting life.

---

5   A folk song on guitar with a Celtic feel

Trio then Chorus

From open minds comes maturity
Frees us from insularity.
Rich in our diversity
Exploring shared humanity.

Chorus

Friendships new, renewing old.
A pleasant stay, it's time to go.
Fond memories we'll entertain.
'À bêtôt'[6], till we meet again.
Au revoir, till we meet again.
Auf Wiedersehen, till we meet again.

Trio
Rhythm, relaxing and style,
Controlling our breathing and mind
For the task. On your marks. Set. Go!
Floating, stretching, pumping, driving hard on to the finish line.
Sharing our hopes and our fears,
Trying our best to achieve, working hard giving blood sweat and tears.

---

6   Jèrriais for goodbye

Sarah took the opportunity to broach the subject of Luke's service days.

'Did you march like that on parade with your regiment?'

'No, we marched at 140 or at the double 180 steps per minute, the repertoire for which is not that great, plus due to cutbacks and amalgamations we had to share bands across regiments. The bugle was the main instrument as we were not a regiment of the line. Though I do believe the Rifle Brigade, one of our forefather regiments, had a very good band.'

Sarah sensed his reticence so didn't probe further and kept it light.

'You don't walk that fast now. You amble or saunter at best.'

'No, well, I'm saving myself,' he said with mock fluttering of his eyelashes. 'It takes rest and patience to achieve bodily perfection.' He briefly took a bodybuilder pose.

'So, you intend to rest for centuries then!' She quickly gave her witty riposte and then reflected on the band's final salute.

After the concert they caught the bus to their hotel where they revisited the last puzzle given to them. Eventually they came to the conclusion that the next likely place to look was either St Helier's hermitage or St Matthew's church, which was known as the Glass Church, so they decided to visit both first thing in the morning.

Their first port of call was the hermitage. Beautiful in its basic simplicity as it was, there afforded no place likely to hold any envelope. Indeed, though open to the elements it was locked with a metal gate to stop access so on they went to St Matthew's.

Sure enough, when they made contact in there, after checks they were handed an envelope and a small parcel. Luke opened the parcel which contained the book *Daily Light*, a daily selection of verses from the living Bible. Initially both he and Sarah thought this might contain clues but realised fairly quickly that this was a gift from Dave to Luke as the inscription said, *'Well done for getting this far in this part of your walk through life.'* They then read the next rhyme that was contained in the brown envelope.

> *Island hop on way back to Blighty*
> *Though not an up between two downs*
> *Pier to pier travel from ticket to Ryde*
> *Find your station in life, be it ever so musical?*
> *Enquire uphill close to nearing the Heights*

'Let's be systematic and list all the islands between Jersey and southern England,' suggested Sarah. This they did with the help of a hotel atlas and online access on the hotel's computer. They whittled away the unlikely candidates that had neither downs nor piers and were left with the Isle of Wight. Luke rang Weston to give the latest state of play. As they flew back to Southampton airport they researched as much as they could about the local geography of the next island to visit.

'There are lots of downs on the Isle of Wight,' stated Sarah.

'Just when things are looking up,' said Luke smiling.

'They certainly are. But which ones does he mean?' Sarah had deliberately ignored Luke's pathetic attempt at wordplay and continued, 'What about this mention of Ryde and piers, and why pier to pier? It seems to suggest some sort of connection,' questioned Sarah.

'Because of the spelling I don't think it is peer to peer as in computer connections. Dave would have been very precise on that, I'm sure,' affirmed Luke.

'There are four piers on the Isle of Wight and one of them is at Ryde and Ryde has two railway stations. There are also a couple of railway lines, one is steam, and I think there might be some old disused sections on the island,' added Sarah.

'What about the reference to station in life?' asked Luke rhetorically and continued, 'As regards stations, it might possibly be one of three that are not inland, that's assuming that one of the piers is not like the one at Wigan. It could be Sandown, Lake or Shanklin, though there doesn't appear to be a pier at Lake. I'll just check the other two.' A couple of minutes passed as they both researched further detail. 'There is a pier in Sandown for definite.'

'I wonder about the musical reference though,' questioned Sarah.

'I'm looking at the station descriptions now. Ah, yes, success! Sandown has live music at the station regularly. The others don't,' exclaimed Luke.

'So, it's a through train ticket to Sandown for us then,' Sarah exclaimed triumphantly. With that, Sarah rang through to Weston to update him.

Arriving at Sandown station they enquired in the café about '*the Heights*', hoping it would eliminate some of the churches in the town from their search. Sure enough, there were only two churches in close proximity to the Heights, almost equidistant. When they reached the Heights, they tried contacting each church as both were closed. Sarah got through to the priest of St Patrick's, who confirmed that there had been no contact with him.

Luke remarked after his call to the other church, 'The church is locked and the contact is apparently away at a conference off island today, but will be back tomorrow.'

'I suggest we get somewhere to stay and find something to eat,' Sarah uttered, a little tired after all their travelling. They found a nice bed and breakfast place along the coast path and started to settle in.

'I think we need to find a laundrette as we haven't brought enough clean clothes with us,' stated Sarah.

'I'll go, if you want to unpack your things. I can always unpack later. I'll tell you what, I'll meet you outside that restaurant we passed when we took a wrong turning. What was it called now? Bellamy's Bistro, that was it. We'll have a bite to eat there,' offered Luke.

After a delicious lunch they decided to walk the bay as they needed to stretch their legs and get some fresh air. First, they walked to Yaverland and then in the opposite direction to Shanklin and back. It was a bracing jaunt – the passing and moored ships on the skyline, the sound of the waves and a section of beach huts with amusing names.

'Was it easy to find the laundrette? Was it busy?' asked Sarah.

'I had no problem finding it. The Chapel Laundry is in Wilkes Street, off the main thoroughfare. They were busy with lots of hotel business but were very accommodating actually. Bizarrely, perhaps, I met some really interesting people with good conversation while watching the clothes go round. There were quite a lot of regular locals who popped in and left their washing and so I got the lowdown on the locality. You just don't expect that from a laundry. It felt such a happy place too and they said that there was no need for me to hang around, they would unload and fold it, and to return at about 4.30 when the ironing would be completed.'

That evening they chose to have a romantic meal at the Bandstand, which overlooked the ocean. The good food and wine perfectly capped off what had been a very tiring day so they retired early. The next morning, they met the churchwarden of Christ Church at nine o'clock. He opened up the building and went to the office, taking time to check the photograph sent with Blagdon's envelope. Sarah and Luke looked around the church.

'I'm so sorry you had to wait. Here is the envelope.'

'Did you know Dave well?' Sarah asked her customary question.

'We first met at a conference in Ashburnham and then became co-leaders on a narrowboat cruise for a Scripture Union teenagers' holiday some time back.'

'Is that a drum kit I spy underneath that black cover in the corner?' asked Luke.

'Why yes, but nobody's played it in a long while.'

'May I have a look?'

'By all means, though, like I said, it has not been in use for, oh, five or six years.'

'Why not?'

'The drummer died and he bequeathed his kit to this church. Apparently, he used to play in the worship group here. Mind you, this was before my time here at Christ Church.'

They took the black dust cover off, to Luke's delight.

'Wow, that's the same make, model and colour as mine, although he's got rototoms.'

'Really, no wonder he died!' japed Sarah.

'Oh, ha, ha,' retorted Luke and then turning to the churchwarden added, 'Tell me about him. Is he buried in the churchyard?'

'Well, I'm actually preparing a little information sheet about him to place by the kit. He wouldn't be buried in our churchyard because it has been full for years. I can't remember from my research whether he was buried or cremated. Rumour has it that he said to his wife, "Surprise me," concerning his funeral arrangements. It was quite strange too that at his funeral he had requested a trainee minister who had not taken a funeral before to conduct it. He wrote the talk for them which was quite humorous, apparently, as well as including a gospel message. Among the Christian songs he requested he had also asked for a special version of "Sing, Sing, Sing".'

'Don't tell me, the 1938 version by Benny Goodman,' offered Luke.

'Yes, how did you know?' replied the warden.

Sarah interjected, 'You don't want to go there! He'll give you chapter and verse.'

'Please go on,' requested Luke.

'He composed a bit but always joked in his old age that he was doing more decomposing than composing.'

'It's nice to know someone has trodden a similar musical path to me but it sounds as if he got a lot further along on his one,' observed Luke.

'I don't suppose you would be available to play this Sunday? They rehearse an hour before the service if you are interested.'

'No. Thanks for the offer, but it seems likely that we will be off the Island this afternoon.'

They replaced the dust cover and left, walking down to the seafront before thinking about opening the envelope.

'Before we open it, can we just enjoy being here for a while?' Sarah suggested.

'Sure, let's treasure some time out from our quest. It'll be nice to enjoy a moment or two together like this.'

The mesmeric sound of the rhythmic waves beating against the shore lulled them into a state of peace-filled relaxation, almost at one with the elements and with each other. The vastness of the ocean and its restless oscillation of tides and moods caused them to reflect on their insignificance in the general grand scheme of the universe, and the smallness of their current predicament, which for this brief moment seemed far, far away. They had each other and together they felt complete if only for this transient time. Eventually Sarah turned to Luke with thoughts returning to their main aim.

'What do you think?' asked Sarah.

'Well, we are in a mess and, being honest, I'm not too hopeful we will get out of it unscathed. Are you scared?'

'Yes, but I think I'd rather be with you than anyone else.'

They decided to have an early lunch at The Reef on the seafront, enjoying the sea view, the food, the cider and some relaxation before attempting to decipher the latest verse. In the back of their minds, though, was still the thought of where to next, from their brief sojourn. After their dessert, they moved out to the exterior decking of The Reef, taking their teas with them so as to enjoy some final fresh air and some wintery rays while contemplating the next clue. It was here that they heard for the second time via someone's loud car radio tuned to a local station, 'The Island Games Toasting Song'. This rendition, however, was sung by local athletes to raise funds for their own team's travelling expenses. They sat and listened while slowly turning over in their minds the stanzas Dave had left for them. The car eventually drove off, leaving the gulls to produce the soundtrack to their final moments of repast.

> *Glad you made it but now it's back to mainland*
> *My future intended was not what was planned*
> *With masts aplenty though placed inland*
> *The game is on, odd ball in hand*
> *But this game is deadly, does not enthral*
> *Ask again within red brick wall*
> *Further Information to catch the crooks*
> *Receive directions near poetic Brooke*

'Hm, "intended", was Dave Blagdon ever married or engaged?' asked Sarah.

'Yes, I believe he was engaged once but if I remember correctly, they mutually called it off. I think in the end they both felt it was the right thing to do.'

'Did she come from Essex too? What was her name?'

'No, I'm not sure, but I vaguely remember her being from somewhere in the Midlands. Her name? It might have been

Carol but I'm not sure. I certainly never heard her surname mentioned. I think the odd-shaped ball has got to be rugby!'

'But is the clue the actual town of Rugby or where the game is played?'

'Hopefully the masts and Brooke should determine if it is or not.'

'Does the Brooke mean running water or something else?'

'I think the *poetic* is the qualifier here. It could mean picturesque or a poet called Brooke.'

After conferring with Weston, they booked a through ticket by train to Rugby, as he was able to confirm that there was an association between Rugby and the poet Rupert Brooke.

— CLOSE TO RETRIEVAL —

Nichols was convinced that unless Blagdon had posted the device it was still somewhere on the UK mainland. Once he had received a transaction alert on Luke Aylmer's account and traced the ticket destination to being back on the mainland, he decided to increase the surveillance on him. Aylmer must be close. *This could be the final piece in the jigsaw*, he thought. It was very convenient letting Aylmer do all the legwork. Wanting Arif and his connections to remain in the capital for the time being, he decided it was time to enlist Ruby in one of her many disguises to follow Aylmer. She was so good at shadowing folk at a distance; besides she had had time off while Aylmer was out of the office. He telephoned her.

'Ruby, I'd like you to shadow Aylmer and Manning. They are on their way to Rugby by train but not due to arrive for several hours. I think they are getting close. Obviously, you'll need to disguise for this because you've worked in the same office as him and, of course, Manning works for you.' He became irritated at himself for stating the obvious but continued, 'I take it you've not put in a workday appearance at your own office just yet but we both like being cautious, don't we? Investigate each contact they make and let me know instantly if they pick up a package or suchlike.'

'Have there been any revealing phone calls from the Manning woman in the office suites?' Ruby asked.

'No, nothing all the time she has worked for the Corporation.'

'OK. I'll drive up there and wait for them to arrive at the station.'

– THE HUNT CONTINUES –

Sarah and Luke's train journey involved a ferry, at least three changes at different stations and a bit of waiting around for the connections to Rugby. They caught a cab to the town centre which, unbeknown to them, was only a minute or so's drive away. They decided to have some tea and a snack after the long journey and gather their thoughts to come up with a plan for their next bit of research. Tom Brown's teashop was very old and quaint. It was tucked away through an archway and was quite small inside, having space for about nine tables. There was a plaque on the wall dedicated to 'Woodbine Willie' from the First World War.

Ruby had donned a disguise and was parked close by. She waited for them to leave before following wearing a wig and outsize, understated clothing in neutral colours.

'I know you've already been through this before but tell me about Dave. What was he really like?' questioned Sarah.

'He was a biological computer systems specialist who loved mind games, word plays and puzzles. He was remarkable for studying engineering, biology, mathematics and was also steeped in an electronics background. Dave produced quite a few prototypes using 3D printing methods. Because of the way management structures work he never got promoted but that didn't matter to him.'

'I mean what was he like as a friend?'

'Fun, open, loyal, trustworthy, gentle and very, very zany,' Luke opined.

After some tea and sandwiches, they decided to make for the library to see what the locality had to offer and had a short list of questions to research, speaking in hushed tones while in the library.

'What about the masts?' enquired Sarah.

'Apparently there used to be quite a few near the A5 on the edge of Rugby but they've been replaced by warehouses and a housing estate.'

'What waterways are in the area?' Luke asked.

'There's the river Avon and the Oxford canal,' replied Sarah while Luke wrote down her findings and ticked the question off their list.

'What about brooks or streams?'

'There's a Rains brook but it doesn't have an "e" on the end.'

'OK, I think we've confirmed that it's got to be about Rupert Brooke.'

'Is there anything to do with Rupert Brooke on the map?' Sarah questioned.

'There is a Rupert Brooke house and a statue. The clue must be near one of these,' Luke observed.

They walked first to the statue and then looked around and reread the clue. Ruby surreptitiously sat on the bench in the Jubilee Gardens, watching and occasionally using the reflection in her makeup mirror. She could partly hear their conversation and lip read any words slightly out of earshot using her compact mirror while pretending to fix her makeup and hair.

'It's facing roughly in the direction of the Baptist church. Would Dave have known anyone there?'

'Maybe, he had connections with Baptists, Roman Catholics, United Reformed, Methodists and all manner of folk,' stated Luke.

'Well, let's start with asking the minister or assistant.'

Fortunately for them the church was open for a cheap lunch for office workers. They were directed by the kitchen workers to the small office.

'We're trying to trace a friend of a chap named Dave Blagdon. I believe he might have known someone in your congregation. Can you help at all?'

'Well, I could make an announcement in the Sunday services.'

She was a jovial, extrovert sort of woman and was examining Luke quite closely.

'And who should I say they should contact?'

'Oh, I'm sorry, we didn't introduce ourselves.' Luke completed the introductions. The assistant went to a small store room filing cabinet and checked a photograph supplied by David of himself and Luke. She then riffled through the filing cabinet to find a sealed envelope which she gave to Luke.

'My minister knew David very well, though I've only heard about him second hand. This has intrigued me ever since it arrived in the office. Are you into these treasure hunt mind games that Dave is?'

'Being honest, no, and I'm sorry to say David died a few months ago.'

'Oh, I am sorry, I didn't know.'

'Thank you for this,' said Luke as he and Sarah exited the building. They opened the envelope by the statue.

Almost visible from the poet's abode
Spiritual solace found across the road
Beyond the trees is the right track
Look behind you and take steps back

'We must be getting close. The clue is in the same area. Shall we walk to the poet's house?' suggested Luke.

'I'm very cold. I'd rather go back to the library and do a bit more background research on Rugby should there be another clue.'

'OK, you keep digging in the library and I'll try the next likely location. Meet you in the park near the council building by the musical instrument sculpture in, say, two hours.'

'Seems good to me. I'm getting tired of traipsing about and like I said I'm getting a bit cold. Take care, though, and please ring or text me if something transpires.'

'Likewise, will you phone or text if you discover something significant?' 'Will do.'

They briefly kissed and when Luke was gone Sarah ensconced herself in the warm library.

Ruby decided to follow Luke. He made his way to the poet's house and stood outside rereading the latest clue. Sure enough, across the road on the corner was a sign for an athletics track and close by on the other side of the road was a United Reformed church. To double-check he walked down the road to the athletics track to see if there were trees and if there was anything in between the track and the church. Apart from an offset leisure centre and indoor bowling building there was nothing of note. *The church has to be it*, he concluded and made his way back. The church was open and he searched for someone in the small rooms attached. He entered the church and found a minister in the office. A similar conversation ensued concerning Dave Blagdon as previously held at the Baptist church, including the photograph check. Again, a sealed envelope was produced which Luke decided to open a little later after he had found somewhere warm to give it his full attention.

As Luke left and very slowly sauntered along the road, the minister quickly locked the church, caught him up and joined him, deciding to grab a quick sandwich from the town. Ruby, who had followed Luke into the church, was left locked in. She took the opportunity to visit the office and started to riffle through the filing cabinets. Unfortunately for her she was discovered by the minister who had had to return to the church because he had forgotten his wallet.

Immediately she took the initiative and held a knife to his throat to force him to talk about what had been passed to Luke but he knew nothing save that a brown envelope had been left for him. He tried at first to reason with her and then, thinking that being a man he would be stronger, attempted to disarm her. Unfortunately, in the scuffle that ensued her loose-fitting wig fell off. As she could not risk possible identification, she killed him. In the struggle his facial expressions of surprise, then fear, and then desperation while gasping for air registered no empathy within Ruby but did evoke a fascination, right up to his final death throes. She had no emotion for her victim at all, but she did feel a taste of excitement, exhilaration even, and satisfaction she had never felt when she had killed before. That had always been at a distance by a silenced rifle or pistol. Fortunately, she had ensured through wearing the right sort of garb that there would be no DNA trace and did her best to make it look like a robbery that had gone wrong before rushing out to catch sight of Luke's slow bummel towards the town centre.

Luke stopped off at a nice little hostelry out of the main thoroughfare called The Merchants. It was somewhere out of the cold where he could sit and consider the contents of the envelope before telephoning Sarah. Ordering a pint of Herefordshire cider he sat down by the fire to warm. Ruby entered by a side entrance, ordered a soft drink and sat where she could see Luke but remain hidden from his view. She needed to report to Nichols about what had happened. Quietly she telephoned him and spoke in hushed tones, using the prearranged code words they had often used in past assignments.

Phone calls to and from Nichols were habitually cleaned and/or wiped from records but he always took as many precautions as he could to ensure no evidence could be traced and held against him. It was their little joke to always use a gemstone to name her, and for this expanding operation it had been Ruby.

'It's Ruby, a black jet stone has been destroyed but I've removed all its dust from the carpet and there were no other jet stones around. The emerald and jade are still available.'

'What's this? Expertise slipping, Ruby?'

'The breakage was unavoidable. Previous owners may be upset once news of this breaks. Do you still want me to continue to trace other gems?'

'A moment while I think, Ruby.'

He had no doubts concerning her professionalism but pondered this development and what best to do next. He thought quickly. They both knew the murder would soon be discovered and a fast decision was needed. After a half minute of contemplation, he instructed her to kidnap Sarah to get the answer or at least put pressure on Luke to provide his answers so far and maybe later to use Sarah as a bargaining chip.

'Take the emerald instead for an exchange in the near future. It can be quite captivating.'

'Do you want me to deliver it to the usual place?'

'Yes, as usual.'

'What about the jade piece?'

'Don't bother I can control any transaction for it once I have the emerald.'

'There could be a window of opportunity now before the emerald and jade are reunited. I will endeavour to secure the emerald for you.'

With that she rang off, exited The Merchants the way she had entered and scurried past the window by the fire, taking care not to show her face if Luke were to peer out. Ruby returned to her car, took out some folded clothes from the boot, spotted a public convenience she could change within and having changed returned to her car. Her new disguise was a loose-flowing burka. Back at the car she drove as near to the meeting place in the park as she could and parked up. Then, opening the boot of her car, she assembled a wheelchair after which she reached in the passenger side glove compartment and carefully checked the contents of a box she had stored in there: a syringe, a couple of clean swabs, two bottles holding different liquids, one of which was larger than the other. One of the bottles had a large atomiser spray device for its top. She placed the box on the wheelchair together with one of the bottles. The bottle with the atomiser she placed in a large pocket of her robe, ready for quick access. She made her way to Caldecott Park and awaited her prey.

Sarah, thoroughly warmed through, felt she now needed some fresh air so returned from the library a little early. She sat on a bench near the sculpture of a tuba, waiting for Luke. She spied a woman pushing an empty wheelchair coming slowly towards her who seemed to be enjoying looking at the flower beds. Every once in a while, she would stop to check something on the chair as if it wasn't working correctly. Ruby awaited her chance when no other people were in the vicinity and approached Sarah with the wheelchair.

'Excuse me, I'm having trouble with this wheelchair. Something is not quite right about it. Would you mind trying sitting in it as a test for me, please?'

'Not at all if it will help,' Sarah replied readily complying.

As she sat in the chair a spray was immediately produced and squirted into Sarah's face, which incapacitated her for a short time during which she felt a needle applied to her arm. The next thing Sarah knew she had been arranged in the passenger seat of a car as if she were asleep, with a blanket covering her body, but she was unable to move. Everything appeared blurred, echoey and distorted. Within seconds she became unconscious again. Ruby drove to the outskirts of London keeping an intermittent eye on her quarry. Before disposing of Sarah to a Corporation satellite laboratory, Ruby searched Sarah's handbag and clothing. There was nothing noteworthy for taking. Certainly nothing of monetary value. She had to be content with snipping a piece of Sarah's hair. Another trophy for her collection.

– A WAIT IN VAIN –

Luke had tried calling Sarah while thawing out in The Merchants but she had not texted a reply so, armed with the new verses and thoroughly warm by now, he sat on a park bench awaiting her. A tall policewoman with a long, plaited pigtail approached Luke while he was waiting at their prearranged meeting place. Her colleague approached him from behind as a precaution.

'Excuse me, sir, have you visited the United Reformed Church today?'

'Yes, I was there about ninety minutes ago.'

'Have you any identification on you, sir?'

'Well, yes,' he said producing his driving licence from his wallet. 'Why, what's happened?'

'Would you mind accompanying me to the station to help with our enquiries concerning a criminal incident that took place there earlier today. Just to eliminate you from our enquiries.'

'Well, I'm waiting for someone actually.'

'Can you phone them to say you will be late?'

'OK.' He tried ringing Sarah but got no reply, assumed she had turned her phone off in the library and forgotten the time, so sent her a text: '*Will be at police station.*'

'Thank you, sir, this way, please.'

He duly got into their car and was checked in at their reception desk, having to hand in his wallet, phone, laces and belt, and then had his fingerprints taken before being led to an interview room. A DNA swab was requested and at his agreement was also taken. He was assured he wouldn't have to wait too long before being interviewed and that they were awaiting the availability of a detective to interview him. Sure enough, shortly after, a detective entered the interview room.

'A suspicious death has occurred and as stated earlier we need to eliminate you from our enquiries.'

'Death, what death?'

'The minister at the United Reformed Church in Hillmorton Road. Did you visit him today, sir?'

'Yes, but he was alive when I left him. In fact, he came out from his office with me to get a sandwich but had to go back because he had forgotten his wallet.'

'Did anyone see you leave together?'

'I don't think so. I really don't know.'

'What was the nature of your meeting with the minister?'

Luke was in a quandary about how much he should divulge concerning his visit and so asked to call Weston.

'All in good time, sir. You will be entitled to a phone call for your formal interview.'

'Well, it was personal. Would you please call Mr Weston on my behalf?'

'Just a few more questions, sir. Did you know the minister well and how long was your meeting?'

'I did not know him. I only met him today having called in on the off chance.'

'Do you have anyone to corroborate that, sir?'

'Well, Sarah Manning can confirm some of the details but not about the actual meeting.'

'The brown envelope in your possession contained this single sheet. What does this strange verse mean?'

'I really don't want to say anymore until you contact Mr Weston.'

Eventually the detective did call Weston who explained his department's role and stated that he would travel up to confirm his identity and answer any further questions. Weston did ask to speak to Luke towards the end of the call and was disturbed to learn that Sarah was not contactable. Luke was detained until he arrived but was made a little more comfortable.

When Weston showed up, having confirmed Luke's story and satisfied the detective's other questions, he asked to listen to the interview tape of the town ranger on patrol who had given Luke's description to the police. He then asked to review the town's CCTV to try to obtain Sarah's last known whereabouts. The CCTV had previously only been examined for people in the vicinity of the United Reformed Church. Though there was no CCTV in the park there were some cameras near the entrances. He quickly ascertained that Sarah had entered the park but was not seen leaving it, but did notice the woman, or someone in a woman's garb, with an empty wheelchair who left with the wheelchair fully occupied. He asked for a copy to be made so that it could be enhanced by Setford back at his office. He rightly deduced that Sarah had been abducted and finally requested that the police statement given to the press would have even less than the usual restricted information.

Weston finished his liaison with the inspector before Luke's final processing for release was completed, so they agreed to meet at The Merchants once Luke had been fully discharged. Luke had also spent some additional time giving Sarah's description and details to the police for local search purposes, though they all felt that the prospect of Sarah being in the local area was unlikely. When Luke did eventually emerge, he took a circuitous route in case he was followed and, leaving separately from Weston, ensured that there appeared to be no link between Luke and Weston should anyone be observing.

– CROSSED PORPOISES –

Joan, Edna and Bert's daughter, was now at the age of being immensely influenced by fashion and what was deemed 'cool' as well as all the usual peer group pressure that went with someone of her age. Fortunately, though, not peer group idiocy. She was much too sensible for that. However, she was still struggling with the raging hormones that emotionally are so hard to initially cope with and these were a major influence on her mood swings. Her pop idol crush was in full swing, including flights of fancy and imagination at full throttle with an imagined life with her dreamboat. She had a close friend in the same predicament and they would write to each other fantasy letters, pretending to be the other's idol on tour. It gradually became more elaborate as they had, of course, secretly married their idol before the tour began.

Much later in life, she would be reticent to admit it, but at this time she was a little ashamed of her family and upbringing, being a girl brought up in a Cockney family with low achievements as far as she could see, compared to the glossy lifestyle portrayed to her in the media. Her life was the antithesis of all that was portrayed. Here she was stubbornly anchored by her family from all that she aspired to. She was just coming to the end of the phase of being much of the time judgemental, dismissive, sometimes antagonistic and yet still needing and loving the security and love of her family. She could often be seen rolling her eyes up at her family and shutting herself away in her bedroom. Their lifestyle was so boring compared to what she could see on television and as for the abode they lived in, well! Here she was, still at the mercy of all these contradictory moody emotions mixed up with new possibilities. Even she, though, found it hilarious being party to the conversation she witnessed between her mother and father talking at cross-purposes. She laughed herself silly while in her bedroom above the kitchen, a silent witness to the interchange below her room.

Bert had arrived back on his bicycle having taken a shortcut through the cemetery and was just taking it through to the backyard when Edna called him from the kitchen.

'How comes you were so quick? Did you get everything?'

'Of course. I took a shortcut through the cemetery.'

'I hope you didn't speed through it.'

'No, I didn't. I was just making sure that if they were stocktaking and were one short, I wouldn't be it.'

By this time Bert had unloaded the shopping in the hall and was in the yard maintaining his pushbike. Edna was still in the kitchen overlooking the yard but had the windows and doors closed. They shouted to each other intermittently, not really listening for a reply, or only half hearing as married couples of many years often do.

'Bert, did you get the littlun's underwear?'

'I got two lots.'

'What did you get culottes for?' And then muttered to herself, 'Never trust a man to clothes shop. I'll have to take them back to Marks and Sparks now. Should know by now never to send him clothes shopping. It just creates more work!' She then busied herself in the kitchen. 'Bert, I'm in the kitchen preparing the steaks for tonight's dinner. I'm just about to tenderise them.'

'Well, you've got tender eyes too, my darlin.'

'Don't come in and dirty the kitchen.'

'No. We haven't been fishing for quite a while. Not sure when we'll go again.'

'I'll just do the dishes.'

'What's judicious, sweetheart?' Bert half-heartedly waited for a reply and then carried on with his maintenance.

'Rose went out with her friend Alice earlier. I wonder what Rose met her for.'

'Did you say check the floor or what's a metaphor?' As no reply came Bert started muttering to himself. A couple of minutes later Edna suddenly remembered two shopping items she had missed.

'Can you nip round the grocer's for brussels and carrots later? I forgot to get some.'

'What? Your cousin Russell has bought a parrot on his pension?'

Edna finished her cleaning and preparation.

'Now you can come in.'

'I've already done the bins!'

Edna opened the door.

'What do you mean, you deaf old codger?'

'You know, sometimes, Edna, your diction is terrible!' replied Bert.

In later years Joan not only realised how lucky she had been to be raised in such a loving family, she became very proud of her parents and loved them to the point that she would get quite tearful at the sheer thought of them.

– WESTON AT THE MERCHANTS –

Weston secreted himself in The Merchants pub to await Luke. The pub suited him very nicely. He casually eavesdropped on some interesting conversations as he had gradually manoeuvred himself into a snug little corner. These conversations seemed to range from astronomy, music, cars, to various sports and business matters. On some benches nearby sat two people, oblivious to their surroundings, investing their attention in their own private mobile phone world. Whether they were known to each other it mattered not as their gaze seldom, if at all, raised from their multicoloured screens. The attractive food served for their consumption sat cooling and ignored.

Weston was in the midst of contemplating the possible courses of action to be taken next concerning Sarah when a short, very old, white-bearded, balding, slightly decrepit man sat down close by him and started a conversation by bemoaning some aspects of modern-day life. Some surreal comedian would have described the old man as having his head on upside down such was his baldness and massive beard. Weston, always the gentleman, didn't want to be rude and so listened patiently while half hearing a conversation progressing close by concerning black holes and quasars. The old man launched into a polemic.

'The country is going to the dogs! That's what it is. Practical skills are plummeting just like the trouser waist levels. Who wants to see men's bums, underpanted or not, peering over their silly baggy jeans?' He took a quick sip of his pint and continued, 'Outsource everything because it's cheaper on paper and lose all your in-house knowledge, experience and skill sets. There's no turning back once it's gone, you know. Short-term, fast-buck, knee-jerk leadership, if you would call it that. Yet further down the line the company ends up paying through the nose for a disaster that could have been avoided if they had listened to experienced people in the job in the first place.' He took another sip of his pint. 'No apprenticeships for youngsters now, just recruitment into drug gangs on estates. That's what is happening. As long as the politicians look to short-term gains to ensure their re-election then long-term planning and investment is a poor second. Give a committee of MPs a task to design a horse and you'll end up with a camel or a giraffalump.'

Weston started giving the old man his full attention and found himself nodding in agreement as there was an element of truth in what he said, though the delivery of the disjointed observations was difficult to follow and in a different situation would have been quite amusing. Each utterance, though a sweeping generalisation, merited thought in isolation. Besides, Weston thought, maybe the old man felt isolated in his dotage by the new generation, but he kept an open mind on the aged chap. Eventually he got the feeling that there was an enquiring and questioning sharp mind behind all these unlinked comments he was making.

Weston's own work experience had also led him to be quite cynical. A brief amalgam of meeting attendance experiences with people he had trained and seen being promoted above him by using lots of management jargon like 'blue sky thinking' had soon led him to this attitude. They could talk the talk, but often couldn't walk the walk. Indeed, at one point in one meeting when it came to asking questions at the end, his frustration led to flippancy, which went down like a lead balloon with his managers. What was it he asked now at the end of the presentation? Ah yes. *'If you shot the statue outside New York would it be a dead liberty?'*

'I suppose you could add the old boy network, the sycophants and the management theories that tend to support the wrong people being promoted to the wrong positions,' Weston offered from his own experience to the surprise of the old man who was put off his stride momentarily but soon found his voice again.

'Politicians, nice work if you can get it. Lovely pension as a reward for stitching up the country. Throw in a position or two on company boards and maybe even an honour. Lucrative speaking engagements. You could even migrate to the Lords to claim expenses and fall asleep. Late night sittings? My arse! Whatever gets them the next vote leads to short-termism in policy planning in my book. Bad for the country.'

Now in full flow again he added, 'Government or business employ external "independent" consultants to often confirm or report exactly what they want to hear or in fact what others want to hear. I've lost count of the job title name changes for performing the same tasks in my job when I was working.' He took a couple of gulps and paused. Only for a second, mind.

'When I was a wee nipper, though I liked my grandfather, he had hairy ears, missed bits when shaving and had whiskers because of it. He even occasionally smelt a bit. Now I'm exactly the same. It's not fair growing old! Not fair at all! I want to be young but with my experience so I don't have to waste time on what's not important and spend time on what is. How much time do we spend worrying about this and that, whether it's management crap or what the government's doing?! Answer me that, eh, answer me that!'

He paused for a moment as if to judge the measure of the man he was talking to and then with a little initial hesitation partially apologised.

'Sorry about my rant but it gets to me sometimes how much time humankind, and me in particular, wastes wrapped up in worthless pursuit. Worthless pursuit of what advertising fantasies offer, and, well, I don't know what!'

Fortunately for Weston the old man spotted someone he knew and after shouting a greeting walked over to him and continued his diatribe. Weston, somewhat relieved, concentrated once again on the situation of Sarah and Luke. His mind began to run through possible options to take and further precautions on Luke and Sarah's behalf. He felt sure that because the Corporation still did not have the device, they would deem Sarah more useful alive than dead but he was still very worried nonetheless. However, later that night he briefly reflected on the old man and concluded that no wonder the man was a little odd, having to try and make sense of the madness of life. Perhaps he was the sanest one of all.

– THE BEGINNING OF REALISATION –

Once Luke had left the police station and had partially recovered from the startling murder accusations his thoughts fully turned to Sarah. Apart from being anxious about her safety, his heart was beginning to tell him how deep his feelings really were for her and he began to feel the pangs of how much he missed her. As he slowly made his way through the town centre to meet with Weston he occasionally stopped to try and collect his thoughts, peering in shop windows but not really looking at the displays of goods. At one of these halts, he heard a ballad broadcast from an electricals shop which really expressed the way he felt and the arrangement stayed with him till he met with Weston.

When Luke eventually arrived at the pub the two men talked about the day's events and the last clue. Weston passed the details on to Setford. Luke was in no state of mind to attempt fully interpreting Dave Blagdon's last clue.

MISSING YOU[7]

I am missing you, yes missing you so bad.
My heart embraces you, my body aches for you, I'm so sad.
I can't wait, barely take, the empty days, till I see you again
To touch your face, your smooth-skinned face. You captivate,
the thoughts in my muddled brain.

Flowers are out in bloom, notes float by from a wonderful tune
But you are not here, not here, to share it with me.
Fine birds in my garden sing and fly
So yearns my soul but it feels it will die
Cause you are not here, not here to share it with me.

I am missing you; I should be kissing you so tenderly.
I get no peace or rest, I'm just a nervous wreck increasingly.
I can't work, I can't live, can't take much more of this, without
you in my arms.
To see your smile, your soulful eyes, it's such a while, it's a trial,
I must try to keep calm.

---

7   Lament on guitar

Awake all night it seems, yet you fill my sleep with sweet dreams
Variations of plot but you always the theme.
You're the first thoughts of my morn and I still can't help feeling so forlorn
Cause you're not here, not here to share it with me.

Yet these feelings inside force me to overcome and go on, and on and on.

My mind I cannot free, it's as though you've become part of me
But you're not here, not here to share it with me.
And so, this cycle goes on, dawn to dusk each day follows on
And I miss you, yes miss you constantly.

Won't you come to me, please run to me, fly to me sweet one.
Place your charms in these loving arms and see, you'll be safe from harm.
Come to me and rest, place your head on my chest, I'll run my fingers through your hair.
When your deeds are done, come to this lonely one and be here not there.

CAUGHT IN THE WEB, WORLDWIDE OR OTHERWISE

SARAH WAS OFFLOADED SEMI-CONSCIOUS FROM THE car into another wheelchair and wheeled into the back of one of the inconspicuous satellite Corporation buildings. They were met by a man in a nondescript white coat with an equally nonchalant set of expressionless features. Together they lifted Sarah onto a hospital trolley, relocked her handcuffs and pushed her down the corridor. While Sarah was desperately trying to keep awake, she noticed through an ajar door some people dressed in strange suits behaving as if they were not aware of where they were or how they were dressed. She was pushed into what appeared to be an operating room. The man in the white coat was just about to scrub up before preparing an anaesthetic in an adjoining cubicle when the telephone rang just outside the room. He picked it up and listened intently. His curt answers bore the frustration of interruption.

'She's in pre-op now. Why? OK, OK then. I'll keep her in a holding cell till you want to move her. I'll administer a strong sedative and take her to that address once you've given the green light. What's that? One of Arif's flats. Will he be there? Who do I liaise with? Louise? Is she trustworthy? Oh, so Abdullah Alam will contact me when? Sorry, I know you're paying the big bucks but it's annoying, these changes of plan. Point taken.' With that last remark he hung up.

A day or so later Alam telephoned to ask for Sarah's delivery to one of Arif's flats.

'Louise would be looking after her for the day till I collect her for an exchange.' Alam then rang Louise to explain the arrangements and, much later, followed up with a further call to check that Sarah had been delivered.

'Louise, telephone me when she comes round. Is she still handcuffed by one arm to the bed? Put some water and a few sandwiches by her bed, other than that let her be. I should be there early evening after some business. If not, it will be Fazul.'

Sarah had no way of marking how much time had elapsed during her incarceration or indeed if she had been held in other locations aside from the two she had some recollection of. All she vaguely remembered was having several sedatives administered, and then being wheeled to and from a car.

Several hours later she partially awoke but was still in a state of deep drowsiness. Groggily she gazed around the room and tried to get up but could not. She felt so heavy. Opposite her, sitting across an armchair, legs sprawled over its arm was a woman working her way steadily through a vodka bottle. Sarah moaned and, fighting with all her might to stay awake, asked, 'Where am I?'

The woman turned to look at Sarah, initially peering into the distance to where she thought the sound had come from, her head and gaze unsteady. Then, trying to use the glass on her outstretched arm she tried to refocus her gaze onto Sarah. She then muttered partly to herself as much as answering Sarah, 'Don't worry about where you are, luv. It's where you are going. Now that's what you should worry about. You'll be just like the others, though you seem a lot older than they normally are,' adding with a very brief sympathetic tone, 'Never mind, never mind. You could end up like me.' She raised her glass to take another sip then fumbled to pick up the phone and made three attempts to dial a number.

'It's Louise, she's coming round.'

With that she replaced the phone and clumsily poured herself another drink.

Sarah attempted to get up again, even though her body felt like a ton weight. Having made the effort, she felt totally exhausted and weariness washed over her in waves. It was all so dreamlike. Everything appeared to be in slow motion and the woman's voice sounded as if she were in an echoey tunnel. She wanted to go to sleep but fought the sensation.

'Help me, please,' gasped Sarah.

A twinge of pity passed over Louise's face for an instant, followed by her usual vacant expression.

'No, luv, I love him, see. Or thought I did. Too deep now, too deep. I always help him. I always do what he says. I'll cop it if I don't.'

Her tone was softer and her words became slurred as her mind began to wander in its befuddled state.

Louise then placed a CD in a player and selected a repeat button for a specific track as she had so often done in the past. She mouthed the words to the music as she had done so many times before but now no longer with the energy or inclination to sing them as she once did.

Identity dented, to you now cemented.
Ebbing and flowing, entwined and choking.
Persona Excessia, nearing dementia.
My ego grated; self-worth subjugated.
Exposed in the nakedness of my soul.

Still the words pounded into her numbed brain as the CD's gravelly bass voice almost whispered the rhythmic melody soon to be joined and contrasted by a plaintive tenor crying a melancholic air. The heavy-metal guitaring reinforced the acoustic twelve-string guitar riff building up to a crescendo of voices in angst.

Louise would have been a beautiful girl but unfortunately had prematurely aged and was marred by her pitiful experience of life – brought up in 'Giro City', as Leeds was once unfortunately known, with matching expectations of that time; child of a single parent. She had multiple siblings from different fathers. None of the half siblings or fathers she knew. All the fathers had abandoned her mother. Early on she had gone into local authority care as did some of her half siblings. She was bright but surrounded by low aspirations and even lower expectations. A lot of girls at that time from the poorer housing estates had made a conscious, or indeed unconscious, decision to take a career in children. That is, to have children and live on benefits, it being one of the easiest options available. Some, again, making the same mistake as their mothers of having children with quite a few different partners, some not even wondering why the fathers didn't stay. To them it was the norm played out from generation to generation. Too many children were brought up with absent, errant fathers who in turn had never been taught how to be real fathers, coming from broken homes themselves.

Louise, though, was brighter than most but unfortunately for her, due to her upbringing in institutions, was groomed at a very vulnerable age. Having never known a father, too early an interest from men had made her feel special and grown up. It would have been hard for her to resist the feelings of being made initially the centre of attention and receiving lots of nice gifts. No one had ever got her gifts like this before. Gradually she was introduced to alcohol and became dependent on it quite quickly, so that her groomer didn't need to feed her the usual cocktail of alcohol and drugs.

Her 'lover', Fazul Arif, hadn't even needed to resort to violence and threats in her case as he had done with other girls. She was far too docile. He spotted early that she would be of a better purpose to him than simple prostitution and hard drug dependency. Although that was after she was passed around his connections. Slowly, bit by bit, he had steadily manipulated and dismantled what few feelings of self-esteem and self-worth she might have had, to the point where she was in total subjugation to him and his needs and principally governed by only two desires: his wishes and her own for the next available drink, both of which would lead to her destruction. It had all become a vicious spiralling downward circle of negativity around her. A nightmare from which she would not be able to wake.

Now that Louise had become an empty chattel and felt she wasn't worth anything anymore she drank out of need, habit, comfort and the numbness it provided from the residing pain of her existence.

PERSONA EXCESSIA PART 1[8]

Just got it together!
The world won't touch me anymore.

No expectations, no disappointments
No more pain, never again, for guilt and blame, such cost and shame, too high a price to pay.

Whispered: *Lighten up.*

I'm so impregnable at least that's what I thought.

Whispered: *Keep calm, that's cool.*

Let you close to me.
Your beauty within blew me away, blew me away.

---

8 'Persona Excessia Part 1' – a heavy rock/metal piece with two voices

Violated by your vulnerability.
You crushed me with care and concern.
You tore me down with a tender touch.
Drowned me in the depths of desire.
Exhumed my emotions buried safely away.
Shot me through with sweet words of succour.
I'm dashed upon the rocks of openness.
Poured out on the seas of softness.

Through emotional ringers, yet my brain still lingers.
On those things you've said. You fill my head.
I rage within, rationality dimmed,
to a wind-lashed sea, of clashing emotions.
A churning foam, welling up from the deep,
grinding my gut. Thoughts of you eat me away.

Becoming possessive, for my love is obsessive,
It's dependent perception beyond realms of reason.
My sense of proportion is just a distortion.
The truth or illusion aids my confusion.
Identity dented, to you now cemented.
Ebbing and flowing, entwined and choking.
Persona Excessia, nearing dementia.
My ego grated; self-worth subjugated.
Exposed in the nakedness of my soul.

(Second voice)

    I'm a man that raves, feeling betrayed.
    Reliving the past, moribund at last.
    Yet in future, friend, you'll kill me again.
    By fear paralysed, I'm dying inside.
    Yet dying and living my mind is unwilling
    To relent to the crying in the depth of my heart.

    You broke my heart reaching out to me in your need.
    I'm battered and bruised by your beauty.
    Hammered by offerings of certain hope.
    Impaled by urges born of your inspiration.
    Pierced by your arrows of innocent impulse.
    You gutted my core with your gentleness.
    Wore me down with your waves of warmth.
    Without a selfish motive in your head and heart.

(First voice)

Darkness calls me to its womb, as I face the walls of my bedroom.
Entombed with pain myself consumed.
Exposed the bareness of my soul, wrapped lies and falsehoods now enfold.
Come jealousy's hot flames embrace, despair's cold fingers poke and grate.
Yet… I'll… survive.

From brokenness can come new life.
Welcome to the human race.

– ABDULLAH ALAM –

Her original groomer, Fazul Arif, was in his early thirties, of Middle Eastern extraction, and held a condescending attitude to women, particularly Western women. He had passed Louise on to Abdullah Alam who was in his late twenties of South Asian extraction. Increasingly frustrated with his own life and his place within it, Alam's limited mindset was such that he could only really face life now as how he wanted it to be and what he could cope with, rather than what it actually was in all its complexity. Any personal blame or responsibility he would externalise to anything or anyone apart from himself.

Louise was now just a trophy to Alam, of how much he could control people and impress his friends. In spite of this kudos he was still restless, not knowing or feeling where he truly belonged. He was struggling to search for some form of meaning though centred entirely around himself. He wasn't enamoured by his Western lifestyle but bought readily into a rediscovery of his roots or rather a particular interpretation of his roots.

Lately he had come under the influence of a Daesh recruiter and handler, who seemed to have all the answers, pointing to the many deficiencies in Western society and offering a rose-coloured view of the Islamic golden age in history and the one to come. The decadent Western imperialist crusader society was portrayed with all its faults and none of its redeeming features. Likewise, the romanticised fictional interpretation of history, particularly of religion, contrasted well and gave him a sense of justice needed to be righted and a sense of being an active proponent of justice and righteousness. He was impressed by the way the man talked and his offering of a way to paradise. It was so simple; all his wrongdoing could be resolved in one final act when the time was right. It would make his empty life meaningful. Paradise would be his.

His attitude had become far more extreme lately since Daesh's radicalising. Now he had fully become a religious bigot, racist and fascist in outlook, especially to white girls who he regarded as easy targets as they were often brought up with more freedom than Asian girls. Both he and his Daesh handler, and indeed Arif, viewed women in general as expendable and would groom them for sex with alcohol, trinkets and drugs if they caught them early enough, particularly if they were vulnerable and in social care. With Asian and Black women, they would try to blackmail them through shame-to-the-family-honour ploys, to get what they wanted. He and his cohorts took pleasure in what they perceived as power over 'their' unfortunates. They regarded them as mere chattels to service their private pleasure and to make money from. They had to target very young girls in their early teens, ideally in care, as they were vulnerable, and easy to impress and influence.

In reality, were it not that many of the men in their circle were in arranged marriages, they would have found it difficult to attract a mature woman at all, such was their limited general appeal. They would not have been given the time of day by the discerning. Arif was cleverer than Alam and used him and his connections for muscle and donkey work when needed, but kept him sweet by feigning loyalty to his cause and taking on the higher and supposedly more useful role of jihadist sleeper in the Corporation. When the time was right Arif's plan would be to fake his own death and disappear with the funds he had accumulated from selling the Corporation's technology to Daesh. Arif knew he was eventually going to lose Alam completely to Daesh as he was becoming increasingly indoctrinated and already desensitised to a great extent.

To Alam, Fazul Arif seemed to be in a position of power not only in the cause but also imbedded in a position of influence in the Western commercial culture. He seemed to show all the characteristics of what Alam regarded as a 'good' Muslim, to be absolutely right on every aspect including disparaging other Muslims who did not agree with his view. Abdullah was fooled by Fazul's feigned discipline of holiness and respected the sacrifice he was making in secretly having to work within Western corporate companies for the greater cause.

– FAZUL ARIF –

As for Fazul Arif, his petty criminal record had been buried for convenience by his Corporation mentor, who for some reason appeared to Fazul to think of him as an intelligent enforcer. For Fazul, he saw this initially as a chance for advancement, greater recognition among his associates outside of work, ascendancy in the pecking order so to speak. He felt he was on his way to eat at the top table. Latterly he had become a little dissatisfied with his lack of progress. Maybe, just maybe, this small element of dissatisfaction would lead him to actually believe in Daesh's ideology but for the moment he stuck to his own agenda.

He was ostensibly employed by the Corporation in their security department but had been recruited by Nichols due to him having access to, and control of, some unsophisticated and unscrupulous muscle and criminal connections. His family, cultural and religious contacts also could prove useful. Unbeknown to Arif, Nichols was well aware of his low-level contacts, even with his new terrorist extremist connections. Nichols also knew about Arif managing to convince the jihadists that he could be part of a sleeper cell waiting to obtain the technology under development at the Corporation and that he could be useful for their cause. He was not aware, however, of the newest developments concerning Arif and Daesh's latest plan.

Nichols felt he knew him for what he truly was, and that was one only out for himself. He strongly suspected that as far as Arif was concerned, Daesh was there to make money from, and Alam and his cohorts were really only useful as expendable cannon fodder. Their cause for the moment served Arif's purpose. Arif, he knew, could easily give the impression of being completely loyal to their cause while using it for his own ends, just as he was feigning to Nichols about his work for the Corporation. Nichols strategised it would be a matter of appropriate timing as to when would be best to deal with Arif permanently. He felt confident that he held all the cards.

As far as Arif's latest allocated task from Nichols was concerned it peeved Arif a little. But just as Nichols had offloaded the problem of temporarily incarcerating Sarah to him, he could delegate this to Alam. Ultimately, Arif calculated that this would be another feather in his cap within the Corporation but all the same it made him feel edgy. The plus side was that he now felt superior to the agent who had created this new device problem in the first place. He or she must have messed up big time. Not that he knew who it was. After all he had done, all he was asked to do in Brazil, he justified, conveniently forgetting that it was actually his mistake that had caused the device to be lost.

– NICHOLS' ARRANGEMENTS –

Nichols eased back in his chair and reviewed the situation and his course of action thus far. His top operative had committed murder, again. No surprise there, but this was unplanned. Was she getting careless? Mind you, he reminded himself, she was the best there is for what she could do, not just in murder and mayhem but in manipulation and information extraction. She was indeed the best of the best. He knew she would ensure that she was untraceable. Thinking about it further, she had, under his instruction, abducted Sarah. An abduction which had in fact provided an opportunity to get what was needed back maybe more efficiently than the elimination of Aylmer, though what to do with him after might prove awkward. He could use it to at least put pressure on Aylmer.

He turned in his swivel chair and looked out at the London skyline through the smoky glass windows, musing on his other operative Arif, his associates and their combined limitations.

He observed a spider in the centre of its web on a corner of the outside window, the wind whipping through the web making it oscillate. Yet it and the spider held firm. His plans too were being battered by circumstances but they too would prevail.

His mind reverted to his original contemplation. He had reassigned Sarah temporarily into a holding room and when the time was right for the exchange to the even more temporary care of Arif. Knowing Arif's contacts and history this would actually mean Abdullah Alam, his henchman, or rather Louise, Abdullah's virtual slave, who would have to do the babysitting. Oh yes, he knew what Arif would do. He knew too about something of Abdullah's other interests and investments, or so he thought.

Ah, Fazul Arif, he thought, the one who had failed again to produce the relevant information even with the help of his low-level thuggery, pimping and criminal colleague Abdullah Alam. They would eventually become a problem not worth covering up. What if he was to clear up some of these issues with a short-term plan? A smirk appeared on his face at the latest subplot to his ultimate goal. Fazul had often been a liability in the Corporation's office environment, particularly with his attitude to women. Maybe it was time to terminate his employment permanently. He had the luxury of giving him maybe one more chance. Picking up the phone he set up an untraceable call by rerouting through various networks and pseudo sites. Luke Aylmer answered on his mobile.

'We have something of yours and you have something of ours. I believe we can arrange an exchange to our mutual benefit.'

'I'm sorry, I don't follow you,' answered Luke initially nonplussed and added, 'Who is this?'

'We have Sarah Manning, your girlfriend, and I believe you have a device, or can obtain it, which belongs to the Corporation.'

'Is she OK?'

'She is quite unharmed. Say nothing to anyone. We will be in contact with details for an exchange in a day or so.'

With that the phone call ended abruptly. The spider sensed the vibrations of an insect caught in its web. It moved quickly to further entrap the insect, spinning further silk around its victim ready for devouring at a later time. Nichols watched it as in his mind he revisited the silk string of limited information he was feeding Luke Aylmer that would achieve the same poetic result. The other flies in Nichols' particular ointment would soon be disposed of too.

– AN INFORMATION WEB IS WEAVED –

Weston had stayed behind in Rugby liaising with the local police regarding the murder but had advised Luke to return to London and await contact from the kidnappers. He was certain that Sarah was not murdered and convinced Luke of the same as she was too valuable a bargaining chip. Contacting Setford, Weston requested that he investigate any CCTV that was available to known Corporation satellite sites around England but particularly London. They might get lucky and spot Sarah being unloaded and pick up a car registration. As a further long shot Weston was hoping they might be able to tie in a car registration with one of the Isle of Wight ferry lists, just in case they had been followed to the island. This was later to prove fruitless.

After many hours of painstaking viewing Setford managed to identify a car arriving with two people but leaving with only one at a West London site. The car description tallied with some indistinct images of those obtained from Rugby CCTV. Specialised software allowed Setford to clarify fuzzy pictures of part of the registration plate. Bit by bit, by a process of elimination he identified the specific car. From then on it was a matter of piecing together data profiles of the suspect and her known contacts. One or two leads began to emerge. When Luke called Weston to inform him of the kidnapper's phone call, Weston assured Luke that some progress had been made and new leads were being pursued. Knowing that things would soon be coming to a climax and time was of the essence, Weston did his best to reassure Luke as well as prepare him for what was likely to come.

'Let me know of the later contact when it happens. Leave the rest to me. Tell me, what do you know of the Corporation's satellite site in West London?'

'Nothing, to be honest I didn't know they had one. I'll try and find out when I get back to work.'

Weston finished their conversation with an assurance and a warning.

'Be careful, they obviously suspect something by following you, the murder and Sarah's abduction. I suspect your time back at work will be either short and restricted or they want to continue to monitor you. I'm convinced it will be the latter.'

From conversations with the police in Rugby, Weston learned of an undercover operation concerning child grooming, prostitution and drugs based in Leeds but with links to Oldham, Bradford, Rugby and London. He spotted some familiar names from the suspect lists but one in particular caught his eye. It was one of the security officers at the Corporation that Sarah had highlighted. The addresses associated with this suspect were passed on to Setford. Weston asked to be updated by the police undercover teams that had these addresses under surveillance. In addition to this, one of the addresses in London had been associated with some Daesh chatter from his own department. Within a couple of hours, a report came back from one of the surveillance teams to say that a female had been part pushed in a wheelchair and part carried into one of the London addresses. Having collated all the information Weston liaised with the officer in charge of the investigation to see if he could effect a rescue of Sarah if need be without jeopardising their work. As an incentive he promised extra resources for the operation from his department if they were needed. He knew that if he could justify helping the police operation due to the terrorist chatter element, this might free up some of his department's resources. Knowing his department, this was skating on very thin ice. For the rescue to be successful then, timing would be the key issue. It had to be as close to the exchange as possible.

– WESTON REMINISCES –

It was about eight o'clock when Weston took time out from the investigation and sought out the rather nice hostelry which not only sold one of his favourite brews but pulled a decent pint correctly. So rare these days.

'A pint of Herefordshire cider, please.' Being a connoisseur of beer and cider he first took note that there was no head on the pint of cider as it should always be, unlike bitters or lagers. He was very particular about that sort of thing. As far as he was concerned there was a certain level of head for bitters and stouts but it didn't seem to matter too much about lagers. Then he took in the scene of the many groups of drinkers, all in various stages of conversation, their voices sometimes quite loud in order to be heard above the general hubbub.

He found a corner to sit in and took out a photograph of his wife from his wallet and reminisced about the times they had shared. He thought of her student nursing days, the long shifts and all the study she had had to do. The words of a song filtered into his thoughts and memories and it stuck there as more memories were resurrected. How she struggled over the course notes and revision while still working tough shifts. Coming off nights, not knowing whether she wanted breakfast or something more substantial, her body clock all out of kilter. He never could understand the reasoning behind the NHS shift system. It made sense to him to have at least a three-week shift system. How could you give of your best for patient care and continuity if you were not fully functioning yourself? Still, what did he know? He reflected on how tired she was when she crawled off to bed after a long shift. He even remembered how on occasion they would debate the issue of the NHS having to put right the mistakes of the private sector, particularly concerning plastic surgery or the people wasting NHS resources because of their careless and selfish lifestyle.

Then there was the time, for quite a while, they both individually sought some solace by immersing themselves in work in trying to escape their grief after losing their twin babies. The initial shock followed by mutual support, eventually running out of words, suffering the pain in silence, the comforting hug, caress or kiss barely making it bearable. Nothing, but nothing, could really fill the void, though they eventually got through it together but were forever changed.

HANDS[9]

− MELODY 1 −

Hands, frozen by life's rawness,
such soreness.
Piercing grief, chilling pain, numbing loss.
Hands skilled to heal.
For other lives to rebuild
She will toil.
Walks by the ocean shore.
Restores her strength once more.
Creation sings to her.
Quiets her soul.

Memories of shared pleasures, she treasures.
Work and chores herself immerses.
Time dulls the pain.
Broken heart begins to mend, to grow and bud.
Now bathe in warmth and love.
Come touch anew.

---

9 'Hands' − a pen picture for two voices and guitar

She needs to hold again.
Needs healing too.

Reach out though an uncertain future's there.
Faith to grasp at what life offers now.
Courage to choose new paths. She must try.

Soul restored her beauty shines, lips of wine.
Eyes a-sparkle, holding on, standing strong.
She has overcome.
Hands a-glow embracing life, at peace with the past.

– MELODY 2 –

Life's hard knocks have caused retraction.
For a while she needs protection.
Caught between the hard place and the rock.
She just needs some time to take stock.
Time to see through the glass dimly.
Time to be with friends and family.
Time to clearly see to judge her next step.
To break free to be.

Finding knots in life's rich tapestry.
Struggling to make sense of mysteries.
Overcoming fear and doubt to grasp
Life in all its fullness again at last.
Making peace with all that's in the past.
Resting in the present and holding fast.
Leaving future cares and wants to God.
Taking strength from love surrounding her.

– HONES AND NOOR –

The Reverend Peter Hones and Imam Mohammed Noor met again for their fortnightly game of chess.

'Ah, with this game you may think you've wangled a strong position but I have a cunning plan, so cunning and secret in fact that even I don't know it but rest assured I will prevail,' asserted Peter Hones.

'You always say that before you lose,' replied Mohammed Noor.

'I can't help it! It's my desperation call of defiance and request for pity at the same time.'

'Any results from your lunchtime availability sessions?' asked Mohammed intrigued.

'Well, yes, there is actually. A nice chap, ex-army. Obviously, I can't confide personal details but he is very honest to the point of admitting his interest has been sparked by a woman and I think his thoughts are only about the woman. I suspect he doesn't know it yet but I think he has fallen head over heels in love with her. She, being a committed Christian, has raised initial questions from her beliefs with him but lately he has started asking about it from a very personal aspect.'

'OK, well I think I might try that at the mosque and see what happens. Checkmate, by the way.'

'A distraction policy, eh, but it's all part of my exceedingly cunning strategic plan to lull you into a false sense of security.'

'Well, it's working. What's that now, fifty-three games to twenty?'

'Well, it's more blessed to give than receive! After the symposium, what do you say we take Martha and Ayesha out for a meal?'

'It's high time they met. I know Ayesha is very keen not just to meet Martha but also to get the lowdown on what I supposedly get up to.'

'Yes, well, I could spill the beans about all the romantic soirees you've not been going to,' he said pulling his friend's leg.

'I think they deserve a treat, especially for putting up with us two. It'll have to be vegetarian what with you needing halal meat and me being against that type of slaughter. Do you want to choose the restaurant?'

'Okey-doke, I have one in mind. I'll arrange a reservation. Is the loser paying?'

'I thought that was the winner's prerogative!'

'Dutch then?'

'Double Dutch?'

'Just like your chess strategy!'

Peter Hones had a strong empathy and affinity with Imam Noor, knowing that he was having to battle on several fronts. At that time for Mohammed, there were two specific cases of domestic abuse in his congregation, wrapped up in cultural values of family honour and loss of face – the misuse and incorrect interpretations of hadiths and blasphemy laws and the cultural male chauvinism oppressing women down the centuries. Now on top of all that was the terrorism committed in the name of Allah, where innocent people, often fellow Muslims, were being butchered as well those of different beliefs, some of which were easy targets within the multicultural communities.

Peter was only too aware of how many bad things had been done by people using the label of Christianity too. The Protestant and Roman Catholic conflicts and the mistreatment and torture endured in both as well as the crusades, much of it fired by the thirst for wealth and power and, of course, general ignorance. But he felt sure that there must have been a proportion who were indeed honest, sincere and full of ardour about what they were doing, though misguided, thinking they were truly serving God.

But who was he to judge them? And even if he could, he would need to judge them by the standards of their day. Not to mention the cover-ups, well meaning or otherwise, of the ill treatment meted out under the cover label of religion. Depressing though this was, he tried to cheer himself up with all the good things that had been done by people of faith. His mind quickly flicked through a dozen or so from Henry Dunant and George Dawson to the Earl of Shaftesbury.

6

THE JAILOR BECOMES JAILED

— EXCHANGE IS NO ROBBERY? —

Nichols having checked a few things decided on the time and place for an exchange. It had to be somewhere in public but under relatively controlled circumstances. Too much could go wrong amongst the crowded London streets. At night on a bridge with limited exits. That sounded good. The scaffolding could afford cover for Ruby and a good vantage point, he already thinking to escalate the exchange to assassination. Nichols selected Luke Aylmer's mobile number having already set up an untraceable route to his own phone. Luke was just starting to make tea when the phone rang and he answered it immediately.

'Mr Aylmer. We want you to exchange tonight. You have the device?'

'Yes. Yes. Where do you want to meet?' asked Luke pretending he had the device.

'There are some bridge repairs being undertaken at Blackfriars. There will be no working on the road surface or bridge structure tonight but it will still have the barriers up so there will be no traffic or pedestrians. On both sides are overhanging scaffolding walkways. Come alone. Approach from the south and take the right-hand walkway. We will meet you midway.' He then issued a time for the meeting.

'How do I know Sarah is still alive?'

'You don't, but you will see her there,' and with that Nichols hung up.

Luke straightaway called Weston on the other phone Weston had given him, to say what the meeting instructions were. Weston knew that now was the time to act on the information they had built up. He quickly contacted the grooming investigation lead officer and requested an update from the surveillance team that had been detailed to observe the comings and goings at one of Arif's flats. Then with detailed knowledge of the geography of the flat and surrounding area he formulated a rescue plan for Sarah. He knew the likely outcome if she were not retaken before the exchange and he would not be able to protect her and Luke Aylmer from both ends of the bridge at the actual exchange. That is, if the Corporation planned to actually carry it through. Timing of the rescue was crucial. If her rescue was discovered too early, that may give the Corporation time to change to alternative arrangements. Too late and she would be gone.

– A BREAKOUT FROM WITHIN A BREAK –

Edna met Marwenna in the doorway as she returned from finishing her tour of four of the floors with the tea trolley.

'Oh, Marwenna, I took a phone message for you while you were on your rounds. Your uncle left a message to call him. He said it was urgent. Here's the number.'

Marwenna recognised the number as one of Weston's many phones and dialled as quickly as she could.

'Hello, Uncle.'

'I have a job for you this lunchtime between one and two or preferably later if you can. Can you make it?'

'Yes, I think so, my normal breaktime starts at one.'

'We are going to deliver and collect "a parcel". It should take about fifty minutes to get there and back but you will have to change on the way. We'll pick you up outside your building entrance.'

'Righto, Uncle. Edna, there is a health problem with a distant uncle. There might be a possibility I will be late back from lunch. Is that OK?'

'Oh yes, dearie, go, you go, I hope he is alright.' Marwenna finished her other rounds and was out of the building a shade before one o'clock.

Weston and Setford were already waiting in a car outside when Marwenna left. Weston briefed her on the way.

'We know something of the past criminal activities at this address where we think Sarah Manning is being held captive. The police have had the premises under surveillance for quite some time and the sole male guard is usually out at this time which has been confirmed for today by the surveillance team. They are sure that another woman is resident at the address but don't know if she is an accomplice to the kidnapping. They are sure she is still there. You'll have to change into this Royal Mail delivery uniform. Whoever is there will suspect a woman less than a man. A dummy large parcel is beside you, which should get them to open the door as it is too big to leave without a signature. Setford and I will hide till we can rush the door once it's opened. Say that the parcel is for a Mr F. Arif.'

'Apart from gaining entry is there anything else you need me to do?' asked Marwenna whilst changing her top clothes.

'If Sarah is there, she might get greater comfort from the presence of another woman. So, your task will be to assure and comfort her.'

Just then the car lurched, nearly hitting the kerb.

'Watch it, Setford,' Weston shouted.

'Sorry, sir, it's the excitement of the mission,' Setford replied uttering an embarrassed lie to save face.

Though desperately trying to avoid looking in the mirror, Setford had succumbed to temptation and looked in the rear-view mirror at the scantily clad woman he adored and hence the near accident.

The package they had was very light but very bulky. Ideal for the purpose. They arrived ahead of the expected time of arrival and parked out of sight of the flat. The surveillance team confirmed there had been no change in circumstances in the flat. After the go-ahead from the surveillance team, Weston and Setford took up their positions. Marwenna grabbed the parcel and signature machine and then walked to the door and pressed the doorbell. After some time she heard a noise behind the door and guessed someone was looking through the door spyglass.

'Who is it?' said a woman's voice with slightly slurred words.

'A parcel, madam,' Marwenna announced with a smile.

The door opened a little but was on a chain.

'Just leave it there.'

'It's a big parcel. You might need help lifting it in, besides I need you to sign for it.'

As soon as Louise undid the chain on the door Marwenna pushed against it and then held her against the wall while Weston and Setford rushed from around the corner and pushed past them both into the flat. Louise was so surprised she did not even attempt to put up a fight. They found Sarah still under the influence of drugs chained to a bed in a small boxroom. Weston, having surveyed the rest of the flat and noticed several empty vodka bottles lying about, viewed some old scrawled notes on a pad. He dictated a message that Louise had to write before Setford quickly administered a sedative to her.

The Jailor becomes jailed

The woman has already been collected. Have gone to get some more vodka. Louise

Weston placed the notepad back in its usual place. He double-checked the shaky handwriting before they speedily departed, leaving the flat in good order and folding down the empty cardboard box to take with them. Setford and Marwenna gently half walked and half carried Sarah and Louise out to the car.

Louise was placed in the back-centre seat and now, subdued by drugs, did not put up much of a struggle or even attempt to escape. Sarah was placed behind Setford, and Marwenna had to quickly change clothes again in the even more restricted space in the back of the car behind Weston. They sped off quickly to drop Marwenna back to where she worked at the Corporation. The whole rescue took little more than three minutes, including the planting of listening bugs on behalf of the grooming surveillance team. Setford cagily stole a quick look at Marwenna in the rear-view mirror but this time Marwenna caught his glance.

'Keep your eye on the road, Setford, we don't want accidents, do we?' she commanded.

'Just checking on our passengers,' he lied.

Marwenna just managed to get back to her job in time, having been dropped off a corner away from her office to ensure that Sarah and Louise did not know where she worked.

'How is your uncle?' asked Edna, concerned.

'It was a heart problem scare, but he is OK,' replied quick-thinking Marwenna.

'He's not due for one of those, what do yer call it, open plan surgeries, is he?'

'No, he won't need open heart surgery, thank goodness,' Marwenna summarised, already starting to interpret Edna's misplaced words.

Both Sarah and Louise were taken to a secure health clinic where they were separately medically checked out. After this, Sarah quickly described all that had happened to her, including seeing the unusual behaviour of the people in the strange suits. Setford was able to explain what he thought she had seen.

'Some time back, scientists were able to produce glasses with liquid crystal display screens used by programs generating virtual reality; other computer clothing soon followed that showed a whole new virtual environment to the wearer. Then they became mobile. We think that in order to deceive, coerce or delude people into living in a false reality they may have developed a miniature version possibly engrafted on their eyes and in their ears.'

'What, like contact lenses?' suggested Sarah.

'Yes, but permanent ones. Although as far as I was aware there is still research going on regarding touch and smell. They could well be streets ahead in that area.'

'They must be very small.'

'A substance for data storage which exhibits the photo-refractive effect, a reaction to laser light, is only found in rare crystals at the moment. It can store up to 1000 bits of data in the area the size of a pinhead. Twenty-five times more than the densest memory chip. Maybe they have found a way of manufacturing it.'

Then, when reasonably recovered, Sarah stayed at Weston's London flat as he could not use another official establishment and they were not sure if her flat was being watched. He loaned her some money to buy some new clothes, specifying that they should be dark in colour just in case they had to move her quickly at night. She felt so much better after a shower and change of clothes, quite refreshed in fact, considering her ordeal.

Louise remained in the secure clinic. Here, Weston briefly questioned her but he did not expect to get much information from her in her drugged and alcoholic state, and he surmised she was more likely to be a victim than anything else but considered it might be useful to build up a fuller, detailed picture of Abdullah Alam, Fazul Arif and any associates that may also have been involved. He knew she would soon develop withdrawal symptoms from the alcohol and any other substances that she might have been hooked on, but he had time to think about that and what would help her long term. In the meantime, a senior police officer from the undercover operation interviewed her to gain as much detail as possible. Setford shared his concern with Weston that Louise did not appear to be the woman in the CCTV they had investigated.

As for Louise, for years she had not smiled and it would be a long time before she would smile again, what with the agony of alcohol withdrawal and the emotional turmoil of losing contact with her other reason for living.

Once the women were safely dispatched, Setford had motored back to the office to continue his technical work. Weston ensured that he arrived a lot later, so as not to arouse suspicion, having walked from the secure clinic. Glad to be back in the office Setford tried to immerse himself in his work but could not help thinking about Marwenna. Before she had arrived on the scene, he had come to a state of almost angst-free stability regarding the possibility of romance. Oh, he liked women alright, but he had come to the conclusion that he was no good, and never would be any good, at the social interaction required. Fundamentally he was a good man, a kind man and deep down a very passionate man, but much of it he kept hidden from view, being quite shy. But then Marwenna walked into the office and had unsettled him from the safety of his emotional cocoon. He had often witnessed those men who had the gift of the gab with the ladies and could flirt easily. Sometimes he had envied them but after a while realised he could not be true to himself by playing a similar role. He felt he would not be able to provide the laughs, the excitement and sex appeal, which is what he thought all women wanted. It was so much easier to bury himself in his work, after all there was no embarrassment or rejection there. After carrying out some normal duties, Weston then returned to Louise.

'You can't keep me here. I know my rights. I want a solicitor,' she bellowed, thumping on the locked door having revived from the sedative. Weston entered.

'All in good time, all in good time,' he said in a calming fashion and sat down at the desk and gestured to her to do the same.

'Tell me about Abdullah Alam and Fazul Arif.'

'I'm telling you nothing.'

'Even if you were to have a solicitor now, I can tell you that you won't be seeing Abdullah or Fazul for quite some time, if at all.'

'What do you mean?'

She became less antagonistic once Weston explained to her that she was being held as an accessory to kidnapping and unlawful imprisonment and what a vulnerable position she was in and to consider her future and the possibility of a fresh start. At the end of the conversation he arranged for her to be put in a temporary secure hospital unit. There, after many sessions of counselling, it was learned how she had been groomed, raped when she was only fourteen and initially passed around Arif's and then Abdullah's male relatives and then passed on to others for business transactions. Subjugated at such an early age and laden with guilt she had lost every vestige of self-worth and respect, becoming a slave to Abdullah's controlling will.

– UPDATES –

Setford updated Weston concerning the latest clue of Blagdon's. It had literally finished in a dead end. The last contact name had died and their belongings had been disposed of in a house clearance. Weston, already back at his flat, reported to Luke by phone that Sarah was now safe and had been rescued not more than four or five hours ago and then pondered out loud, 'I wonder how he knew there will be no work undertaken tonight?' but then quickly asked, 'Now we have Sarah back are you still up for the supposed exchange?'

'Do you think they'll still show once they know Sarah has gone?'

'They want the device, don't they, and there's a chance that they won't realise she's gone until it's too late and will try to bluff you. We will have concealed backup on one side of the bridge and should that fail, Setford and another operative from my department will be on the other. You know you don't have to do this,' Weston added, concerned.

'I know, but they had taken Sarah and I don't think they will leave us alone till they get what they want and even then, I suspect we will be regarded as an unnecessary risk to their plans. Can I speak with Sarah?'

'Of course! Here she is.'

Once they had chatted for a while, reassured and glad to hear each other's voices, they arranged to meet up after the exchange as it was too risky to meet before in case Luke was being shadowed. He and Weston had a final brief few words to agree on a rendezvous location and time for a final check before the exchange was to take place.

– THE PLOT THICKENS –

Because he did not fully trust Arif's loyalty or even his ability, Nichols had telephoned Ruby as a backup before even calling Arif. He didn't bother with code words for Ruby this time.

'I have a job for you this evening. Can you make yourself available? It might be just a case of shadowing but it could easily turn into disposal.'

Ruby had in fact no plans for the evening but made it sound as if it was awkward to acquiesce to his request. This was purely to try to bump up the price. Together they talked about all the possible scenarios from shadowing up to having to kill Arif, Abdullah, Manning and Aylmer. Above all, they both knew she had to be flexible. To cover all scenarios, she double-checked her disguises and weaponry, though Nichols had promised to supply a weapon with a night sight.

Straight after the phone call to Ruby, Nichols called Arif to ensure he had worked out the details for the exchange.

'How are you going to ensure Manning is kept quiet before the exchange?'

Arif paused for a moment. Thinking quickly, he lied, 'I have an associate who can act as a guard.' Arif had already agreed other plans for Abdullah.

'I take it he or she is trustworthy and capable!' Nichols had already guessed who he would use but maintained the pretence of not knowing all of Arif's contacts.

'Of course.'

'OK, Arif, I want you to terminate both Aylmer and Manning after securing the device. You got that?! Make it look like a lovers' joint suicide if you can and dump the bodies in the river.'

With Abdullah Alam already assigned a different task Arif decided that Louise could act as the calming influence. He could cuff them together till the exchange. Louise was expendable and he could make it look like a love triangle tragically gone wrong, with Aylmer, Louise and Manning all dead and dumped in the river.

After Nichols' phone call, Arif rang his contact in Daesh, stating that it was likely he could get the device that night and that their plan for Abdullah Alam would have to be initiated as a diversion. He also added that there was an added cost on his part to obtain it. After the coded conversation they agreed on a plan. His Daesh contact then telephoned Abdullah Alam.

'Whatever Arif asks you to do, do it. It is time, my brother. The honour to become a martyr for our cause is for you. Tonight, just think, you will be in paradise.'

– EARLY EVENING WORK –

Edna turned to Marwenna, saying, 'I've got some orders for teas and biscuits for late meetings at the Shellac building. Shouldn't take too long though. Would you be able to do that for me, luv, as their tea lady has gone home ill?' Marwenna nodded. 'Oh, thanks, dearie, let me just get my specs on so I can read the details. You know the optician said that at my age I could use those, what do you call 'em, er, you know, er, bisexual lenses.'

Marwenna couldn't help but to laugh.

'Oh, Edna, you are a hoot sometimes. You mean bifocal.'

'What did I say then?' Edna then realised what she had said and laughed.

'Oh, bifocals, that's the ones.'

– BETRAYAL TO THE DUPED –

Arif and Alam met up in a park and kept walking so as to maintain security and secrecy.

'Abdullah, my brother, the time has come for you to finish your jihad, to be rewarded and be at peace in paradise. A plan is in place and you will be contributing greatly to our ultimate victory. I will be stealing a phenomenal weapon for our cause but I need a diversion to be successful. Your part is to be that diversion, and, of course, strike another terror blow against these unbelievers. This will ensure I get the weapon to our brothers.'

'What is the plan?'

'A suicide bomb in a carriage on Westminster station. It will take away resources from where the weapon is being exchanged. I need enough time to deliver it before being traced and if you just place the bomb, they will be looking for you and so could discover me. This is why, my brother, you can't just plant the bomb but must be a martyr.'

'I understand.'

'I will meet you later after I have collected the equipment you'll need.'

Now he had to collect the bomb from the Daesh contact, who had arranged its assembly that very day. He drove to the bomb-making flat and obtained details of his escape to another country should he need it. Having carefully stowed the bomb in the boot, as well as the drug that would make it easier for Alam, he then drove to Abdullah Alam's main flat. Together they went over the plan and rehearsed it many times.

'Here is the haversack with the bomb in. All you need to do to activate it is press these two switches here but it must be in this order. Now, my brother, prepare yourself for prayers and worship and after you have completed these we will go over the plan again and double-check everything. I have also brought you a drug to make it easy for you when the time is right. After our final check do not contact me. I will be on my way to my part of the mission. I expect you to complete your task at our agreed time. Tonight, you will be in paradise with all you could possibly want. I envy you, my brother.' They both praised their god as they understood their god to be and embraced. After further prayer and meditation and the departure of Arif, Abdullah Alam triple-checked his timed route before starting out.

– VERBAL JOUSTING WITH LOVE –

Peter Hones opened his front door with his key to be greeted with Martha shouting from the bedroom while making the bed.

'Did you get to the dentist on time?'

'Yes, five minutes early actually. You know, it's very tiring trying to keep your mouth open.'

'Well, you shouldn't have such a big one then, should you.'

'At least mine is not open most of the time. How's your sunburn?'

'What sunburn?'

'The one on your tongue!' She came into view with a pillow in her hand and hit him with it.

'So, you've finally been to the barber's as well!' said Martha with hands on hips, pleased he was present and correct and adequately spruced up for the big meeting that night. 'It's about time too,' she added.

'Yes, he did not only my hair, or what's left of it, but my eyebrows and the hairs on my earlobes as well.'

'Good, now, next time get him to sort your face out!'

'Oh, ha ha,' Peter Hones replied.

'You've got just two minutes to get your things collected for the symposium.'

'You know, I've been neglecting you. I haven't annoyed you lately like I used to, have I?' he added while pushing her onto the sofa and tickling her all over.

Between her giggles and trying to fend him off she shouted, 'Careful, you'll lose what hair you've got left!' She then embraced him, gave him a deliberately sloppy wet kiss and dismissed him saying, 'Go get 'em, tiger!'

With that, he left ready to meet Imam Noor at the underground station on the way to Westminster. How Martha loved Peter and was very proud of what he was doing. Having ensured her man left smartly and on time, she turned her thoughts to Sunday school preparation and what best tactics to adopt with little Johnny Swale who had attention deficiency issues. A lovely boy but a real handful.

– LAST JOURNEY TO OBLIVION –

Abdullah Alam still had some reservations about his appointed task and he considered his two choices to make. The second depended on the first option. Should he blow himself up or leave the bomb on the train and, if the former, should he take a drug to make the action easier for himself? Abdullah had also independently studied the means and the wherewithal to trigger a bomb remotely. But another influence for his decision to commit suicide was that he already suspected that the local authorities and police were closing in on him, as investigations into his grooming and enslavement activities had been started and were being escalated up. He knew this as one of his cousins had limited access to information from the local police and had kept him informed.

At the planned time he caught a bus to his nearest tube station that would lead him into the heart of the city. His backpack made him nervous, having consciously made the decision to not carry it in his hand till he boarded the train carriage. Once seated on the tube he would stow it by his feet, making it easier to leave and/or to detonate it without suspicion, or so he hoped. This part of the plan had run smoothly, and though a little later than originally envisaged did not alter the timing for the bomb detonation.

Trying to look at ease and unconcerned he sat down, adopting as inconspicuous a pose as he could. There weren't many people in the carriage at first but it would grow crowded the further into the city the train travelled. There were several tourist families coming to the end of a long, enjoyable and educational day. The children out with their parents were very tired but in spite of this appeared to be the only folk curious about him. Most other passengers were either playing with their phones, reading or had headphones on listening to music. During his journey by bus and train he had done his best to avoid close scrutiny by any of the safety and security cameras in the stops, stations and platforms. Westminster station was where he had been directed to unleash the bomb so as to draw the attention of the emergency services away from the Blackfriars Bridge area. He was almost there. Today he could be a true martyr and his jihad would end, he kept telling himself. All his crimes and selfishness would be blotted out and he would be in paradise with many, many women at his beck and call, or so he thought and justified to himself.

– CARRIAGE OF HOPE, CARRIAGE OF DESTRUCTION –

The Reverend Peter Hones and Imam Mo Noor had left the symposium a shade late and walked briskly to Westminster station. It had gone well and both men were looking forward to a very late meal with their wives. It would be a great time to relax and for Ayesha and Martha to really get to know each other. The men dutifully waited on the platform, which was fairly empty in comparison to rush hour, and then they boarded the train. They stood by the doors as they only had one stop to go in order to change lines.

Abdullah Alam was already in the carriage and saw Hones' dog collar and was ready to trigger the bomb when he saw the unmistakable Muslim dress of Mo. He initially baulked and started to panic at his own intention, wondering whether he should abort the mission, but the drug helped to calm him and to acquiesce to the thought that the imam would forgive him in paradise and with that he pressed the button just as the train was leaving Westminster.

The explosion totally wrecked the carriage. People lay dead or dying from horrific burns. The children were lifeless, their clothes in pieces as were their bodies. Both cleric men were thrown against the carriage doors as their bodies were ripped apart by fragments and what was left of them lay in two crumpled heaps. Both very close to death, they instinctively reached out to each other and just as their fingertips touched, they breathed their last within a few seconds of each other.

The scene of smouldering desolation was eerily silent within what was left of the carriage after the blast, and seemed in a different world to the screaming, groaning and crying occurring in the attached coaches. A half-burnt dismembered dolly lay on the floor, its missing arm still held in what was once a young girl's innocent hand. As is so often the case, innocent lives had been snuffed out by unrelated hatred that neither cared nor concerned itself but dismissed their lives as of no real value, a necessary cost, collateral damage, justified by an ultimate aim which in reality would never be achieved.

– HUNGER FOR FOOD AND NEWS –

Independently in their separate dwellings, Ayesha and Martha readied themselves for the evening meal out. Both were keen to meet each other, as both were more than a little curious about the other. Having showered, washed their hair, preened and made their faces up, Ayesha and Martha donned their best casual outfits. They found some things to occupy themselves before being picked up. As time passed, they grew a little concerned as their men were running late. Initially they put this down to finishing some follow-up work at the symposium. Independently, however, they quickly came to a conclusion that it was uncharacteristic for them to be this late. Checking their watches and clocks they intermittently tried their husbands' mobile phones. Neither man answered.

Martha then telephoned Ayesha.

'Hi, Ayesha, it's Martha here, Peter's wife. Are they with you?'

'No, I thought they probably were with you.'

'I expect there has been some sort of signal trouble or delay on one of the tube lines or some such thing that has made them late. I'll check on the internet for service delays.'

Martha and Ayesha agreed to telephone the other as soon as their men walked through the door. Both began to get a little worried and then, while trying to find the latest on travel news, they caught the main news on the internet. They hoped against hope that their men could have just been delayed by the explosion or that they were ordered to stay put at the symposium venue, though that didn't explain why they had not phoned. They both began to fear the worst. They offered up their heartfelt prayers to their respective gods.

After several hours they managed to get through to an emergency helpline set up concerning the terrorist incident and were able to give their missing husbands' details and their own contact numbers. Martha even tried phoning the Queen Elizabeth II conference venue, which by that time had been taken over for treating victims of the blast. No information was available at that time.

Martha had to tearfully give the news to their children and contacted their church's prayer support chain. Offers of help poured in but really, aside from wanting Peter to turn up at the door, all Martha wanted at that time was her family to be by her side. Ayesha, in total shock, managed one phone call to a family member who spread the news to the family, friends and mosque groups. Both families independently arranged for a family member to stay with Martha and Ayesha while waiting for further news.

BATTLES WITHOUT
– AT BLACKFRIARS BRIDGE

AFTER WORK, THAT IS, WHEN WORK DEMANDS allowed, Setford had taken to the habit of waiting outside Marwenna's workplace to check she was OK and not followed. Usually he would secrete himself behind a pillar opposite the entrance to the corporate building. He knew she was more than capable of looking after herself. In fact, much better than he would be able to, but nonetheless it eased his mind. He always made sure she never saw him. This particular day he had not seen her leave so after waiting about twenty minutes he phoned her work number. He could always use the pretence that Weston was checking where she was and to let her know the latest concerning the exchange, but he would have to do that part in disguisable terms. It rang for a while and then Edna answered.

'Oh, is Marwenna there, please?'

'No, she's gone to do a special conference at the Shellac building on the third floor.'

'I see, thanks. Is she liable to be long?'

'About an hour. She left about twenty-five minutes ago. She'll be clearing up in the morning, I expect. Who's calling?'

'Just an old friend.'

'Can I take a message, dearie?'

'No, it's OK, I'll catch her later.'

The Shellac building wasn't too far away, just across the river in fact, so he thought he would just take a stroll to see her leave from there, having time to fill anyway before being a backup to the night's exchange which was not too far from the Shellac building.

As Marwenna pushed the trolley from the conference rooms in the Shellac building she passed Sarah and Yvonne's office. Yvonne looked up, pleased for an interruption to her humdrum long day with a boss she despised. She had often toyed with the idea of putting laxative into his coffee but had so far refrained. It felt an especially long day as Sarah wasn't there to talk to. She spotted Marwenna in the corridor and called out to her, 'Hello, I've not seen you before. Our regular or Edna on holiday?'

'No, Edna is back at Penguin House, your regular is off sick, but you're right, I am fairly new.'

'Hi, I'm Yvonne.'

'I'm Marwenna,' she replied from outside the door in the corridor.

Fazul Arif was ensconced in his adjoining office running through in his mind the operation for tonight. First there had been the collecting of the bomb and drugs from the Daesh contact, then preparing Alam for the bombing, then there was still picking up Louise with the Manning woman and finally negotiating the device and killing all three. He then evaluated his options concerning whether to take Daesh's money and disappear or take their money and stay undercover at the Corporation. He felt sure he could convince Nichols that either Aylmer did not have the device or that in a struggle it disappeared into the Thames. It was then that he heard Yvonne's voice talking to someone on the phone, or so he thought. This disturbed his deliberations. Already tense his patience snapped.

Striding out of his office into hers he started raising his voice and berating her out of frustration. Not aware initially of Marwenna's presence in the corridor he stood over Yvonne aggressively. He then lost his temper and slapped Yvonne on her cheek and raised his hand again to strike harder while Yvonne moved to avoid another blow.

'Oi! You can't do that!' said Marwenna, outrage welling up in her.

He spun around, surprised but still fuming, and replied, 'I can do what I want.' As far as he was concerned, he did not have to pretend and maintain his cool, polite facade with these minions, female minions at that. 'I can get you fired for a start, you're a nothing, a nobody.'

Losing his temper even more he paced aggressively towards Marwenna. He was used to women being easily cowed, browbeaten and scared of his physical presence. Moving to strike her too, this 'tea lady', and make her cry like he did so often with the staff temporarily assigned to him before, he raised his hand.

Marwenna blocked his attempt, punched him in the face, kneed him in the unmentionables, threw him over her shoulder and while he was lying on the floor poured the last of the iced water over him from her trolley.

'You third rate excuse for a man. Hit a woman, would you? Crawl in your hole, worm! I'm reporting you to Human Resources,' and with that she shoved the trolley temporarily into a convenient cubbyhole near the end of the corridor, grabbed Yvonne by the hand and they marched upstairs to Human Resources to make a formal complaint. *Blast it*, she thought on the way up, *I've probably blown the assignment, but I'm not putting up with that chauvinist ignorant crap.*

Luckily there were people working late in Human Resources and so Yvonne and Marwenna started the formal complaint procedure there and then. The personnel team seemed to be more than a little used to complaints about Arif, though nothing could ever be said publicly about his employment problems. Privately, however, they had often wondered how he had been allowed to get away with so much in the past with just token disciplinary slaps on the wrist. Other staff would have been sacked but he seemed to live a charmed life. Usually they were instructed to reassign the staff affected, get them to sign non-disclosure agreements with compensation and hush it up. Once again, they would have to contact Nichols, his line manager. Nichols, on this occasion, made his mind up that he would defend him no longer.

Yvonne was shocked and upset at the face slap, then astonished at what then transpired between Marwenna and Arif. Then, after having some time to calm down, she experienced stifled amusement over what she had been part of and witness to. She was very grateful to Marwenna for defending her and boy was she glad he'd got some comeuppance.

When Fazul Arif eventually recovered from the shock of a woman fighting back and himself having to overcome losing face in his own eyes, let alone anyone else's, he retreated to his office more than a little flustered. He then quickly thought that he had better complain and counterclaim to Human Resources and insist on them being fired before the women could complete their report. However, he was too late as the women had already started the process. So, instead he insisted on giving his report first as his time was too valuable to be waiting. He would smooth things over with Nichols as he always did later, or so he thought, after all, he had done so before. Nichols would deal with it and fire them both. He was sure he was far too valuable to him and his plans. Besides, if there was a problem, as long as he managed to get the device and pass it on to either Nichols or Daesh then he could disappear anyway if need be. He was unaware that

Human Resources had already contacted Nichols before he had got there.

The ladies had been ushered into another room to avoid any further conflict with his presence and continued to report their side of things. Yvonne was asked to make and fill in a statement first, and eventually went home still upset but relieved. She had signed witness statements and chose to sign a non-disclosure agreement linked to compensation and had been assured verbally and in writing that she would not have to work with him again and that Marwenna would not be disciplined.

Marwenna was still angry, not only at Arif but also the fact that it complicated her information-gathering role. *I won't resign or sign a non-disclosure agreement*, she thought. *If nothing else I'll make him sweat a little*. Even at that early evening hour the unofficial channel of in-house gossip, often faster than official communiqués, spread the news of what had happened very quickly. The chatter about what Marwenna had done spread like wildfire. The next day there would be quite a lot of amusement in some quarters and jubilation in a few select offices whose workers had had direct experience of Arif.

Nichols pre-empted Arif by calling him while Arif was making his statement in Human Resources, which caught him off guard. Arif excused himself and moved out of earshot from the person recording his statement.

'I take it you'll be delayed for some time,' stated Nichols.

'Hopefully not too long here but I will need to avoid the late rush hour traffic.'

'Will you have time to meet your associate and pick up the woman? I can arrange for someone to collect her and meet you or your associate if you are going to be late.'

Arif now had to quickly think about his phantom associate without giving anything away to Nichols, who was unaware of this latest bomb plot, but was pleased with his improvisation when he replied, 'That will be fine. If I don't pick her up in time your operative can meet me directly at the bridge and take the place of my associate. I'll let my contact know about the possible change of plan.'

Nichols followed up with a final question. 'I know the address you are holding her at but what about entry to it?'

'There should be someone there but if not, then there is an emergency spare key taped under the fourth stone on the right which props up the dustbin. I'll call you if I'm going to be late.'

Arif thought that he could make this work greatly to his advantage. If he later called claiming to be running late at an appropriate time, it would save him a journey and he could get the lowdown on the other operative of Nichols'. Maybe even compare notes with the operative before killing them. His main priority was still getting the device to pass on to Daesh and killing Aylmer, the other Corporation operative and Sarah, ideally in that order. As for Louise, he knew that she did not pose a threat and so could be spared elimination till last. He then had the possibility of remaining undercover within the Corporation and lying about the whereabouts of the device, saying that the other operative had it in their possession when their body fell in the river after they had been killed by Aylmer. All four bodies eventually would be found in the river, of course, minus the device lost in the Thames. His other option was to flee with the money reward to the suggested sympathetic country of safe haven after passing the device to Daesh.

By the time he had finished giving his statement and interview Arif's clothes were almost dry. On his way out he concentrated his thoughts again on his imminent mission. He was becoming even more edgy, the nerves building for what he was about to do. This was the first time he would actually have to kill in England, let alone four people. In the past Nichols had always arranged for someone else to dispose of people that he had been involved in investigating, the exception being his bungled murder attempts in Brazil. What if the other Corporation operative with the Manning woman didn't show? He would have to bluff Aylmer into parting with the device before killing him. What if the operative turned up late? Depending on if he had time to dispose of Aylmer, he could concoct a story to put them at their ease before killing them as well as the Manning woman.

— MARWENNA GETS THE POINT —

By the time the complaints procedure was gone through it was quite late. Marwenna was considerably later than the other two, due to her refusing to sign a non-disclosure contract. Three times they had upped their compensatory offers and given Marwenna ten minutes each time to consider. On her way down from Human Resources she needed to collect her tea trolley and at least arrange the equipment ready for an early clean-up in the morning. Just as she was about to move the trolley, she overheard half a telephone conversation coming from the other office that adjoined Yvonne's. Quickly and quietly she moved closer after slotting the trolley further down into a corridor dead end. She listened intently. It was a woman's voice, a voice Marwenna thought she had heard before but could not pinpoint the person or a place of association. It was the subject matter that really caught her attention though.

She edged along the corridor to see if she could glimpse the conversant through the narrow gap of the door that was slightly ajar. All she could see was a jewelled hand playing with the phone wire as the person sat at a desk. Marwenna tried to remember where she had seen that jewelled hand before and place the voice. All she could think of initially was a black-coffee drinker but where and who?

After checking everyone had gone home from the office the purposeful jewelled hand had surreptitiously picked up the antiseptically squeaky-clean corporation telephone. The hand bore no marks of domesticity and was immaculately manicured. It belonged to a very attractive brunette with considerable charms. Knowing that all external calls were monitored she had decided to enter the building, which she rarely did, and call Nichols on an internal phone. Out of habit she had meticulously avoided the CCTV cameras, the location of which she knew so well. Relaxing, she put her feet up on what was her own allocated desk, though it was never really used. Nichols answered and they adopted their usual coded, guarded words in their conversation.

'Just thought I'd do a final check to confirm our latest business project for the Blackfriars Bridge merchandise exchange. Is it still the original agreement or are there any further developments I need to take into account?' she asked of him.

'Ah, perfect timing as usual and well anticipated. The plan has been upgraded. Our main exchange agent has been delayed. You may have to collect our merchandise and take it to the exchange location because of his delay, that's if he has not done so in the meantime. At the moment he is uncontactable.' Nichols then gave her the address of where Sarah had been held. She repeated it back to him while committing it to memory and checking she had heard it correctly. Marwenna recognised the address at once. The woman then repeated where the key was to be found. He then confirmed the location and time details for the exchange.

'If you have the Manning woman you can meet Alam and Arif approximately forty-five minutes before the supposed exchange at the bridge and for their benefit, and to all intents and purposes make a show of departing for home. There should be some good vantage points in the bridge work to set up for closure.' He continued, 'He has messed up too many times and now needs to be removed from the business in hand. In fact, all sellers and buyers need to be removed permanently from this business project once the transaction has taken place. The river should be a convenient disposal method. After this little project we will close down operations for a while. Then you'll have some well-earned rest and have time to enjoy your new purchases.'

'You know I will want more for this escalation and extra service as this was not part of our original agreement.' She enjoyed toying with Nichols, making him think that money was her main incentive. Indeed, she liked to ruffle his feathers on occasion, just to let him know that he wasn't necessarily in control of her, but she was always careful to not overdo it. This she calculated was in case he thought her a liability too, though she was already making insurance plans to make herself untouchable by him. If the Corporation could double cross and kill, and she was often instrumental in that, then it could do the same to her. In the long term she knew that there may come a time when she would have to deal with him permanently, but for the moment the pay and the lifestyle was good. She turned her thoughts to the kill, and the excitement started to take a hold. Pumped up with a little adrenaline she impatiently said, 'Let's cut the coded messages, you'll arrange to filter and edit out where necessary anyway. You want me to wait for the merchandise to be exchanged and then eliminate all the parties, retrieve the device and dump the bodies in the river. I repeat, I want more recompense for this service.' There was a short silence at the end of the phone.

'The usual method of payment?' came the delayed reply.

'Yes, but I want a particular stone this time. There's a jewellery piece I've had my eye on for some time to add to my collection.'

'You normally do,' came the response.

'It's sitting in the centre of a Tudor rose in the left-hand window of Garrard's. They won't split the setting.'

'But of course, why would they?' He could see the price tag increasing exponentially.

He always paid for her stones and jewellery out of his own personal wealth, and always in cash, so as not to trace it to the Corporation. As far as the Corporation was concerned, she was a reasonably paid business troubleshooter, nigh on eleven and a half months of the year out of her office troubleshooting somewhere on the globe.

Though sounding as amenable as he could, Nichols thought that she was getting more and more expensive and less controllable. Her usefulness may eventually become a possible liability but she was oh so useful to him and oh so good at what she did. He could not but help admire her. With terms agreed Nichols reflected on the situation.

It's time Arif's secret Islamist agenda came to an end. In fact, he'll get what he wants in his terms of 'martyrdom' in the service of his cause, only just not in the way he planned. Although most people on the planet would say, '*just desserts for an evil man with an evil agenda based on a fascist view of heaven and the world*', he would not, because he wasn't most people. No doubt there may be some small group that would mourn him, thinking him sincere to their common beliefs but Nichols knew you could be sincere, but sincerely wrong. An afterthought appealed to him, which was that with any luck they would all kill each other. He wouldn't have the device but it would be a mere delay to his plans on obtaining another one.

She lifted her other hand to admire the sparkle of her rings, turning her hand gently to enjoy every facet of lustre.

'I'll return the device by the normal method.'

She put down the phone quickly and just glimpsed a movement of a shadow in the general office as she did so. She got up slowly and walked quietly to the door. Improvising quickly, she returned to get a letter opener, turned the lights off and made as if to leave the building by exiting using the lift. Then quietly doubling back up the stairs she began to investigate, holding her improvised weapon at the ready, which, if need be, she would dispose of later. At the top of the stairs she surveyed the corridor and then silently checked each office and section, spotting the tea trolley in the dead end.

Marwenna had entered the office as soon as the other woman had left in the lift, and turned on a desk light in order to dial Weston's number. It was Marwenna's turn to be eavesdropped on, though her conversation was to be cut short. She dialled quickly and started her report. Weston answered.

'It's Marwenna… it's a double-cross, she's going to…'

Just as Marwenna was about to elaborate a jewelled hand covered her mouth and a knee jerked into her back as she felt a piercing sensation in the chest. Marwenna's forces training kicked in and she brought her elbow back hard into her assailant's stomach whilst she tried to turn around and face her attacker. The pair struggled for some minutes, both trying to gain ascendancy with the letter opener. Marwenna gradually began to weaken with the loss of blood and once more the letter opener plunged into her but this time in her stomach and she was pulled to the floor where she continued to fight for her life. The noise of the lift could be heard and as Marwenna stopped struggling she was left to die in her own pool of blood. Her assassin, taking the letter opener with her, made her escape calmly down the stairs after replacing the phone and whispering in Marwenna's ear before leaving, 'I only wish I had time to watch you die, bitch!' Her last action after spotting a Cornish gold ring on Marwenna's finger was to rip it off.

The professional assassin knew that her fingerprints would be counted as normal as it was her own office and no one had seen her enter the building as she had circumvented security cameras, as she often did. She had a legitimate right to be there anyway. Her alibi could be established easily and she knew what precautions to take to deceive any forensic investigations. More importantly for her was the emotional reward she got from the encounter and became even more excited with the idea of what was to transpire that night. What a buzz that would produce, she surmised with anticipation.

Setford had been scanning the windows of the building from the other side of the road when he spotted Marwenna on the third floor as she switched on the desk lamp. He had caught sight of the start of the struggle as Marwenna was grabbed from behind. He rushed through the main entrance, vaulted the security barrier and raced up the stairs. Security, taken by surprise, were slow to follow-up.

He ascended to the third floor and checked each office till he found Marwenna in her pool of blood. He called for an ambulance immediately. Then he took Marwenna's hand, initially feeling for a pulse, then held the two folds of skin together where the blade had entered while stroking her forehead with his other hand. Marwenna, now semi-conscious, opened her eyes and vaguely aware of his presence weakly uttered, 'Roger, I'm cold… hold me… please.' It was the first time she had ever used his first name. She thought she was dying and did not want to die alone.

Setford, on both knees now, placed his jacket around her, rested her torso on his legs, cuddled her from the back while placing one hand over her wound to stem the flow of blood and the other to hold together the skin folds of her other wound. She then fell unconscious. Setford shouted and shouted for help till someone came and he told them to alert security as to where to send the paramedics within the building and that an ambulance was on its way. Once the paramedics arrived, he identified himself to the building security and called Weston. In the meantime, security had called the police and for a very short time Setford was held under suspicion of attempted murder. When the ambulance crew had done their work to stabilise her as best they could, he was allowed to travel with her in the ambulance. At the hospital, Marwenna was placed in a cubicle where she quickly deteriorated and a crash trolley was summoned from which the emergency staff worked on her for quite some time. Setford was ushered out and had to wait in the corridor until she was eventually stabilised and then rushed for emergency surgery.

– LIFE AT THE END OF THE SPECTRUM –

Like the murder of the URC minister before, Ruby didn't register with any significance, understanding or empathy with Marwenna's signs of distress as she struggled to cling onto life, but was a little fascinated by her facial expressions. Such was her unusual nature; she was indeed at the zenith of the female psychopath spectrum.

The assassin's unexpected kill gave her great excitement in a new way. She couldn't decide what was the best thrill, planning killing, the hunt and kill or tonight's improvised homicide. This would satiate her deep inner desire for satisfaction, at least for a short while. Over the years, her toying with people by skilful manipulation and mimicking of required emotions became less rewarding, particularly where men were concerned. Although they provided greater opportunities, they presented less of a challenge and she sought greater challenges. They were becoming too easy. She was naturally very attractive and could ape vulnerability exquisitely. The different challenge of assassination with its inherent risk and danger, the more dramatic and greater the cost for the win, the greater her sense of achievement and pleasure.

Now her senses, heightened by the thought of killing at least another three people and retrieving the device, were into new levels. She had never killed as many people in one attempt. Triple the danger, triple the risk, triple the excitement, yet she was still in a mode of total control. Calmly she drove to the address Nichols had given her. Having knocked at the door and got no reply, she found the key and entered the flat. She found Weston's dictated note in Louise's scruffy handwriting, locked the flat, replaced the key and sat in the car. So that part of her assignment was a cinch. She called Nichols to report in and confirm progress.

'The package had already been collected.' She also took the opportunity to report her latest killing. 'By the way, a snoop overheard our previous conversation at the office. She's been dealt with. I have an alibi. We can pin it on Arif and I'll make sure he'll not live to deny it.'

By this time Nichols, along with much of the Corporation hierarchy, had been informed of the stabbing. His creative devious mind had quickly assimilated possible outcomes. He knew it had to be Arif or Ruby, surmising that it was likely to be Arif.

He reasoned that if the stabbing was fatal, with no positive identification of the assailant being made, then the evidence would stack up against Arif. If Arif was then killed at the bridge it would be an easy open-and-shut case for the police. However, if the stabbed victim provided evidence that it was Arif and he survived the bridge then, if need be, Nichols would have to get his own hands dirty and eliminate Arif himself. If it was Ruby who was identified and she survived the bridge then that would be a far more difficult prospect to solve. His best plan would be to offer Ruby an escape route because he knew he was no match for Ruby's expertise. His best hope was that the woman would die without identifying anyone and that Ruby and Arif killed each other. The only other option open to him was to kill the victim before she could identify anyone. Not an easy task if she was under police protection. His best stance would be to await the result of the bridge encounter before deciding the next step. If all went well, the deaths could be explained away by Arif having a complete breakdown and killing four Corporation employees before killing himself. Now that Nichols knew that it was Ruby, he was a little relieved as he knew it would have been done professionally and she had never let him down yet.

Ah, tough decisions in corporate management! I was made for this. He found his mental comment to himself amusing before verbally replying to Ruby.

'Excellent. That gives you ample time for your final part. The hardware you will need will be dropped in the usual manner at the usual place close to Trinity Square.'

Tempted though she was to retain the letter opener as an additional trophy, she disposed of it in the river on her drive to Trinity Square. She arrived spot on schedule, three minutes after the drop had taken place. Looking around she studied the commercial litter bins for a few moments. Then, warily and professionally scanning the scene, double-checking to make sure there were no passers-by, she left the car and walked briskly to the slightly over-full litter bin second on the left. Having donned gloves previously, she quickly lifted the lid and collected a black compact carrying case which held the short-barrelled sniper rifle with the additional night telescopic sight.

Ruby then drove to a multi-storey car park where she had an excellent view of the bridge. In addition to her normal small derringer attached to her garter, which she wore as a matter of course when on a killing assignment, she decided to pack a handgun and silencer because of the number of targets to dispatch. Here in the car, unobserved, she assembled the short-barrelled rifle and attached the night sight. After use, these too would be destined for the river. Though there was no time to zero in the weapon, she should still be close enough not to miss, being an excellent markswoman. She cocked the weapon but it jammed. There was something wrong with the fitment. After reassembling several times and retrying without success, she decided to abandon its use and fall back on her handgun and get in close. Words would be said with Nichols about this. Her frustration increased but so did her sense of excitement. The thrill would be greater anyway with the handgun and it was quicker to use.

If Arif did his job correctly then only he and a possible accomplice would be alive and she had dispatched two targets easily before. If she could not finish them off there and then she knew the route Arif was to take after the exchange. This would be a contingency if she couldn't get a clean kill for those two survivors. If he could not carry out the killing of Aylmer and Manning then her calculated killing order would be Arif, Aylmer, any accomplice and then Manning in order of likely threat. After all, Arif was the only one certain to have a gun. A significant number of emergency vehicle sirens started to sound and the vehicles she spied were converging on Westminster. She watched in silence and judged by the mixture of ambulances, fire engines and police cars that this was a response to a major incident. Turning on the radio she heard on the newsflash that it was a suspected terror incident on the underground station. Due to this she could not drive any closer, so decided to walk to check out the bridge for the best aiming points and concealment places.

The bridge was closed at night and off limits to the public for structural repair work before resurfacing could take place, which was due in a week or so's time. At street level at the side of the bridge and hanging below it were scaffolding and walkways which skirted around the pillars as well as the spans. She walked nearer to Blackfriars Bridge, taking the opportunity for a closer inspection before choosing where she would hide. The scaffolding along one side and underneath the bridge would be ideal. She could traverse under the bridge to the other side if need be. *Perfect*, she thought as she walked back to the car.

There was plenty of time to complete her disguise, prepare and secrete herself into a hiding place, but she would need to wait for when the clouds covered the moon. From the boot of the car she took out the special black burka that allowed plenty of free movement should she need to run or fight and to help blend into the darkness. The face veil would dissipate any trace of breath in the cold winter air. The cunningly hidden splits in the sides allowed easy access to the handgun and even the derringer if needed. She was glad that she did not have to hide the lightweight short-barrelled rifle under her garb though. Once suitably attired in this Middle Eastern get-up that conveniently broke up the shape of a person to Western eyes, she took out a black walking cane. In fact, it was a single-shot walking stick but she had no intention of using it as such, unless out of necessity as an ultimate backup.

At the allotted time she shuffled along from the car like a bent old woman, using the cane for walking support till she neared the confines of the bridge. As what was visible of the moon disappeared from view and checking that no one saw, she hid herself amongst the scaffolding close to a column, merging into the shadows out of sight from the rendezvous point but in a good vantage point for getting shots off. She double-checked her weapon, attached the silencer and then was ready to take the safety catch off when the time was right. She took care to breathe into the column to try to prevent any hint of hot breath in the cold winter air giving away her position should the veil fail in its purpose. She relaxed and deliberately stared into the blackness of the Thames to accustom her eyes to a lower light level than the one on the pre-planned allotted exchange point.

It was a crisp cold night, the full moon for the most part hidden by clouds, occasionally emerging to shine on the murky fast-flowing waters, the undercurrent making little whirlpools on the surface especially as it flowed past the bridge's stanchions.

– WESTON'S EXCHANGE PLAN –

Weston was still in the flat where they had placed Sarah for safety when he had received the interrupted call from Marwenna. Sarah overheard the brief exclamation from Marwenna and Weston's unsuccessful attempts to ring her back. Aware that something had seriously gone wrong with one of Weston's personnel, she made sure she overheard all of Weston's calls regarding the changing situation and the organising of backup for the exchange. Her unease increased when Setford's call came through and the subsequent change in backup arrangements was made by Weston. As it was, Weston had earlier on called in quite a few personal favours to have unofficial backup personnel on hand for the exchange at Blackfriars Bridge. Though becoming more fearful, particularly for Luke's involvement, she insisted on going with Weston to the bridge but had to begrudgingly acquiesce to his equal insistence of her staying hidden in the car. Weston had refused her the chance to see Luke before the exchange. Likewise, Luke had kept his distance from Weston as a precaution should he have been tailed until their agreed pre-exchange meeting about a half hour before the actual exchange. This was to go through the final details and possible scenarios.

Weston arrived a shade late for the planned pre-meeting with his cobbled-together backup team before the bridge encounter, due to the delay in establishing Marwenna's situation. Sarah, as agreed, remained in the car. Midway through briefing each backup operative, they were interrupted by the sound of a lot of emergency vehicles noisily travelling along the other side of the river. Within the space of fifteen minutes, each one of the backup team in turn was officially summoned to tasks concerning the terrorist bomb blast at Westminster and the resultant intelligence work required.

'Sorry, Weston, but you know this official summons takes precedence over your swap scenario,' was the general comment as each member had to leave the meeting. The final member just gave a helpless gesture and shrugged before leaving. Weston understood, of course, but that left him in a real jam. On his way back to the car he decided to stop the mission and so telephoned Luke and advised him of the situation and suggested it would be wiser to abort.

After some discussion Luke Aylmer persuaded Weston to continue. Luke's thinking was that he and Sarah would always be at risk if this was not resolved. He also had in mind the legacy that Dave Blagdon had left him and the likelihood that someone had affected his own health at the office. But the convincing argument he used to persuade Weston was his army experience of one or two operations involving a foul-up somewhere along the line, though not of their making, and having to adapt and overcome.

'What did Luke say?' asked Sarah of Weston having half heard the latter part of the conversation and getting more concerned by the minute.

'He wants to continue.'

'What! Let me talk to him, please.' Weston handed her the phone.

'You don't have to do this. You've heard what Weston said. You realise there is no credible backup. You're being stupid and stubborn. Don't be some dumb macho idiot trying to prove something. I've experienced how dangerous these people are.'

'Don't you realise we will never be shot of them till this is resolved?' he said calmly. She knew deep down he was right. But why should it have to be him? Why when she had found someone so, so… she couldn't find words to describe how she felt. She lost her temper.

'You're a bloody fool and if you come to harm, I'll bloody kill you,' she said, thrusting the phone back to Weston as she started to cry out of frustration and fear.

'We'll meet at the agreed time and place before you walk the bridge,' confirmed Weston.

In spite of her fear Sarah insisted on going with Weston to witness the exchange from the safety of his car. Then she could be with Luke as soon as it was completed. The time came for Weston to park up in order to walk to his rendezvous with Luke in plenty of time before the exchange was due to take place.

'If you'll just wait here in the car. I'll be less than a couple of minutes,' Weston assured Sarah. The rendezvous was in a sheltered spot on the South Bank very close to where Weston had parked. Weston reassured Luke as best he could and, giving final advice: 'I again apologise for the backup team being withdrawn but the bomb at Westminster takes precedence. Just stay long enough for identification during the negotiations for the device. Stall them by saying the device was in a safe place close by but you needed to see Sarah safe and well first! It looks as if they still think you are working alone and have either not realised Sarah's absence yet or have and are going to bluff you into giving over the device. Any sign of trouble, withdraw immediately, don't take any chances. Above all else, stay safe and alive,' Weston emphasised and then added, 'How is your fitness should anything awkward occur?'

'I'm out of condition compared to my service days,' he said patting his stomach. 'And yours?'

'First thing in the morning, up and down twenty times and then I do the same with my other eyelid. I am inspired by the sight of giant tortoises that live for hundreds of years and do everything physical slowly!' Both men laughed. It helped to deflect the build-up of nerves and deep concern they had for what was about to take place.

Luke relaxed a little, having been reminded of all the operational briefs he used to give or be part of in the army. It was almost like old times. They then went their separate ways, Weston back to his car and Luke strolling slowly to the bridge and towards the end of his journey taking in every last detail he could of the surroundings. It was like being on patrol again. Sarah sat in the car looking at the bridge. Weston handed her some night vision binoculars and mentioned he also had infrared binoculars available if she needed them.

– BLACKFRIARS BRIDGE –

It was a very dark, wintry night and because of the repair work on the bridge the street lights on it had been switched off. Arif had been waiting at the north end of the bridge for the arrival of Sarah, who was supposedly in the control of Nichols' arranged promised help. So far, they hadn't showed. He thought it pointless telephoning Nichols who would be unlikely to know exactly where they were. *No matter*, he thought. *I will infer that they are sheltering at the end of the bridge. As long as I bluff Aylmer in order to get close enough to be certain of killing him, it won't be a problem.* He had already planned for when they did arrive. Having collected the device from Aylmer and dumped his body in the Thames, he could then ask for their help in searching for the supposed missing device which had been dropped in the supposed fight. Having then led them to the centre of the bridge to make it easy to dispose of the bodies, he could kill them while they were searching. Checking his watch, he started to slowly walk to the centre of the bridge along the scaffolding walkway.

Luke had arrived ten minutes previously and had kept out of sight. Finally, he climbed up to the walkway and started slowly traversing along it. Weston handed back the night vision binoculars to Sarah, who had briefly used them when she noticed an indistinct movement of a dark shape. It was hard to make out so she swapped to Weston's infrared set of binoculars.

'There is definitely somebody else there,' she worriedly stated passing the binoculars back to Weston. By the time Weston had focused through the lenses and honed in on the shape, Sarah had left the car and started running to warn Luke, desperately concerned for his safety. Sarah made it to the bridge end in a flash and climbed to the level where she had seen the shape. As Sarah closed in on the silhouette that she had spotted, she saw the shape moving as if to take aim at the two men. Her heart leapt at the thought of losing Luke and she sprinted as fast as she could. Weston, taken by surprise at Sarah's reaction, had done his best to follow but was easily outpaced by Sarah's youth and fitness.

The two men stood facing off three yards apart. Luke recognised Arif.

'So, you had the device all along?'

'No, not at first. Where is Sarah?' Luke demanded, trying to act concerned and distract his opponent at the same time.

'She is at the end of the bridge.' Arif gestured behind him thinking he could bluff Luke and part hoping that the other operative of the Corporation would arrive in time with Sarah. 'Have you got the device?'

Luke touched a pocket and nodded.

'I need to see it.'

'After I've seen Sarah.'

Arif reached for his revolver, the silencer making it a little difficult to extract from his open overcoat quickly. In that split second Luke knew he had to attack or be killed. Luke launched himself at Arif, initially knocking him to the ground, causing the revolver to fly out of his hand. There they rolled about struggling on the wooden boarding.

The dark mysterious-shaped figure took aim and fired at the two men wrestling on the ground. One of them slumped over the other as the assailant re-cocked the weapon. Sarah launched her lithe body full length to disrupt the secondary aim of the assassin just before a second shot rang out. The gun went off as the revolver was knocked away. The only advantage Sarah had was her dance fitness and flexibility and for her to do the unexpected as she had never trained in fight techniques. Ruby had previously trained in martial arts but had been taken completely by surprise. The two of them grappled with each other. Sarah fought for her life and for Luke's too for that matter. Ruby's head covering came off and much of her garb ripped as they wrestled. Ruby tried scrabbling quickly for her derringer but was too slow. In the scuffle that followed Ruby's locket chain broke and came away in Sarah's hand as she tried to grab her assailant. Ruby, thinking she was gaining the ascendancy, took one of her gloves off in order to inflict greater pain on Sarah with her rings. Sarah, however, managed to bite a restraining hand and ripped a ring off the finger of her adversary in the process. Still fighting they both toppled over the bridge scaffolding into the cold, dark waters below.

Weston arrived breathless immediately after the action had subsided. He checked for pulses on both Arif and Luke and called an ambulance. Then he searched more thoroughly for Sarah and her assailant but could find no trace. He called in what remaining backroom staff he could muster to secure the site ahead of the police as he knew they would be busy with the aftermath of the train bomb, as would the ambulances that were needed. He took quick stock: one dead body and another unconscious but breathing with few visible serious injuries aside from bruising, Sarah and her assailant missing and Marwenna in hospital. There were two handguns and an unusual single-shot walking stick on which forensics should hopefully find fingerprints and of course DNA evidence.

Previously, Weston had tried contacting Setford after receiving the cut-off phone call from Marwenna but he had not answered until reporting back to Weston after the stabbing and on the way to the hospital. Now it was time in the aftermath to reflect on what had happened to Marwenna. He called Setford to find out how she was and queried why he was in the area of the Shellac building at the time.

'How is she?'

'Still in surgery at the moment.'

'How was it that you were so quickly on the scene?'

'I just happened to be passing, sir.'

Weston accepted his response at face value commenting, 'I'm jolly glad that you did. I doubt if she would have survived if it wasn't for your timely discovery.'

Eventually, post-Marwenna's operation, Setford was allowed to sit in a chair next to her bed while she slept. That evening's experience changed Setford when he had held her for the first time, and in that moment the thought of losing her triggered a growing change in him.

As all the news organisations were tied up in reporting on the terrorist attack on the train, Weston had time to liaise with the police first on the scene to restrict the information released. Fortunately, all the press reporters were preoccupied with the terrorist atrocity. When interest was eventually shown the police liaison officer chose not to link the body on the bridge with the major terror incident in spite of press speculation, his closing statement being, 'It's too early to say.'

BATTLES WITHIN
– THE SEARCH FOR SARAH

Edmund Athelstan Weston had wanted to retire early but was persuaded to stay by his department due to lack of resources on their part and to his needing something to do after his beloved wife Susannah had died. Work kept him from home; it filled in the time while he drifted from his mountain of loss through his valley of numbness along his river of loneliness to some form of basic life beyond breathing in and out a mere existence. Though trying to escape into normality as best he could, when at home he still sometimes caught himself half shouting, 'Shall I put the kettle on, Suse?', inevitably answered by a melancholic silence. Even when it came to cleaning the kitchen surfaces, he would still think how *Susannah would have been pleased with me doing this.*

Initially, it had been returning from work to an empty house which had been so daunting, then the strangeness of having eventually to adjust to sleeping in the middle of the bed with no one to cuddle with or wrestle the covers from. In their life together, many was the time he had actually got up and walked around the other side of the bed in the middle of the night because Susannah had taken up most of it, and mainly on his side. Now for him light sleeping had become a habit followed by uhtceare[10] mornings often forcing him to rise, drinking pots of tea and pottering before getting into work very early.

He missed sharing things with her so much. Little things. The male blackbird with the white tail feather and his offspring's antics, the menacing cat that would leave its mess in the garden that Weston would have to clear up. The regular echoed conversation amplified through the courtyard between a father and his very young son while waiting for the bus before school. He and Susannah had unintentionally at first eavesdropped but then regularly listened with much shared amusement. Over time they began to subconsciously measure the patience of the father and the sometimes-dubious replies as he tried to answer all the questions beginning with *'Dad, why does…?'* He missed too their mutual quoting of lines at each other at opportune times from their favourite much loved and watched films.

Planned holidays and thoughts of a retirement together had gradually been put on hold as slowly Susannah's health deteriorated. They had originally had it all planned. Their budget just about allowed early retirement, but they were still undecided as to where. However, their last couple of years together had been in uncertainty as the cancer re-emerged after several temporary successful treatments. Susannah had been a highly qualified, experienced nurse and knew exactly the likely outcome as the disease progressed. Knowing this, she did her best to prepare him and taught him many things by her attitude and from her Christian faith before she passed on. Even when she was dying her thoughts were for him and his future without her.

For his part, he had devotedly nursed her as best he could until her final stay at the hospice. There he would sit and read to her, for she loved the sound of his soothing, gentle voice. Since

---

10   To wake before dawn because you worry or care

then, for many months the job had acted as an anchor after he drifted, lost as to what to do while mourning her in his own private way. Susannah had asked her pastor to look in on him after her death from time to time just to see if he was coping and if he wanted to talk. Weston did not feel comfortable talking to people about his loss. That was not his way but the pastor encouraged him to write down his feelings and Weston had found that beneficial.

It had indeed been a rare marriage that had lasted well over thirty-five years. When cancer struck, they faced it together, the initial shock and disbelief, the thoughts of, *this can't be... this happens to other folk...*! Then the realisation of what time might be left and how best to appreciate it. Initially Weston was tempted to succumb to the trap of anger and bitterness, comparing perhaps less deserving or less worthy lives that are healthy but lived out in destructive lifestyles to Susannah's, even though an impartial observer would indeed measure Susannah's contribution to society of greater merit. Susannah would have none of it and led him to a better viewpoint. She looked on it as a gift of an approximate known time spent to put things and relationships in order. A time for reconciliation and completions wherever possible. Another thing he had to thank Susannah for.

They both agreed to make their limited time together as precious and memorable as they could. Such was their love that at their final hug, kiss and holding of hands they both gazed at each other and whispered, 'Thank you,' both being so grateful for the life they had shared together.

– THE MORNING AFTER –

Weston stared out through the window at the view from the Bouncing Banker public house which directly overlooked the river close to Cannon Street Bridge. It was 11.30 the morning after the night before. Things had gone badly, very badly. Even the pub did not serve a decent English cider, or brown ale for that matter, so he swapped to a local stout. He was fed up with all that over-marketed, hyped-up, fashionable, taste-bud tat that targeted the young. Still that was the least of his worries. What a mess, and it was his fault. He had already fended off phone calls from his 'superiors' as they often thought themselves, but in his value judgement line managers promoted to a first level of incompetence beyond their abilities, or seduced by the perception of career power and status.

They would be quick to blame him, although that did not worry him. He was past worrying about such things but just felt so deeply for Marwenna, Sarah and Luke for whom he felt responsible. Arif was shot and killed outright but it was a mystery as to what had happened to Sarah and her assailant. The likelihood was that they both had drowned. A police launch was by one of the Blackfriars Bridge supports while divers were busy searching for evidence, unlikely though that any was left, what with the strong currents and the passage of tide and time. Up above, Forensics were busy doing their bit in the cordoned-off area.

He perused the pub surroundings closer and traced the wording on a brass plate screwed onto the bar, which in other circumstances Weston would have found amusing – '*On Saturday 23rd September 1989 at 8.33 pm Declan Smith admitted he was wrong.*'

Luke was at Westminster Hospital recovering from the previous night's fight where he had been knocked unconscious by a glancing bullet. Though normally St Thomas's would be the place for emergencies, Weston had arranged for Luke's and Marwenna's dispatch there. Here they could be treated in a very controlled environment away from prying eyes. It was the least he could do. Weston had left Luke a message to call as soon as he was able. He reached in his pocket and felt for a piece of embroidery. The phone ringing stopped him brooding. It was Luke who had just regained consciousness.

'How are you feeling?' asked Weston and added after Luke's reply and further question on the latest situation, 'It's now being handled by the police. Everything is being done that can be done to find her, though we have imposed a temporary news blackout and are not releasing any new details to the press just yet. We are still not sure exactly what happened to her apart from what I saw and what you said before losing consciousness again. If you think of anything to add to what you said previously then ring me straight away.'

Weston explained what he had witnessed again. 'All I can remember is Sarah running towards you having spotted a dark silhouette shaping up to aim a weapon. She disappeared into the gloom, two shots rang out and then what looked like two people fighting falling off the bridge. It being so dark it was difficult to make out. Your assailant is dead, shot by presumably the other assailant fighting with Sarah, though we don't know for sure yet.'

'You will keep me updated, won't you?' asked Luke seeking reassurance.

'Of course, I'll be along later to tell you in detail anything new. The river police are working out the likely places the current would have taken her.' Weston sensed Luke's anguish and frustration. 'When there is anything practical you can do, I'll let you know but as an ex-soldier, you know very well it's best to leave it to us as you will just get in the way.'

Weston looked in later on Luke who was so desperate to try anything useful to help. Just before leaving to visit Marwenna, Weston suggested to Luke to try a chat with Sarah's pastor and contacts.

'Something to do, right?' stated Luke, knowing that was Weston's ploy.

'Hopefully more than that! But you've been in the services and you know that well-meaning enthusiasm may be counterproductive to the mission.'

'Yes, you're right but I feel so...'

'You never know what might be useful. Just get better quickly and try to remember anything else you can think of that might be useful in finding her and dealing with the Corporation.'

– MARWENNA –

On a different floor of the same hospital lay Marwenna. She had undergone emergency surgery and was sedated. Setford had stayed with her all night and was now dozing in a crumpled, tired and worried heap in a chair near her bed. While she had been asleep under sedation Setford had talked to her, holding her hand, occasionally caressing her forehead and stroking her hair. Finally, before dropping off himself he kissed her hand and whispered, 'I love you.'

The utterance of the words triggered something subconsciously deep inside him. He had never really acknowledged the depth of feeling he had for her to himself before, certainly not out aloud. Weston, who had already had his fill of hospitals, poked his head around the door.

'How is she doing?' he asked Setford, who woke with a start.

'The doctors say she has lost a lot of blood and should be OK but the next twenty-four hours will see if complications develop. They are concerned about the likelihood of peritonitis, sepsis or organ failure,' replied Setford.

'They are keeping Aylmer in for another twenty-four hours for observation but it is only as a precaution. He should be fine. You look all-in, Setford. I think you need to go home. You can't do any more good here. Leave it to the medics to do their job.'

'You will call me, sir, won't you, if there are any developments?'

'Of course, but go home and get some sleep.'

Weston got the latest information from the doctor concerning her condition, which was stable. He then left for the office.

Luke's anxiety about Sarah had made him restless but he knew that he had to stay at the hospital a further day for observation. Silly though it was, during that time he tried to keep abreast of the news coverage for updates, even though there was a blackout and in spite of the fact that Weston had promised to update him if there were any developments.

After receiving all the salient points from the forensic reports and passing relevant information on to the police investigating the grooming circle, Weston travelled back to the hospital and called in on Luke to update him. He then went to see how Marwenna was. Luke was making his way to the lavatory when he spotted Weston entering the lift and noticed that Weston, the sole passenger, stopped at a different floor from the ground floor. Intrigued, Luke decided to explore the floor in question. There were a number of private rooms as well as the usual wards. Luke stayed in a discrete waiting area where he could see the main corridor and waited for Weston to leave, making a note of which door Weston exited from. Could they have kept some horrible truth from him about Sarah and were keeping her there or, worse still, her lifeless body? He sneaked a peek around the door. He could not see the patient's face but noted that the hair was a different colour to Sarah's. Could this be Sarah's assailant? As he pondered he heard footsteps, so hid in an empty room and spied Setford entering the mystery patient's room. With that he slipped back to his own room and turned on the hospital radio programme.

'*And here we have a special request for Sonia in ward D from her husband, "Missing You"*[11]*, by Edward King and the Potatoes*,'

---

11   'Missing You' – a lament on guitar and voice

announced the disc jockey. It was the same ballad as the one from the electricals shop. The record again summed up how Luke felt but it brought no comfort at all.

– DARK BATTLES WITHIN –

After a very long night and day with little sleep Weston made it home. He had always been susceptible to dark moods, even when young, but these had progressively got worse since the loss of Susannah. The quiet house often reminded him of his own personal emptiness so he often switched on the radio just to fill the void with sound. This time he did so and a plaintive melody on cello cut through the air.[12]

Weston had been with Susannah through all her treatment and at the hospice where she had spent her last days. He was the closest witness to her battle against pain, internalising and suppressing all his own feelings of anguish and hurt to support her as best he could, needing to be strong during these times, always positive, always cheerful, while on occasions nearly falling apart inside. At the end he was a shell of his former self having reached the limit of his emotional resources. Now those feelings began to bubble to the surface. Now, maybe for really the first time, he was being forced to deal with them.

Susannah had been a keen gardener and had kept their small garden in pristine order until the final few months of her life. On her death, he took up the mantle of gardening as something to do and it made him feel somehow closer to her because she had loved it so much, but gardening was not really him and he did struggle with it. What kept him going was that it somehow kept a piece of Susannah alive, or so he thought. Now in times of stress he reverted back to it. It was one of the tricks he used to overcome his sorrow, loneliness and depression. Other times

---

12 'A Vision in a Dream' – cello and classical or twelve-string guitar piece

he would revisit his writings, prompted by the pastor's urging. Writings for his eyes only. When the pain got bad it was there to remind him of the love of his life and perhaps how he had progressed a little since his loss. Of course, he would remember the good times, grateful for so many, but sometimes that made him feel his hurt even more keenly.

He remembered how, towards Susannah's end of life, he had pushed her in her bed on wheels around the grounds of the hospice when the weather was warm or if there was a clear winter night and they could stargaze together, so long as she was kept warm. The hospice was absolutely brilliant for stuff like that. He cast his mind back to some of her words just before their final farewell as she was dying: 'Go on and make the most of what's left, don't waste it moping, I'll be looking down to see what blondes or redheads you pick up and expect to see loads.'

Sometimes he would reminisce about their early days at school. Susannah, her close friend Cobby and he would walk home together after school and then stand chatting at her friend's gate. When he and Susannah moved on from saying goodbye and out of sight, he would carry Susannah's books for her. He reflected on when he first became aware of how she felt about him and from the resulting argument how he realised he felt about her. She had first really intimated her feelings for him when she became very jealous about him giving a St Christopher away to a Welsh girl called Rhyian Wilson Davies on a school boat trip across the Channel. The argument and reconciliation that ensued brought them closer. So much so, that Susannah had insisted that the daughter of their twins they had had for such a brief time should be called Rhyian as a reminder of the girl that brought them together. It was a pretty name after all and of course it was a victory over her earliest rival. Now Susannah lay buried with Rhyian Wilson Aethelflaed Weston and Harold Cedda Weston both aged three months.

– A SURREAL ASIDE –

Just for the one moment in her senior years, Rhyian Wilson Davies broke off from what she was doing and wondered whatever happened to that English boy who had given her a St Christopher on a school trip. Would he have been a better husband than the one she had now? After all, at the time, she was dead set on marrying an Englishman. Would he have given her such lovely children as she had now? She quickly glanced at a photograph of Rees, her loving husband. In an instant, she dismissed the mere thought and prospect and carried on with her ironing. As far as she was concerned, she had made the right choice.

– THE ISOLATION OF GRIEF –

Weston still tried to enjoy life's experiences and recognised its value on all the known levels to him but on occasions he could feel he was crying inside, sometimes the more in company, the more alone he felt. In the aftermath of Susannah's death, he had cried till there had been no more tears left. He had endured the emptiness, the numbness, the feelings of guilt, the frustration, though he had never felt anger in the way that some folk do during bereavement. The exhaustion of it all. The one surety in life is death, he knew, and he was aware of the differing philosophical values to life. In the West it was maybe overvalued, and in the East, it was maybe regarded too cheaply. Bottom line for him was his better half had left a massive chasm that could not be filled.

– LOVE MEETING PAIN –

When the deaths of their husbands were confirmed Martha, forever practical, picked up the phone.

'Hello, Ayesha, this is Martha, Reverend Peter Hones' wife. I know we have never met but I thought we could at least share our grief together.' They both fought back tears as Martha went on. 'I know the Muslim tradition is to bury quickly and that you are probably busy arranging the funeral but I would like to stand with you in our loss and you are welcome to stand with me and my family when Peter is buried.'

'Thank you, it's very kind. I'd like that. Mohammed often spoke of you and Peter with great affection.'

As soon as Mohammed's body was released the arrangements were made. Ayesha's family, in-laws and members of the mosque were very kind to Martha. Ayesha even invited Martha to sprinkle rose water on the grave, as was the custom from where her family had originally emigrated. Likewise, when it came to Peter's funeral, Ayesha stood with Martha and her family as well as Peter and Martha's church family. They too were equally loving and supportive to Ayesha and her family. Over the weeks the two women kept in contact and a strong friendship grew, initially out of their situation. In fact, both wider families grew quite close. Eventually, several months later, a memorial service was held for the whole of the broader church and mosque congregations to share their loss together and salute the contributions both men had made.

Aside from meeting to discuss funeral arrangements and the memorial service both women started meeting on a regular basis. They shared their grief and often talked about their husbands and their long friendship, and elaborated on the small, quirky foibles particular to their husbands. It somehow brought a little comfort to them both and at times raised a brief smile amid the tears.

'Mo used to fiddle with his beard a lot when musing on the Koran. I'd tease him about it.'

'I noticed Mo did that too when they played chess. Being honest, Peter could be annoyingly frustrating at times, particularly administrative-wise, but I'd swap anything to have him back once again.'

Both Peter and Martha had already planned and financed their own funerals years before because they didn't want to burden their children with such things. Some of the details, though, they had kept personal to themselves. Peter Hones had left strict instructions concerning a few aspects of his funeral, allowing freedom for the family to express their grief, but also making a few compulsory wishes for himself. Though he couldn't dance for toffee, as Martha would often say, he had loved to see it in the worship services and wanted a worship one at his funeral. It also reminded him of seeing Martha for the first time. So, he had insisted that 'Teach Me To Dance'[13] should be played and if those who turned up at his funeral were up for it, to learn the dance beforehand and dance at his funeral.

He had stated in his farewell note that he would be learning to dance in his new body in praise of God in heaven and have at least eternity to get the steps and body movements right. As it turned out, at least three quarters of the usual congregation made the effort, although some of the ageing ones had to make compromises concerning the more enthusiastic moves.

Belatedly, almost too late, Luke Aylmer had discovered that Peter Hones was one of the victims of the bombing. He managed to obtain details from the church secretary and asked to go to the funeral to pay his respects. Thankfully he was way at the back of the church when it came to the dance.

Martha had held her emotions together up until the poignant final verse of '10,000 Reasons'[14], which struck her very hard. At this point, she lost the battle of control and started to sob quietly and eventually totally broke down.

---

13 'Teach Me To Dance' by Graham Kendrick
14 '10,000 Reasons (Bless the Lord)' by Matt Redman and Jonas Mylin

– THE SEARCH FOR SARAH –

Weston had advised Luke not to call in to his workplace yet, as he wanted to try to monitor any Corporation moves.

'After all, we don't want them knowing you are alive just yet,' he had added. Luke, illogical though it was, even to him, and knowing that it was pointless, still kept questioning the situation to himself. Why no body? Was she alive? If so, why no contact? He just could not believe or accept that she was dead. He was in limbo, frustration growing, totally at a loss as to what to do while waiting for news.

Several days later, out of desperation, Luke put a missing person page on Facebook. He looked at the messages the following day – some supportive but with no information and some from trolls. He initially could not believe how sick people could be. They seemed so full of bile and hatred. Did they hate him and Sarah that much? Then on reflection he thought most of the troll messages suggested that fundamentally the originators had never left the primary school playground in terms of intellect or aspirations. Perhaps their sole satisfaction was now bound up in derision and hatred, indicating that they had become so dissatisfied with their own lives, which to them were devoid of fulfilment, that this was one of their major or only outlets.

After the initial hurt it had caused him, he came to realise that all he felt for them actually was pity and sadness. How could a human being be so reduced in humanity to get one of their main pleasures from someone else's pain and misfortune? Life had become so empty for them and all they had left was scorn. He took down the page reflecting on how futile it had been. Then, out of frustration, still keen to do something positive, anything, anything that might bring him closer to Sarah, he sought out Sarah's minister.

– A WISH AND A PRAYER –

Sarah's church was in Tooting and as he journeyed there, he thought he might meet some of her church friends, but if nothing else, he would just be glad to be in a building she was associated with and where she had danced. He met her pastor and told him of her disappearance, spilling his story out as best he could while still limiting the information to what he thought Weston would allow. The minister listened intensely and sensed that Luke was holding something back and so asked, 'Are there any parts of your story that you do not want sharing with a prayer group?'

Luke indicated that he was content that the limited knowledge he had given could be shared. The minister then led him down to the prayer meeting room below the place of worship where six or seven people sat in an informal circle. He waited for an appropriate time to interrupt them and told of Sarah's disappearance and asked them to pray.

'This is our intercessor prayer group,' he remarked to Luke and each one either nodded or smiled at Luke. There was quiet for some considerable time as they prepared themselves and waited on God. Then, one by one, silently or with mouthed whispered words each prayed one or several prayers. Silent tears slipped down the cheeks of one or two of the ladies. An occasional vocal prayer did break the silence.

Luke felt a little uncomfortable at first, in this quiet room full of strangers, listening to their prayers or rather those that said them out loud. Gradually he felt at ease and at one point Luke felt peace flood into him and a huge weight lift off him. He was in total self-control, yet he knew he still needed to deal with his emotions. After a considerable time, the prayer session ended and the minister was about to usher Luke to leave when one of the seven piped up, 'I believe I have a picture that has come into my mind. A picture of a bird sitting brooding on a nest in the junction of branches in a tree. A violent storm raging around it and causing the branches to sway considerably. Yet the bird is resting.'

Then, another, this time a lady in the group, shared verses she felt impelled to utter.

'I have these words for you. Seek and you shall find, knock and the door shall be open to you.'

The minister waited for an explanation of the picture and the words but none was forthcoming and so he took Luke aside and spoke in quiet tones.

'Normally, we have an independent person within the group who would verify such a picture so I am a little concerned that there is no independent corroboration within the group. Does it make any sense to you? How do you feel? Do you want anything explained?'

'Actually, I can confirm the picture,' said Luke and continued, 'The picture is something that a work colleague described to me a couple of weeks before he died. He said it represented peace. The bird had faith that it would not be destroyed and therefore had peace, even though the circumstances surrounding it could cause fear and panic. I always understood what he said intellectually but it is not the same as knowing inside, is it? It is like my situation now. The situation and my emotions are out of my control, like the storm, but since this meeting I have a strange sense of peace that has flowed into me, which I have never felt before. I can't explain it. It's not an emotion, although it affects my emotions. It is outside of me yet fills me. Does this sound bizarre? Do you know what I mean?'

The minister nodded.

'I see and what about the verses that the lady said: "*Seek and you shall find, knock and the door will be opened to you*"?'

Luke hesitated for a second before replying.

'I'm not sure. It could mean many things. For instance, does it mean search for Sarah or something else?' replied Luke.

'Perhaps either or both and maybe more besides. I do know one thing though. That it is for you to find out, nobody else can do it for you in your situation. You have to knock at that door or doors. We will of course continue to pray for you both.' The pastor then scribbled the verse references down and added two of his own and gave the note to Luke with a twinkle in his eye and a firm handshake as they said goodbye. His additions for Luke read:

'Many waters cannot quench the flame of love, neither can the floods drown it. Love is as strong as death.'[15]

'Peace I leave with you; my peace I give you. I do not give you as the world gives. Do not let your hearts be troubled and do not be afraid.'[16]

'Let us know any news of Sarah and come back and tell us how you get on,' added the minister while showing Luke out. As he waved Luke off, he remarked, 'God always leads you one step at a time at a pace you can cope with, so try to be patient.'

Luke left for home feeling a lot more positive and dared hope that Sarah was still alive.

– WESTON AND LOUISE –

Weston visited Louise to advise her of what had transpired and to prepare her for the interviewing she would have to undergo. She was now drying out in a secure room of a safe house – sometimes antagonistic, sometimes withdrawn. Initially all she would want to play was the single CD track and occasionally mouth some of the words having no interest in television or radio.

---

15   Song of Songs 8 v 6,7 (NIV)
16   John 14 v27 (NIV)

*Becoming possessive, for my love is obsessive,
it's dependent perception beyond realms of reason.
My sense of proportion is just a distortion.
The truth or illusion aids my confusion.*

*Darkness calls me to its womb, As I face the walls of my bedroom.
Entombed with pain myself consumed.
Exposed the bareness of my soul, wrapped lies and falsehoods now enfold.
Come jealousy's hot flames embrace, despair's cold fingers poke and grate.*

'Can I get you anything? Books? DVDs? CDs?' asked Weston.

'Don't want to read no books. Just get me out of here?'

'I'm afraid I can't, well, not for the time being anyway but eventually you will go after we learned what you know.'

'But I've told you all I know.'

'Well, events have moved on since then, my dear. I'm sorry to say that both your colleagues are dead.'

'No, you're lying. They both can't be.'

'Abdullah Alam blew himself up along with a lot of innocent people on the tube. Fazul Arif was shot dead in a kidnap exchange. Not by us, I might add, but by someone we think who worked for the same boss as Arif. You might possibly know them. Both deaths were on the day we arrested you. It's taken us a while to confirm the body pieces of Alam.'

She sat stunned, open-mouthed, sometimes trying to form words but none came.

'In the meantime, is there anything I can get you while you are here? Do you enjoy reading? If so what type of books would you like?' he asked for a second time. Louise was unable to respond. With that he departed, leaving Louise in shock, still trying to grasp the truth about her lover, captor, Svengali, torturer all rolled into one. He knew she would need time to digest the bad news he had given her.

Weston, as a favour, had asked Pastor Grinstead, Susannah's pastor, to look in on Louise, which he did, unaware of the true nature of the house or hardly any of the facts. All the pastor was told was that she was a valuable, vulnerable witness possibly under threat.

He sat and listened to her for a long time and left her with a bible and some verses to think about. If nothing else it took her mind off the worries that were beginning to surface in her, as well as the debilitating desire for alcohol that gnawed at her. Weston just popped back as the pastor was leaving and the two men conversed outside her room.

'Thanks for visiting her, I know it's not your area of work but she has no one to trust and she certainly does not trust me. How is she holding up?'

'As you know, she is really in a bad place emotionally as well as physically. You know she told me, and not in confidence I might add, that she didn't feel she could love anyone ever again, but I think what she had was not love at all. It might have started out as love, but become something hideous that ate her up. Before she can love again, and I believe she can, she has got to learn to love herself and in order to do that she has to get to discover herself again. That was something her previous relationship robbed her of – her own sense of identity. He, whoever he was, certainly screwed her up so terribly that she had no control of herself. The only control she had was his. Her view of self-worth had been subjugated so badly that her sense of being came from living for him, but in doing that she was destroying herself even more. I can't even allude to our loving heavenly Father as she has never known a loving father and would not be able to relate.' Weston nodded as he listened to Pastor Grinstead, who continued with much concern in his voice.

'As you know, she is very hostile when she has the energy, taking out her angst on anyone or anything in sight and when tired she becomes very withdrawn and subdued. Louise is so very hurt and damaged. It's a defence mechanism, you know. Her personality had been so inextricably linked with the chap she mentioned. It's as if part of her had died with him. Her anger is all she has left and even that is born out of need for alcohol. Normally it takes the form of self-harm. I've given her some Bible verses to think about because even though she does not hold herself in any esteem they will remind her that God does. Watch out for signs of any self-harming though. Is there anyone to care for her?'

'Not that we know of,' said Weston adding, 'and as far as we know there is no one else she could go to.'

'You've obviously taken an interest in her. Do you think you can help?'

'Well, I can't keep her here indefinitely, that's for sure, but I could personally finance her stay elsewhere for a while. Susannah would have wanted me to do that at least.'

'Yes, she certainly would and she would have been pleased at your decision, if I may say so.'

'Just out of interest which verses did you give her?' asked Weston.

'Psalm 139 verses one to eighteen and Luke's gospel chapter twelve verse seven. She needs to start loving herself. I told her that she is respectfully and wonderfully made and that you have to start loving yourself before you start loving your neighbour. Not a selfish love, of course, but a respectful love. Self-worth based on truth, not on illusion. You know, some people get their sense of value and worth in total from what they do,' he said looking directly at Weston, 'others from their relationships, for others still their belief validates them.'

'Ah, because her sole reference, her anchor, if you will, is dead, she is lost,' stated Weston.

'I gather it was a very sad and pitiful life she has led.'

Weston touched the embroidery in his pocket and uttered his own response to the pastor's observations.

'Indeed, it was, the poor mite. She's totally lost.'

'Not nice for you, I grant you, but she's letting out her hate, frustration, rejection, bereavement in a way and the beginnings of fear for the future. The only thing I can say is that it is good for her to let it all out and kick against something, or in your case someone. She is rediscovering her emotions which were blotted out by the drink.' The pastor then grasped Weston's arm with concern. 'You know it's nothing personal.'

'Well, the way things have gone I certainly deserve some sort of retribution,' remarked Weston.

'What she needs now is a lot of love, time and patience and if whoever looks after her has faith, then prayers for healing.'

'I trust you will do that part,' replied Weston.

'You know Susannah never gave up on you so I won't either!' said the pastor with a grin referring to Weston's agnosticism.

'That's one challenge I can do without at the moment,' smiled Weston. The pastor made to leave but Weston had one final question for him. 'How is it you keep so cheerful when you see so many problems every day?'

'I have my heroes of faith to inspire me.'

'What, like St Francis of Assisi?'

'Well, actually more recent folk. When I was in training, I used to visit a lady who had four stumps for limbs and lived on the third floor of a tower block. Even with all the modern paraphernalia it was difficult for her to leave her flat. Her faith was very strong. She was always welcoming and open. She would pray a tremendous amount for other folk. Her care visitors would place her close to the window for much of the day where she could look out on the traffic. Very occasionally, a driver or passenger would look up and she would smile at them and wave her stump. She saw in their faces whether they were worried or harassed with the pressures of everyday life. Sometimes they would smile and wave back. Whatever she discerned from their response she would pray for them accordingly and such was her belief she knew that her prayers brought blessings for them.'

– THE RIVER GIVES UP A BODY –

About a week later Weston got news of the discovery of a woman's body in the Thames. He contacted Marwenna and asked, if he arranged a private ambulance, would she be able to identify the body? Having checked with the medical staff and being incredibly impatient to leave boring hospital she was delighted to say yes. Weston knew he had to inform Luke but wasn't looking forward to it. Luke, aching for news, picked up the phone as soon as it rang.

'I'm afraid we've found a female body. I've been told the water and a head injury has not been too kind. I've arranged for someone to try and identify it.'

Luke's heart sank. He felt badly let down by the pastor and prayer meeting. How dare they lead him on! Making suggestions to people at a vulnerable time. Yet they seemed so genuine. Maybe they were deluding themselves as well as him. All the same, it could be very damaging to folk. Maybe they were just telling him what he wanted to hear or what they wanted to believe or a little of both, but he found it difficult to accept that they were manipulating the situation or him. It just was not like that. They had nothing to really gain. His mind cast back to the prayer meeting. There had been no hassle, no hype, hysteria or pressure, no appeals for money, no soft or hard sell and no mental suggestions. Just a chat where Luke did most of the talking and then the prayers. He started to feel sick inside, like something cold was gnawing at his stomach. He had lost his best friend since his army days and now the person he really loved and trusted had gone too. He suddenly realised just how deep his love was for Sarah now that it was almost certain she was gone. It is sometimes the case that for some men they realise far too late what their true depth of feelings are and how much they really care about the most valuable people in their lives. Luke was unfortunately one of them.

'I'll go. Where?'

'The body is at Shoeburyness mortuary. Are you sure you feel up to it?'

'Even though she may be dead I would like to be close to her at least one last time.'

They motored down mainly in silence as there was nothing meaningful to say. Luke steeled himself for when the sheet was lifted. The mortuary had a small viewing area and at a nod from Weston the face of the body was uncovered. It wasn't Sarah. Luke's legs nearly buckled under him. It took some time before he gathered himself.

'It's not Sarah but I'm sure I've seen her before,' Luke stated with utter relief. After the initial shock and relief, he did feel that the face, distorted as it was and with no makeup on, was possibly familiar, though he could not place it.

'Have a sit down and take plenty of time to think. It's likely to be someone in the Corporation but if not, would it be in the services or from your own interests? There is no pressure, like I said, I've got someone else arranged who may be able to identify the body. I'll see if I can rustle up some tea,' stated Weston. Luke was glad to sit down and recover further.

While obtaining some tea Weston made a quick phone call to see if Marwenna was still able to travel and if she was on her way. Setford was in the back of an ambulance with Marwenna and they were nearing the end of their journey. He passed his phone over to her at Weston's request.

'Are you sure you are up for this, Bowers?'

'Of course, sir, I insisted on coming. I am very bored convalescing, sir.'

Weston and Luke stood drinking tea and chatting when an ambulance pulled up outside and Setford emerged from the back to help Marwenna onto a wheelchair together with her infusion stand. She nodded, smiled and went in to view the cadaver from the viewing area. She instantly recognised her assailant. They emerged very quickly. Setford wheeled her over towards Weston. As Setford pushed Marwenna past Luke in the corridor, Luke did a double-take recognising Marwenna and was stunned to see her.

'Isn't that the tea lady's assistant, Marwenna?' he blurted aloud to Weston, nearly spilling his tea.

'Catering management assistant consultant, if you don't mind,' corrected Marwenna acutely embarrassed at Setford's suppressed smirks.

'Er yes. Quite! What are you doing here?' replied Luke.

'The same as you. Trying to identify a body.'

'So, you work with Weston and Setford,' Luke offered, realising he was a little slow on the uptake.

Weston interjected, 'She's a plucky woman, with real gumption, working undercover who got attacked in the line of duty and was nearly killed. A very brave woman indeed, especially as it was her first assignment.'

'And I hope the last,' muttered Setford.

'Well, thank you, I'm very impressed. Er, what is your real name if I'm allowed to know it?' said Luke as he bent and kissed her hand.

'It is Marwenna, honest,' she replied with an appreciative smile at his gallant kiss, her head held high with a regal air in Setford's direction.

Setford took a silent sharp intake of breath, feeling more than a tinge of jealousy. Would his dream of being something or someone important to Marwenna ever come true? At this moment, his subconscious determined that he would try to win her affections. He did not know how, but if he had to, he would fight for her. Desiring from afar was no longer enough but this did not outweigh his doubts about not being good enough for her.

'Positive ID, sir. She's the one who knifed me. She works in the Shellac building. She was in the office of a Ruby Fenwick, or at least that was the name on the door,' Marwenna stated with a detached professional manner, at the same time hoping to brush over Setford's amusement.

'She had a liking for a lot of jewellery, sir, I seem to remember seeing a lot of rings in the fight.'

'All her rings had been removed by the mortician and given to the police for evidence,' Weston confirmed.

The business in hand completed, Marwenna and Setford turned to leave and Setford couldn't resist jibing back, 'Come on, tea lady's assist… oh, sorry, what was it? Catering management consultant assistant or something like that, time to go back to observation,' Setford stated.

'Typical! How cruel to someone in a wheelchair.' Marwenna rose to the bait.

'That's not cruel. Letting your tyres down, now that would be cruel. Mind you, if you develop an over-inflated ego, then maybe I could.'

Setford was interrupted by Marwenna. 'You cheeky b…'

'Bowers! Remember where you are,' interjected Weston, 'and that goes for you too, Setford.'

'Yes, sir.'

'Sorry, sir.'

Setford took great delight in adding in a louder voice as they left and laughing, 'Come on, it's back to the hospital for you! Personal assistant to an executive department manager, of tea.'

With that they both left the mortuary.

As Luke and Weston were leaving Luke suddenly remembered where he'd seen the body before.

'It was the forensic security auditor seconded to my office. Her name was Sapphire O'Connor! I wonder what her real name was! Sapphire or Ruby or maybe something else?'

As they left the mortuary some reporters milled about.

'Any comment on the body found in the estuary?' one of them shouted.

'Not as yet, no.'

'Is it linked to the terror incident? Is it true that an additional body was found on Blackfriars Bridge? Are the two linked? Was it a suicide? A possible lovers' suicide?' the questions were shouted by a variety of reporters.

'That's pure speculation! Gentlemen and ladies, you know by now that we cannot give details out without letting the next of kin know. At this point in time we cannot confirm the identity of the deceased but will be issuing details once identity is confirmed and relatives have been contacted. I can, however, confirm that the body is of a woman. Detective Inspector Pollock will be making a statement in due course.'

On the journey back Luke kept turning things over in his mind. Why no body, was she still alive? He just couldn't accept that she was dead, although logic told him it was likely. Weston dropped Luke off and went back to his office.

— STARK BATTLES WITHOUT —

At work, Weston was in deep trouble and expected to be dismissed having taken full responsibility for the unauthorised operation. After a strong departmental ticking-off which had come from the top and the strong suggestion that Weston should resign and take his pension, Weston sat at his desk wondering whether to take the offer. As it was, he had been suspended pending an internal inquiry but such were the limited resources in the department that he was allowed to semi-officially carry on and clear up the mess he had made. He did, however, argue convincingly and successfully that Marwenna and Setford thought they were doing the official department's work and therefore deserved recognition of some sort. In spite of the suspension, Setford agreed to keep unofficially working for him in the clearing-up operation as well as acting as an unofficial channel for further developments or subsequent investigations. This was in addition to his official allotted tasks.

After Susannah's death Weston had immersed himself in work but deep down no longer had much enthusiasm for it. Much of his job now seemed to be undermined and what kept him going was kicking against some of the management and departmental balderdash that came his way. Did any of it really matter? What value was it? He did feel useful, however, doing his best to shield Setford and Marwenna from most of it, particularly Setford because of how it would affect his career more than Marwenna's. Being a 'techie' there was no hierarchical progression that management could bestow due to the restrictive thinking in terms of reward, recognition and responsibility. Financial remuneration was linked to bums on seats, as Marwenna would say, or in polite parlance, management of personnel or financial budget responsibility. The fact that Setford's nurture may be far more useful to the organisation, nay the nation, did not fit with the limited way departments are run, particularly in the public sector, though some private companies were just as guilty. Marwenna's career would definitely progress but could be hindered by outmoded thinking at certain levels, which he did his best to challenge, but he knew she was too bright and positive to be held back for long, whereas Setford was quite shy and certainly less assertive.

Weston knew he was responsible for the situation and some of the extenuating circumstances that had led him to risk going unofficial but he had never expected this result. His many battles in the department over the years had been on different levels and areas but was this how it was all going to end, in mess and failure? He had come a right cropper, and had no one else to blame but himself for the foul-up. Not that he cared what happened to him or his reputation, such as it was, but now all he could think of was Marwenna, Setford, Sarah and Luke and, for that matter, even Louise. They were young, their whole lives ahead of them. Slowly he plodded home.

He suddenly felt very exhausted, too tired to be cynical or bitter, just an air of resignation hung over him. He slumped into the armchair not wanting a drink, just drained, numb and empty. He fought the blackness which he sensed was drawing in to all but consume him. He had developed little strategies for coping with the usual triggers that could send him into sombre, black, depressive moods. It was too wet to attempt gardening and so he picked up an exercise book left out of its home in a drawer. He thumbed the poems he had written at the pastor's behest, and they did indeed articulate his own feelings of loss, pain and loneliness. It fell open at the words of his lowest point in bereavement. He started to read.

I dreamed a dream of you but you are gone.[17]
The cancer did for you. Can I carry on?
Bits of me inside are now dead. Yet I'm still loving you.
I wept till there were no more tears, parched sunken eyes
in vacant stare.
Alone in silence, time stood still, yet life continued all around.
My numbed senses tired of constant ache, to the living it's
so hard to relate.

---

17 'A Vision in a Dream' – guitar and cello piece

Rather than bring solace it seemed to emphasise the pain from an old raw nerve and so he tried to quickly remedy this by moving on to a poem written later on in his bereavement journey. This attempt at an emotional rally failed abysmally and so he placed the notebook back in its home. He switched on the radio as a distraction but the melody playing matched the word scan of the first poem, the melody almost mocking him by having the same rhythm as his first set of stanzas as his brain involuntarily matched the words to the melody. He switched the radio off.

This sense of emptiness led him deep into depression, which racked him again and again till he finally surrendered to it, descending the spiral staircase in his soul to the very bottom where light was a stranger, relinquishing his struggle and embracing the despair that would imprison him there. He was just too tired to fight against it anymore. Oh, how he missed Susannah, just to hug her, to look into her eyes, to hold her hand, to know she was beside him. He physically ached for her.

OLD AGE AND TIME ROLLS ON[18]

Myriad golds, greens and browns.
We autumn leaves danced on gentle breeze.
Indian summer's final flourish of glory
Then we too fall down.

Hard winters we've had to endure.
Sweet summers we've shared in our lives.
Our springs of romance and passion.
The storms and the lulls and the calm.

I am thankful for what we had.

Time and travail etched their marks
Now fading looks and waning powers.
Our goodbyes said, a new door entered.
New life for you but I go on.

---

18 'Embracing the Loss' – guitar and voice lament

Dancing Into Danger

The child, the woman, my lover, my wife, the mother,
my closest friend.
Friend to others, giver of blessings, God-fearing woman,
soul mate to the end.

And it's hard to go on alone.

I looked in the window of your soul.
I read what your life had to say.
Your dreams sacrificed on the altar of self.
Serving the ones, you loved.

I talk to you at your grave
Reflecting past times, ruing words unsaid
Yet knowing that love covers all
Including the parts of me now dead.

Our love transformed lives on.
And on, and on and on.

How he would love to join her. Now maybe it was time for an ultimate act to end his desolation, succumb to the blackness and emptiness forever. Capitulate from a world that neither seemed to know nor care.

He left his abode and ambled through the quiet but echoey courtyard and past buildings in the main thoroughfare. The strains of Dave Brubeck's rendition of 'Koto Song' drifted out from an open window of a cellar from one of the old three-storey Victorian houses as he trudged by.

A final look at the village field of green where children for the most part in their innocence had once regularly enjoyed country dances decades before. The duck pond, once quaint had become a dumping ground for litter and shopping trolleys. In his wandering, he found himself at the park close to the school field.

– THE STRUGGLE –

Aside from work Weston felt increasingly out of step with today's values. His world had shattered when he lost Susannah and all that he had held dear now seemed to be disappearing. He often battled depression on several fronts: ideologically, the political systems and their limitations; the madness of humanity in general, repeating the same mistakes throughout history; in culture, generational; and spiritually, seeking some form of meaning for this world, or at least trying to find some peace with the thought of no meaning or the pointlessness of it all.

Culturally, gone the old England with teashops, manners, respect, reserve, where gentlemen were exactly that, gentle men, and where consideration was given to others, where fair play and good-natured fun were the order of the day. He saw brief reminders of how things could be or used to be but he struggled. Manic philosophies were easy to spot and try to counter but the gradual subtle wearing-down of family values had been relentless from the heady days of almost innocent, banal, successful lifestyle commercials of the 1950s to the obscure alternative lifestyle statements of perfume and car commercial television adverts of the 2010s. Had it all been a delusional dream? Had he invented a sort of life created by fictional media? He did not know what to believe anymore. Yet he looked at what appeared to be there now tinged by his depressive mood, coloured by his negativity, his perceptions and value judgements. Life seemed to offer little.

All he seemed to see was the worst aspects of oppressive consumerism, pressure to conform to some fictional advertising lifestyle, isolation within communities of fear, selfishness and the culture of celebrity with no substance where the only kind of communal bonding among the young appeared to be the gang. What hope was there for the next generation? He feared for it, what with it being bombarded by froth and celebrity, and having fewer positive adult role models in the media. He didn't condemn those trying to make a living solely being a celebrity but to him it was all such a waste of energy and endeavour.

His head spun with the complexities of views, trying to make sense of it all, his world collapsing in on him. He sighed as he moved along the pavement. His mind flicked from the personal to parochial to national to global, families, systems, governments and to the conundrum of mankind itself. So many depressing things crowded his thoughts. It was like being bombarded by semi-musical sounds. He felt empty and judgemental. So much selfishness, greed and demands to meet needs, perceived or real. Man's history being not so much for survival as thirsts for power, aggression and selfishness. People were still hungering after power and prepared to perpetrate heinous deeds to gain it or hang onto it. What hope was there for them to embrace something meaningful? He struggled to get a grip and was in meltdown and he knew it. It was perhaps a jaundiced view, he knew, but he felt so despairing. It was easy to see the negatives. A very black dog mood indeed.

His mind tried wrestling with many perceptions on different levels all at once. So much information, much of it transient, circumstantial, relational. So many layers to comprehend, not that one was necessarily superior to another, and so many that were still to be discovered. After all, the value of such information to society and personally was mainly subjective. He remembered a line from a film he had seen with Susannah on a rainy afternoon. It was a Superman film, yes that was it, a remark by the villain Lex Luthor concerning chewing gum wrappers. How the line of dialogue had thrown into contrast our perceptions of life.

Which way would he turn? He did not mind change or even fear it but the sheer pace of it wore him down, though he did care about what was worthwhile being lost. He sat on a park bench as the winter early darkness shadows began. His wife had died, no job of consequence, could he face the pain of getting involved with Louise? Weston's mind went over the events of the last few months. Would he shrug off the workings of his old department with cynical acceptance? He mused on the Corporation.

– INNOCENCE IS A POWERFUL THING –

As he sat on the bench for what maybe would be his last time, a little girl approached him. She was probably only seven or eight – he was never good at judging ages – her mother looking on. The girl had been playing near the pond, playing hide and seek and feeding the ducks, skipping back to her mother on numerous occasions. Her mother, when not playing with her, constantly watched her. A few other mothers sat or stood, taking more interest in their mobile phones or conversations, but would occasionally look up to check where their particular offspring was. The little girl had come over to him and smiled and pointed to the pond.

'There are ducks over there!'

He smiled, trying hard to control his emotions which were already starting to generate tears deep within his soul that were beginning to well up, inching ever so slowly on the journey to his eyes.

'Yes, there are, my petal,' he almost whispered.

'Do you like ducks?' she asked.

'Er... yes I certainly do, poppet,' he replied.

'I know a joke about ducks,' she continued and then proceeded to tell her joke. It was about a man asking a little girl if the water was deep in a ford that he was going to drive through in his expensive car, to which she replied, *'No, it's not deep.'* He then proceeds to drive through it and gets stuck halfway across in about two feet of water.

Stuck, he winds down the window and shouts to her, *'I thought you said it was not deep.'*

To which she replies, *'But it only comes halfway up the ducks!'*

Such was her age the little girl proceeded to explain the joke in case Weston did not get it. He mustered a smile and cheery reply.

'Little girl, I thought that was quackers! But a very good joke.' He smiled at her sense of achievement. Weston thought her so cute and sweet that he wanted to cuddle her but such was life today that it would be regarded as suspicious. He had reached the point where he felt he could not even enjoy watching children play or approach them for fear of being suspected of being a paedophile or pervert. That was what this modern world had become as far as he was concerned. His eyes started to moisten; a lump came into his throat. He dreaded losing control and so swiftly departed, leaving an empty bench as a silent witness to the encounter, just as the girl's mother called her and she skipped away.

He had desperately wanted to cry but found it easier to laugh, firstly at the innocent little girl's pathetic joke, then at the absurdity of the situation and lastly, and mostly, at himself. Little did Weston know that later on that day the little girl showed the opposite side of her sweet nature. As children so often do, she had learned swear words in the playground. Having learned how to swear (but not knowing the meaning of the words), hands on hips, she stood defiantly in front of her friends in a designated play area for small children. There she confronted some youths who shouldn't have been there.

'Play up your own end, you bloody bugger sods!'

It actually made the youths laugh but they did wander off.

Weston walked back to his abode. Feeling drained, he sank into his favourite armchair again and started to try to get a grip of himself, his mind focusing on Marwenna, Luke, Sarah and Louise. If nothing else, a steely determination resurrected itself in him, to not give up on himself, because he had to see this job through for their sakes. Sure, he knew maybe his days of survival were numbered, certainly at work at least, but he could still laugh at himself and more importantly hang onto the resolve of finishing things as best he could for the four of them.

'*Come on, you silly old fool,*' Susannah would have said and she would have been right, as usual, he said to himself. *Strategy: think about others, not myself.* Be thankful for what he had had in his life, Susannah and their times together. Now he had to battle. *Life will go on with or without me, but I still have things to do*, he concluded. He tried to concentrate his mind on the situation but tiredness won out and he drifted off to initially a disturbed shallow sleep which eventually gave way to a deep, soothing dream.

– THE DREAM –

In it he saw his wife who he recognised, but she was somehow different. She shone, yes, she shone and there was a young woman and man next to her who he felt he should know but could not place. The woman nodded and smiled and pointed at him while half embracing his wife. They were all smiling.

His wife's body had changed beyond superficial recognition. There was a radiance about it, yet somehow he knew totally and unquestionably it was her. He felt sure he should know the other lady and man with her but frustratingly could not connect the faces.

His wife mouthed to him with no sound, 'Go on, Edmund… go on,' and the other woman mouthed, 'Live and overcome.' He woke with a start. It was morning. Looking out the window he reflected on his dream. The latest rational explanations would be that his brain was refiling all his concerns, worries and recent events into some sort of order, or his subconscious was bubbling up related and unrelated items again in an automatic sorting process, or that merely a network of neurons and associated axons were replaying previous pathways. Even if this was the only truth, would this be how one aspect of destiny is experienced and could the physical and the ethereal relationship be so easily summed up? Was it more than the sum total of its parts, he reasoned? For one thing it was positive and not driven by fear or sense of loss unlike most of the dreams of the past. However, he was convinced that this dream was different from many others he had experienced since the loss of Susannah. How he still loved her and that would never change. He could even hear her voice urging him on to '*go find a woman to knock your socks off*' on her death bed. The dream was as if there was a whisper of certainty from somewhere unknown voicing that this was his destiny.

He tried another philosophical tack to try to reason it away. *Our essence and perceived value of being,* he argued to himself, *is so bound up with our search for a place in respect to our experience of the universe that our view is distorted in terms of proportion to it. But then,* he counterposed, *I suppose that is all we have. Whether it is the artist who insists his or her contribution is vital to contribute to the view of life or whether an expression of the spur of the moment. Oh, blast this!* he thought. *At least it is more real than the latest fashion in management gobbledygook nomenclature bullshit I normally have to put up with at work.*

He then thought of Sarah, Luke, Marwenna and Louise. Marwenna in hospital, Louise's situation. What a disaster. He could not let them down now, not after the mess he had created. Weston found his thoughts continued to return to Louise. She had been kept isolated from phones because of security of the operation, not that she really had any family or friends to contact or would be missed. Weston had money left over from the nest egg he and Susannah had been saving. With it he could finance a drying-out clinic for a short while and then maybe set her up in digs till she got herself straight. For the second time in his life Weston would become a rock. Though this old rock had been worn down by wave upon wave of pain and grief to the point where fissures had developed. This time he would become a rock to stand against the waves of pain and growth in Louise's life. Outside observers would likely speculate from a broad spectrum of possibilities as to whether this was two deep-seated needs being addressed by each other from circumstance, or whether this was a loving God that provides a way back from brokenness for both parties. Neither could be proven as the correct interpretation of this developing relationship.

He put on the heavy metal rock song about the extremes of love that Louise had kept playing and thought about her known history and how the words would have been absorbed by her psyche. Did it just reflect how she felt or was it somehow catalytic in influencing how she felt? He tried to remember how music affected him in his early teenage years and early twenties. How powerful it was or could be, the two almost fighting voices of the music illustrating the confusion in her very being. What would she become? He studied the words. Then he let the first part of the song pound through his brain over and over again to try to get at least a little into her mindset.

Poor child, he thought, for in his eyes she still was a child, never being allowed to grow up in healthy maturing relationships, ill-used and abused. He listened to the second track on the CD. But the repeated small link line changed everything: '*From brokenness can come new life.*' Could it be true for her and her future? He hoped so.

The rest of the tune and words reminded him a little of his feelings for Susannah in his youth with all the passion and mind-blowing desire of love.

> *I'm besotted, euphoric and almost psychotic with the love that I have for you. I'm ecstatic, quixotic and feeling erotic with the passion of love's full bloom.*

That takes me back! Ah, first love, in all its purest power, he reflected. By listening to the track, it enabled him to take an emotional step further back from the situation he had found himself in. His contemplations turned to long-term goals for Louise. It would be a difficult path for her to recover, but he hoped, he wished, she would get to the stage of exploring life in all its fullness. To think, she had missed out on so much, all the arts, nature, history, science and real friendships, even expectations of a family of her own.

— WESTON'S FURTHER VISIT TO LOUISE —

The next evening Weston visited Louise again. He found her in a foetal position lying on her bed in a darkened room. She had been crying but was worn out with the effort. Weston could not think of any comforting words so found a book and started to read a few pages. Eventually Louise momentarily stopped him, confessing, 'It's painful experiencing feelings again, especially ones that I would like to forget. The drink helped to numb them.'

'Do you want to talk?' asked Weston.

'No, not really, carry on if you like.'

'Books, what book would you like? Science fiction, classics, poetry, historical?'

'Romance, I liked romance, I mean I like romance.'

He started reading and after several pages she again interrupted.

'Why are you interested in me?'

Weston was initially lost for words.

'Well, my dear, you have been a victim much of your life but there is life out there that is much better than you have experienced. You can still grasp part of it and enjoy some of it. Hopefully put some of it under your own control but it will be tough, at least initially.'

Weston fingered the embroidery he always kept in his jacket pocket. Not knowing really why, he pulled it out and offered it to her. He had nothing to give save this unfinished embroidery that Susannah had been working on before she died. He had always kept it with him. Did he get comfort from it or was it a subconscious reminder that their life together felt unfinished to him?

'Taken to needlework, have we, or is this for me to do? I suppose you want your washing done as well,' said Louise bitterly adding, 'I don't do embroidery.'

'I thought that you might like it… I didn't do it… my wife did,' he said softly.

'Ah, did the little woman at home have pity for the wretched bitch you've come across at work?'

'Er, no, it's actually the last thing she worked on before she died.'

'What did she die of? Boredom?' Louise uttered still antagonistic.

'No, cancer.' He hesitated then continued, 'My wife taught me many things, especially in her final months before she died. She explained it to me this way. Some people view life as this thread here. Do you see how it comes and goes,' he traced the running stitch with his forefinger and continued, 'and meanders but seems to have no definite direction? But life for her was like the rest of this piece. See all the knots and rough bits on this side of the embroidery. They represent the pain and problems we encounter in our lives. But when you turn it over.' Louise then saw a beautiful picture. 'This is the pattern that God sees and we will see one day, at least that was what she believed.'

Louise was stunned, partly by the gift and partly by the explanation. She remained silent for quite some time.

'I'm sorry for what I said. When did she die?'

'Two years, five months and twenty-two days ago.'

'You must miss her.' He just nodded at first but partly trying to cover his awkward silence and partly to engage her.

'Yes, but I carry on, I breathe in and out, I work, I eat, I sleep and then there's always the challenge of tasting a new real ale, stout or cider.' He smiled as he said the latter statement.

'Turn over that old vinyl version of the CD you have been playing. It's just like this embroidery, there are other sides of life, and love.'

Louise had long forgotten about the other side which had increasingly become irrelevant. Never good at philosophy, it was all Weston felt he had to offer at that time.

With each visit the pair relaxed a little more in each other's company and Louise began to look forward to Weston reading to her. It was a welcome interruption to the abstinence from alcohol. Louise, just for something to do and to while away the time, had started to learn embroidery. Occasionally she would take out Weston's gift of Susannah's embroidery and think about what was said concerning it. Doing this helped her through some tough times on her own.

Weston became very much aware of her withdrawal symptoms and the fight she was enduring, keeping a careful watch for signs of self-harm. With this in mind he brought her a little devil figure.

'Susannah, my wife, had this in her room when she was in the hospice. It represented her pain but she threw it away a few days close to the end. I fished it out while she wasn't looking, I'm not quite sure why. Maybe,' he hesitated, 'I don't know,' then continued, 'some fight pain, some endure it, some embrace it. I think at various times she tried all three. But I do know she overcame and had a peace that I've never known.'

Whenever they met, the ritual of reading, around which conversation gradually grew, suited them both as they reached out in their separate ways via a comfortable format. Louise settled back at ease, experiencing a new sensation for her. When he read to her, she found his voice somehow soothing and comforting. For the first time in her life she felt really secure. Perhaps he was the father and grandfather she never had. He was old, quiet, reassuring, unthreatening, yet with an understated openness. She knew there was nothing he wanted from her, or for that matter anything else she needed to hold back from him. He knew it all, her shame, her addiction, much of her past. For him, not through his design, but by happenstance, she could have been the grown-up daughter he never had. He may have missed the rebellious teenage years but she may yet put him through the parental emotional ringer a tad as their relationship grew.

– AFTER THE FUNERALS –

'How do you cope?' Ayesha asked Martha.

'Well, I'll miss him of course, and life will never be the same without my other half. It is and will be painful but I'm open to God's comfort and will just have to see what God has in store for me in future. Our parishioners have been brilliant in support and with help concerning the funeral. Practically, it's a choice between trying to use routine at home or taking a little break. I've decided on the latter. I'm going to a place called St Julian's for a week or so, to take stock, but I'm sure it is too early to make any serious decisions. You are welcome to join me, if you like. And you, how are you coping?'

'It's great having family around but sometimes I just need to be alone. The mosque has been brilliant but I feel I've lost a little bit of my identity, I'm now Mo's widow, not quite Ayesha in her own right anymore. Bits of me are missing. A huge chunk belonged to Mo. I will have to rethink my role in life as well as coming to terms with life without Mo.'

'Actually, Ayesha, you've caused me to rethink. What do you say to finishing what Peter and Mo started? In our own right. We both believe in what they were doing. What about organising and finishing the symposium that our men could not complete?'

'That's a great idea.'

'Then I'll put my break on hold.'

– NEVER FORGOTTEN –

In the early months after Susannah's death, if Weston did take a break, he would often visit the places they had gone on holiday together. At the end of these mini-breaks he always visited the graves of his wife and children. This was in addition to his regular visits to the graveside. As he stood there on this occasion a council worker who was hoeing nearby turned on a radio. A gentle lullaby rose into the air.

Whenever Weston visited Susannah's grave, he spent some of the time thinking about their children as he did about her. Their remains were buried next to her. He pondered on what might have been. How old would they be now? Would they have had successful careers and had a family? Would he be a grandfather bouncing children on his knee? He remembered some of the protective thoughts and feelings he had experienced from the very moments he had held them for the first time. Sadly, the concerns and cares of parenthood were all too short for them both. So much emotion and love had been wrapped up in those little bundles of joy soon to be taken from them. Years later Susannah once said she saw them surrounded by a loving gold radiance but Weston never registered or experienced such a dream or vision. For him there was little solace. The radio music played with his memories and heart.

He whispered to his children's grave, 'This time, Rhyian Wilson Aethelflaed and Harold Cedda, I'm looking at the future which should have been yours, not the past. I'll try and live it for all of us. For you and Mummy. There is a young woman in trouble and as your mother would say but for the grace of God you or she could have been. I'll do my best to help her. Goodbye, all, for now. I love you.'

DOODLES OF A PARENT[19]

When I held you in my arms
My new-born precious child
O the sanctity of life
The wonder of it all
As I looked at you each night
Heard your snuffles and your cries
Shared your discoveries of life
Its beauty through your eyes.

Hugs for tears, tickles for fears, twitches while dreaming
Nightmare frights, pillow fights, goodies and baddies.
Times you're sick, hide and seek, you're Superman.

Imaginary friends, paper aeroplanes, silly jokes and songs.
Heroic deeds are read when it's time for bed after chats and prayers.

You make me laugh
You make me cry
Make me see the reasons why
There's so much joy in the gift of life.

---

19 A song with twelve-string guitar and flute

You're still so innocent
Unspoilt by life's events
I'll never stop loving you.

As you progress through your teens
Peer group pressures, new feelings.
Puberty you'll undergo
And you'll question status quo.
Examinations they now loom
Sanctuary sought in your bedroom.
New responsibilities and chores
Idols, friends, views to the fore.

Making sense of life, spawns internal strife, causes confusion.
Over-confidence, yet self-doubt descends, emotions they seesaw.

I'll teach you right from wrong. Help you grow up strong, an independent man.
Mark a place of constancy, a reference in your sea of swinging emotions.

There's so much danger now around
Perverts, drugs and cults abound.
My fears I have to keep in check

Time to do time to be
Growing naturally.
I'll never stop loving you.

Dancing Into Danger

Career, life choices need to make
Learn from successes and mistakes.
New relationships and roles
Enjoy the journey to your goals.
Learn how messy life can be
Gone the childhood certainties.
More responsibilities
Now to adult you are grown.

To overcome, to be at one, the continual challenge
To give your worth, to keep life's thirst
till life is all over.

Embrace life while you can, and try to understand, appreciate
the good times.
Trials you'll need to overcome, your limits discerned, learn all
you can from them.

To find your niche, to find true friends
To find your way in the world of men.

To make your mark, decide your path
Enjoy your life before it's passed
To meet with God and know yourself.

While your working life through
Don't lose the child inside
I'll never stop loving you.

OUT OF THE FRYING PAN

Sarah's barely conscious body clawed its way to the surface in the fast-flowing tidal waters of the Thames. Both hers and her adversary's heads had just caught a glancing blow from the bridge bastion as they fell and disappeared from view. Fortunately for Sarah the main impact was taken by her opponent's skull which had made the direct contact with the bastion before clashing with Sarah's.

As she travelled down the river she drifted in and out of consciousness, the cold shock of the water leaving her numb and hyperventilating, the weight of her clothes pulling her down. In her remaining brief conscious moments, she just managed to half clamber onto some driftwood, her torso and head above the water on the wood, her legs and feet immersed in the water. She then blacked out. The cold and her now relaxed state eased the blood flow of her head wound considerably. At the mercy of the current she drifted for quite a while.

Downstream a large motor sailing vessel was moored close to some barges, its mast secured away. In the blackness of the night, shapes of a couple of men could just be made out. They appeared to be surreptitiously moving boxes from a barge to the boat. A third shape at the other end of the boat stood with boat hook in hand acting as lookout and retriever should any boxes get spilled. He glanced down and spotted what he thought was a dropped package, pulling it in with the boat hook. As he reached down to lift the supposed package, he realised it was a woman. He did not know what made him do it when logic dictated to leave well alone, to avoid detection and complications, but something instinctive from his gentle nature took over. Lifting Sarah aboard he checked for a pulse and for breathing as the driftwood continued on its journey. Then very quickly and quietly he secreted her in the cabin below, placing her in the recovery position and putting some blankets around her to gradually warm her. Back to his post in a jiffy he continued his duty. In the back of his mind he considered her plight; the possible shock and hypothermia she may have undergone were his biggest concern, yet he was still vigilant in his task.

Once their loading had been completed, they weighed anchor, quickly changing the name and number of the boat as they raised the mast. They began slowly moving down river to the open sea. Just past Purfleet, Bert, the billhook operative, approached his skipper to tell him what he had found.

'Bert, you wally! You know we don't need complications as it is. What are we going to do with her?' The captain was very well spoken whereas Bert had a London East End accent reminiscent of a previous Cockney generation, which made their unlikely pairing strange to say the least. They had often 'borrowed on a permanent basis' but sparingly so as not to draw too much attention concerning their thefts.

'I'm sorry, skip, I just couldn't leave her. Me daughters aren't much younger than her. We could leave her at a hospital or something. She's been unconscious all the time and hasn't seen any of us or the boat or nothing from the journey.'

'OK, OK, once we are docked you can take her in the car and leave her at a hospital. Borrow a wheelchair to take her in but make sure you are not picked up by security cameras and asked any awkward questions. I'll tell Chalky.' Bert could hear Chalky's reaction.

'What an absolute plonker!' he exclaimed.

The captain placated Chalky who gave Bert a filthy look when he eventually left the boat the following day.

'We'll load the van and then go on to the store. It's probably a suicide attempt, the poor mite,' surmised the captain.

'I don't think so, skip, as she was half on some driftwood.'

'Maybe she changed her mind.'

'You could be right but I dunno, there's something about her that doesn't fit.'

The skipper knew well to trust Bert's instincts. They sailed around part of Kent, hugging the coast through much of the night, slowly so as not to attract attention. Bert stayed with her most of the time and occasionally the captain popped in to see if anything had changed. Even though she had a massive bump on her head and quite a few bruises the captain thought her very attractive, perhaps because of her vulnerability. *Maybe another place, another time and another lifetime*, he thought. Her hands were still clenched whether from the cold or the struggle but as Bert started to rub her hands, one of them opened and in it was a locket and chain. The captain stared at the locket not quite believing what he saw. He recognised it immediately and examined it very closely. His face and demeanour changed markedly.

'Keep her safe, Bert, I need to know what happened and where she got that jewellery from.'

'She could have gotten that anywhere.'

'No, not this piece. I'm sure it is unique.'

'But I thought you said to drop her off at a hospital, leaving a false name and address.'

'Yes, well I've changed my mind. But she won't be able to stay here on the boat. Any ideas?' Bert wracked his brain as he looked at the wrapped-up Sarah who gradually drifted in and out of consciousness into a restless, deep sleep. Then he noticed the dove necklace she was wearing. It reminded him of something. His sister had one just like it.

'Me sister might be able to help.'

'What makes you say that?'

'I think that dove represents the Holy Spirit which means that this girl could be a Christian. My sister has got one similar and her situation may prove very convenient. She lives in a Christian community of women in Sussex not too far from the coast. It's unlikely that questions will be asked 'cos they don't have telly or nothing. More to the point my sister trusts me. They do have guests there on a regular basis too, though they tend to be paying ones, not personal guests, mind, like Flo will be, but I'm sure she could look after her for a while with not too many questions.'

'Flo?' exclaimed the captain quizzically.

'We've got to call her something till she wakes. So, I thought Flo, short for flotsam.'

'How are we going to move her without her knowing too much about us?' asked the captain.

'We can't really blindfold her as she's been through a lot as it is,' ventured Bert then turning to the captain added, 'I know, we'll move her at night.'

'Can you fix it with your sister in the meantime?'

'No worries, skip.'

Sarah slept for some time. Eventually she did rouse. The rhythmic throb of the boat's engine was soothing as was its gentle rocking. Bert looked in again on his new charge.

'Ah, you're awake. We dragged you out of the river, luv. What's yer name?'

'I am... my name is... I don't know... I can't remember.' Her hesitation, frustration and fear grew greater with each utterance.

'Can you remember anything?'

Her voice trembled at the realisation. 'I don't remember anything.'

She felt strange, frustrated, panicky as she struggled to remember.

'Don't worry, luv, you're safe, looks like you had a nasty bump on the head. Tell you what, I'll call you Flo for now, till you remember your name. Short for flotsam 'cos we pulled you out of the drink, see. Speaking of which, like some tea?'

As soon as Bert told the captain that Flo was awake, he slipped into the darkened cabin but ensured he stayed in the shadows as he did not want two people she could recognise again.

'Where did you get this?' he asked quietly, presenting the locket and giving nothing away of his initial shock at seeing it.

'I… I … don't know… I can't remember.'

'She don't remember nothin', skip, not even her name,' said Bert trying to ease any further anxiety or pressure Sarah might be experiencing when attempting to answer.

'Don't worry, luv, you're still safe but we will need to take you somewhere safer, see,' added Bert reassuringly.

'Are you a Christian?' asked the captain.

'Am I what? I'm not sure. Am I?'

'Well, your necklace indicates you are,' he further stated and then, deciding that he was getting nowhere with his questioning, looked across to Bert.

'Don't worry. Your memory will come back in its own good time. Get some more sleep. I know someone who is a Christian too and she will help you,' he stated, assuming his sister would readily comply. 'We'll take you to her. You'll be safe there. It's just that you can't stay here, luv, as this is a working boat see, and well… what we do is… well… is covert, shall we say. It'll take a day or two depending on tides,' Bert offered, doing his best to reassure her, sensing her growing confusion and fear. 'I'm afraid we've only got some old clothes that obviously won't fit properly if you want to get out of your wet things.'

Bert and the captain left and she donned the ill-fitting clothes which were dry and warm. She felt exhausted and drifted off to sleep knowing only for certain that the mate was very kind to her and that she felt safe with him. After the dispensing of their main cargo and dropping off the rest of it, Bert left a telephone message for his sister at the community and arranged to be at a public telephone box at a set time for her to call back. In the meantime, he purchased some cheap jeans and a T-shirt for Sarah. In her phoned reply, his sister Margaret confirmed that she would look after Flo. Bert reported the outcome back to the captain.

The captain stated, 'Then it's settled. We'll anchor off Worthing and you can drop her off to your sister at St Julian's in Coolham.'

During the voyage the captain and Bert kept monitoring the national and local news to see if anything had been reported about missing people, particularly with respect to the terrorist incident, as they sailed further along the coast. They pondered whether she could have been a victim of the tube bombing, but couldn't come up with a plausible explanation of how she ended up in the Thames, plus the fact that after a day of the latest bulletins on the bombing there were no reports of missing people. Then there was the locket in her hand. The captain was desperate for an explanation of that.

Quite late the next morning Sarah awoke to the smell of food cooking.

'There's nothing like an English breakfast to build your strength up,' Bert shouted to Sarah as he made a fry-up. She ate heartily.

'Well, at least there's nothing wrong with your appetite,' he exclaimed, taking the empty plate away.

Sarah stayed on the boat for a day and a half not knowing who she was or how she had got there, apart from what the mate had told her. They eventually moored off Worthing, the winter swell subsiding. The weather was very cold but had been good for that time of year, particularly when the wind dropped.

The gentle lapping of the wavelets against the side of the boat and its even gentler rocking had a calming and comforting effect on Sarah as she waited for Bert to take her to wherever it was that was safer. Though he was a rough and ready sort of character, and from his lined face appeared to have had a tough life, there was something reassuring about his cheery, caring nature. As for the captain, he kept himself to himself but was polite enough when he went to the cabin. The early darkness of a winter evening beckoned their departure.

'It's tonight then?' asked Sarah.

'Yes, but before then, I'll put to shore to get the newspapers and stores.'

She had watched the cargo ships in the distance sail by during the day and occasionally a few small yachts manoeuvring close to shore, the enthusiasts of which were practising their tacking skills. As dusk turned to twilight the first stars appeared in the cloudless winter sky and the newly switched-on cargo ships' lights and shoreline property lights mirrored their twinkling in the hoary air.

Bert finally took her in the skiff to shore and they drove off in a van into the night, heading north.

– ALL AT SEA –

The captain was a very private man who chose, or maybe felt forced, to live on the edge of society. Amongst those he associated with, no one knew quite for sure why. It had never been discussed. Nor were questions raised by the occasional extra casual crew member as to how the captain and Bert had met, but at various times they had noticed an unusually strong bond between the two of them. It was as if they shared some secret or tie which locked them together, even though they seemed an unlikely team to the casual observer.

The captain was a quiet, withdrawn man and fairly easy going but was very tough when he had to be. He was in his mid-thirties unlike Bert, his mate, who was in his fifties. To an outsider the captain looked after his ageing mate and provided him with some form of job security and the mate protected the captain from unwanted attention, particularly when the captain was in one of his black moods. He would then retreat to his cabin with several bottles of beer or spirit.

– SIBLING STRINGS –

Margaret met Bert and Sarah at the end of the drive and walked them back in the dark using a powerful torch to her very small cottage in the extensive grounds. Fortunately, Margaret was of similar size to Sarah so could lend her some clothes, albeit not at all fashionable for someone of Sarah's age. She first of all made Sarah very comfortable and ensured Sarah was safely tucked up in bed on a spare put-you-up, before turning to Bert for greater explanation.

He tried initially lying to Margaret but, being his sister, she saw through him straight away. She looked at him in a quizzical and doubting way not used since their childhood days when, even then, she knew if he was prevaricating in order to dream up some little white lie.

'You said on the phone she might be in some kind of trouble. Why didn't you take her to the authorities?'

'We fished her out of the drink. She doesn't know who she is and I think she might be in some kind of trouble or danger, sis. Can you put her up for a while? Please.'

'Why here?'

'I thought of you because of her necklace and she is safe with you. Doing Christian fings might jog her memory. My boss needs to know more about her and he'll pay for her upkeep at least for a month if need be.'

'That won't be necessary.'

– DISCOVERING –

The next morning after a long sleep and a healthy breakfast Margaret suggested they walk through the grounds as she described the nature and routine of St Julian's. She started by stating, 'Please don't ask any questions about the man who brought you here. I won't lie but I would refuse to talk about him as he is someone dear to me and I suspect he may be in trouble if you name him. Feel free to wander round the garden or punt on the lake, or you can help me with the gardening if you want or just enjoy the peace and quiet.' She continued, 'I'd better tell you about our community and its running. This is called St Julian's, named after a Sussex saint, and it was founded by Florence Allshorn. We are a small community of Christian women and we offer stays for people needing respite from their daily lives. There are sixteen rooms in the main house and we can look after up to twenty-three guests.'

Sarah discovered over the week that for guests, breakfast trays were left outside their rooms in the morning. At lunch and dinner, book rests were provided as no talking was allowed at meal times. It was the only rule that guests had to adhere to. Afternoon tea and cakes was the time if people wanted to socialise and guests would optionally abandon their studying, walking or reading for polite chit-chat. Nothing else was mandatory. Sarah ate in Margaret's cottage for most of her stay to avoid awkward questions.

After the gentle walk together, Margaret went to her duties and Sarah found herself back in the very small cottage in the grounds of an extensive wooded garden with a lake close by a large house. The lake and grounds backed onto fields. There were one or two small cottages in the grounds. The community looked on serving their paying guests as part of their vocation. Some of the community lived in the small cottages while the others lived in the main house. Paying guests, who tended to be clergy or missionaries, stayed there recharging their batteries and recovering from the rigours of the world. There were, however, on occasions, others such as teachers and youth workers, and a few recovering from crises in their personal lives. It was a chance for them to read, to contemplate, to listen and to enjoy company when it suited them and was congenial to do so. Guests were asked not to use mobile phones unless it was an emergency and all seemed more than happy to comply. There was one landline telephone used for business by the community but most of them chose not to own a mobile and would walk to the phone box at the crossroads if they needed to make a personal call. Wednesday evening was the social highlight of the week when the ladies of the community dressed up in their best dress to sit and listen to classical gramophone records. There was no radio or television but there were broadsheet papers in the library together with nature and Christian magazines.

At first Sarah stayed close to the confines of the cottage where she would enjoy short walks to the lake but as she felt her strength return, she explored. She found a little boathouse with one punt in it but the weather was much too cold to use it. She also discovered a wooden chapel not much bigger than a longish shed. This had a glass end wall that looked out onto a pond that adjoined one end of the lake. A highly polished, pine wood, uneven table with two candles was placed in front of the glass wall. Above this hung from the apex of the roof a transparent cross. There were about five rows of four or five old wooden chairs separated in the middle by an aisle, and straw was laid on the ground save at the table end. It was always open and people could go there any time of day and sit and look out or contemplate or pray or just enjoy the silence. Twice a day a short service was held in there for about ten to fifteen minutes. These were always announced by a half-minute small bell ring to remind those who wished to attend.

Sarah asked Margaret about the short services.

'Someone of your generation may struggle with the words but by all means come along.'

She did decide to go to one or two of the short evening services where compline was sung or said. When they were sung, always in plainsong, she felt the urge to slowly sway with the music. She did not know quite why. This she confessed to Margaret after one compline. Margaret thought for a while and suggested Sarah go with it next time and see where the movement took her. Sarah did find the language of compline unfamiliar. Indeed, had she remembered who she was and her personal history, it was an entirely different experience of church to what she was used to. Her own church experience, before her memory loss, tended to be for the most part very lively with choruses, drama and of course dance. However, she did find compline comforting, even though the words seemed archaic and hard to understand. There was a reassurance in the ritual, that it had continually been going on for many years and there was a peace there too.

'We might have something more in your line at the local church on Sunday if you are interested. There's a travelling group of Christians from Brazil sharing their worship experience.'

'Sounds interesting,' replied Sarah. Sarah enjoyed the conversations she had with Margaret. 'Your life seems idyllic. You seem to have all the answers here.'

'Far from it.'

'Margaret, do you mind me asking you, what do you do in your devotions?' Sarah enquired.

'My quiet times? Oh, well, I quiet myself down on my own. If it's nice weather, somewhere outside that's out of the way in the grounds, where I can't be disturbed. If it's inclement weather, then either in my bedroom or the chapel. Here I will read a small passage of the Bible and meditate on one verse of it. Sometimes I use notes, say from Scripture Union for example, to help me understand the context. Or, having read a passage I might meditate on some aspect of creation to see what I can learn of God from it. A bit like trying to understand the artist from one of his or her paintings, I suppose.'

She continued, 'At the moment I'm using *Living Light*[20]. I pray, which obviously involves praise, requests, listening, confessing, waiting and thanks. Aside from this I study. I've set my own little prayer rota up too, which is fairly flexible. For instance, Monday might be mainly some aspect of world affairs. Tuesday might be for some of the local folk. I always try to set it so that my focus is on international, national, local, close and casual relationships and of course personal issues over the course of a week. Sometimes I might fast. You see the discipline is there but there is flexibility. Besides, it isn't all plain sailing. Sometimes it's tough to pray, or to wait, or to believe. Then there are always the tricky doctrines to wrestle with or the personal struggles on issues to surrender to God!'

'Wow, it sounds complicated.'

'Not really, at the end of the day, life is simple, messy but simple, and we make it more complicated than it really is.'

'Are you struggling with anything at the moment?'

'Yes, quite a few things actually. My perception of some aspects of life. I have a tendency to look on the gloomy side to

---

20   ISBN 0 902088 79 3 Coverdale House

the point where my perceptions almost totally mask reality. I hesitate to generalise and use labels because that is inaccurate and unfair, but you'll get my drift.' She took a deep breath. 'Firstly, as the world moves on, supposedly progressing it recreates old problems under new labels either through poor stewardship, like pollution, the excesses of commerce and political systems as well as personal thoughtlessness, selfishness and greed. People making more money than they need and not thinking through the consequences of their pursuit of more profit. By our lifestyles we seem to be increasing the volume of illnesses. The waste of resources due to war and the suffering it causes. Man's, or woman's for that matter, inhumanity to humankind. I have a friend who often says if women ruled the world there would be no wars. I have to remind her about the behaviour of some on a big sale day!

'Secondly, as the world moves on, particularly in England, we Christians are becoming increasingly marginalised. At best, we appear an amusing niche, the innocent, ineffective and bumbling vicar in a play. Sometimes at the opposite extreme as a dangerous, narrow-minded, right-wing bigot, out of touch, or a redundant organisation that tries to browbeat and judge the world. Internationally there is a lot of persecution too, particularly in the Middle East, which goes underreported.

'Thirdly, I am struggling with the Church's various ethical and belief stances on homosexuality, transgender and detransitioning issues. On a personal level it isn't really a problem. I accept people at whatever stage they are in their life and with God's help try to love them just as I try to love myself. I know that God has a purpose for them just as he has one for me and I try never to condemn anyone as I am not a perfect person myself.' She paused and raised her hand in a pointing gesture.

'I always think that any hand with a pointed accusing finger actually always has three pointing back! And of course, there are the verses about the beam and splinter in eyes.

'I and they are, after all, loved by God equally. Thankfully, the friends I have that happen to be homosexual or lesbian are very loving, supportive and understanding of my quandary. Yet scripture seems to condemn the act. One of my favourite verses from Psalm 139 is that we are respectfully and wonderfully made knitted together in the womb. Thinking about it with my very limited scientific knowledge, there is a lot to be said about the amount of testosterone in the womb and maybe even the temperature at conception. Are there specific genes or gene associations? Is it a moral, biological or lifestyle choice? A bridge not crossed into adulthood? All these theories that experts put forward or argue about. I have to leave it with God and may never come to a conclusion. All I know is that I love my friends dearly and that we will all have to answer to God. It is a little upsetting what one prominent homosexual said, though, and that was that he was at war with the Christian Church.' Margaret paused, surprised at herself for talking so much.

'Gosh, I'll get off my soap box now.' She laughed and added, 'Just as well God gave me a sense of humour so that I can laugh and not take myself too seriously. In the meantime, I think we need to sort you out a better bra or as my mother used to say "over-shoulder-boulder-holder". Which of the four types do you fancy?'

'Four types?'

'Yes, you know, which of the four religious types do you want?'

'Religious types?'

'Yes, Catholic, Salvation Army, Presbyterian or Baptist?'

'Sorry, I don't follow.'

'Catholic supports the masses, Salvationist lifts the fallen, Presbyterian keeps them staunch and upright and Baptist makes mountains out of molehills,' Margaret stated while giggling.

Throughout the week Sarah gradually discovered who the other guests were, mainly as they sometimes chatted to her, assuming that she was part of the community, while she was helping out with the gardening. There were a very elderly missionary brother and sister. Both were small in stature. The sister, who was also very thin and looked very fragile, surprised Sarah greatly when she described doing all the mechanics on their Land Rover when in Africa. Each guest that did stop to chat always had something interesting to say. There was a lady youth worker who worked with autistic children from the East End of London, a doctor from Twickenham who had worked in India but had to come home due to some malaise he had caught there, a middle-class vicar from a middle-of-the-road to high church background keen on opera, a young youth leader still a little wet behind the ears, and a woman who was recovering from the devastation and shock of a sudden separation and divorce after twenty-two years of marriage. The latter was not up to much conversation but would enjoy walking in the gardens. A few days in, Sarah ventured into the library and browsed the books, finding one on dance in worship that, though she was not sure why, appealed to her.

– THE CAPTAIN –

The captain, for the most part, engaged in low-profit legitimate work but when the opportunity arose to hit at the Corporation, he was keen to partake in a little 'iffy borrowing'. This thieving was only ever against the Corporation, such was his enmity against it. He always made sure that the thefts were never that great so as to remain under the radar. This property loss would cause no great concern or warrant investigation.

The news blackout of the bridge incident had lasted a couple days before the national press and media eventually broke the news that a man's body had been discovered in suspicious circumstances on Blackfriars Bridge and that a woman's body had been washed up in the river estuary. The identification of both was being established but it was thought that they may have worked for the same company and there was speculation that it was a relationship that had had fatal consequences. The captain was shocked when he saw the picture of Ruby, taken several years previously, broadcast on the main news. He read and reread the later article in *The Times* concerning her and the circumstances of her body being found. The same body that he had cherished and had known well. Bert had watched him turn white and stare at the picture of the dead woman as it was flashed up onto the screen and she was named. It was she who had engineered the captain's downfall into the twilight world he now inhabited. It was he who had given Ruby the locket.

Now she was dead he was free, but he needed to know what had happened, still not quite believing she was gone. In spite of all she had done to him, up to this moment there was still a part of him that had never stopped loving her. Now their dark secret that had kept him from moving on had died with her. For him, the woman he had fallen in love with, who had ill-used him, ruined him and his reputation, was now a spectre from the past. Yes, he had tried, somewhat unsuccessfully to rebuild his life but the wound had always festered, having never really healed. Now at least it was a final closure of a sort. Now he was free from the half-life existence he'd been living. Now the main catalyst for his bitterness and attempts at payback to the Corporation was dead. He still would hold the Corporation to account, or rather the director he strongly suspected who had helped crush him.

Bert and the captain had a strong unspoken bond between them. The captain, though younger than Bert, had taken the older man under his wing when he was on his downers. He had spotted straight away that Bert was at his lowest ebb in life to the point of being desperate enough to commit suicide. Nothing was ever said between them, or indeed about them that gave a hint to their strange, unusual bond, but some folk with similar stories to tell could recognise something in that bond.

Bert had been struggling very badly when finding it difficult to adjust to civilian life after leaving the army. In the army, the rules of responsibility were definite and fixed for the most part, though creative thinking and initiative were encouraged and rewarded. In civvy street, life seemed far more fluid to Bert and he initially found it hard to adapt.

Bert loved his wife and family very much and wanted to provide for them but his failure to cope was exacerbated by how well his wife was seemingly able to cope and the allowances his family were happy to make on his behalf. This, magnified by the desperation and the sense of guilt he had about it, had locked him into a sort of reinforcing negative set of feelings and thought processes. His family were brilliant, but what he had really needed was specialist help, which was just not available at that time. The support structure was not in place during that decade he left.

It was no coincidence that the rate of ex-soldiers becoming gentlemen of the road or committing suicide was quite high. Many just did not want to leave the army and when they did, it proved too hard a change. It was like a bereavement really. There was the loss of friends, the importance of the role they had played, the regularity of the environment even though situations were varied. The whole regimental family backup just seemed to disappear overnight, and of course, pride on his part for being useful as part of a team and needed. His sense of self-worth and pride took a major blow.

Likewise, Bert had recognised that occasionally the captain would suffer from some form of permanent emotional wound, shut himself away and hit the bottle. Bert never presumed to ask why, as the captain was protective of his privacy. Such was the nature of their relationship that sometimes occurs between men, their bond didn't need to be vocalised.

The captain, again from habit, retired to his cabin with a whisky bottle, one minute quietly laughing, another crying to himself, enduring perhaps for the last time the grinding mill of pain cutting deep into his gut. Burt, his loyal mate, ensured that he would not be disturbed.

– GOODBYE TO THE OLD, HELLO TO THE NEW –

After an hour, unusually early, the captain emerged from the cabin and asked Bert to join him and started to toast.

'To John Cadbury, Joseph Chamberlain and Robert Owen.'

'Who?' said Bert, knowing that the toasting stage allowed the captain to tend to show off his knowledge, probably making up for his feeling of inadequacy after his ruination. This would progress to the next stage of keen socialising and finally Bert would have to put him to bed. Bert found it difficult when the captain got philosophical.

'We celebrate what they did for the common man, woman and child in their separate ways, Bert!' He took a swift gulp of spirit. 'To Thomas Paine for his common sense influence on the American Constitution and the French Revolution. Bert, come and join me in toasting. You know I hate drinking alone.' Bert took a very small measure in a glass. The captain had already ignored Bert's last question. 'To Jill Saward for what she did for rape victims and women's rights in law.'

'You always toast people I've never heard of,' said Bert. He continued, 'I'd prefer to toast my old regiment, the Royal Green Jackets or my dad's regiment, the King's Royal Rifles, if it's all the same to you.'

'But they don't exist anymore, Bert.'

'They still do in The Rifles.'

'Of course, Bert, to all three!' They downed the sixth of a gill. 'The Tolpuddle Martyrs and what they did for the working man.'

'Now you're showing off.' They quaffed another snort together.

'Alright then, to Mary Seacole and Florence Nightingale! I'm sure you've heard of them, Bert. For what they did for nursing in their different ways.'

'Aye, captain, a belt to them.'

'Bert, you know that work is the curse of the drinking classes, don't you?' he added, starting to laugh and continued, 'You know, Bert, I drink to make other people seem more interesting.'

'Oh, thanks very much, I'm sure! Well, in that case here's to the biggest fishing fleet in the world in 1850.' The captain looked quizzically at Bert. 'It was based in Barking and my ancestors were part of it.' They downed another sixth of a gill.

'Well, I didn't know about that, Bert. Do you know, Bert, we English applaud and celebrate the Scots, the Welsh and Irish cultures with them but what of our own eh, Bert, what of our own? I bet your son and daughters don't know any English folk songs or dances. Oh, sure, they'll know Shakespeare and Dickens and maybe the odd bit of poetry but what of the English heroes? Like every nation, we do have things to be ashamed of. You know, like the suppression of speaking Welsh in the early 1900s but at least in most cases we admit it and apologise and repair where we can. We're not like those countries who deny their bad history or conveniently cover it up because of loss of face or whatever.'

At this point the captain started to spill a little of his drink as he waved his glass around drunkenly philosophising.

'Going back to my original point, Bert, have any of your kids heard of the Battle of Brunanburh?'

'Well, no, but I haven't heard of it either. Why should they know about it?'

'As usual, Bert, I shall need to explain.'

'As usual, you are getting steadily drunk, skip!'

'A drunk's words are a sober man's thoughts, Bert.'

'Aye, sometimes, I grant you.'

He became less coherent as the drink took effect. He struggled to express his final attempted toast.

'To oblivion, nirvana, reincarnation, heaven or paradise, whichever you prefer.' With that the captain started to drift into a drunken sleep. Bert removed the half-drunk glass and associated bottle and then put a cover over him on his bed like he had always done.

When the captain awoke the next day, he took a huge lungful of air and stretched. Bert noticed that there was something different about him. He didn't take long to recover from his mild hangover and there was a smile on his face Bert had never seen before. There was a lightness in his demeanour too, as if a load had been lifted. Perhaps a new purpose was kindling in his soul.

The captain announced with one less deep furrow on his brow, 'Bert, I'm going for a sail, this time for pleasure, are you coming?' As they readied the boat he added, 'You know, Bert, some days you can feel like the pigeon and some days you can feel like the statue.'

'And what do you feel like today? As if I didn't know.'

'To be honest, Bert, I'm not sure, maybe a little of both. Actually, thinking about it, this pigeon is going to fly away.'

As the skipper was in such a rare good mood, Bert took the opportunity to enquire, a little hesitantly, 'I've never asked before but I've always wondered, why did you stop and talk to me when I was on the bridge?'

'Well, I spotted the signs of you being ex-military. Your bearing and stance gave it away. Figured you were having a tough time adapting. You see, my great-grandfather served in World War I as a rifleman in the 18th Battalion King's Royal Rifles. He suffered from what was then known as shell shock and underwent experimental electric shock therapy at Colney Hatch. He was so bad he was only allowed home four days a year and when at home he kept falling out of bed. It affected his children considerably, my grandmother particularly and in turn her daughter, my mother. Besides it was the decent thing to do. I couldn't have you polluting the river, now could I?'

Bert briefly revisited his own dark days and remembered how he had hit rock bottom, thinking to end it all and not be a burden to his family anymore. Since then, he had often marvelled and wondered how Edna had managed to stick by him and cope with the family at the same time in the way that she did. How he was now grateful to live, and to see his family grow up and still be part of it. Bert, by nature, had always been a kind-hearted man and due to his upbringing, opportunities and schooling, had taken a simple outlook on life. Now, although involved in occasional dodgy dealing, at least he could put food on the table, provide and strive to ensure his kids had a better chance to grasp opportunities that were not available to him when he was growing up. What loving parent wouldn't want the same opportunities for their children?

– CONCERN AND LOVE ALWAYS FOLLOW UP –

Sarah's pastor contacted Luke to see how he was getting on and if there had been any new developments. They talked a lot about Sarah, and Luke took the opportunity to confide about his earlier judgement on the prayer group.

'It's perfectly understandable given the circumstances. Just keep those verses in mind and we will continue to pray,' stated the pastor at the end of their conversation.

— MUSCLE MEMORY TO THE RESCUE! —

Margaret hurried back to the cottage during her break to find Sarah pottering through the chores she had set herself. Sarah saw Margaret's excitement.

'What's going on?'

'Remember that there is a Brazilian Christian samba group visiting our nearest local church tomorrow! We've never had that before. All of us in the community that are off duty are going. Well, I've just learned I can go as I'm off duty all day! Why don't you come? It's a once-in-a-lifetime treat for us.'

Sunday came quickly enough and the two of them arrived a little late but managed to squeeze in by standing at the back of the church, which was crowded. The Brazilian leader explained what a Batucada samba was and how they had adapted one from street parade music to worship, making more of a subtle song in the process, but still with only percussion instruments to accompany the voice melody line. After a few bars of music Sarah felt compelled to move with the beat and as the singing began, she felt an even stronger urge to dance. Margaret sensed Sarah holding back so encouraged her by also moving as best she could with the music, after all they were at the back of the church and no one was watching.[21]

After the service Margaret asked as they walked back to her cottage, 'Are you a dancer, Flo?'

'Oh, sure I used to dance a lot at our church.' Both Margaret and Sarah stopped in their tracks. Some memory had returned. It felt right, it felt natural.

'I can remember moving like this before.' Sarah fought hard to remember. 'I do dance, I love it, my name,' she hesitated

---

21 'Echoes from the Psalms' – samba with drum set, percussion and voices

trying so hard to search her mind, 'my name, it's Sarah.' She started to get excited. They began walking again but hesitated whenever Sarah could recall something else. Finally, just outside the cottage, Sarah turned and looked at Margaret.

'Luke, I love Luke.'

'Take your time… Sarah,' replied Margaret offering a comforting hand on Sarah's shoulder.

'Luke was in danger. There was a struggle. Is Luke alright?' she asked panicking, her memory returning piecemeal.

'Let's go in, sit down with a cup of tea, take time to remember and then I will contact my brother to see if he knows any of the outcome.' Margaret in the excitement had inadvertently let slip who had brought Sarah to her.

'It was your brother who saved me then?'

'Yes, please don't give him away as I suspect he'll be in trouble.'

'No, I won't but would he know what happened to Luke?'

'I don't think so. Because of whatever activity he is involved with and because of the jewellery you were holding he could not go to the police. All he knew was how he found you and what you were holding in your hand.' Over several cups of tea Sarah tried very hard to remember more.

'It's coming back, bit by bit. There was a struggle. She was going to kill Luke. We fell in the water. What happened to her? I must try and contact Luke and Weston.' They walked to the telephone box at the crossroads and there tried telephoning Bert and then Luke on his landline as Sarah could not remember his mobile number or for that matter any of Weston's numbers. Both men were out so they had to leave messages on their answering services saying that they would be at the phone box at a certain time. Bert responded first.

Did he know any more and would he collect Sarah and deliver her home as Margaret had no car and could not drive? Bert suggested that Sarah might still be in danger so to avoid her flat. They decided to drop her outside Weston's office the next day.

Bert duly came and delivered Sarah to Weston's office block. On the way, Sarah recounted as much as she felt able to Bert of what had transpired. In turn he shared that one male body had been found on the bridge that had worked for the Corporation. He couldn't remember the name though vaguely remembered it sounded foreign, but he was almost certain it wasn't a Luke Aylmer. As she exited the car she leant over and kissed Bert on the cheek and thanked him for saving her life and being so kind. She reassured him that he would not get into trouble with the authorities.

Weston, as soon as he was summoned to reception, met her and ushered her into a small interview room. There she disgorged her story. Weston contacted Luke who dashed across London to be with Sarah. As a precaution Weston arranged for a short safe house stay while checking out risks to them.

– LOUISE REFLECTS –

After several weeks of drying out, the initial fight and animosity Louise had originally displayed evaporated as she now considered her future.

'What will happen to me?' she asked for a second time.

'For the moment, you are safe here while I try and find you somewhere more permanent so that you can fully overcome your addiction and hopefully build a new life,' replied Weston.

'Will I go to prison?'

'Unlikely, I see you more as a victim than a perpetrator.'

Louise had Weston and occasionally the Pastor Grinstead as visitors. Because she had no other friends or relatives she started to really look forward to Weston's visits. Arif had cut off any friendship bonds she might have had early on as he came to domineer her. Even the few friends she might have had ended their days in a worse position than she was, that's if they lived long enough. Gradually, as she improved, she asked and learnt a restricted amount about Marwenna and Sarah from Weston. She reached a point in her recuperation where she wanted to write to them both to apologise and ask for their forgiveness as she felt considerable guilt in the role she had fulfilled. At that time, she had felt too ashamed to think about facing either of them. Weston delivered the letters and explained the situation to the recipients. Both women replied to her accepting her apologies and wishing her well. Eventually both would visit her but not till she felt she could cope. She gradually stopped playing the CD track. Eventually Weston persuaded her to do a little voluntary work behind the scenes in a charity shop. Just a few odd hours and mornings to build up her confidence and her social skills.

– BROKEN LIVES FROM A BOMB OF HATE –

In the light of the bombing, the symposium had been cancelled but during the following months, Ayesha and Martha joined forces to finish what their men had started. Indeed, it had been therapeutic for them to reinstigate the symposium. They both gave a joint opening address, the gist of which was that the planet was far too precious to be left in the hands of politicians, dictators, generals and big corporations, which was very well received. It was after this, however, that the gaping vacuums in their lives became very apparent to them and the grieving process became more acute again.

At this juncture Martha revisited her original idea and suggested to Ayesha that they take a break together to take stock and see what direction they should individually go. As it turned out, they ended up for a week or so at St Julian's enjoying the solitude or each other's companionship as the mood took them.

Ayesha felt no pressure concerning her having a different faith from the community and just enjoyed the quiet countryside around them. While there, they took time to count their blessings and explore possibilities for the future.

'You know, we've a lot to be thankful for. Not every woman gets what we have had,' stated Martha.

'You are so right. I suppose that's one of the many reasons we miss them so much.'

Then, during their conversations, they discovered that both men had wanted to visit St Catherine's in Sinai and had never had the chance. They decided to visit it together on their husbands' behalf. It would be a tough journey, fraught with difficulties at the best of times, but particularly as they were women. However, they were up for the challenge and would bring back to their mosque and church photographs of the Greek Orthodox working monastery and the mosque that is within it together with a photograph of the copy of a charter signed by Mohammed, *'in aid of the Christians'* with its gold handprint.

— FAREWELL TO THE OLD, HELLO TO THE NEW —

After a bracing day at sea alone, enjoying the elements, the captain moored up for the night. He retired to his cabin and opened a final bottle. Alone he decided to make some final toasts.

'To Bert and Edna and their family. May they continue on their path of health and happiness!'

A GOOD TO BE ALIVE DAY[22]

Verse
Infectious laughter, Silence shared.
Humanity discovered; Profound moments rare.
Significant milestone. From millstone set free.
The turning to friendship from past enemies.

It's a good to be alive day.
A great to be alive day.
Sunshine, cool lapping waves.
Fun times, salad days.

Verse
The fruit of hard labour, a job well done.
The joy of creation, fears overcome.
Deep friendships of old, discovering the new.
Good old dependables, surprise from the blue.

---

22 'A Good to be Alive Day' – laid-back song on guitar, drums, flute and bass

It's a good to be alive day.
A great to be alive day.
Living life right to the full
Though parts can be hard and cruel.

Sometimes caught up in the rat race, such fast pace.
Our vision mis-focused to a grind in a rut.
Seduced by pretences or passing fancies
Or fashions or fads with no substance just floss.

Verse
Scenic panoramas, takes breath away.
Deep stirrings of love which no words convey.
The wonder of nature, first sight of new birth.
Relief in belonging, a sense of true worth.

It's a good to be alive day.
A great to be alive day.
Sublime days (you wish to) should never end.
Times shared with family and friends.

'To all the downtrodden peoples that are treated as subhuman that the world forgets. The Yazidis, the Orang Rimba and the Kalasha hill people and those I've no knowledge of yet. Good health to them and may they overcome and prevail in life.' The captain picked up the bottle and looked at it and spoke to it. 'And so, my friend, I will toast you now as I won't be seeing you for quite some time and only then when I'm celebrating. Here's to alcohol, your use for deadening the pain and dulling the senses.' After this he emptied the bottle for one final toast and placed it in the recycling bin on board. 'To the future and most importantly my future.'

Little did he know that sometime later he would be recruited by Weston in a common cause. Indeed, the future was to hold him as a strange bedfellow with the intelligence services concerning their common adversary.

He turned on the radio and a cheerful laid-back song eased its way out into the ether. It certainly was a good to be alive day! *A new start requires some new destinations*, he thought and so pulled out some charts.

– SILENT WITNESSES –

Repair work on the bridge was complete, the scaffolding now gone. As ever, old Father Thames kept rolling along, the ebb and flow having washed away all trace of previous events. The metal outlet of the once meandering river Fleet now encased in concrete, its final few miles of passage out of sight, out of mind, close to the bridge, was now perhaps the only constant silent witness to what had transpired.

– A FRUITFUL RELATIONSHIP –

As they recovered from their ordeal, Sarah and Luke's relationship blossomed further, deepening as the days went by.

The adventure had focused their minds and accelerated their awareness of how much they really cared for each other. Though Sarah had never thought of it in such terms, aside from when her memory returned, she had fallen deeply and passionately in love with Luke. He, for his part, had known since her disappearance how much he loved her but he had held his counsel, giving Sarah plenty of time and space to get to know him. Now it just felt right to ask her. There would be nothing he could do if she refused. So, after a lunchtime concert at St John's Smith Square, they walked through St James's Park and there by a weeping willow tree Luke proposed. Sarah, a little surprised, though not shocked, still felt she needed time to think about it.

'I do love you but just feel I need some time before I will answer. After all, it's a big commitment. I need to not just listen to my heart but my mind too and I'd like to pray about it and maybe talk to my pastor. Just to be sure.'

'Take all the time you need,' replied Luke, much relieved at not being refused outright.

Sarah did take time to pray and talk to her pastor. He advised they come to marriage preparation classes if her answer was to be yes, adding at the end of their conversation, 'A marriage consists of many things: lovers, a working partnership, friendship and putting your partner before your own needs, and adjustments of expectations. Over the years you will both change and grow and you need to allow each other space to do that. Normally you can find six people in a marriage.'

'Sorry, I don't follow.'

'Well, the values, behaviours or reactions to them; expectations, from both sets of parents of each one getting married, are brought into the marriage, even though the parents may be dead. That's aside from the personal as well as society expectations. Then there's your own individual expectation of what married life should be as well as aspirations about children.'

'Wow, that's a lot to think about.'

'That's why it's good to attend preparation classes. In centuries past people didn't need it as everyone's roles were known and defined. If you were a farmer's wife, you knew exactly what that entailed.'

Sarah went home, thought about it, prayed about it and telephoned Luke.

– A MINOR SETBACK –

Nichols consoled himself that the death of his operatives was at least fortunate in damage limitation. He had already made sure that nothing was traceable to himself. Arif had become a liability anyway, so it was indeed useful that he had been killed. As for Ruby, well, it would be difficult to find a substitute in terms of usefulness and skill and there would be a delay in finding someone similar and the developing of a new 'business' relationship with them. He quite missed her, but had always been very careful not to invest any real sentiment because he knew how dangerous she could be.

With regard to the device, he thought it was more than likely lost in the Thames. A slight delay in the scheme of things but he was sure that after a period of quiet he could resume his long-term plan of control and could always switch continents while England would be conveniently dormant for a while.

Then there was Aylmer and Manning. It would be well to leave them to carry on their lives. They obviously wanted to start a new life without the Corporation. They were of no more use to him and from their recent behaviour were not a threat so were really of no further consequence. In fact, by not having further contact with them it would prove to any investigating authorities that the main Corporation culprits had already been killed and a line could be drawn under the whole episode.

– MARWENNA AND HER VISITORS –

The wounds Marwenna had received during the struggle had unfortunately developed complications so her stay in hospital was a lot longer than normal. While convalescing Marwenna had had a succession of visitors. Setford had initially left her his favourite book to read, *Operation Emerald*, though he knew she may not be keen on that genre of book but it was all he had to hand. Weston and Setford took it in turns to keep her abreast of the progress of the follow-up investigation. She was particularly surprised at Edna's husband's involvement in rescuing Sarah. Luke and Sarah popped in several times and learned of Marwenna's interest in poetry as it was something she could do while stuck in hospital. Luke made them both laugh when he explained his very brief attempts at writing poetry or rather the lesser literary ambition of attempting to create marching rhymes his men could use. This, he explained, was found hard because of the marching speed of The Rifles. On Sarah's last visit she announced her engagement to Luke and asked Marwenna to be her chief bridesmaid.

Marwenna, who was sitting up and quite mobile now, her recovery much improved, was only too pleased to accept but then had a few misgivings about fulfilling the honour after Sarah had left. It certainly gave her things to think about and do. Because she knew Sarah took her Christian faith very seriously, she wondered whether there was anything special needed to fulfil the role. Her own experience of religion was fairly limited being mainly church parades while serving in the forces and some childhood memories from Sunday school at St Enodoc, Trebetherick. So, with this in mind, she asked to talk to the hospital chaplain.

After brief introductions Marwenna explained about the wedding and Sarah's interest in dance within worship and her own lack of knowledge to do with church.

'What do you want to know?' said the kindly young chaplain.

As Marwenna put her questions and concerns, the chaplain jotted a list of Bible references for her and gave some advice on interpretation and context for some of them. When Marwenna mentioned about dance in worship the chaplain hesitated and finally replied, 'Well, I've heard of it but sadly never seen it. Few churches in Britain have any experience of it, which is a real shame. There may even be some opposition from some quarters, which again is sad but not unprecedented. Even King David was looked down on for dancing in worship in an Old Testament episode. I'm afraid I can't really help you on that one but I will see what I can find out concerning any books on the subject and let you know. Here are my contact details if you are discharged in the meantime.'

'Oh, OK, thanks, John,' said Marwenna, grateful for his input.

'What I can do now, though, is add to your biblical understanding of our English word "love".' He then continued, 'In New Testament Greek, there are a variety of words for what we translate as love. They are: Eros, which we think of as romantic or sexual love, agape as brotherly love, phileo, love of God, and charity, love of our fellow man, plus also there is the inference that love can also be an act of will. Let me give an example. When Peter replies to Jesus having been asked if he loved Jesus, Peter replies three times that he does. However, on the final time the word used is phileo, equating to love of God, whereas the previous times it was agape meaning brotherly love.'

'Thanks, you've given me a lot to read and think about.'

Marwenna then set about her research, jotting down notes and toying with ideas for some poetry. A few days later it was Setford's turn to visit. Plonking some fruit down on the bedside cabinet he noticed Marwenna's jottings.

'What's this… thinking of weddings?' said Setford picking up her early attempts at verse. For the very first time, she was slightly embarrassed by him and actually squirmed a little. He might get entirely the wrong idea about her. Of all people, she did not want him to think that she was thinking of romance. Why should she be embarrassed or even care what Setford thought? Would he sense a weakness in her usual dominant self? Afterwards she was puzzled as to why. Setford, however, did pick up on her embarrassment.

'That's right, pick on a poor invalid when she's recuperating. It so happens, I'm chief bridesmaid!' she announced with pride and defiance.

'I see your mouth has fully recuperated then,' he replied. Setford, answering back? Another first! What was the world coming to? Slightly flummoxed she recovered in time to scold, 'You oaf, have you no feelings! Kick a girl when she's down!'

'I would never do that, maybe when she's not looking but never down!' he replied feigning hurt feelings.

Marwenna, frustrated, could only mutter under her breath a mix of English and her native Cornish, 'Garrulous[23] empak!'

It was at this juncture that the chaplain poked his head around the door of her room.

'I'm sorry, I didn't know you had visitors. Shall I come back?'

'No, it's fine, I was just explaining to my troglodyte colleague here that these are the first attempts at verse for my chief bridesmaid role.' The two men shook hands.

'How are you doing?' asked Chaplain John of Marwenna.

'She's getting back to her usual contradictory self,' Setford replied on her behalf.

'No I'm not!'

'See, she's in denial too!' Setford said, winking at Chaplain John.

---

23 Boffin in Cornish

'No I'm…' she hesitated having fallen into his verbal trap again. 'You are my biggest pain! Isn't it about time you went?'

'She always has to have the last word too!'

'Buzz off, you… you… blockhead.'

'How did you get on with the readings?' the chaplain interceded, offering an olive branch to the bickering pair as he pulled up a chair.

'I found the "Song of Songs" very hard to follow. It's a bit racy for the Bible, isn't it?'

'Well, if you know where to look there's the equivalent of sex, drugs and rock and roll, albeit in different terms in the scriptures. People have not really changed in thousands of years. Look what happens with Adam and Eve. Prime illustration of people trying to blame someone else for their mistakes. Adam blames Eve. Eve blames the serpent, etc. There's even a verse about motorcycles if you look at the appropriate version.' He winked at Setford without Marwenna seeing.

'Really?' exclaimed Marwenna genuinely intrigued.

'Sure, I'll add it to my scribble. I'll jot down the details of a good commentary for you on the "Song of Songs". I'm not sure the commentary is in print now though, so you might need to get a second-hand copy.' She quickly read the scribbled note.

'Mm, Hudson Taylor's *Union and Communion*,' she read aloud checking with the chaplain that she'd understood his almost indecipherable scribble. 'Make yourself useful for once, Setford, and get me this commentary, please,' she half scolded while passing the piece of paper to him.

'Okey-doke. Anything else, O budding Sackville-West, before I do thy bidding?' Setford touched his forelock and half bowed mockingly.

'No, you can shove off, unsympathetic moron.'

'Your wish is my command, O she of the grumbling written appendix, well, grumbling anyway, pleased to meet you,

Chaplain John,' he replied exiting the room, making a show of bowing and scraping to Marwenna.

'I just don't know what has got into him recently,' she said out of frustration. 'He used to be so, so, what's the word?' she hesitated searching for an appropriate word.

'What?' asked the chaplain.

'Shy, quiet and, well, pliable.'

'That's three words.'

'Don't you start!'

– HOSPITAL FRUSTRATION –

Setford dropped in the commentary together with the version of the Bible the chaplain had mentioned for the motorcycle reference. While Marwenna excused herself to the ladies' lavatory, steering her drip stand of intravenous antibiotics with now experienced ease, he caught sight of Marwenna's completed verses. Surreptitiously he took a photograph of them with his phone. *That was 'convenient'*, thought Setford.

When Marwenna got back she looked up the reference Chaplain John had left her in the delivered Bible version. She read '*mounted on his Triumph*'. Thought for a split second. 'Oh, ha ha,' she was tempted to say out loud but did not want to give Setford any satisfaction at her expense.

'You look a trifle flushed!'

'Suddenly everybody is a comedian,' she exclaimed.

'Everybody?'

'Never mind!'

Marwenna did, however, express to Setford her feelings of guilt about fooling Edna. He suggested she write a note and he would deliver it to her, which he duly did. At his next visit he confirmed the delivery and could see Marwenna was still feeling bad about it because Edna had been so welcoming and genuine.

'Come on,' said Setford, 'I'll take you to her. You should be discharged soon anyway for malingering. I'll check with the staff now and if the green light is given, I'll ring ahead to see if it's OK to visit. I take it you'll want to stop off at your place to change and freshen up as well as purchase some flowers for her.'

Marwenna was not used to being organised by someone else, especially Setford, but was glad for once.

'We can pick up some of the wedding invites on the way,' stated Marwenna.

'Wedding invites?'

'Yes, Sarah Manning and Luke Aylmer have asked Mr and Mrs Ackroyd to the stag and hen nights as well as the wedding. I think there might even be one for you, though I can't see why.'

Having been set free by muttering his words of love to Marwenna when she was unconscious, Setford decided to set himself the task of putting music to her words. It would be his gift of love for Marwenna, though she would never know it. His love, after all, was unselfish and he was well prepared to let her go to become the woman she was meant to be. He would, of course, still take an active or inactive interest in her, from afar, depending on what was right for her, till his dying day. She would be free to reach her potential whatever that meant career-wise, love-wise or anything else but he was no longer cowed by any negative result as far as his personal future with her was concerned.

— TIME IS CONSTANT, BUT RELATIONAL, DEPENDING ON — THE GRAVITY OF THE SITUATION

Several months had passed during which Luke and Sarah had attended marriage preparation classes. Sarah's pastor conducted these and included some unexpected questions and observations, which initially threw them a bit concerning their preconceptions about married life.

As for planning the actual day, Sarah had used the time well, especially since she had enlisted the help of Marwenna after she had left hospital. They had started to meet on a fairly regular basis to discuss the wedding arrangements. From the off they had developed a strong bond between them to the point where people might have thought them sisters were it not that they looked nothing like each other, nor had similar personality traits. Marwenna was tallish with red hair, whereas Sarah was slightly under average height and blonde. Choosing dresses, flowers and the like together gave them the opportunity to get to know each other a lot better.

– WESTON AND LOUISE AND A PLAN –

Weston had now taken to visiting Louise several times a week. He had to move her from the temporary safe house she had resided in to a drying-out clinic and then on to a small bedsit. This he personally funded out of what was left of the savings he and Susannah had accumulated. The awkward silences between them had become a thing of the past. Louise had grown in confidence to the point where she would converse freely and really looked forward to his visits. Towards the end of each visit she would always insist that he continue reading whichever book they were following. She felt comfort in this as she fought her reliance on alcohol and the struggles of rediscovering what was left of her personality. For her part she felt an assurance in his voice and could immerse herself in the story. It was almost as if she was catching up on a childhood she never had. As time passed a strong bond of respect and trust developed between them. She began to venture out and had started volunteering to help part time in a charity shop. This gained her further confidence and got her to the stage of having a part-time paid job. Weston was gradually teaching her how to handle her own finances and they both explored cooking together as neither was good at it. For the first time it brought laughter to them when they had to each share culinary disasters.

– CLEARING LOOSE ENDS –

During the debriefings and subsequent follow-up investigations, Weston and Setford had learnt and shared with Marwenna the information and contacts discovered. When Marwenna learned that Bert was married to Edna she became very keen that no action should be taken against Bert and tried with all her persuasive powers to ensure it. Setford picked up on this straight away and added his weight to her arguments. Weston bowed to their pressure and it was finally decided that no action should be taken against Bert and even the captain regarding their shady dealings.

Having seen the mission through, Weston decided to retire and on leaving he inferred to his immediate line manager that someone very high within the government should be investigated. After all, he had been subtly warned not to follow his instincts concerning the Corporation. He did, however, receive a lot of unofficial congratulations from colleagues in the know. Having reaffirmed to the official channels that Setford and Marwenna thought their assignment was official, he made sure that Setford was recommended for a commendation and that Marwenna for commendation and a special bravery award, together with a recommendation for early promotion. Typical of OHMS, it would be weeks at best, more likely many months, before any decisions would be made.

When Weston finally cleared his desk, it became the catalyst for him to finally take stock after Susannah's death. Looking through his desk drawer there was not much to show for thirty-five years of intelligence work. He reflected on how eager, ambitious, naive and patriotic he had started out. He picked up the photograph of his beloved Susannah that had always been on his desk and while brooding a thought occurred to him.

He lifted the telephone receiver and dialled a number and left a message for a certain boat owner. This would be the last official piece of work he would do, or so he thought. He decided to clear his life too, putting much into storage, placing the house on the market in order to downsize. He needed a clean break from the reminders of the house he and Susannah had shared, but he always would keep some precious reminders of Susannah with him. His London flat he would retain for the time being in order to visit Louise easily. He took a couple of short breaks, the last of which was based in Rugby to explore the Midlands.

After a day exploring parts of Warwickshire or Northamptonshire, he would oft return to The Merchants pub of an evening. Here, installed away in a little corner, he would muse on life while supping his favourite brew, people-watching, happy with his own company and thoughts. He liked the hostelry because occasionally he could seek out company for some very interesting conversations and there were decent papers to read, not to mention watching the rugby or cricket when in season.

However, this was a Tuesday night, which usually entailed live music. It was bound to be crowded which meant he could merge in with the background as he liked to do and enjoy the pint and the music while, again, people-watching.

On this particular night, the singer in the band opened the second half by announcing that the next song was 'in honour of all the barmaids who have served in the pub, for that matter in honour of all barmaids up and down the land', adding to the barmen serving, 'Sorry, chaps, you don't get a mention!'

It was a catchy little upbeat song with a Latin American feel.[24] Weston's thoughts returned and focused on his former colleagues,'

---

[24] 'The Barmaid' – moderately fast Latin piece for two voices, drums, percussion, flute or sax

Louise and especially Sarah and Luke and their upcoming wedding. He still felt very bad about what had happened to them. The words of the song seeped into him, stirring past memories of times before he was married to Susannah, times that seemed to belong to someone else's life now.

Then a young man, footloose and fancy free, he would get a little merry and check his intoxication level by how much he fancied the barmaid. Once he started to really fancy her, he knew he should have left earlier and would leave. That was unless before drinking he was really attracted to her in the first place. Every plan has its shortcomings.

How could he make it up to Sarah and Luke? He looked down and saw his foot tapping in time. *This would be a good tune to dance to*, he thought. *Hang on a minute! Dance! Dance! Yes, that's what I could do. I could arrange and pay for some dance and music for their wedding. What an inspiration. That could at least go some way to making up for their trauma and involvement. It's also something I can share and chat about with Louise, as I know she likes romance and weddings. Besides, she's young, she'll know what youngsters want at weddings these days.* His concern for Louise's welfare had grown, indeed it contributed to the first few steps of leaving his stagnant cul-de-sac of mourning for Susannah. There were still painful steps ahead but attempts at growing a life since Susannah had now begun.

He consulted Louise at the very next visit to her bedsit. It had been a very long time since Louise had been asked her opinion about anything. To think that someone was interested and may even act on it was quite alien to her, such had been the years of ill treatment she had endured. Louise thought about it for quite a while and then offered some practical suggestions, pointing out the obvious issues.

'You know, you've really got to ask them as it is their wedding. They may have already organised some or were planning some.

They may have very strong preferences. Who is her chief bridesmaid? She might know.'

'Ah, that I do know, I'll telephone her now.' Weston dialled Marwenna's number and came up to speed on the arrangements thus far. 'She does not know but thinks they have not decided. She will find out from Sarah,' explained Weston to Louise.

Within half an hour Marwenna got back to Weston who in turn reported the upshot to Louise.

THE BARMAID [25]

People their worlds diverse, ebb and flow
She drinks in their lives as they come and go
She serves their choice with professional care
Unknown the heart that burns for her there

    The man from bleeper, phone and PC likes to hide
    Needs a break from treadmill to a better life
    Older lads who boast how much that they can drink
    Two hours on their heads thrust down into the sink

        She listens, she watches, she smiles as she mingles
        She's pleasant while serving, she knows all the wrinkles
        The stag and the hen nights. The live bands and odd sights
        Men out for aggro who live just for fist fights

What dreams, hopes, needs lie deep in her breast
Desires masked by agate eyes, yet still suggest
Exudes subtle charm unaware of inner glow
She hides her fears in outward stoic show

---

25 'The Barmaid' – moderately fast Latin piece for two voices, drums, percussion, flute or sax

Dancing Into Danger

Office girls share latest on the dating scene
Who's done what with whom and when, they sit and scheme
Wheeler dealer hustles on without a break
Hooked on making money from this dream won't wake

What passions, ambitions, what in-hib-itions
Inspire her, and fire her, guide her decisions
Admirer ponders her mystery alluring
No outcome for love just feelings enduring

Filofaxing poser mobile phone to impress
Are they lacking something 'neath designer dress?
Lady looking lounging lizard seeks to devour
Cares not for the women that he tries to deflower

Couples eating grilled lunch tabled out in the nooks
Courting couple eating, t'other hid in the snook
Businessman with buying clients tries the soft sell
Man from CAMRA eulogising lists of real ale

'Apparently they are having headaches about service and reception dance music. They can't make up their minds and are hoping for some outside input or inspiration,' reiterated Weston.

'Do you know anything about dance and for that matter dances at weddings?' asked Louise.

'Well, no.'

'Do you know anyone with this type of experience?'

He thought for a while.

'Actually, there is an old friend from school. I'm sure she would know. At the very least she could offer dancing lessons for them. I'll give her a call. Yes, I'll give old Cobby a ring.'

For Weston, Louise could have been the daughter he never experienced growing up. In some ways, they mutually healed and supported each other, though never completely. Weston was too worldly, cynical and weary to be a doting father, but there would be more than an element of her eventually twisting him around her little finger as their relationship grew. Louise, however, would never attempt to selfishly manipulate him, as she knew only too well how despicable that could be. She grew to really love him as her father and he too grew to love her as his own.

– SEEKING FORGIVENESS –

Setford and Marwenna took flowers to Edna to apologise for Marwenna's deception, after Marwenna had written a note to her from hospital asking to visit, which Setford had delivered. On opening the front door to them Edna became excited and glanced at the car they had arrived in.

'Is that one of those plain clothes cars?'

'No, Edna, we didn't come in an official unmarked car. That's Setford's old banger, which frankly could do with a clean inside and out,' replied Marwenna with a dismissive look at

Setford, then turned to Edna and softened considerably. 'Sorry for deceiving you and letting you down concerning shifts,' Marwenna blurted out as she went to embrace Edna. She didn't understand why but she became quite emotional.

'Now, now, luv, what's all this? From what I understand from your young man you've been in the wars. You will stay for tea, won't you both?' Edna insisted. Though not relating the true nature of Marwenna's hospital stay Setford had passed on the general gist of it.

'Thank you for the flowers. I'll just put them in water.' When Edna returned, she asked Marwenna, 'Did you have a local antiseptic for your operation?'

'No, I had a general anaesthetic,' replied Marwenna exchanging a knowing look with Setford whose puzzled expression changed to a smile.

'Edna, we have an invitation for you, to a wedding and hen night,' Setford added.

'What, you getting married, Marwenna? Oh, how lovely and to such a good-looking fella!'

Marwenna quickly drew Edna aside and quietly corrected her. 'No, no, he's not my young man, and it's not my wedding.'

'I'm sorry, dear, I'm always making *poe fars* according to the family.' Then whispered, 'Mind you, you do make an attractive couple.'

Bert arrived home, locked his old sit-up-and-beg bicycle to the railings by the front door and half shouted to his daughters while releasing the bottom of his trousers from his socks.

'It was tough cycling away from all those excited women of Poplar at the sight of my trim ankles again.' His routine jape usually brought groans and smiles from his daughters.

'Dad, we've got guests,' said the youngest in an embarrassed, subdued voice.

'Oh, who is it then?'

'Someone from Mum's work.'

'Oh, best behaviour then, where's your mum?' Before anyone could reply Edna called to Bert.

'Bert, Bert, I have a wedding invitation!'

'That's great, Duch', who's getting married?'

'Oooh, in the excitement I haven't looked yet.'

'There's a letter and invitation for you too, Mr Bass,' interposed Setford quietly whilst Edna was rereading her invitation for the third incredulous time.

Bert took his letter and opened it. He sat down momentarily stunned.

'I don't know no Sarah. Is this a mistake? How does she know me?' said Edna somewhat confused.

'Look at the man's name, his Christian name in particular,' Setford assured her and Marwenna added, 'Research Department on the third floor, decaff tea with milk, no sugar.'

'It's not that nice young Mr Aylmer from work, is it? Oh, Bert, Bert, you've got one too. How lovely. I wonder why they sent them separately.'

Bert pulled Setford to one side and spoke out of earshot.

'I've been asked to be best man,' he explained disbelievingly and continued, 'I don't even know him. By the way, it's Bert to you, young fella.'

'It's Roger,' as they shook hands. He then quickly and quietly told Bert that this was the Sarah he had saved.

'I'd push the regimental connection if I were you should Edna get curious but I'll leave that to you once we've gone.'

Bert looked at Setford and knew instantly that he knew more than he was telling and just nodded.

'So, you know then,' Bert said. Setford nodded.

'What do you know?' asked Bert.

'Well, let's just say we are aware of your permanent borrowing and who you work with.'

'Please don't tell my Duch'. I did plan to tell her but have sort of put it off. She thinks everything is legit. I know it looks bad but I owe my captain a lot. Not money, you understand, but as a friend. He saved my life by stopping me from doing something stupid when I was at my lowest.'

'I'm sure you will tell her when the time is right and as far as our department is concerned, we are not furthering our investigation, we don't have the resources,' assured Setford.

'What are you two talking about?' Edna asked.

Just then an emergency vehicle siren blared out as it passed and Bert, like a lot of fathers up and down the land, took the opportunity to use the Morecambe and Wise line *'They'll never sell ice creams going along at that speed'* whilst thinking, *Saved, literally, by the bell.*

'Dad, you always say that,' said Rose, his second eldest daughter.

'Well, I'd better make some tea,' asserted Edna.

'Here are two other invitations for your sister and your skipper, Bert. Could you pass them on?' requested Setford. Bert nodded still a little stunned.

Meanwhile Marwenna had been looking at a framed poem about Edna on the wall in the kitchen.

Two score and ten does not describe
The life that you've lived and the journey so far.[26]

'What a beautiful poem. Who wrote it?' asked Marwenna.

'That's Joan's, our eldest. She's always writing stuff. Takes after her grandfather, she does.'

'Do you have anymore?' enquired Marwenna of Joan.

'Yes, do you want to see them?'

'Yes please.' The pair went off to Joan's bedroom and perused her poems which were often accompanied by delightful sketches.

---

26 See Appendix 1

'Here's one of my grandfather's about his experience in the North Atlantic convoys.'

'This is another one about Mum, only it's funny. It's actually a rap about her dodgy hip before her operation. I got my sisters to do the drum sounds.'[27] Marwenna read through it and started grinning. 'I'm glad I've got you on your own. Do you mind if I ask you something?' requested Joan.

'As long as it is not about writing verse. You are much better than I am,' replied Marwenna admiring the presentation of her verse.

'Are you and he an item or going out or anything?' enquired Joan.

'Who? Setford? No, we're just colleagues,' Marwenna half laughed.

'Is he seeing anyone?'

'Not that I know of.'

'Oh good, he's rather dishy, isn't he?'

'Is he?'

'I think he is.'

'Well, he's not a drop-dead gorgeous Adonis or beefcake, is he? But I don't know, I suppose he is a little attractive, in a certain light. I'd never thought of him that way before.'

'What are his interests? Any chance of you pointing him in my direction?'

'Well, his interests... Do you know, I haven't got a clue! I think he once babbled on about music and I have seen him reading a few sci fi books by Hulta Gertrude but that's all I know, I'm afraid. He did loan me his favourite one when I was in hospital.'

'Do you think I might have a chance?'

'I honestly couldn't say, he's a bit of a closed book and seems, or seemed, to clam up a lot. I can't even say talk to him about

---

27 'Edna's Rap' – a rap for drum set and voice

his work because he's not really allowed to talk about it. I will mention your name and what lovely poetry you write on our journey back though.'

'Oh, thanks.'

They had a delightful tea where the family reminisced about funny episodes and regaled about Edna's predisposition to get words mixed up, much to everyone's amusement and Edna's slight discomfort.

'Do you remember the time, Mum, when you ordered cham clowder instead of clam chowder?' The girls started giggling.

'Oh yes and the time you called that motorcycle a Harley Dickenson and the car a hunchback instead of hatchback,' piped in Rose.

'And what about the time you said "getting all historical" instead of hysterical,' added Joan while trying to catch Setford's eye.

'No wonder your mum gets confused with all you girls to look after,' Bert offered in her defence.

'Your mum is exceedingly good at her job,' said Marwenna, adding her support to a mildly embarrassed Edna. Later on, when Marwenna and Setford had left, Bert told Edna about the invitation to be best man.

'Well, I don't remember you ever mentioning him before when I've spoken about him from work,' said Edna a little suspicious.

'There are lots of blokes in the services called Luke, Duch', I just didn't know your Luke was one of the ones I might have known. Besides, you know we often went by nicknames.'

''Ere, Bert, did you know that Roger Setford was telling me that Marwenna got stabbed by one of those cyclepaths and was lucky to keep her life.'

'You don't say, Duch".'

Bert passed the invitations on to Margaret and the captain as well as news of the actual wedding plans and details of the stag and hen nights as they became available. The captain politely declined the invitations and added he would be offshore during that week. He was particularly relieved to know they would not be prosecuted but realised that they were on notice to be fully legitimate so took the opportunity to think of what he and Bert could do in future. Since the aftermath of the bridge incident and his own emotional anchor had now dissolved, he just needed some time to think a bit more about a positive future.

10
THE EBB AND FLOW OF LIFE

– AN OLD FRIEND TO THE RESCUE –

Weston thumbed an old business card and dialled the number.

'Cobbald Dance School, please leave your name, telephone number and message after the pips,' the answerphone chimed.

'Hi, Cobby, it's me Westy, er, sorry to call you out of the blue but I have a favour to ask. Not really for me, you understand, but for a young couple that have been through a lot. I'll pay you well if you are available and are up for it. Can you give me a call on…?'

The receiver was picked up midway through him leaving a message.

'Hello, Westy!' A woman's voice sounded hesitant, almost shocked.

'Oh, you're there.' There was a short awkward silence before he continued. 'It has been a long time.'

'Yes, not since… Susannah's funeral.' She was reticent about mentioning it. Weston then proceeded to explain his idea about a dance gift and a few thoughts of his own.

'I think we can do better than that,' she initially responded. She, being more practical than him in such matters, asked contact details of the bride and chief bridesmaid and was intrigued to hear about Sarah's interest in dance.

He ended the call with, 'Thanks, Cobby, I'll pay whatever it costs! Actually, if you are asked by them, Her Majesty's Government will be paying.'

She knew him too well to know that he would actually be financing it but didn't want any gratitude or a fuss. Having replaced the receiver she mused about the fact that it was rare for Weston to take a special interest in people, especially a couple, particularly after Susannah's demise. She decided there and then to pull out all the stops for him, or was it them? She wasn't sure.

Idonea Boudicca Cobbald BA (Hons), LRAD, ARAD, RADRTS had always been a dance teacher and had poured her life into her art and her pupils. Having been classically trained in ballet, which was her first love, she was a real stickler for discipline. As the years passed, she became more focused on dance as an expression of community. She was in the throes of organising one of her many dance festivals when Weston's call came. This particular one was a folk and community festival with cross-fertilisation from different cultures. It was mixing North Country and Appalachian clog dancer sets with some Andean dancers of the Huayno, as well as several Morris and English country dance troupes. She was so proud of how some of her pupils had progressed and she used these festivals to give as much experience to her pupils as possible. Her only professional fault, if you could call it that, was as she got older, she would get the music muddled up during the examinations of her pupils but it always eventually got sorted out and it never affected the results.

Ms Cobbald, or Cobby for short, had been a friend of the Westons since childhood and indeed had been Susannah's best and closest friend. All three had been in the same class throughout their school years. The three of them, Cobby, Westy and Suse, had always kept in touch up till Susannah's funeral. After a few tentative approaches to Weston after Susannah's death, Idonea stopped trying as she did not want to intrude into Weston's mourning as he seemed not to want to be with anyone. His memories of Susannah were precious and maybe she would have been too much of a reminder of them. Then days grew into weeks, weeks into months, during which neither Weston nor Cobby tried calling the other for fear of bringing hurtful memories back.

For several minutes after she put down the receiver, she thought about him and Susannah and how things were between the three of them. She remembered how Susannah had been with Weston, their many ups and the few downs. How solid and supportive he'd been when they'd lost their children. He never did show much emotion about the loss. He was too busy supporting the woman he loved. Cobby had always loved them. Her feelings for Weston had always run deep – neither he nor Susannah ever knew how deep. She reflected on the biggest temptation she had ever had to come between Susannah and Westy early on in their relationship, before they were married. The temptation to have him for herself. If she had been a manipulative, mercenary woman she would have taken advantage of a big argument they had and would have engineered the situation to replace Susannah in Weston's affections.

Susannah had flown into the kitchen in almost incontrollable rage. She was so angry, frustrated, flustered, confused and so full of different emotions all at the same time it brought her right on the verge of tears and yet she wanted to strangle Weston at the same time. She was beyond words… all she could shout was, 'So there!' before slamming the door of the lounge and walking into the kitchen.

'Well, that told him!' Cobby said trying to lighten the mood.

'Stupid man, why can't he be like... be like,' she stopped, lost for words. Cobby turned to her with love and understanding in her eyes.

'But you love him the way he is,' she said calmly. Cobby could have easily stoked the fires of their disagreement, have gone to him initially as an understanding friend, and then maybe his thoughts would have turned to her. The temptation had been there, but she loved them both too much.

– ARRANGING A WEDDING –

After initial phone introductions Sarah, Idonea and Marwenna arranged to meet up to discuss the wedding arrangements. Sarah and Marwenna had just finished shopping for wedding dresses and arrived at the teashop on the outskirts of London just before Idonea. First, they discussed what cakes and teas they would like. Having ordered, they then set about preliminary planning, getting to know one another in the process. It was initially hard for Idonea as at least the other two knew each other, though they both did their best to make her feel welcome.

'Call me Cobby,' Idonea said on introducing herself and added, 'Westy said you wanted some dance arrangements for your wedding. Did you have anything particular in mind or specific ideas for you and Luke to dance at your reception?'

Sarah replied, 'We're not sure really. We're more concerned about all the folk we've invited, that they can take part and enjoy it. Luke is not particularly well co-ordinated, bless him, although he has improved. I'm sure he would give anything a go.'

'I see, what experience of dance have you had or like?'

Sarah stated her passion for all dance, her experience of worship in dance and most of the types of lessons she had had with Luke. She admitted most of the lesson times tended to be comprised mainly of instruction for Luke to try to put his feet in the right places, finally explaining that she had never had any proper formal training. Cobby was intrigued to the point of asking if she would be able to see some dance in worship, ideally with Sarah dancing.

'Regarding all the people coming, how about the pair of you attending the international folk dancing festival I have been arranging and is due to start next week? My students will be performing as part of it.'

'I'd love to,' said Sarah excitedly.

'And how about you, Marwenna? A special chief bridesmaid dance, perhaps?' asked Cobby turning to Marwenna.

'Me? I'd not thought. We haven't discussed anything. I'm not sure I could. Stomping around handbags is my limit!'

'Do you have a prospective partner if something is arranged for you?'

'No.'

'Don't worry, Marwenna. I have no such plans for a special dance for you. That is unless you would like one. I want you to enjoy the day just as much as I will. You don't even have to dance with the best man if you don't want to, though I'm sure it will be fun.'

'Who is it? Some handsome hunk that Luke knows from the services?' asked Marwenna.

'I must admit Luke hasn't told me yet. I think he is waiting for a reply.'

'I would like to go to the festival, though, and also see you dance, Sarah,' added Marwenna.

'Then it's agreed,' affirmed Cobby in a businesslike manner.

Their first encounter had warmed quickly as Sarah shared her love of dance with Idonea, and Marwenna was intrigued about Cobby's association with Weston. Any apprehension from any of them soon disappeared when they discovered that they all got on like a house on fire. Marwenna, initially a little wary, really grew close to them both over time, though it took longer for her than the other two. Idonea took to Sarah straight away because of their mutual love of dance, their experience of which contrasted greatly. Idonea had all the formal training, Sarah had none but danced from her heart. Marwenna, who had no great desire dance-wise, gradually got caught up in the enthusiasm of the other two.

Over the course of several weeks the three women met up quite a few times during which they attended the festival, watched Sarah in a church service and decided to meet for a plush high tea at a swanky hotel to conclude the plan for the wedding. Cobby had said she was relieved that the festival had gone so well and was glad that someone else had controlled the music CDs and tapes as in the past she had had a few foul-ups with selecting the wrong music for the wrong dance. Sarah had loved it all and felt she was just like a child in a sweetshop. She particularly loved the sight of a Tahitian dance performed by a mature couple in waltz timing. It looked so romantic as arms outstretched and back to back they turned together and then faced each other. As for Marwenna, her eyes were opened to Huayno, Afoxes, Appalachian and Northern Cloggers and she found she actually had a real soft spot for the jolly old Morris dancers, maybe a little more than the stately English dance examples.

Sarah was far more laid back than Cobby and Marwenna, not really having a major ambition in life as such. She had interests, of course, but was not driven like the other two. After watching Sarah dance in the church service both women were intrigued by what she did, but Cobby particularly from a professional point of view as well as her heart being lifted by Sarah's movement.

'How do you go about it?' asked Cobby. 'I mean, do you plan every movement? What is your approach?' she clarified.

'I quiet myself, focus on the scripture or hymn or song and meditate on it. I suppose I become emotionally involved with it and am moved by it to the point of wanting to express my reaction to it or rather the being behind it. I suppose basically I'm saying in my dance, "Look what I have discovered, how wonderful it is." That is when I am ready to dance. Group dances are often different. The movement, the costumes, the banners are symbolic. Sometimes they demonstrate a story or truth and sometimes group worship and harmony in community.'

She elaborated further. 'There are a few hurdles for some Christians when learning to dance. To overcome self-awareness either with embarrassment or self-aggrandisement and ego-massaging. You face the question, "Is it a performance or worship or elements of both for God?" At the end of the day, you can only be honest with God and offer your efforts with all their occasional suspect motives, wandering thoughts and nerves to be transformed into something acceptable. The more you do, the freer you become from these hindrances. I've spoken with some Christian musicians and they have the same barriers to overcome. Does that make sense?'

Cobby thought for a moment.

'There are perhaps similarities. From my background you rehearse your body so much that you need less to think about technique and feel a greater freedom to express in body shapes and stances. There is also an element of response to audience on occasions.'

Thinking back on this conversation a little later, Cobby decided to liaise with Sarah's pastor regarding worship dance to see what input he could add. In the event, he couldn't add much, and only from his experience as an onlooker. For him the dancing was a visual interpretation of the words of the song or text, though sometimes he didn't always fully understand it.

Marwenna learnt more about Weston from Idonea than she had ever learnt while working with him. She had often wondered about his background as he gave very little of his personal side away in work. Cobby was far more forthcoming.

'You know Weston from?'

'We went to school together. I knew his wife, Susannah. She was my best friend. They adored each other.'

There were some highly comical stories she told about Weston's youth. Of course, Weston would have been acutely embarrassed knowing that he was the subject of such amusement. His reputation at work was tenacious, quiet, reserved and single-minded in a very understated manner but with flashes of brilliance. People generally thought of him as a little stuffy, formal and staid. When Marwenna shared the general office impression of him Cobby was quick to respond.

'Not if you really knew him. He turned many a girl's eye in those early days, you know. He never had any idea how attractive he was, never clued up where girls were concerned. He couldn't even chat up a paper bag but boy there was many a heart made faint by him.'

'And yours?'

Idonea just smiled and continued, 'No, I was Susannah's best friend right up until the end, in fact good friends with both of them.'

'What happened?'

'She died of cancer.' Cobby's eyes moistened a little.

'What happened after her death?'

'He turned inward on himself and wouldn't or couldn't open up. Wouldn't let anyone near him.'

Cobby's thoughts quickly ran in directions she did not want to go. Maybe now that Weston was finally coming out of the bereavement process it would be OK to wish that there was a chance to spend their last years together, at least as friends again. Would he ever see her for herself rather than Susannah's best friend? She had got on with her life all these years, burying all feelings of love for him and yet there was still a small part of her that had dared to hope, to wait. Sharing the sunsets and the silences together would be enough. Could she adapt from her life as it was? She'd waited this long. She could wait a little longer. Even quicker, she dismissed these thoughts from her mind. Marwenna interrupted her thoughts with her own musings.

'I wonder how he managed to wangle the department's contribution to the wedding out of the budget?' Cobby quickly headed her off at the pass, so to speak, by changing the subject.

– COBBY'S GIFT –

Cobby threw herself, heart and soul, into planning the wedding dances.

Subconsciously she would do it for Weston just as much as she would for Sarah and Luke. It would be her expression of love to him, even though he would never know it. The love of her life, for the love of her life. She was delighted to find two new young friends, one of which was just as passionate about dance as she was, albeit from an unschooled history.

It was now the last meeting before the hen night and the wedding. They had their tea in a walled garden of the plush hotel which had many fruit trees growing close to the walls. A blackbird sat very close to them on a neighbouring bough and sang sweetly. Initially Cobby was on her phone texting and Marwenna was on her phone looking at a Facebook page of one of her brothers. Sarah was the only one really listening to it sing. Eventually she called them to order.

'Ladies, please, can you cease your technology playing. Honestly, if it's not Facebook, it's emails or texting or if not, then Twitter,' as she pointed to the blackbird. They ceased their keying and smiled.

'You have our full attention,' stated Cobby. They discussed the progress of the dresses, flowers and other arrangements. The conversation then took a humorous turn when they discussed all sorts of dances that they would discount quickly but could try and get Luke to do for the wedding.

'A courtly one to a madrigal?' offered Sarah.

'A clogger one for bride and groom?' suggested Marwenna.

'How about leading in with full Morris kit, hankies and bells and all? Marwenna could be the one with the balloon!' suggested Cobby.

'I don't think Luke could cope with clogging. Being a man of honour, he'd have a go but I think he would struggle, bless him. He certainly did when we tried Lindy hop.'

'You tried Lindy hop?'

'Yes, it was great! Though sadly, we weren't.'

'Cobby, what do you do to make the girls work in your lessons?' asked Marwenna suddenly.

'I drop the temperature in the room, just a shade, to make them work to keep warm and threaten them either with being rusticated or made to perform the Threeple Hammer Damson.'

'The what?'

'Oh, it's from one of my favourite dance fiction films. I watch it if I feel I'm getting too serious about my work. The Threeple Hammer Damson doesn't really exist, but they don't know that.'

'What film is that then?' asked Sarah.

'*Morris: A Life With Bells On*! It's a mockumentary.'

'Would I learn much about dance if I watched it?'

'Not much. Let's just say, it's more about people than dance. It's certainly at the opposite end of the spectrum to *The Red Shoes* or *Dirty Dancing*. But I love it. It always brings a smile in spite of the little bit of swearing in it.'

'By the way, I've found out from Luke who the best man is,' Sarah stated while winking at Idonea without Marwenna seeing.

'Oh really, who?' asked Marwenna.

'Now, to break the ice at the reception I'm going to get the wedding group to lead off with a La Marcha dance around the room in the Mexican tradition before the buffet. You know the sort of thing, bride and groom, followed by maid and best man. I'll designate a couple to lead off,' Cobby elaborated.

'Oh, who am I dancing with?' asked Marwenna again, which Cobby and Sarah ignored, and Cobby carried on.

'After the buffet the bride and groom will dance, to which the best man and chief bridesmaid will join in.'

'Well, who am I dancing with?'

'What are you like at the Rhumba, Marwenna?' Sarah asked.

'What?' There was panic in Marwenna's eyes.

Cobby continued, 'Then there is the option of a Norwegian dance of two rival ladies to a single man or I'll get my junior group to demonstrate an English country dance or maybe both. After this dance each child will take an adult to partner them for the first barn dance. The child will then introduce their adult to another adult for the next dance and the children can then relax and feast on buns and lemonade till their parents collect them. Of course, there will be safeguarding of the children's welfare throughout until that time.'

'The best man is a real hunk.' Sarah's lips slightly twitched.

'Oh, who?'

'So I gather, though he's a little too young for me, but I think you might have met him,' Cobby elaborated to Marwenna.

'How come Cobby knows and I, your chief bridesmaid, doesn't?'

'Cobby needed to know to assess his dancing skills,' Sarah asserted.

'You'll have to dance a lot better, you know. He's very light on his feet!' Sarah smiled further.

'Of course, I'll polish up my footwork,' replied Marwenna unconvincingly and more than a little nervous. 'But who is it?'

'I think some other woman has got her eye on him, anyway,' Cobby chimed in, adding to Marwenna's tension. Cobby and Sarah started to smile broadly.

'Don't worry, I've finally chosen a simple waltz for my dance, not a Rhumba so you should be OK,' Sarah giggled.

'WHO IS IT?!' Marwenna demanded in frustration.

Sarah and Cobby looked at each and said together, 'It's Edna's Bert.'

They all burst out laughing. Marwenna after calming down finally stated, 'I'm sure I can manage that! You rotters!'

'Aw, are you very disappointed?'

'More relieved than anything.'

'Now you know Bert is best man, who are you going to dance with after? Is there no one you fancy?' asked Cobby.

'Nobody comes to mind.'

'What about Setford?' suggested Sarah.

'No chance, besides he's a boring colleague at work, though come to think of it, he has changed lately,' she said reflectively.

'What do you miss about Cornwall, Marwenna?' asked Cobby taking pity on Marwenna after their leg-pulling.

'Oh, well, I miss the smell of the sea and the sound of the waves crashing on the shore and the ragged coastline. I miss Mum and Dad, of course, and even my brothers in a funny sort of way. They could be such pains when we were young but that prepares you well for dating later, I suppose. I used to like walking to church when I was a child because of the sense of danger.'

'Danger?' Sarah and Cobby said together at exactly the same time.

'Yes, we had to walk through a golf course to get to St Enodoc and there was always the unlikely threat of being hit by a ball. When you are young the danger is considerably magnified. In actual fact all the golfers were always very, very careful.'

– SETFORD, A MAN OF PASSION –

Unbeknown to Marwenna, but with Sarah and Luke's consent, Setford had liaised with Sarah's minister to have a band and singers perform in the service, after the signing of the registers. This was to perform the music he had written to Marwenna's words. It was in one of these rehearsals that the minister popped in to listen.

'I was intrigued as to why you said on the phone that you did not want an organist playing it. You seemed very passionate about it.'

'There are three things I'm passionate about: music, Essex and science fiction. I have nothing against organists *per se*, aside from the sound which, like Martin Luther, I'm not crazy about, but there are often timing issues. Firstly, there is a time delay between pressing an organ key and the sound escaping. Secondly, they often come in late at the start of a verse. This is often deliberate to give singers a chance to breathe but sometimes due to choir conductors conducting by phrase rather than strict time. The idea behind this is to give added expression to the music. To my ears this is overused and rarely works as it is too unsubtle. The problem is that organists, and for that matter choirs, often add up to two beats extra between verses. It gets them into bad habits and while I am venting my spleen, like Beethoven, I am not in favour of changing keys on pieces. They were written in the original for a purpose.'

'Oh, I can see you are a bit of a purist. Listening to your piece, tell me, what was behind the use of different aged couples for two of the verses?'

'It's a reflection of how love grows with age. Marwenna did a good job with the words and even kept to the "Song of Songs" format of having a witnesses' or friends' section.'

'Oh, so you are familiar with the "Song of Songs"?'

'Only for composing purposes. I have to admit I'm not a believer as such. About the only religious thing I remember is a story from a sermon about Essex monks and music. As I mentioned before, music, Essex and science fiction are my passions.'

'Really, do tell. I might be able to use it.'

'An abbott and his monks lived in the Essex marshes and because of this, their voices were often affected by the dampness and their singing was often quite rasping. One day a very famous singer with a wonderful voice was travelling through the area and they asked him to sing matins. He did and the monks sat and listened and enjoyed it very much. That night the abbott was given a dream and in it, God said to him, "Why were you not singing to me today?" The abbott explained about the wonderful singer and his superb voice. God replied, "He is not heard in heaven but you are! He may have a pure voice but you praise me with pure hearts!"'

'That's excellent. I'll definitely be able to use that. Thanks for relating it. I must say you and Marwenna have done a great job on this. What did she think when she heard it?'

'She does not know about it. I thought I'd surprise her at the wedding.'

'I'd better let you get back to practising. Just one final thing, are you sure there are only three subjects you are passionate about?'

— THE STAG NIGHT —

Luke's best friend from the forces, who was Fijian, wasn't contactable and nearly all of Luke's regimental friends were on tour in the Middle East, which was fortuitous in one respect as it meant there would be no hard-drinking exploits and associated idiocies. A meal, a few games of bar billiards, snooker, ten pin bowling and then on to a jazz club to try to catch Steve Smith's drumming was what he wanted and that's what he arranged. He had invited Bert, Setford, Weston and the captain too, but only Bert and Setford could make it. A few ex-army buddies that he could trace, some of which were still coping with physical or mental disablement, made up the rest of the stag night. It was an enjoyable enough affair. After the jazz concert all his ex-army buddies were seen into taxis, leaving just the three of them, Luke, Bert and Setford, the latter being a little worse for wear due to him drinking more than he usually would.

During the night, Bert and Setford discovered they actually had something in common too.

'Pardon me, gents, but I would like to toast my favourite football team,' announced Bert.

'Who?' they both said.

'The Hammers!'

Setford exclaimed, 'I thought I was the only one!'

'You too! I hope you're not one of these malcontents that is never satisfied with anything the team, manager or chairman do.'

'Sadly, there is that element in most clubs,' stated Setford.

'So, you're both football fans!' exclaimed Luke.

'Can anything be more important? Worldwide hunger? War? Cancer? What could possibly be more important than twenty-two men kicking a bit of leather between six sticks?' replied Setford.

Bert added, 'Years ago, the players came from and represented our area but now you might get one or two from the local area at most.'

'Ah, the tribal element! Don't get me wrong, I appreciate the swerving ball, the precise dribble, the incisive pass etc,' commented Luke.

'How about you?' Setford asked of Luke.

'I'm more a cricket and rugby union man myself. The sound of leather on willow, Bernoulli's law affecting the cricket ball, but if push comes to shove, I suppose Yeovil is the club for me, though I quite like Forest Green.'

'It's about time you gave a toast, Roger. What'll it be?'

'OK, let's see, er, to Hulta Gertrude.'

'Who?' they both said at the same time.

'She's my favourite authoress. She writes science fiction books.'

While Bert went to the gents', Setford and Luke chatted about music. Luke and Setford discovered they had a shared a passion for music and had a long and deep conversation concerning quality music. They got on so well that Setford started to pull Luke's leg concerning drumming and dating.

'I can picture it now. A romantic candlelit dinner with seventeen musicians playing soft, soaring harmonies. A cool zephyr gently disturbing the drapes as an enigmatic musical phrase oozes out a lydian scale adding to the soft ambience of the evening air when a hanger-on of the band, sometimes known as a drummer, adds to the air of sophistication. Subtle as ever: "Fish and chips, please, and go easy on the vinegar!"'

'It's wicked to mock the afflicted!' Luke replied.

Then suddenly Setford became very serious, turned to Luke and blurted out, 'You know when we were at the mortuary, I was a little bit jealous.'

'Why?' asked Luke, surprised at this admission.

'I thought you were going to make a move on Marwenna.'

'Oh, I see, so you are keen on Marwenna, well what's stopping you making a move for her yourself?'

'I'm not her type. Besides, she's too good for me.'

'How true,' Luke quickly retorted, pulling Setford's leg but then added, 'What is her type then?'

'An all-action man, I guess.'

'You guess! Don't you know?' exclaimed Luke seriously. 'Listen, why don't you try asking her out? You'll never know unless you try.'

Setford nodded and, succumbing to the alcohol, started to drop off to sleep. When Bert returned, they decided to have a few more toasts from their final pints and then get Setford back to his flat.

'To The Rifles.' Luke raised his glass and swallowed a few gulps.

'Swift and Bold,' counter-toasted Bert.

'Kidney Ridge.' Bert lifted his glass again adding before supping, 'My dad, along with all the other Londoners from my area, fought in that.'

'This is getting like a regimental dinner!' reflected Luke mainly to himself and raising his glass once more. 'To the Royal Green Jackets.'

'First in and last out,' Bert reciprocated, downing the last of his drink adding, 'I'll get a cab for us all,' while exiting. During Bert's absence Luke finished his pint with one last toast.

'Here's to you, Dave, whatever mansion you are in that God has for you and whatever musical instrument you are learning to play, and to you, Peter Hones, may you dance to Dave's tune for God's glory. Thank you both,' and with that he woke Setford and helped him outside.

– THE HEN NIGHT –

The hen night on paper looked as if it was a disaster in the making to Marwenna who felt very responsible for it as she was chief bridesmaid. She had been used to girls in military service having either very raunchy, bawdy or drunken hen nights, or some at the opposite extreme of acute disappointment, the highlight of which was dull conversations with dull company, a disappointing meal and dancing around handbags. Neither extreme was to her fancy. *What would be successful for Sarah, her church friends, Margaret, Edna and Idonea?* she thought.

In the end, it turned out to be one of the best hen nights she had ever been on. She organised an ice-breaker with 'match the question with the answer'. The chatter and laughter increased as the evening progressed over a superb meal. At one stage Edna stated after several wines that she liked the occasional spirit but was 'no drin ginker', much to everyone's amusement. Idonea, who very rarely drank alcohol, got very merry on three Babyshams and a sherry. She kept saying in her prim and proper way, 'I'm awfully sorry but I'm a little squiffy. Isn't this fun.' In her tipsy state, she opened up a little about Weston when Marwenna probed about him again.

'So how did you meet Mr Weston? I've forgotten,' asked Marwenna being a little disingenuous.

'Ole' Westy! We were school friends. Susannah, Westy and me, Cobby!' pointing to herself and now starting to look more than a little bit sozzled. 'Every day the three of us would walk home together. My home was first. We would stand chatting for a while and then the two of them would continue homeward. Susannah was his eventual wife,' she elaborated further without prompting.

'Yes, I didn't know how much he liked her till one day I was looking out the window and noticed that when Westy thought they were out of sight he used to carry Susannah's books for her,' she added wistfully as she briefly gazed into the distance.

'To think if I'd lived further away, I might have been Mrs Weston.' Her voice died away with more than a hint of regret. She quickly recovered and then refocused. Marwenna had an inkling that somewhere deep in Cobby's heart and psyche there were maybe long-suppressed feelings that were unresolved.

Idonea herself was probably not aware of them or the extent of them. Marwenna caught herself thinking what Edna would have said in such a situation. Probably she would have said, 'inkled a suspect or two for suspicions'.

Why did she suddenly think of Edna? This was starting to get a little bit weird. Nevertheless, she continued with her questioning, though she was not sure why.

'Did you enjoy school together?' Sarah asked.

'Oh yes, we did country dancing and sang English folk tunes, among others.' She moved her arm in a grandiose gesture nearly knocking the glasses over.

'Such as?'

'Oh, "Scarborough Fair", "Dashing Away with the Smoothing Iron", "Soldier Soldier Won't You Marry Me", "My Grandfather's Clock", oh… and "The Drunken Sailor".'

'The Drunken Sailor?'

'Yes… Don't you know it? You've not heard it? Shame on you.'

She then started to sing it. *'What shall we do with the drunken sailor…'*

The whole table stopped their conversations at this. She then proceeded to teach them it. For their part, they joined in as best they could. Cobby then with her finger gestured to Marwenna as if to whisper as she did not realise she was speaking loudly.

'I know what I'd like to do with a drunken sailor,' she giggled and then proceeded to change the last line of the verse.

They all started to laugh and giggle and started singing the chorus of 'The Drunken Sailor' again. This then rapidly turned into a game of inventing new risqué lines to end each verse, the rest of the group taking it in turns to add their last lines. Things got very silly. When it came to Idonea's second attempt, Sarah intervened with, 'Whoa, hold your horses. Too much information,' to spare her embarrassment. Then quietly she whispered to Idonea, 'I think I'll need to see you home.'

Marwenna interjected, 'Don't worry, I'll see her home, I am chief bridesmaid after all.'

'Where are you going to live? A flat or apartment?' asked Margaret of Sarah.

'Americans call them "condom-minions", don't they?' added Edna, hesitating after the second syllable, much to the amusement of everyone else. More than a few smiles beamed around the table.

'I think we'll stick with a flat,' replied Sarah stifling a titter behind her hand. The conversations multiplied as the women chatted to their adjacent diners and the murmur increased in volume and laughter. After a while it all went suddenly quiet as various conversations reached their natural ending with the exception of one. Edna was finishing speaking about a neighbour of hers and the whole table heard what turned out to be the final statement on her neighbour: 'She had a camera scan up her bottom which can result in those, what d'yer call 'em? Polaroids.'

Marwenna quietly translated to Sarah. 'She means haemorrhoids!'

Edna continued, 'And then she had one of them, what d'yer call 'em, you know, oh, erm, hysterical rectomys.'

Uproarious laughter erupted at this and no one could say anything for quite a while. Finally, wiping tears from her eyes Idonea piped up in her plummy voice, 'Oh, Edna. You made me laugh so much I nearly wet my knickers.'

'Oowa… fancy that… an' you a dance teacher an' all!' Edna exclaimed bringing more bouts of laughter. Earlier on in the evening Sarah had taken an opportunity to explain to Edna how Bert had saved her and looked after her.

'You know, he's never said a word to me. That's just typical of him. All through his service days he never let on about things, no matter how bad they got, in case I worried. Of course, that never stopped me from worrying. I could kill him sometimes if I didn't love him so much.'

'I think I've already experienced that with Luke!' Sarah affirmed.

During the course of the evening Edna had met by chance Marwenna in the ladies' and asked Marwenna, 'How's that young man of yours?'

'I don't have or need a young man. What young man?'

'The chap who came with you to tea.'

'Who? Oh, Setford. He's not my young man. He's OK, I suppose, though I think he's got above himself lately.'

'You know, there's something about him. Quiet, honest, loyal and a lot of qualities that are understated,' Edna asserted in her best English.

'Sounds like a dog.'

Edna suddenly turned to Marwenna and grasped her arm.

'Now listen, my girl. I've brought four kids up and I think I'm reasonable at judging folks' character. He may not be exciting but you could do a lot worse. Maybe you should think about what you could offer him.' She hesitated. 'Sorry, Marwenna, I'm talking out of turn. It's just that when my daughters get a little bit above themselves, I like to bring them down to earth a bit. Now, I apologise. I've said my piece and had no right to, but, well, though you're not one of my daughters, I would love you to be.'

Marwenna could have been angered but sensed the love with which the mild rebuke had been said, so she hugged Edna and added, 'I'd like that too. Let's join the party again.'

– THE MORNING AFTER –

The next morning Sarah telephoned Idonea to see if she was OK. Marwenna answered.

'She's sleeping now. Last night when we got to her flat, she wanted to waltz, then to polka, tried walking up the wall and then wanted to be sick. I stayed here all night to make sure she was OK sleeping and generally in the recovery position. I've contacted her clients for the day and told them that she is indisposed.'

Marwenna looked down at Idonea's desk as she was talking and noticed some photographs that Idonea had obviously been reminiscing about before she had gone on the hen night. They were principally school pictures of her, Susannah and Weston, but what caught her eye was that there were some well-thumbed pictures of Weston on his own. Sarah said, 'You truly are a chief bridesmaid!'

Marwenna laughed. 'I don't know about that but I'd better go as I can hear Idonea stirring, or shall I say groaning.'

'Tea or coffee?' Marwenna asked as she popped her head around the bedroom door.

'Oh, tea, please. What's the time? I must get to work. Oh my head.'

'It's OK, I phoned your clients for today to say you were indisposed.'

'Oh thanks.'

After a pot of tea between them they breakfasted together.

'How long has it been since you were on a girls' night out?' said Marwenna smiling.

'Not in years, in fact the last hen night I was on was Susannah's, Westy's wife. That was a long time ago. I'm afraid I'd forgotten that I don't tolerate alcohol very well. I'm not sure I remember everything from last night. I hope I didn't embarrass myself.'

'No, you didn't. How long has it been since you were on a holiday?'

'Well, I've been to a few dance courses over the years.'

'Have you always loved dance?'

'Oh yes, it's my life, my passion.'

'What about men?'

'Well, no, not really, there's never been anyone special. Perhaps once, but it could not become anything,' she looked into the distance, 'besides, like I said, my first and only true love is dance.' Marwenna looked at the pictures of the three of them. Idonea recounted the tale of Weston and Susannah's first major row as school friends concerning a Welsh girl on a ferry.

'When they got back together, neither Westy nor me heard the last of it for about a month afterward.'

Marwenna felt that her suspicions were confirmed about there being something more than a close school friendship, leastways on Idonea's part, but did not press the point. Later at home, Marwenna thought on poor Idonea's many lost opportunities, just letting things go like that. How Idonea must have wanted to reach out to him in his anguish, loss and grieving, but to no avail. This made her determined that it would never happen to her, to miss out on love like that.

– THE WEDDING DAY –

Edna, who was in the bathroom, shouted to Bert, 'The tin lids are now at me sister's, I just need to fix me face and we can go.'

'I do want to get there today, you know,' he shouted back laughing.

'I heard that, Bert Bass! Do you want a bunch of fives?'

'No, Duch', I made sure I was in a different room when I said it,' still laughing. They eventually got there early so that Bert could hand out the buttonholes and order of services, which was what nearly all of his duties entailed, aside from standing next to Luke in the service, handing over the ring and then dancing with the head bridesmaid.

It was a sunny morning, the blossom was out, an occasional gentle breeze causing the leaves to shiver. Guests arrived and either chatted outside on the village green way before the early ceremony was to start, or congregated near the two flowered arches between the church porch and the churchyard gate. Idonea had surpassed herself in organising the dances for the wedding celebrations. As one of a few surprises she had prepared for Sarah and Luke, she had some of her younger children students dancing country dances before the wedding on the green by the church and maybe subconsciously half hoping it might raise something in Weston's memory of when they had danced as children. He had nearly always been her dancing partner at school.

Setford had also arrived early, in order to check with the singers and musicians that all was ready for the song. As everything was as it should be, he sat in a back pew. Weston arrived a little later and sat with Setford before he was due to meet Sarah at the door and give her away. He felt incredibly honoured to have been asked and burst with pride when he had told Louise. With five minutes to go Cobby marshalled her dancers into the church hall next door, ensuring there were no last-minute issues or hitches.

Luke arrived next and together with Bert had been welcoming guests as they arrived. Lastly, Sarah and Marwenna arrived. Weston greeted them at the door and offered his arm to Sarah. She looked radiant, as did Marwenna. The congregation stood and they processed up the aisle. Sarah was dressed simply but elegantly in white with a circle of flowers resting on her hair. The bridesmaids all wore smaller complementary crowns of flowers in their hair. It was the custom of this church community to give a copy of the Holy Bible to the wedding couple on their wedding day, often with a reference written in the front that the minister felt led to give to that particular couple.

Cobby, together with her handpicked dancers, quickly joined Setford just as the service began. It was indeed a joyous occasion and Marwenna was totally surprised by her words being sung and was equally relieved that she did not have to read them aloud. Cobby's students actually danced to it as well as a hymn and one chorus as well. Edna cried a little.

THE CHRISTIAN WEDDING SONG[28]

Love, deeper than the deepest cavern, (Male)
Higher than the highest mountain, I feel for you.
Love, wider than the widest ocean, (Female)
Brighter than a blazing fire, I feel for you.
You feel it too. So, (Together)
Come my love, let me hold you in my arms always. (Male)
Hold me close, and never let me go or turn away. (Female)
I will never leave or forsake or turn my back on you. (Together)
I'll protect you. (Male)
Love, rich or poor in health in sickness. (Both but on different parts)
Love conquers all and lasts I witness.
Our love is a gift from God.

She pleases me in all she does, (Male)
Working hard because she loves God and me.
He loves me like Christ loves the church, (Female)
Gives his all, shields me from hurt, serving he leads.
(S)he brings me peace, contentment. (Together)

---

28 A celebration of love for four main singers, chorus singers, guitar, drum set and bass

I am yours and you my love are mine. (Male)
We are one united by God's Spirit, three in one. (Female)
Working to a common goal, one in body, mind and soul. (Together)
Living, being in God. (Male)
God, God the Father, Son and Spirit. (Both but on different parts)
God, God of marriage, his love fills it.
We are, in God, our true self.

Love is so patient so pure and kind. (The witnesses singing)
Phileo, Agape, Eros, Charity.
Love keeps no records or wrongs or lies.
Love is eternal, never gives up, always builds up truth and harmony.
Love by nature makes us want to declare it.
Love by nature makes us want to share it.
God's love, source of all true love.

All true love is a gift from God. (Everyone singing)
Undefiled it shows to us reflections of him.
God loves the world so much he gave.
Jesus crucified to save people of the world. That's you and me, sing.
Come my Lord, says the Spirit and the Bride and he who thirsts.
Come my love, says the Lamb, the son of man to the Bride.
Soon the final wedding day, grief and tears are wiped away.
No more mourning and
Death, all things said and known will pass away.
All things known in part will pass away.
Love, imperfection disappears it will fade away.
Imperfection disappears away.
Love, faith and hope and love will only be remaining.
Faith and hope and love only remains. Love.

Sarah and Luke had asked Sarah's minister from Tooting to officiate and immediately after the service he busied himself shaking hands as guests gradually filed out and waited for the photographs of the bride and groom to be taken. He was so impressed at the wedding song lyrics, he asked Marwenna to write some more verse for a worship song when she had the time.

'Well, I can certainly write some more lyrics but I can't do the music. Do you know who wrote the music?'

The minister realised that Setford had not yet told her and didn't want to spoil the surprise. Fortunately for him Marwenna was summoned for some photographs so he didn't have to reply but shouted after her, 'Whoever it is, you two should team up.'

When Weston exited the church, the pastor turned to him and said the oddest thing as they shook hands but felt he was compelled to say, even though he did not comprehend its real meaning. 'It says in Ecclesiastes there is a time to mourn and a time to dance. You know, I hope you don't mind me saying but, it's now time for you to dance once again.'

Weston was momentarily taken aback. He had expected a general remark of pleasantry. The pastor looked for some recognition in Weston's face to see if what he had said made any sense. All Weston took it to mean at the time was that he was needed to dance at the reception. Always the gentleman, he smiled and shook hands and swiftly moved on.

The pastor talked with Cobby for a long time after.

'I gather everyone calls you Cobby, may I?'

'Of course.'

'Well, Cobby, what wonderful dance. I wish we had that every Sunday. I feel compelled to say something, though I don't know why I need say it. I hope you don't mind.' Cobby looked quizzically at him. 'Patience will reap its own reward. But it will be just a little while longer.'

Cobby's mind was partially elsewhere, concerned as to what was next for her dancers, to fully comprehend what he was saying. She just said, 'Thank you. I must check everything is ready for the Marcha while they are being photographed.'

– AT THE RECEPTION –

The wedding was planned so there would be no exhaustive evening 'do' where the wedding couple's cheeks and feet get tired from smiling and standing for a very long and tiring day. Both sets of parents were already dead, so there was no pressure for obligatory family attendances, no acknowledgment of parents letting go, no disillusionment of the bride thinking it is solely her day and discovering other parental factors and family pressures coming into play.

Before the buffet Luke was particularly grateful to get his welcoming speech over quickly, which was the sole speech of the day, but he did take time to eulogise the work Cobby and her dancers had put in.

For a wedding, what Cobby had planned, to be honest, went more than a shade over the top but nobody minded. It just added to it. The Marcha led to the start of the buffet and was followed by an English country barn dance with real homemade lemonade, cider and real ale for those who wanted it, as well as some of the best English white wines available. Non-alcoholic cocktails with funny dance-themed names were on offer for the youngsters and any others if they preferred.

At Marwenna's insistence Cornish sparkling wine from Camelford was used for the toast. She was adamant that champagne was 'overhyped, overpriced and over here', borrowing from a Second World War British phrase and added, 'If it's that good why do people waste it at the end of car races and other sports celebrations?'

As a surprise, by part cajoling and encouragement, Cobby had arranged for some groups from the dance festival to 'volunteer' to perform at the wedding towards the end of the buffet before the barn dance proper was to commence. Idonea had especially saved an Hawaiian waltz dance couple till last, as it would lead into Sarah and Luke's first dance. Bert danced a basic waltz with Marwenna and was excused by Setford so Bert moved straight for Edna to continue his waltz.

While they danced, Setford said, 'You look stunning.'

'Of course,' Marwenna replied before Setford cheekily added, 'For a tea lady's assistant, that is.'

'You scrub up OK too, for an empak,' was her disdainful riposte.'

*

'Cobby, you've done an absolutely splendid job organising the dancing and music. You look enchanting, by the way. You always did look good in turquoise.'

'Thanks, Westy. It was nice of you to pay for it all.'

'Do you remember us dancing English country dances at school? What were some of their names now?' asked Weston trying to remember.

'Well, there was Sir Roger de Coverley, Yarmouth Long Dance, Circassian Circle, Dashing White Sergeant. It's funny how, thinking back, it was always sunny when our junior school classes were allowed to dance to those old 78s. Do you remember that terribly primitive record player and crackly loud speaker cabinet that was rolled out?'

*

The waltz stopped and so did Setford and Marwenna.

'I may be an empak, as you put it, but at least I don't put on pretentions.'

'You are just a boy with toys!'

'Well, at least I'm not a harridan with a handbag!' he blurted out without thinking and having caught sight of her gaze decided to retreat immediately.

'You cheeky skogyn[29]! Fancy a knuckle sandwich? You just wait till I get my hands on you,' she called after him as he half ran and walked speedily to the gents' for sanctuary, laughing all the way with Marwenna in hot pursuit, both of them trying not to lose too much decorum.

'Come out, you kilgeun![30] You poltroon!' she loudly commanded as she banged on the door. She could hear him laughing inside. In her exasperation she resorted to full-on Cornish, adding a few other choice Celtic words for good measure. She then started noticing the odd looks she was getting from other guests, so withdrew and adopted a bit more sophistication in her demeanour. Idonea turned to Weston and asked, 'Are they an item?'

'Marwenna from Cornwall and Setford from Dunmow? If they ever were, which they are not, I would never see them claiming the Dunmow Flitch!'

Edna turned to Bert having witnessed the exchange between Setford and Marwenna. 'Bert, prepare yourself to cope with a lovelorn older daughter having lost her first love.'

'What?'

'I'll explain later.'

Slowly Marwenna wandered back to the dance floor to join Weston and Cobby just as Weston, in consternation, raised a nonplussed eyebrow at their antics, adding to his last

---

29 Idiot in Cornish
30 Coward in Cornish

observation, 'The youth of today… eh, Cobby. Would never have happened in our day.'

'Ahem… Can I remind you about the time you…?' She started to relate a past tale as she sidled closer to him, feeling very pleased with herself for how the dancing had turned out. Dare she now hope for something that she had denied to herself ever since her school days? Surely, she just had to wait a little longer. He would love her in a different way to Susannah, of course, but he would love her and not any the less. Just to share that sunset, a fireside chat, a comforting silence together, she could certainly settle for that, and what might stir in the course of time? Who could tell?

'Yes… well… that was a long time ago,' he interposed adding, 'Do you remember some of the songs we used to sing at school?'

'Yes, some of them, let's see now. What was that one, "Dirty British Coaster"?'

'Oh yes, I think I just about remember it but I do remember better, "I Don't Like Porridge".'

They both laughed. It felt so nice to be with him. She felt inexplicably suddenly free and joyous.

'Do you remember the favourites of the three of us?' she ventured.

'"Jonah Man Jazz", "Daniel Jazz" and, oh, what was the third one?' he countered.

'"Scarborough Fair",' she added triumphantly.

It was the first time Marwenna had ever seen Weston in such a jovial mood. He even quipped, 'Ah, nostalgia, it's not like it used to be!' adding when they reminisced about school, 'The older I get the better I was.'

Marwenna couldn't help teasing, 'Cobby, I thought your favourite song was "The Drunken Sailor".'

'Yes, well, erm, that was one of them,' she quickly confirmed.

Sensing Marwenna had calmed down, Setford joined them. Marwenna and Setford had never seen Weston so relaxed.

Afterwards at the barn dance, Cobby had the young children dance the first dance and then lead off the next dance by grabbing an adult as a partner. She had asked her star pupil to make sure that she was paired with Weston and to lead him to her. All the adults embraced the start of the barn dance proper, and Weston and Cobby for a brief time were children again. After a few dances Weston, Cobby, Setford and Marwenna all stood watching the dances for a while, smiling and listening to the music, then Weston looked at his watch and uttered, 'Well, I suppose I'd better go and see Louise in a short while.'

Idonea felt cut in half by his remark. How could she not have foreseen the possibility of another woman? No wonder he was happy. Yet, she thought that she knew him so well that there just couldn't be. How cruel life could be that something so deeply dormant in one so mature as her finally surfaced only to be dashed upon the hard rocks of disinterest by this one statement. Idonea, momentarily shocked, held back her tears and excused herself before rushing off to the ladies' very upset. A wound opened up so deep Idonea thought it could never be healed. Marwenna expertly sized up the situation and took after her to the ladies' where she found Idonea sobbing her heart out.

'These magnificent dances you've put together... it's not just for Sarah and Luke, is it?' asserted Marwenna. Idonea realised at once that Marwenna knew something of what was in her heart and part blurted out her confession.

'I just... I couldn't comfort him, you see. Or do anything for him during his loss. He just, sort of cut himself off.'

'You love him, don't you,' Marwenna stated.

'Yes, I suppose I always have, the selfish unfeeling man!' There is an unknown part in everyone that is hidden from themselves and Idonea was caught by her own. Weston was the love of her life, he did not know it, and in some ways as life had moved on, she had suppressed that fact that he still was the love of her life.

Marwenna was normally used to ladies' emotional upsets from the services where the usual conclusion was 'all men are bastards!' but such was Idonea's genteel manner and knowing Cobby and Weston from work, this affected her more deeply. They had become close, which was rare for two women of different generations and similar characters to share. It was a comic, endearing, heart-wrenching and amusing scene all at the same time.

'And yet you love him just the way he is, don't you?' said Marwenna gently.

'Yes,' whispered Idonea in between quiet sobs trying to gain some self-control. She felt so foolish. This was the sort of outburst someone of Marwenna's age or younger would understandably have, but not her. She should be the person to dispense wisdom and be fully in control. It should not be the other way around, but she had never confessed out loud to anyone or even to herself before and the depth of her feelings overcame her. It all just poured out and there was nothing she could do to stop it.

'But he has not got a clue, has he?'

'No,' said Idonea tearfully. The déjà vu moment of Susannah and Weston's argument all those years ago was not lost on Cobby. Marwenna then told her who Louise was and that she was more like a daughter to Weston. Idonea continued to cry but with relief.

'You silly old fool!' she said aloud to herself in the mirror. 'I am a fool, aren't I?' She turned to Marwenna, part smiling and crying at the same time.

'It's the sort of thing you youngsters would do… not an old fossil like me. How am I going to explain this?'

Marwenna hugged her, not out of pity, but out of genuine concern and – dare she admit it to herself? – love. They then hugged each other again and Idonea fixed her makeup while Marwenna made her laugh saying, 'That has given old Westy something to think about! It's about time too! We'll put it down to the stress of all the arrangements or we can pretend it's all their fault, ideally both. After all, it is in a way, isn't it?'

Still in the function hall, Weston and Setford looked at each other both perplexed and put it down to 'women' whom they would never fully understand and were not sure that they would ever want to.

'I've never had so much fun dancing in all my life!' said Setford to Weston, changing the subject.

'I know what you mean. I suppose I'd better go.'

'What and leave me to face whatever's brewing in the ladies'?'

'There are some things a man must face alone!' said Weston, grateful to be escaping, and thinking it was high time Setford asserted himself. After all, he could not shield him anymore at work.

– LIFE'S JOURNEY RESTARTS WITH THE HONEYMOON –

'Do you want me to drive, you must be tired by now?'

'Yes please, in a little while, when it's convenient. I haven't told you, have I, what I do when I get tired driving and can't immediately take a break?'

'No.'

'If it's difficult to take a break, I splash my face with a little water from the bottle, open the windows a bit, put a CD on and sing as loud as I possibly can.'

'What do you sing?'

'Oh, I put on any selection, like this.' He inserted the CD and on came a number and he started singing at the top of his voice just as they were stopping at a toll booth. He looked up at the lady in the booth while giving her the money still singing.

'*I'm gonna make you love me, yes I will, yes I will.*' Her face was an absolute picture with mouth open as they drove off.

'Married only five or six hours and you are already romancing another woman!' Sarah gave Luke a playful slap on the arm while giggling.

'Well, that's taken its toll, in more ways than one!' Luke quipped.

They motored on to Port Isaac via the Atlantic Highway and registered at a hotel that had been an old school. This overlooked the small harbour. A sumptuous seafood meal was accompanied by some Cornish sparkling wine courtesy of Marwenna who thought it would be a nice surprise.

Just offshore a boat had dropped anchor several hours earlier and the captain who had previously been scanning the shoreline with binoculars dispatched a man in an outboard motor-powered inflatable dinghy which steadily made its way past the harbour walls and onto the beach. His field glasses followed its progress and the subsequent journey on land. So, Bert had been right about the honeymoon times and destination after all, he thought and smiled to himself. On beaching, the lone occupant jogged to the promenading couple, approaching them from behind. He tapped Luke on the shoulder. 'These are for the missus,' thrusting some flowers into Luke's hand and then zipped back to the dinghy. Totally surprised, their gaze followed his run back to the dinghy and its subsequent journey out of the harbour. They then read the attached note: '*Congratulations, Flo! – Compliments of your captain.*'

As the dinghy raced back out to sea the captain smiled to himself and felt in a way he had not felt in years. He reread a note from Weston. '*We have friends in common and a common enemy. Maybe we can pool our resources when the time is right.*

I will contact you in future if you are in agreement. A friend. Now he was not alone after all in opposing the Corporation. Weighing anchor, he continued on his voyage of leisure, now looking forward to what might be in store and maybe now, life out of the shadows.

'Who was that?' Luke asked.

'Oh, you might say a passing ship in the night,' replied Sarah laughing.

'Not married a complete day yet and you're already consorting with sailors!'

At the end of their walk they stood savouring the moment, mostly just listening to the waves breaking and the occasional birdsong. Bright lights danced on the water like sparkling jewels contrasting with the cloudless bright blue sky. They mutually gongoozled, as if hypnotised in synergy by the sea, and then almost uniformly their gaze returned to each other. As the evening closed, the lowing cows moved out of sight over the hill, and the glorious pink and gold sunset still occasionally played flashes of light on the water as the tide drew further in.

This was their day. During their stroll they would often turn to each other, while still holding hands, enjoying and studying each other, drinking in each other's humanity and beauty. Sometimes they would reach out and gently touch or stroke as they wandered up and down the port. Then taking a mental step back, they beheld the picture they were making and cast it to memory.

Here was a moment in time, the remembrance of which would stay with them for the rest of their lives. Luke took in the fragrance of Sarah. How it pleased him. From time to time in the coming years, if he caught a whiff of it in a crowded lift or some such place, he would always be reminded of her.

One of the aims from their marriage preparation classes was to do something together as well as allow each other some space for personal interests, ideally to share a pastime or some such and discuss it. They chose to read the 'Song of Solomon' together and decided to start it on their first day of married life after their walk. A brief discussion followed after chapter one and then Luke finished the unpacking while Sarah bathed. Sarah switched on the radio and sang along to the words[31] while waiting for Luke to finish showering.

'It's been a great day,' said Sarah.

'Yes, though I have to say my face aches with all the smiling for the photographs.'

'Well, I think I know a remedy for that. Place your lips here,' she signalled with a pointed finger.

— CONFESSION BRINGS FORGIVENESS —

After the reception, Bert and Edna made their way home, their children staying with a mixture of friends and family.

'OK, it's just you and me, luv. Now what's all this about?' Edna enquired. She was confounded by Bert's request to talk to her alone. She couldn't remember the last time they had been alone like this.

'You know I love you, Duch', don't you.' He'd always called her his duchess. 'How you've coped with me being away when in the army, bringing up the kids so often on your own, me and the problems I had after leaving the regiment. Well, I've done some things I'm ashamed of,' he said with a deep frown.

'What things?' Edna braced herself for the worst and sat down. She had been there with him experiencing some of the nightmares of his service in Northern Ireland and not being able to express her fears, anger and frustration of what he was sometimes asked to do or experienced. Even then, she knew he had not told her everything. The hatred he had endured from

---

31 'A Good to be Alive Day' – laid-back song on guitar, drums, flute and bass

some folk there, particularly some of the protesting women who would harangue his section on patrol. The orchestrated protests aimed at ambushing them. First the children with shaved sharpened penny edges used in the catapult attacks, their withdrawals and then the subsequent terrorist rifle fire after the children had retreated as well as the risky snatch squads, he had been part of.

She had never heard him speak like this before. He had always been her cheery, chipper Bert; even during the tough times there was a sort of undeclared mutual ignoring of how bad the facts actually were. Whether that was from pretence or actual ignorance neither of them would truly know. Even when things were low, he had somehow always raised a smile in the family. The many years after he had left the army when they could not afford to take their annual holiday in Sandown, Isle of Wight because he couldn't get work. They didn't even have the option that their parents and grandparents had of hop-picking in Kent.

'I'm ashamed to say I'm involved in a bit of thieving. Not from people, you understand, but from a big corporation. Not that it makes it any better. I know it's wrong but… I owe an awful lot to the captain I work with. He's a good man but has some sort of vendetta against one business in particular,' said Bert as he began truly unburdening his soul for the very first time. Edna had initially thought it was likely to be financial debt. What sort of hold had this captain over him? she thought and feared.

'No, no, it's nothing like that,' he assured her. He then confessed how he had become suicidal and was at the point of ending it all when the captain discovered him, talked to him and had rescued him from leaping off a bridge.

'At the time, I was so desperate, Duch', I know you would have listened but I couldn't talk to you. You were the biggest victim from my failures and I was telling myself I was not helping you and the kids, which I think was right. I thought it would be best for all of you if I wasn't here. I knew I was causing concern to you and that you were worrying about me and even more my effect on our kids. God knows how I love you and the kids… but I just could not carry on. I was empty.' He started to cry a little. They stayed hugging and crying together for some time until both became exhausted by the outpouring of truths, past fears, concern and relief and then the eventual assurance.

'We've been through a lot together. I knew something wasn't right,' stated Edna. She then continued, 'Bert Bass, you are a good man, who has been through what many men never do and I know there is not a selfish bone in your body. Come here and let me snog your face off,' starting to draw his face close to hers.

'Give over,' he said, so relieved that he had managed to unburden himself, hoping his outpouring had not made her feel and think any the less of him. They kissed and then for the first time in a very long time they looked into each other's eyes, their gaze such as when they had first fallen in love all those years ago; the romance and desire surfaced once more as their love for each other became ever deeper.

– A FURTHER CELEBRATION –

There was a knock on Setford's hotel bedroom door. Marwenna entered with two glasses and a bottle of Cornish sparkling wine from the Camel Valley. She had always preferred it to champagne and as a girl from Cornwall was proud of what her county could produce.

'Typical, it takes our department months to let me know that I've been promoted and given an award. I've just been told! And I don't have anyone to celebrate it with. So, I thought if you weren't doing anything you could stir your stumps, you groovy old dad dancer, and open the bottle,' she added, mocking his earlier attempts at dancing, wishing both to share her success but also to tease him just a bit as she had always done.

'Congratulations, it's well deserved. Weston had often said to me that you were destined for the top and I agree. The next Stella Rimington no doubt in a decade or so. So, for you the only way is up,' he said raising his glass and added, 'Here's to you, you deserve it, and more. Hey, this is nice stuff.'

'Of course, everything out of Cornwall is very good. I mean, just look at yours truly,' she replied in mock pose and self-bragging.

Setford was still a little hesitant. Yes, he had always wanted her but something inside him still could not believe that she would want to be with him, particularly after their recent squabbles. He still felt that she could do so much better than him. They stood on the balcony, imbibing their drinks while drinking in the view and the lyrics of a song that had just started on the radio.

'*It's been a good to be alive day*,'[32] Marwenna quietly sang along. She felt great; life could not get better. She smiled broadly as she turned to Setford. 'It has been a good day, hasn't it?' Marwenna remarked.

'Yes, it has indeed been a great day,' he smiled and chinked her glass with his. They then turned to look at the sunset again.

'Oh, do you know who wrote the wedding song music to my words?'

'Did you like it?'

'Yes, it was great. Oh, so it was you who arranged for someone to compose it. I didn't know you knew someone musical! Who was it, anyone I know?'

'Actually,' he hesitated, 'I composed it.'

'You! How did you get hold of my verse?'

'I photographed it when you went to the loo at the hospital.'

---

32 'A Good to be Alive Day' – laid-back song on guitar, drums, flute and bass

'How come you've not mentioned that you composed before? Was it difficult to write such lovely music to my words?'

'It was easy,' he drew a deep breath and turned around to look at her directly, 'I just thought about you.' Then after a moment's reflection he decided to cast caution to the winds and so added, 'I hope I'm not going to spoil your evening by saying this. But, well, there comes a time when things must be said. I love you, I always have, and I guess, maybe deep down you have always known that,' he said staring straight into her eyes. He continued, 'It's alright, I understand if I don't fit the bill and you don't feel the same way. We could still be friends, right? That's if you don't feel uncomfortable about it. I'll make no overtones and it wouldn't interfere with our work. After all, it hasn't up until now, has it? I know you'll want your independence and your career but I can't bear the thought of this happening to you again especially when we are married… that's of course if you'll have me.'

Marwenna stood mouth open totally taken aback by his directness. More than half of her was awakened to something, she wasn't quite sure what, and in actual fact an enormous blush rose up from the core of her through the whole of her body, enveloping her in a way she had never felt before. She had not expected this! Her original intention, what was it now? She struggled to react. There was panic, the thought of involvement, worse, commitment. Such turmoil. He misread her stunned silence.

'Sorry, bit of a shock for you. Let's just rewind, forget what I said and enjoy the sunset and wine and go back to how we were. Where were we? Congrats!' He raised his glass to her again and then turned to look at the skyscape.

Marwenna, still agog, made a real effort to close her mouth but still could not speak at first. It hit her like a sledgehammer, the realisation for the first time of how much she really wanted him. The conscious denial subsumed for once by honesty with herself. She felt that at this moment in time he would complete her and make her whole. Setford knew about the world she wanted to inhabit, her aspirations; in some ways he knew her better than she knew herself and of course these things mattered to her but now no longer in the same way. It was as if the issue of the words 'I love you' had freed them both, their utterance illuminating the enormity of how much she really did love him.

'One more thing,' he added while going to a drawer. 'Here.' He passed her a gold ring as he returned to his drink and the balcony. 'I know yours was taken. It's Cornish gold. I know it's not the same but what with the rarity of Cornish gold, it's the best I could do. It's antique Cornish gold so they tell me. Put it on whatever finger you like. I'm just grateful for knowing you.'

She slowly stepped in front of him and looked directly into his eyes.

'Setford, you can't expect a woman to hear those sorts of words and then ask her to put them out of her mind. If you really mean them,' she hesitated and took a sharp breath, 'then act on them.'

He reached out slowly and caressed her cheek and then slowly drew her to him.

'And you, how do you feel?' he asked.

'I want you, Roger,' she whispered knowing that she had never wanted anything or anyone more in her life and then she whispered only to herself in her native Cornish, 'My a'th kar.[33]'

– WESTON AND LOUISE –

For Louise, it was something new that anyone valued her opinion. It had been years since anyone had asked for it on anything. Now that she was well and truly on the mend, she took

---

[33] 'I love you' in Cornish

a deeper interest in life in general and in addition was being kept up to date, with limited information, by Weston concerning the aftermath in her case. Her confidence and self-esteem had grown as had her trust in Weston to the point where he was becoming like a surrogate father to her. She even grew some assertiveness. As a child, she had loved weddings and would ask Weston details about the up-and-coming wedding he was to attend. He for his part tried to do his best to explain what was being planned as far as his limited knowledge allowed.

It was early evening when Weston arrived at Louise's bedsit. She was playing a new CD with a favourite new track called 'Five Aspects of Love'[34]. Gone the playing of the repetitious track of before.

'Well, spill the beans… How did the wedding go?' asked Louise, the first of many questions, from 'What dresses did the bridesmaids have?' to 'What was the cake like?'

'I've brought you a slice of cake,' offered Weston.

He then described in detail as best he could at Louise's insistence how things went, up to the point of Idonea's reaction and his total lack of comprehension of it.

'What did you say again before she rushed off?' enquired Louise thoughtfully.

'I said that I was going to see you.'

'And what does she know about me?' asked Louise.

'Nothing really as yet, I didn't get a chance to explain about you. She just ran off.'

'How long have you known her and how long have you been friends?'

'Since school, she was Susannah's best friend.'

'Is she married?'

'I don't think so. She wasn't till a couple of years ago, I'm fairly sure.'

---

34 'Five Aspects of Love' – pen picture on guitar and voice with harmony

'Has she ever been married?'

'You know, with your curiosity and questioning technique you could do me out of a job. Come to think of it I am out of a job,' he laughed. They were now very much at ease with each other, though Louise still referred to him as Mr Weston. For Louise, he was the first man she had ever known who was not intent on using her. She felt very safe with him. On occasions, he allowed Louise to boss him, just a little. This helped grow her self-confidence, develop self-respect and maybe a little bit of gumption. He was pleased to see her progressing well, and his nurturing of her gave him a purpose for living, particularly after his job had ended. She in her vulnerability needed protection, a caring eye to watch over her, her delayed development into a beautiful woman.

A conclusion quickly raced through her mind that maybe Idonea cared for Weston in more than a school friendship way. She thought very seriously about broaching this subject with Weston, and a number of ways quickly filled her developing mind. She could not think of an easy way of telling him.

FIVE ASPECTS OF LOVE[35]

Laughs with her girlfriends, nights of fun on the town.
Hides in a drunken haze she's butterflies on a merry-go-round.
So much love to give, aching, reaching out for love.
Love will find her one day because she's beautiful…
the child within… Beautiful. Yes, she's beautiful. Beautiful, beautiful.

Head on her pillow, as the tears stream down her face.
Heart again broken, the wrong guy, time or place.
Self-esteem takes a blow.
Why always me? She doesn't know.

> Love unrequited… Her love so sweet… It cuts so deep.
> Drawn to her old love… It's second best… like the rest.
> Know that you are worth much more than this… Dear Heart.
> Know that you're beautiful. Don't cry. Beautiful. Beautiful. Beautiful.

---

35 Five Aspects of Love – pen picture on guitar and voice with harmony

Fears, introspection as the years take their toll.
Life cuts her hard, bruising hurts she'll never show.
Gone her natural zest for life.
Hopes, longings subdued.

> I will cover you with all my love and care.
> For I'm patient and gentle, time and space, take all you need.

I'll take all of your burdens, for I love you so very much.
Come my sensuous lover, feel my warm and tender touch.
Rock you in my arms, whisper words of love, share your charms.
Your broken heart we'll mend, let me be your husband, lover, friend… Only believe… Only receive… my love… you're so…
Beautiful, my comely one. So beautiful. Beautiful. Beautiful.

> O see her bloom, see her grow, see her shine.
> All of her wounds are now healed and she is
> Fine are the days, sweet are the nights.
> Gone is the pain, share in her
> Delight in her face, warmth in her smile.
> Love set her free, she's the woman she's meant to be.

She's so beautiful. Beautiful. Beautiful.

In the end, she decided to hold her counsel. He was too precious to her to risk him thinking she was interfering. Instead she looked at him a little disapprovingly and tried to effect an atmospheric silence.

Weston picked up on this. The way Louise spoke to him reminded him, if nothing else from thirty or so years of marriage, that he was in trouble, even though he did not know what for. Suddenly he felt very small. Was this how a father feels after his daughter chides him for wearing socks with sandals, the ultimate fashion sin? Or the embarrassed denouncement and pleadings of a teenage daughter for her father to stop his attempts to dance with some strange out-of-fashion body movements at a wedding? It had been many years since Weston had been in the doghouse with Susannah but he would have given anything to be there if she was still alive. It was strangely almost comforting to be in the doghouse once more, though he was totally baffled as to why. Little did Weston know that not only was his business with Louise becoming ever more open-ended, but even his old department had not finished with him quite yet.

Louise had not only rediscovered lost positive feelings that had been buried for so many cruel years but she had started to care again. Not just for herself but for Weston and to some extent the outside world. In fact, her concern for Weston had been beneficial in developing her further. Caring for Weston started to make her feel useful and outward-looking. Louise could not maintain the silence or the look of disapproval for long. Then an idea came into her mind. It took all her courage to pluck up the resolve to execute her plan. She knew Weston often kept business cards in his wallet and quickly, surreptitiously, selected the Cobbald Dance School business card from it. She put on the radio and said she needed to change for bed ready for him to read to her and went to the bathroom, taking the radio with her. She placed the radio near the door and using the phone Weston had given her she telephoned Idonea. How Weston had helped her, now she could help him was her thought. It was one of her very first personal assertive initiatives.

'Hello, Cobbald Dance School.'

'Hello is that… Cobby?' Louise hesitated.

'Yes?' replied the puzzled voice.

'Hi, my name is Louise, we have a mutual friend in Mr Weston. I hope you don't mind me ringing but it's just that I think you may have a misunderstanding about me as I believe Mr Weston probably hasn't told you about me. He's like a dad I've never had. I care about him and I think you do too. So, I would like to meet you if that is OK. But first you must know, well, being brutally honest, I am a recovering alcoholic amongst other things. I will understand if you don't want to meet. I can give you directions to my digs and we can arrange a get-together. That's if you like. By the way, he doesn't know I've called you.'

'Oh, well, yes, OK,' said Idonea taken aback but intrigued and a little relieved all at the same time. They arranged a date and time.

'Great, that's a date then.' Louise felt good about doing something in return for him. Who's to say, her mind working nine to the dozen overtime, she still might attend a wedding yet. Idonea put down the receiver. Dare she hope still? Louise turned the radio off, returned from the bathroom and settled herself down for Weston to read to her.

'Who was that you were talking to?'

'Oh, that was a radio play. I sometimes listen when I am in the bath. But it turned out that it wasn't the serial I have been following of late.' Louise didn't like her deception but hoped it was worthwhile. The three indeed would eventually spend many hours together.

– A TIME TO MOURN AND A TIME TO SUPPORT –

Ayesha and Martha's latest conversation while still at St Julian's had led them to reliving the various happy experiences in their marriages. The recounting of past episodes brought comfort. These lovely memories, now though tinged with sadness, did produce gratitude for what they had had, both of them remarking how many women had not had the happiness they had experienced. They both knew words could never really convey how they both uniquely felt in their pain and need. Indeed, both women were progressing at different rates and stages in coping with their loss. As they parted on the stairs to their respective rooms Martha uttered, 'He was more to me than a lover, a husband and a friend. He was my soul mate. The same for you with Mohammed, no doubt.'

Ayesha nodded, they hugged and then progressed to their rooms. There alone, they both had a little cry, their emptiness tempered by the solace of the wonderful times they had shared with Peter and Mo. Ayesha then overheard the music of a string quartet[36] from another guest's radio through the wall. It was music that Mo and she loved to listen to together. It cut her heart so much that tears began to flood again and she beat her breast many times such was her pain, but though tempted to cry aloud she chose not to and put her face in the pillow as she lay on her bed.

After her weep, Martha took stock of her emotions and decided to visit the chapel in the hope that it would be empty. She picked up her personal CD player and placed a CD in it, choosing a track that she often used to help other Christians cope with grief. The chapel was empty and so she sat, listened and looked out to the pond and trees beyond. An element of peace and acceptance began to gently ease into her core as she gazed on the beauty outside.

---

36 'Missing You' – a slightly faster string quartet version

A SONG OF CONSOLATION[37]

Teardrops falling without warning. (Sung twice)
Tears in the night, will change to morning joy,
when day by day, step by step, you learn to live a new life.
Cherishing, the moments and the memories,
of the life you love, but have lost, for a time.

                          Dark is the night.
                          Grief will deeply cut you.
                          God's shaft of light is there,
                          To lead and comfort you.
                          To take you through.

Friends are here, to sit and listen, to love and care for,
learning of the life held so high in your heart.
Be thankful for the precious life you love and shared while here
on earth,
through good times, and bad times.
Give thanks for all they gave.

---

37 'A Song of Consolation' – solace from hope on guitar and voice

> Listen to what God says.
> At the end of time. He says…

God shall wipe all tears away. No more death or pain. All crying will end.

Jesus says come to me for rest, all weighed down or hard pressed. Receive of me, my peace.

At the great resurrection, we'll be raised to meet again. Such joy will await us. Singing alleluias to creations amen. Though changed in body we'll know each other. Made new by Jesus to live in rooms prepared. Life will be as God intends it, with peace and joy and love in the Son. Life in God the Father, Son and Holy Spirit three in one. Meet again in the Son.

Joined by God we'll be one.

– LOVE CONQUERS ALL –

Weston opened another romantic fiction book to read aloud to Louise as she settled down in bed. It had been a tiring first month in a new job for her. He had occasionally felt a little uncomfortable with the prose in the past. He wondered, pondered in fact, how could he have coped with a daughter in her teenage years discovering boys? He cringed inside with embarrassment but to all intents and purposes registered no such feelings in front of Louise. The opening up to her need had started to open up the need within himself that had, since Susannah had died, long been capped. A shut up well that he thought had run dry but whose waters had been suppressed for so long.

'Louise, I've bought some more romance novels for you. I'll start with this one. I'm assured it's a recent best seller.'

'Oh great.'

As soon as he cast his eyes over the first paragraphs, he began to regret having bought it as he felt more than a little embarrassed.

*

Bert reached out his hand towards Edna and began gently caressing her face.

*

Roger and Marwenna put their glasses down as he started to stroke her hair as they embraced and began to move to the music.

*

Sarah and Luke stood close up looking at each other, taking in every detail of each other's face. Here was a time not just of great desire but of careful assessment, of no hurry, of being able to let go with no fear, of enjoying being, of being fulfilled, made whole, of being part of something, yes as the cliché said, bigger than themselves. They disrobed. How they wanted each other. Then, oh so gently at first, they approached each other. What a beautiful gift our bodies are and how sensitive they can become. In the subdued light, touch brought with it a heightened sense of enjoyment. Slowly, deliberately, valuing every sensuous touch they caressed.

*

Weston cleared his throat a little nervously. '*The sensuous touch of his hand on her face as he gently stroked her cheek and slowly drew her to him made her want even more to surrender to her deep, stirring inner desires. He caressed her cascading hair. Together they sank to their knees. He then placed his forefinger on her lips to signal the continuance of this silent special moment. They gazed into each other's eyes longingly. This was their moment. Then with unbridled passion they...*'

*

Luke kissed Sarah's body. Gradually in their physical union, passion took over until each wave of hunger and delight swept them on together into a crescendo of physical ecstasy which subsided into quiet fulfilment.

EPILOGUE

Cobby: Idonea and Weston became a permanent item as well as surrogate parents to Louise. They grew very devoted and were always supportive of Louise. Shared sunsets, silences, mutual reading times and the holding of hands increased. Cobby's love for dance always remained but changed. It and she became more relaxed.

Louise, whose mother had died as a drug user and alcoholic, developed good housekeeping skills and progressed to promotion in her job. She eventually married and became a very good mother. Weston gave her away at her wedding. She even carried on Weston's family tradition of including an Anglo-Saxon name in the children's middle names, i.e. Robin Edmund Saexa and Rebecca Mildritha Idonea. If Louise's husband was ever away the children often enjoyed Weston reading to them at bedtime.

The captain became fully legitimate in business and gradually got involved in normal social relations. His work with Weston will be found in another book in the future.

Edna and Bert grew gracefully old together and became doting grandparents. Joan eventually found true love and had children of her own. Their family story from previous generations will be in another book.

Ayesha and Martha remained friends for the rest of their lives and both moved on as best they could in their lives. Both families kept in contact.

Sarah and Luke both found new jobs. Sarah, after consultation with Cobby, decided not to formalise her dance education but drank in other exotic forms of dance language under Cobby's guidance. She continued to develop in her dance and walk with God. Luke progressed to grade eight level in his drumming and played in a band just for fun.

Setford and Marwenna kept their professional life separate from their joint personal life. Though they did not regard themselves as committed Christians, they wrote a lot of music and lyrics together for the pastor. They really enjoyed researching the stories, history and the lives in both testaments for their joint compositions. Their approach, rather than writing the usual type of praise chorus, was more like exploring how people in the Bible felt in particular situations, or they would discover a gem of insight that they wanted to highlight. Perhaps, this was best described as like walking along a sea shore and picking up a coloured stone or shell and holding it up to the light. It brought them ever closer together. The other interest they shared was playing table tennis together. Whenever Marwenna was losing, which was more often than not, she would resort to swearing and hurling abuse at Roger in Cornish. They never attempted to win the Dunmow Flitch.

Nichols: after a brief halt to his actions Nichols continued on his power agenda. His ultimate comeuppance is reserved for another book.

Margaret: The women's community eventually ended and she moved on to where she knew God had called her and provided for her needs. Her spiritual journey, growth and experiences continued until her death and beyond.

APPENDIX

— JOAN'S POEM FOR EDNA —

Two score and ten does not describe
The life that you've lived and the journey so far.

Edna the child, the wife, the mother
Edna the pliant, the strong, the lover
Words don't purvey the traumas and joys
The beautiful daughters and the wonderful boy
The time you've invested, the love and the care
Always supportive, always been there!!!!

It's right that we're thankful of your parts that we know
Though the kernel of Edna perhaps still a person unknown
Hid by our focus defined by your roles.
But we still reach out with arms to enfold
Yes, you're bound in love by the arms of your family
Providing and caring to offspring unstintingly

The years unbegrudged for bringing up babies
On limited budgets, struggling daily
Making things do due to lack of resources
Hard decisions to make circumstances forces
It's hard for us to comprehend
The extent of love you've had to extend.

Two score and ten does not describe
The life that you've lived and the journey so far.

Thank you for giving us life.
Thank you for giving us love.

APPENDIX

— EDNA'S RAP —

No longer impromptu curtsies down the road
No longer doubts of whether it will hold
Endurance now is to relate her trait
Especially when she's doing the 'hip'y 'hip'y shake

Now she can watch *Strictly* on TV
Or on holiday Lindy hop with glee
She'll start a fashion and become really 'hip'
Lindy-'hip'ying about in a championship.

Fame now awaits, her chance to roam
She could appear at the 'Hip'-o-drome!
Her new diet includes Rose hip syrup
The taste now added has a mighty fillip.

Doctors impressed are given new hope
They queue to renew their 'Hip'ocratic oath
Not long now on those awkward crutches
Soon to escape the physio's clutches

Some folks' weight grows and they kick up a fuss!
But Edna is no 'hip'ypotamus
There's nowt to say now Edna's back to stay
Except let's all shout 'Hip' 'Hip' hooray!!!!!

— JOAN'S POEM FOR EDNA'S BIRTHDAY —

What do you get now a year older?
First a slippy hip, now a frozen shoulder
Bosses put right trying to make business leaner
How did they feel being taken to the cleaners?

Could life exist without Harley Dickenson's roar
Or referring to specifics by 'Thingies' galore!
Have birthday spritzers, treat tonight as a Beano
Dressing in style being driven in a Limo

Mother it's time to rest at repast
And show us kids your touch of class
Relax, enjoy the proverbial chill
Dream of toy boys your chores they'll fulfil

APPENDIX

— JOAN'S GRANDFATHER'S POEM —

Taxi! Taxi! The mariner cried.
Was it to cheer those sailing by?
Or a shout of black humour afore he died?
Could it have been in anger, the enemy defied?

The seaman's name we'll never know.
All we can glean is the humanity showed
When his ship went down and the convoy wove
To avoid another deadly tor-pe-do.

Taxi! Taxi! From the abandoned man
As the ships sailed on to the ordered plan.
Left in the sea and the cold as he swam.
What was he called? Tom? Harry? Sam?

Yet the memory remains with those who heard
Till time for them to expire in turn.
What a shout to make when death is certain
But it's all that we know of this sailor's life term.

ACKNOWLEDGEMENTS

– PUBLICATIONS AND FILMS –

Morris: A Life With Bells On. DVD, Twist films.
The Holy Bible – New International Version.
Union and Communion – Meditations on the Song of Solomon by Hudson Taylor. ISBN 85363 056 9.
Operation Blacklight by Hulta Gertrude, from the Obsenneth series. ISBN 9781973825944.
Living Light. ISBN 0 902088 79 3.

– MUSIC AND MUSICIANS –

(that are not part of the optional musical)
Please check out their music and websites.

Drummers Steve Smith and Jeff Hamilton brush duet – 'Salt Peanuts'.
Albert 'Tootie' Heath's solo in Sonny Rollins' rendition of 'St Thomas'.
Dave Brubeck's original recording of 'Koto Song'.

Acknowledgements

Benny Goodman's 1938 version of 'Sing, Sing, Sing' featuring Gene Krupa on drums and Harry James on trumpet.
'Always Something There to Remind Me' written by Burt Bacharach.
'I'm Gonna Make You Love Me' written by Kenny Gamble and Jerry Ross.
The Band of the Island of Jersey.
Louis Bellson's 'Skin Deep'.
Graham Kendrick's 'Teach Me To Dance'.
'10,000 Reasons (Bless the Lord)' written by Matt Redman and Jonas Mylin.

– INCIDENTS IN THE BOOK –

Though fiction, this book includes many real-life incidents. Here are some of them. Identities and particulars have been renamed to protect the individuals and the pigeons in question!

The damaged seat and passenger fall on the tube happened on the District Line to Dagenham East.

The pigeon riding on the tube. It happened at Mansion House tube station. The defecation happened at Mile End.

The comb in the hair happened on a bus one morning.
The pain being represented by a devil figure happened in a hospice in Essex, as did the stargazing outside with the patient still in bed.

Conversation in post office queue between two teenage girls regarding having children rather than work happened in Rugby.

The dancing of the children before Sunday morning service happened at St Michael le Belfry, York. Likewise, the dance in worship in one of their services.

The prayer meetings starting in silence sometimes producing tears, pictures and laughter happened at York, Havering-atte-Bower and at Pilgrims Hatch, Essex, along with numerous other places.

There was once a community of women at St Julian's, Coolham decades ago.

A friend fell in love with a Christian girl and, unbeknown to her, found out what Christianity was all about by secretly going to a different church. He eventually became a Christian, they married and did live happily ever after (that's not to say they did not have difficulties to overcome in life). He eventually became a vicar.

Matador

For exclusive discounts on Matador titles,
sign up to our occasional newsletter at
troubador.co.uk/bookshop